J GRAPHIC CIBOS v. 2
Cibos, Lindsay.
Peach fuzz /

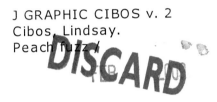

2.12 / 9.13 / 10.16

Peach Fuzz

Vol. 2

by

Lindsay Cibos
and
Jared Hodges

 TOKYOPOP®

HAMBURG // LONDON // LOS ANGELES // TOKYO

Spotlight

visit us at www.abdopublishing.com

Reinforced library bound edition published in 2009 by Spotlight, a division of ABDO Publishing Group, 8000 West 78th Street, Edina, Minnesota 55439. This edition reprinted by arrangement with TOKYOPOP Inc. www.tokyopop.com

Production Artist   Jennifer Carbajal
Cover Design   Monalisa De Asis
Editor   Carol Fox
Digital Imaging Manager   Chris Buford

Library of Congress Cataloging-in-Publication Data

Cibos, Lindsay.
  Peach Fuzz / by Lindsay Cibos and Jared Hodges.
     v. cm.
  Summary: When Amanda begs her parents for a pet and they relent and get her a ferret, the previously calm household turns chaotic, and even worse, the ferret learns to fear Amanda, who knows nothing about how to take care of a pet.
  Contents: Vol. 1. Peach Fuzz -- Vol. 2. Show & tell -- Vol. 3. Prince Edwin.
  ISBN 978-1-59961-572-1 (vol. 2: Show & tell)
  1. Graphic novels. [1. Graphic novels. 2. Ferrets as pets--Fiction. 3. Pets--Fiction.]
I. Hodges, Jared. II. Title.
  PZ7.7.C53Pe 2008
  [Fic]--dc22

                                                                    2008002197

All Spotlight books have reinforced library binding
and are manufactured in the United States of America.

Table of Contents

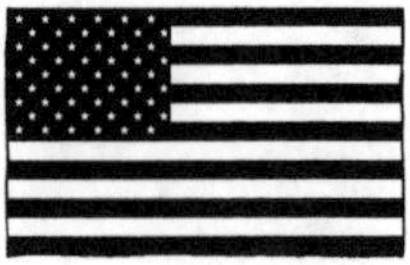

Mushroom Valley Department of Education

ENROLLMENT PASS FOR PEACH FUZZ VOL. 2

Enrollee's Name: ____
FIRST MIDDLE LAST

Date of Birth: ___/___/_____
M D Y

---

1. Required Knowledge of Storyline

☐**Yes** ☐**No**

Before proceeding, it is necessary to verify that the above named enrollee is familiar with the storyline from *Peach Fuzz* Vol. 1. If not, mark the box for "no," and read below.

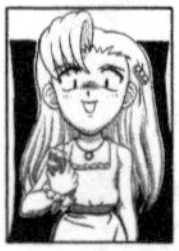

Desiring a pet, Amanda visits a local pet store. There she convinces her mother to take home the adorable sleepy baby ferret she falls in love with. However, Mom warns, if the ferret causes any problems, she'll return it. Inspired by a fruit stand selling peaches on the way home, Amanda names the ferret Peach.

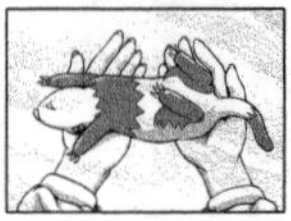

Peach awakens to find herself a prisoner of the Handra--multi-headed, dragonlike monsters, otherwise known as human hands--and tries in vain to flee. Amanda accidentally drops Peach in the struggle. Peach is rushed to an animal clinic for emergency treatment, where she recovers without injury.

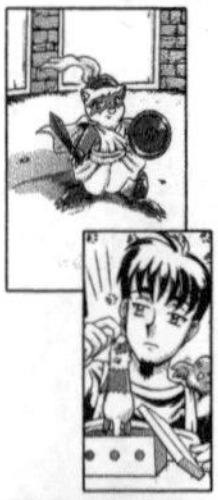

After another escape attempt, the Handra upgrades Peach's cage to a stone walled dungeon. Only allowed out to partake in gladiatorial combat, Peach learns to fight, tearing apart friends, foes, and eventually the mighty Handra.

Amanda endures a particularly nasty bite from Peach, and Mom makes good on her threat to return the ferret. However, an enthusiastic clerk with a product for every conceivable problem sells them a spray called "Bitter Bite" and convinces them to give Peach a second chance.

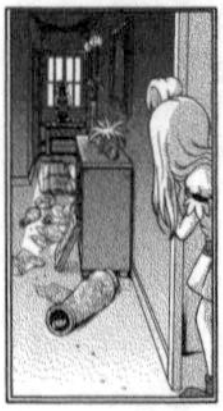

Amanda musters her courage (and her "Bitter Bite" spray) to take responsibility for her haphazard animal training. She follows Peach into her hidden lair and soon gains the upper hand in the battle. Then Amanda soothes the wounded ferret and regains its trust.

But the Handra are tricky creatures to figure out, and Peach's adventures with them are just beginning...

2. Required Knowledge of Characters

☐Yes ☐No

To avoid confusion, it is required that the enrollee have intimate knowledge of the six principal characters listed below. If not, mark the box for "no," and read below.

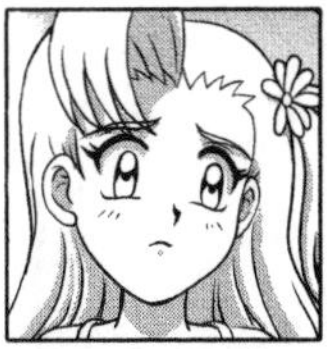

Amanda Keller

Amanda is an enthusiastic but not very popular fourth grader. In search of approval from her peers, she comes upon the idea of getting an exotic pet. The ferret she chooses brings new joy into her life, but also new responsibilities.

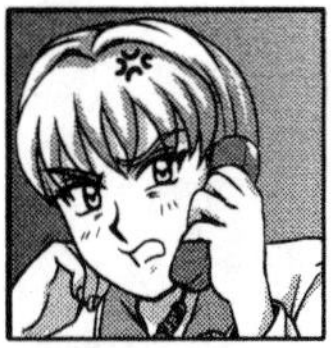

Megan Keller

Amanda's workaholic divorced mom, Megan feels incredible guilt over the effects the breakup of her marriage has had on her daughter. Loving but overbearing, she feels the need to shelter Amanda from the world's harsh realities.

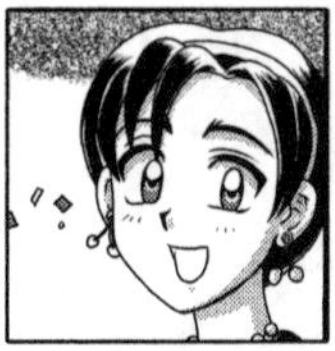

Kim Chang

Short, sassy and always in control, Kim is one of the most popular and trendsetting girls in the fourth grade. By some accident of fate, she's also Amanda's best friend and classmate.

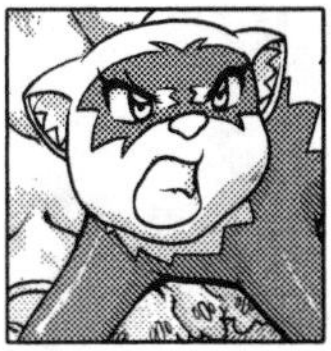

Peach

Amanda's new pet, a bold and haughty sable ferret who thinks of herself as the princess of the Ferret Kingdom. Peach hopes to gain control over the Handra and return to her kingdom.

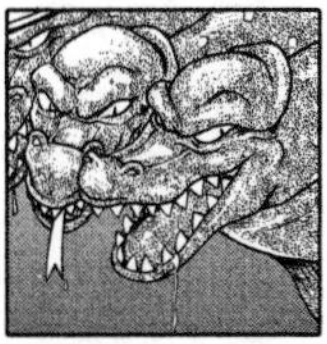

Handra

The human hand, from Peach's point of view. These scaly five-headed monsters of ferret lore capture creatures for shadowy purposes and inflict upon them horrors untold.

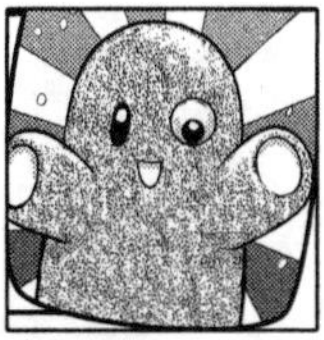

Mr. Fuzzy

A small stuffed toy rewarded to Amanda for a good grade in class. This strange silent character shows up one day alongside Peach in the dungeon. After a few initial run-ins, which result in the loss of his left eye, Mr. Fuzzy becomes Peach's trusted friend.

3. Waiver of Reading Requirements

☐Yes ☐No

If the "yes" box has been marked for requirements 1 and 2, this will be considered a waiver from above reading requirements.

Mushroom Valley · Department of Education · 1859

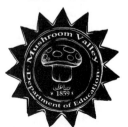

This Certifies That

____

SIGNATURE

has read the description of and/or is familiar with the story and characters.

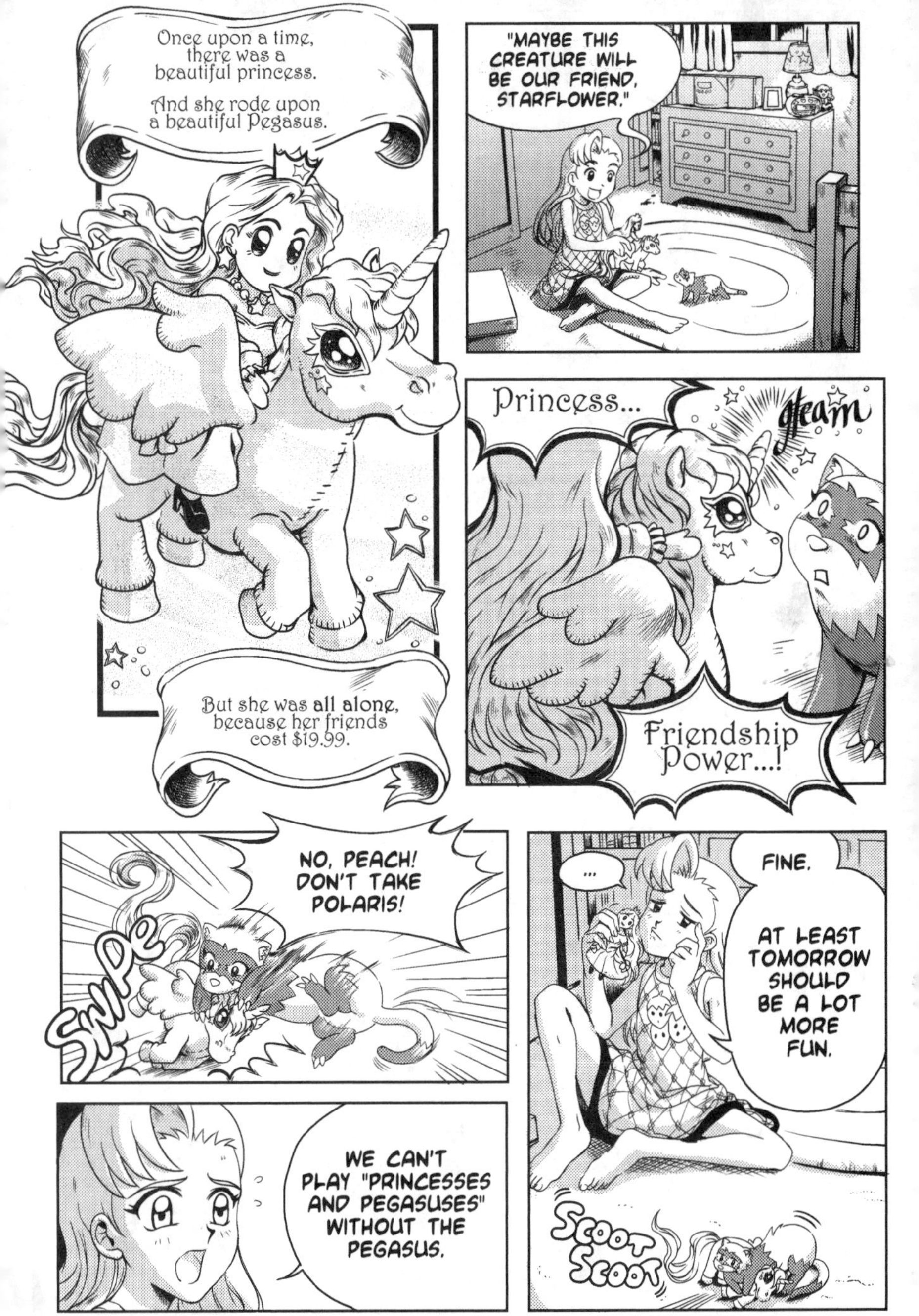
Once upon a time, there was a beautiful princess.
And she rode upon a beautiful Pegasus.
But she was all alone, because her friends cost $19.99.
"MAYBE THIS CREATURE WILL BE OUR FRIEND, STARFLOWER."
Princess...
gleam
Friendship Power...!
NO, PEACH! DON'T TAKE POLARIS!
Swipe
WE CAN'T PLAY "PRINCESSES AND PEGASUSES" WITHOUT THE PEGASUS.
...
FINE.
AT LEAST TOMORROW SHOULD BE A LOT MORE FUN.
SCOOT SCOOT

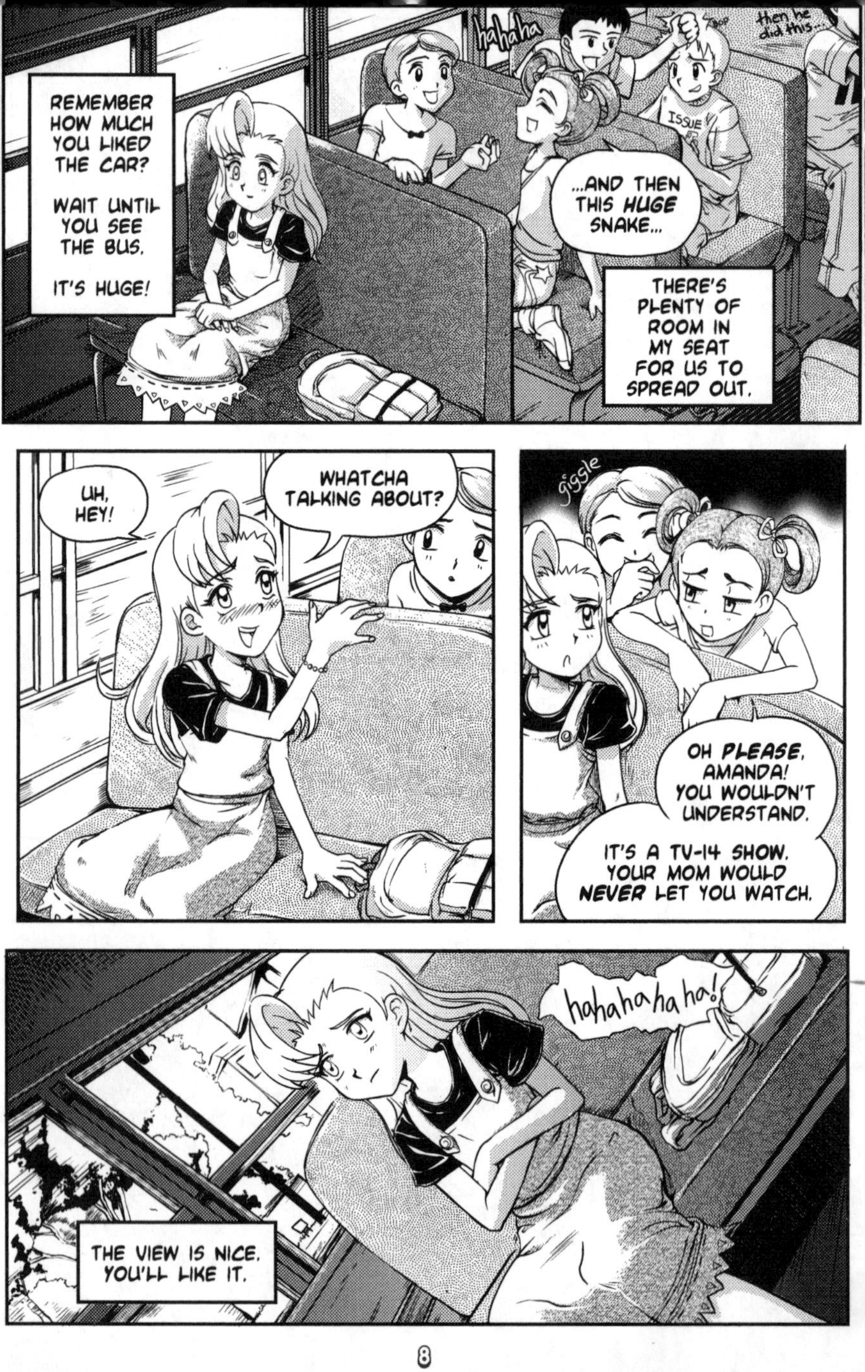
REMEMBER HOW MUCH YOU LIKED THE CAR?
WAIT UNTIL YOU SEE THE BUS.
IT'S HUGE!
hahaha
then he did this...
...AND THEN THIS HUGE SNAKE...
THERE'S PLENTY OF ROOM IN MY SEAT FOR US TO SPREAD OUT.
UH, HEY!
WHATCHA TALKING ABOUT?
giggle
OH PLEASE, AMANDA! YOU WOULDN'T UNDERSTAND.
IT'S A TV-14 SHOW. YOUR MOM WOULD NEVER LET YOU WATCH.
hahahahaha!
THE VIEW IS NICE. YOU'LL LIKE IT.

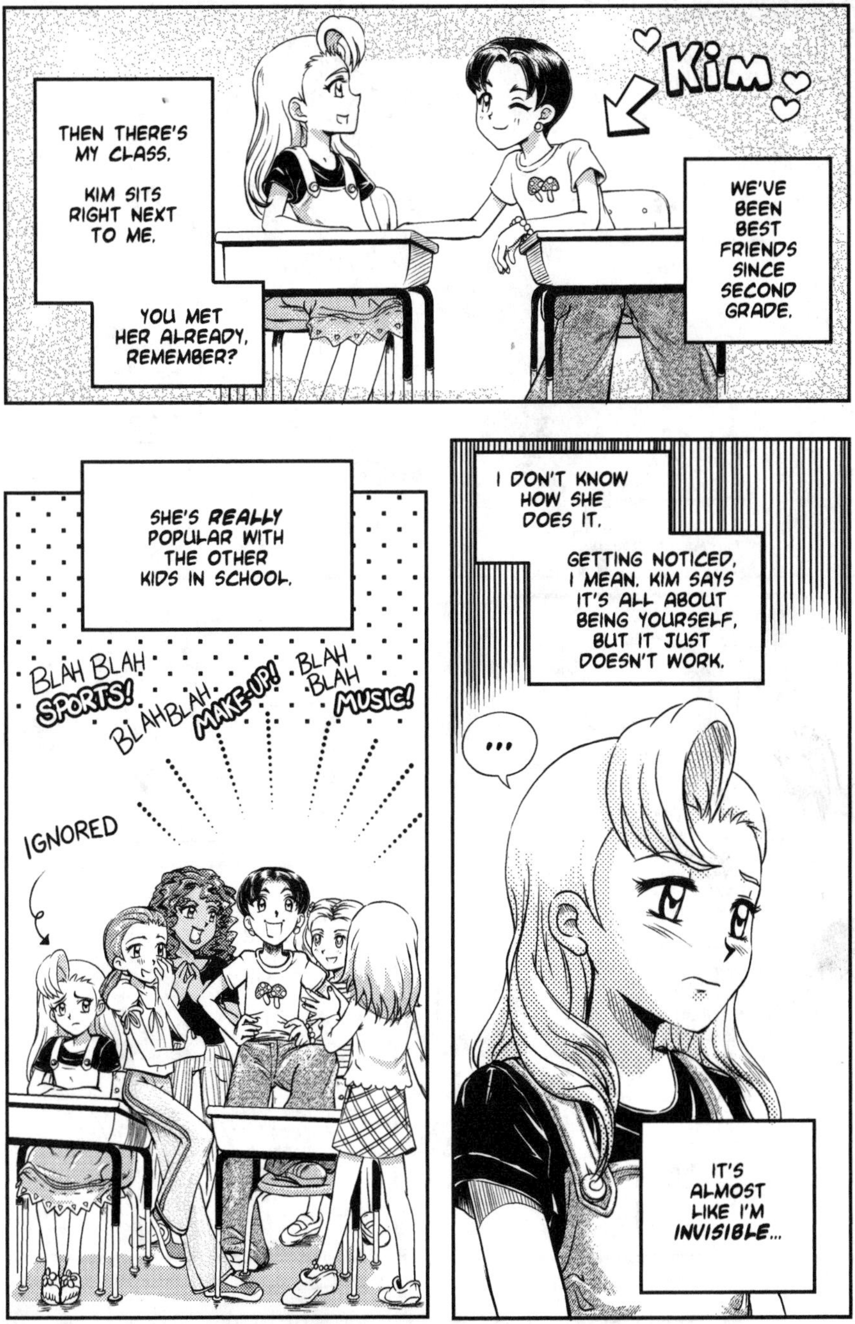
Kim
THEN THERE'S MY CLASS.
KIM SITS RIGHT NEXT TO ME.
YOU MET HER ALREADY, REMEMBER?
WE'VE BEEN BEST FRIENDS SINCE SECOND GRADE.
SHE'S REALLY POPULAR WITH THE OTHER KIDS IN SCHOOL.
BLAH BLAH SPORTS!
BLAH BLAH MAKE-UP!
BLAH BLAH MUSIC!
IGNORED
I DON'T KNOW HOW SHE DOES IT.
GETTING NOTICED, I MEAN. KIM SAYS IT'S ALL ABOUT BEING YOURSELF, BUT IT JUST DOESN'T WORK.
...
IT'S ALMOST LIKE I'M INVISIBLE...

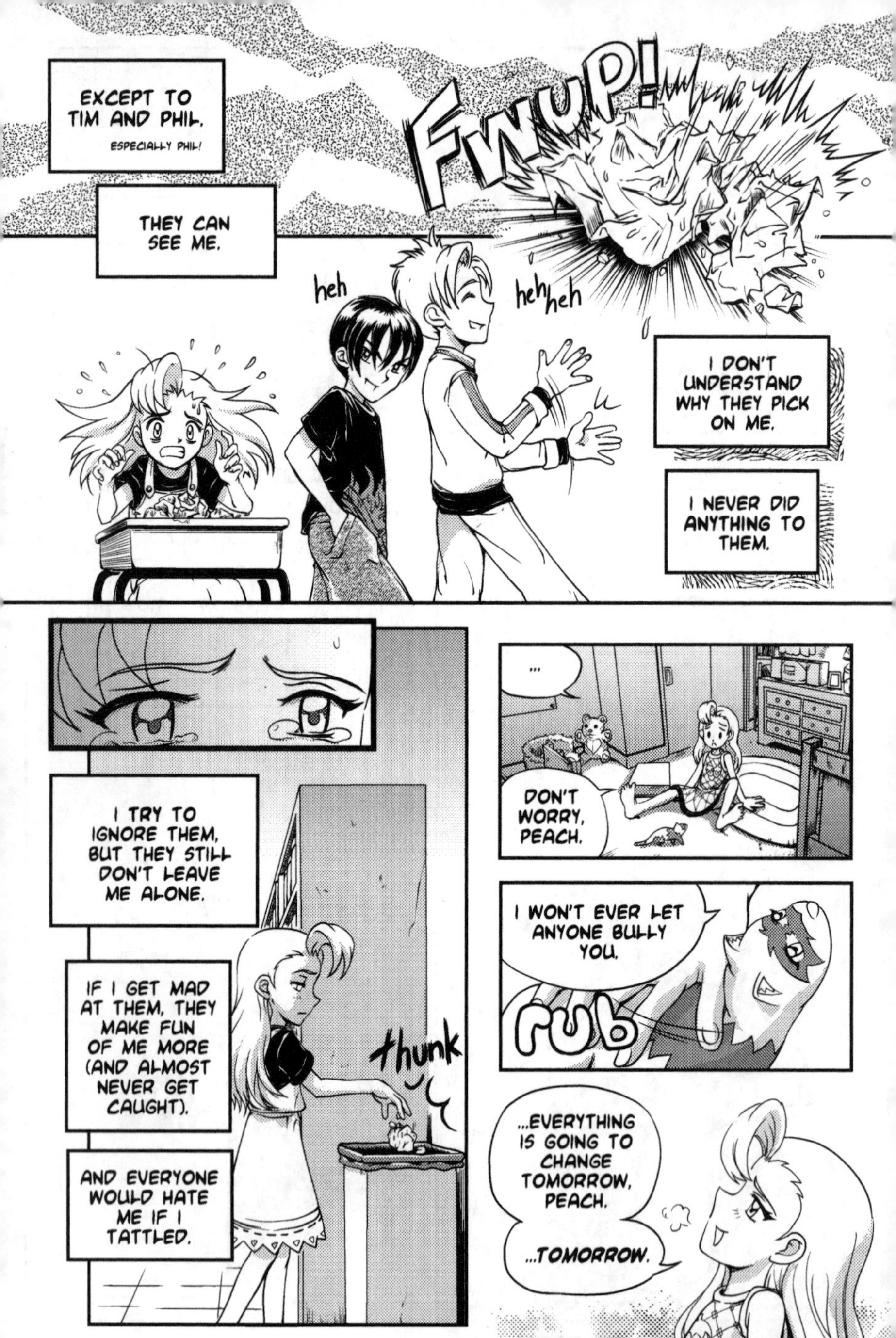
EXCEPT TO TIM AND PHIL.
ESPECIALLY PHIL!
THEY CAN SEE ME.
FWUP!
heh
heh heh
I DON'T UNDERSTAND WHY THEY PICK ON ME.
I NEVER DID ANYTHING TO THEM.
I TRY TO IGNORE THEM, BUT THEY STILL DON'T LEAVE ME ALONE.
IF I GET MAD AT THEM, THEY MAKE FUN OF ME MORE (AND ALMOST NEVER GET CAUGHT).
AND EVERYONE WOULD HATE ME IF I TATTLED.
thunk
...
DON'T WORRY, PEACH.
I WON'T EVER LET ANYONE BULLY YOU.
rub
...EVERYTHING IS GOING TO CHANGE TOMORROW, PEACH.
...TOMORROW.

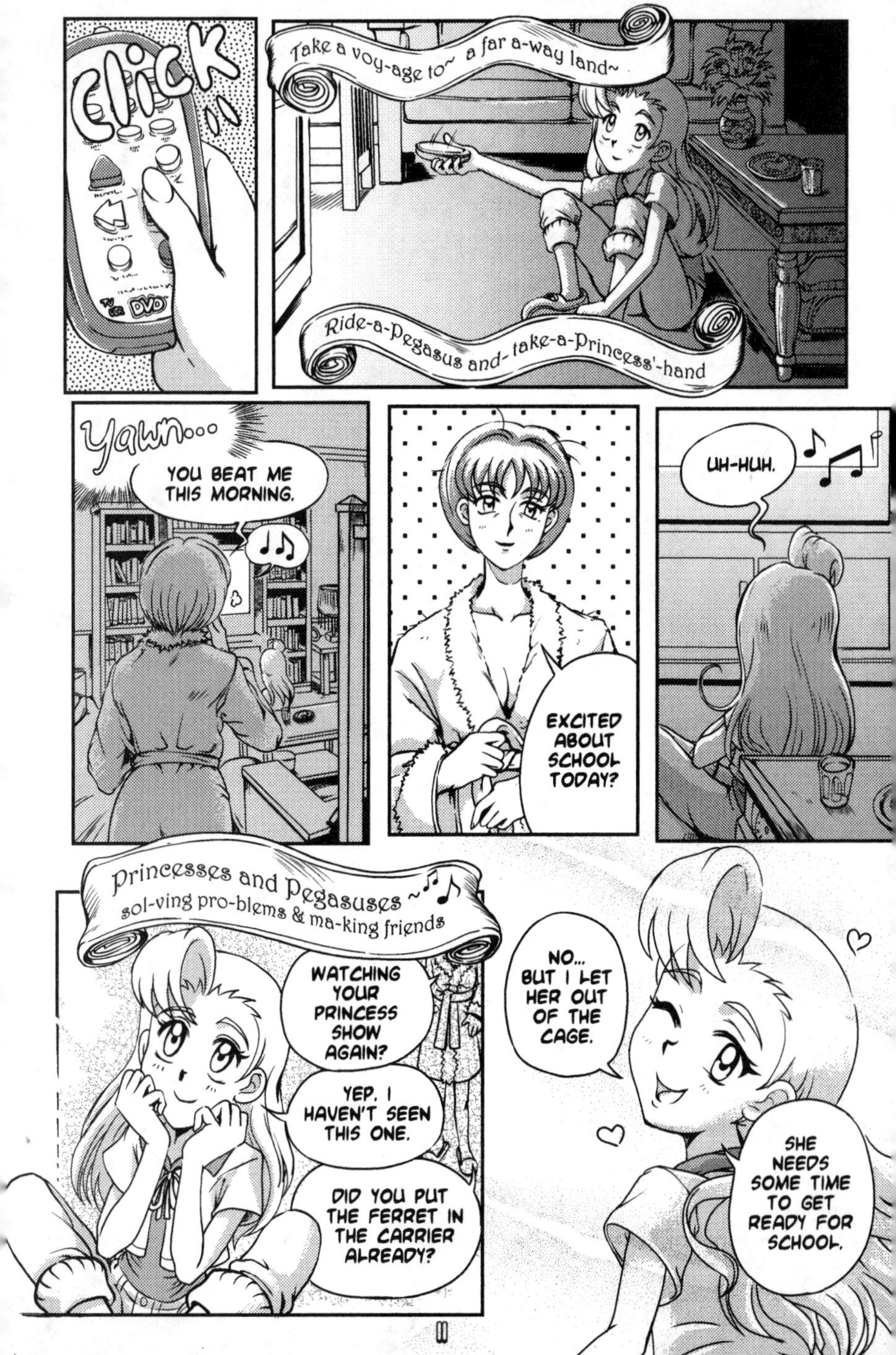
CLICK
Take a voy-age to~ a far a-way land~
Ride-a-Pegasus and-take-a-Princess'-hand
Yawn...
YOU BEAT ME THIS MORNING.
EXCITED ABOUT SCHOOL TODAY?
UH-HUH.
Princesses and Pegasuses ~ sol-ving pro-blems & ma-king friends
WATCHING YOUR PRINCESS SHOW AGAIN?
YEP. I HAVEN'T SEEN THIS ONE.
DID YOU PUT THE FERRET IN THE CARRIER ALREADY?
NO... BUT I LET HER OUT OF THE CAGE.
SHE NEEDS SOME TIME TO GET READY FOR SCHOOL.

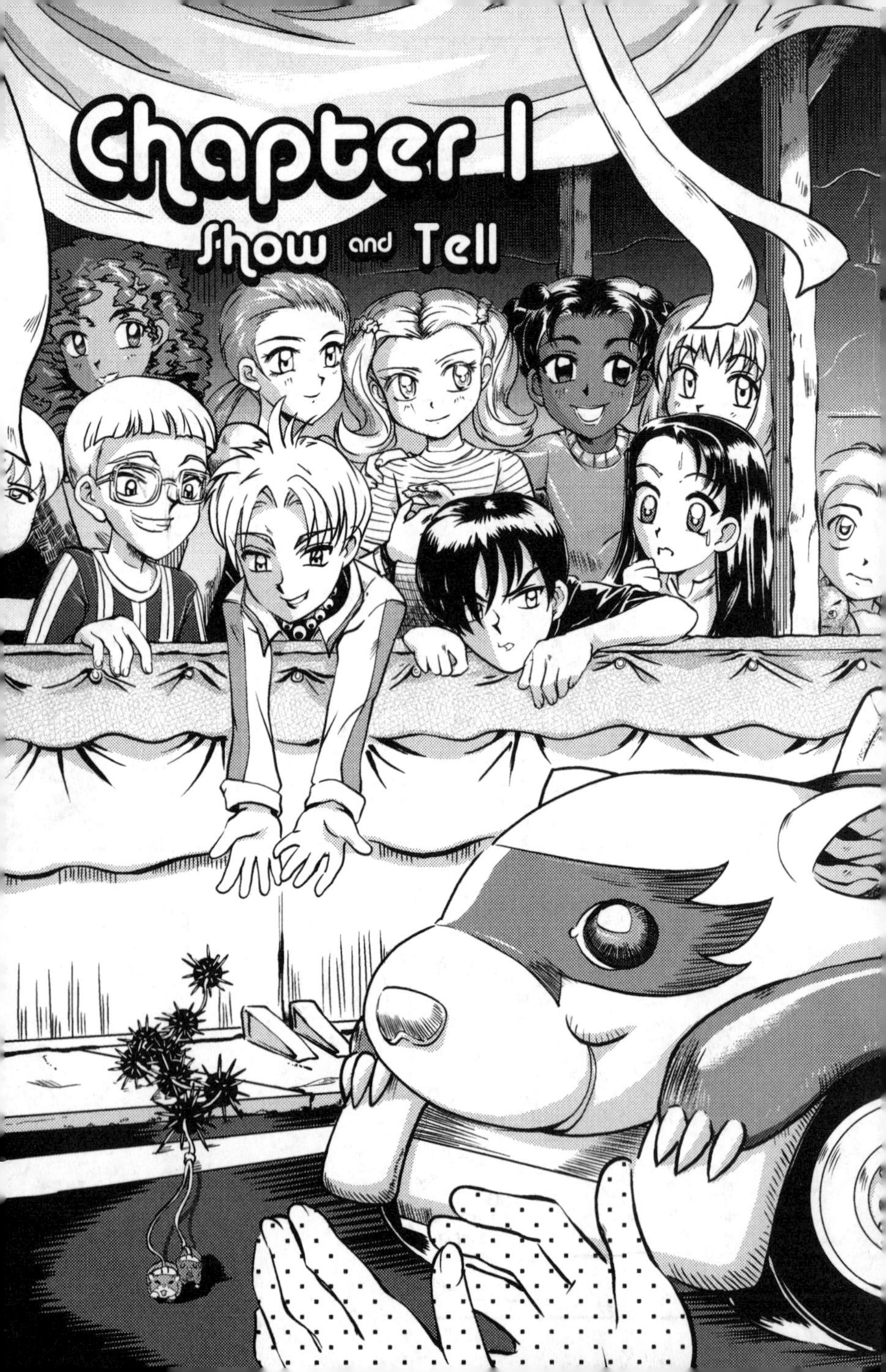
Chapter 1
Show and Tell

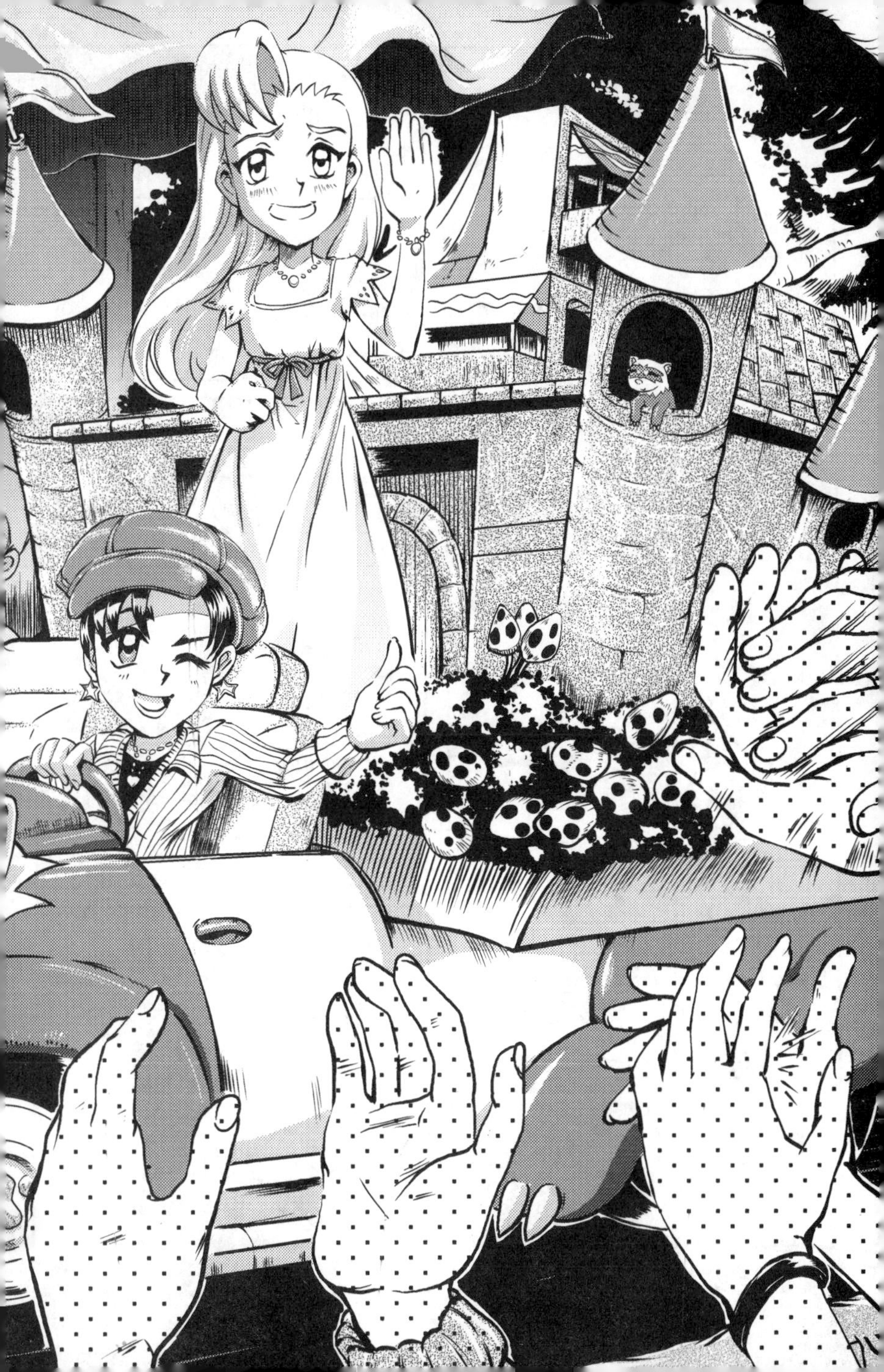

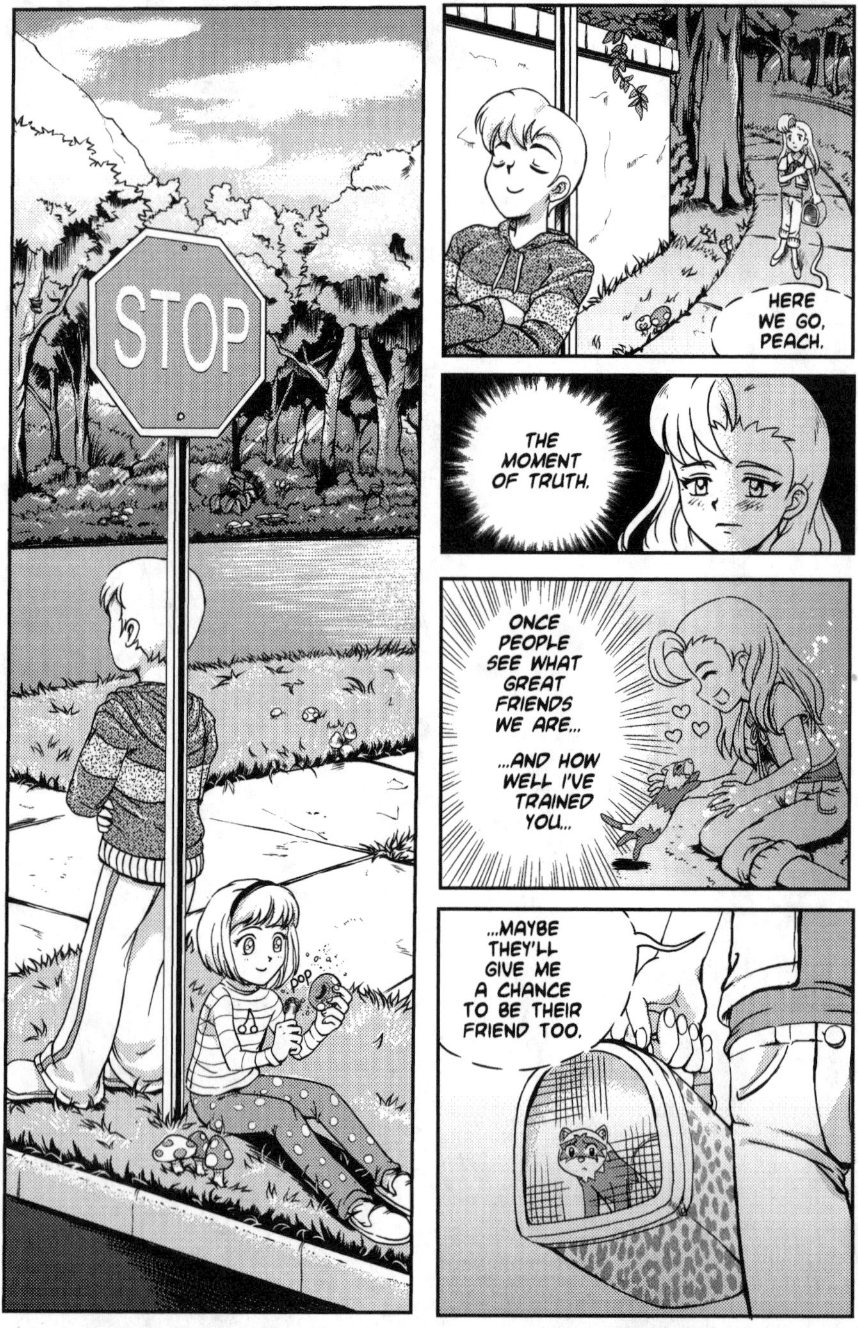
STOP
POP
HERE WE GO, PEACH.
THE MOMENT OF TRUTH.
ONCE PEOPLE SEE WHAT GREAT FRIENDS WE ARE...
...AND HOW WELL I'VE TRAINED YOU...
...MAYBE THEY'LL GIVE ME A CHANCE TO BE THEIR FRIEND TOO.

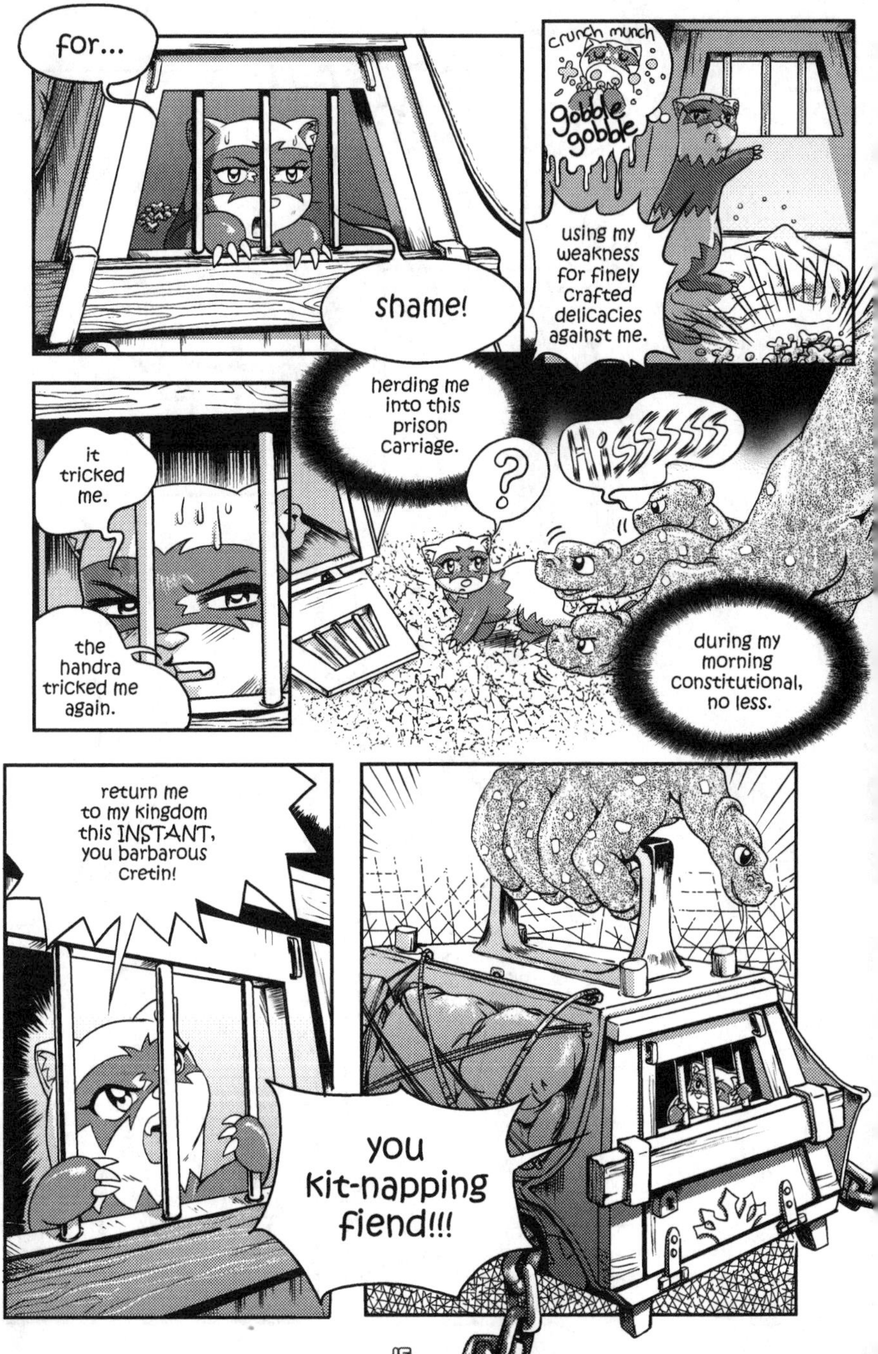
for...
shame!
crunch munch
gobble gobble
using my weakness for finely crafted delicacies against me.
herding me into this prison carriage.
?
Hisssss
during my morning constitutional, no less.
it tricked me.
the handra tricked me again.
return me to my kingdom this INSTANT, you barbarous cretin!
you kit-napping fiend!!!

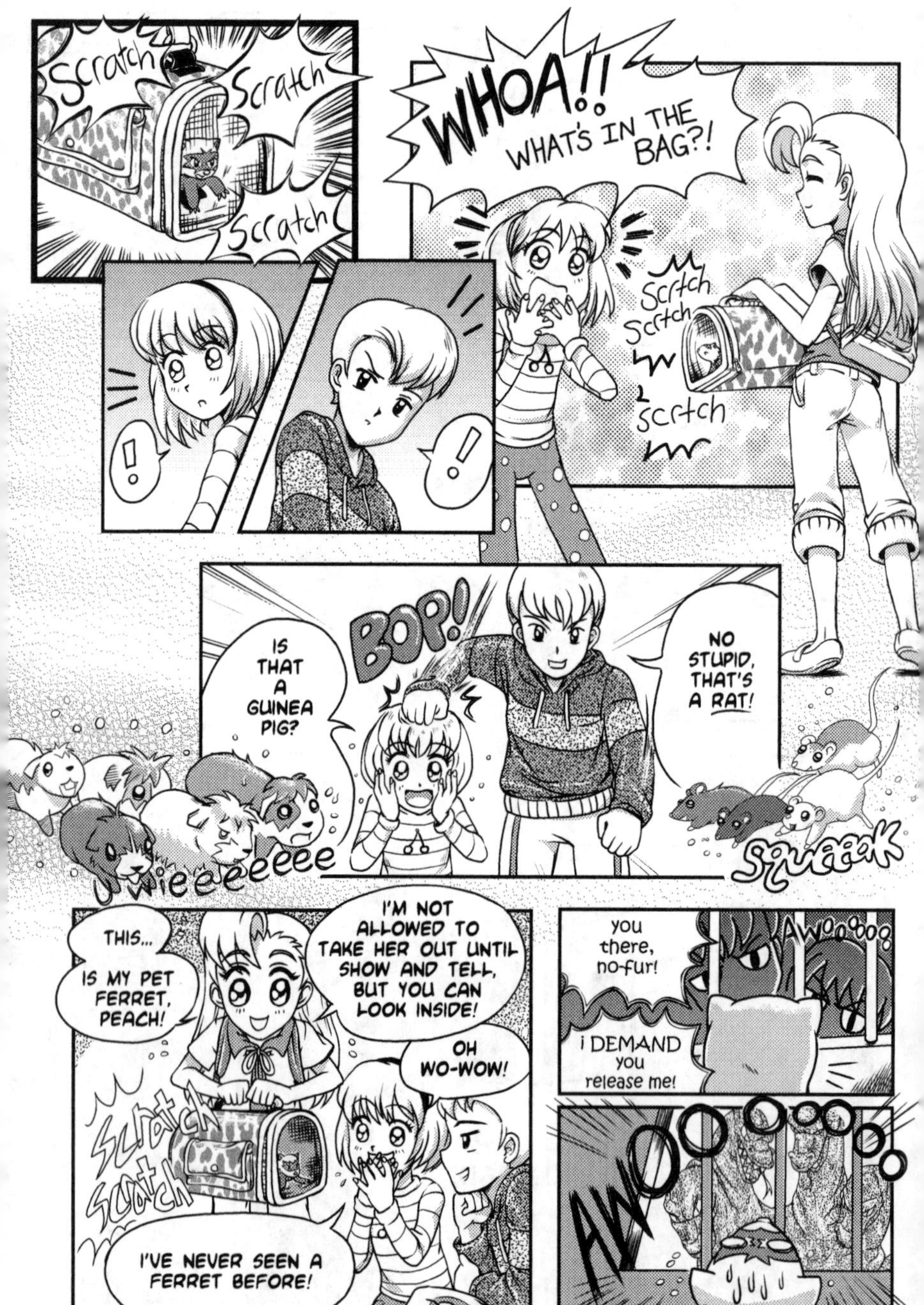
Scratch
Scratch
Scratch
WHOA!!
WHAT'S IN THE BAG?!
Scrtch
Scrtch
Scrtch
!
!
BOP!
IS THAT A GUINEA PIG?
NO STUPID, THAT'S A RAT!
wieeeeeee
Squeeek
THIS...
IS MY PET FERRET, PEACH!
I'M NOT ALLOWED TO TAKE HER OUT UNTIL SHOW AND TELL, BUT YOU CAN LOOK INSIDE!
OH WO-WOW!
Scratch
Scratch
I'VE NEVER SEEN A FERRET BEFORE!
you there, no-fur!
AWooooo
i DEMAND you release me!
AWOOOOOOO

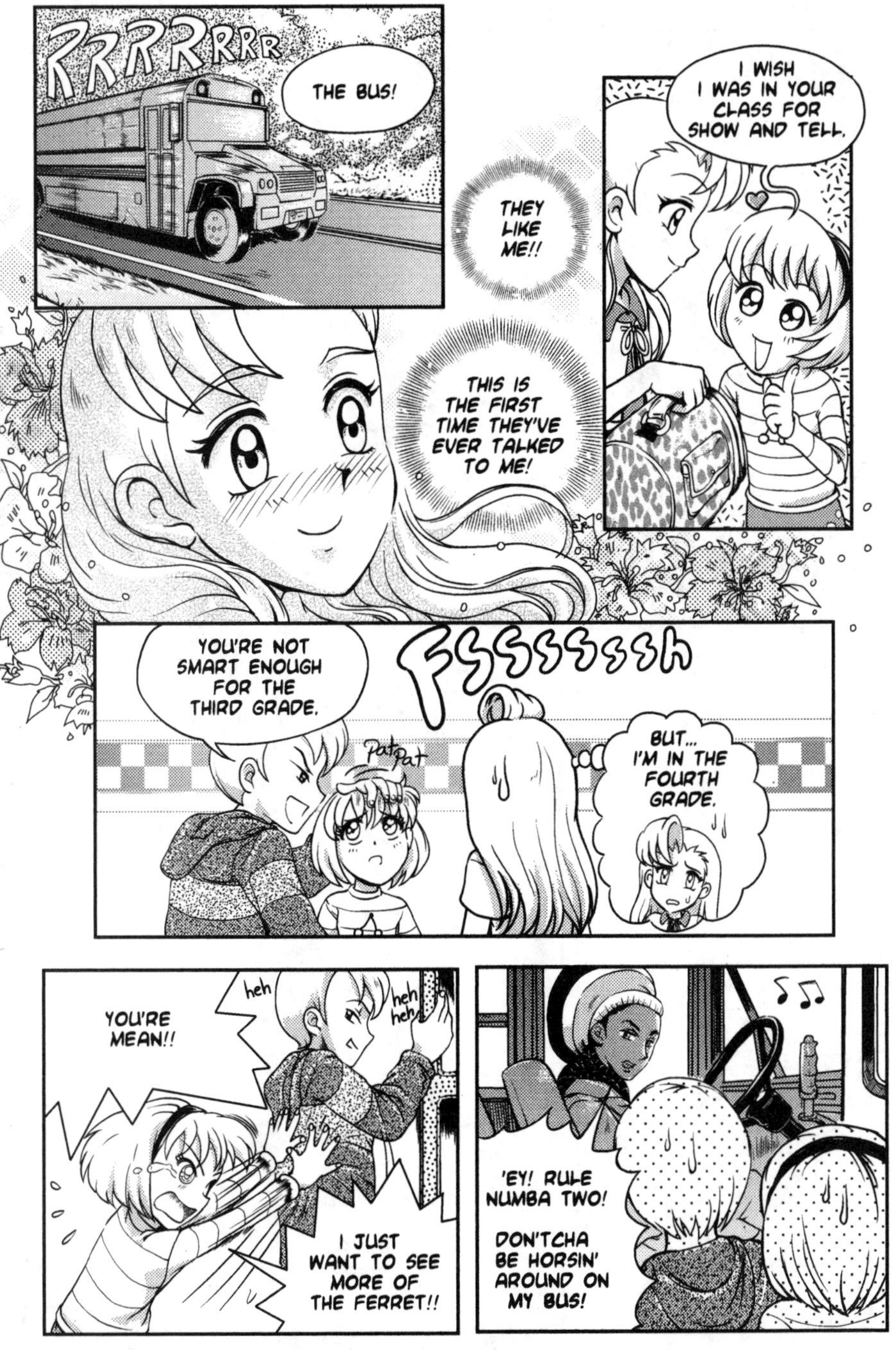
RRRRRRR
THE BUS!
I WISH I WAS IN YOUR CLASS FOR SHOW AND TELL.
THEY LIKE ME!!
THIS IS THE FIRST TIME THEY'VE EVER TALKED TO ME!
YOU'RE NOT SMART ENOUGH FOR THE THIRD GRADE.
FSSSSSSh
Pat Pat
BUT... I'M IN THE FOURTH GRADE.
YOU'RE MEAN!!
heh
heh heh
I JUST WANT TO SEE MORE OF THE FERRET!!
'EY! RULE NUMBA TWO!
DON'TCHA BE HORSIN' AROUND ON MY BUS!

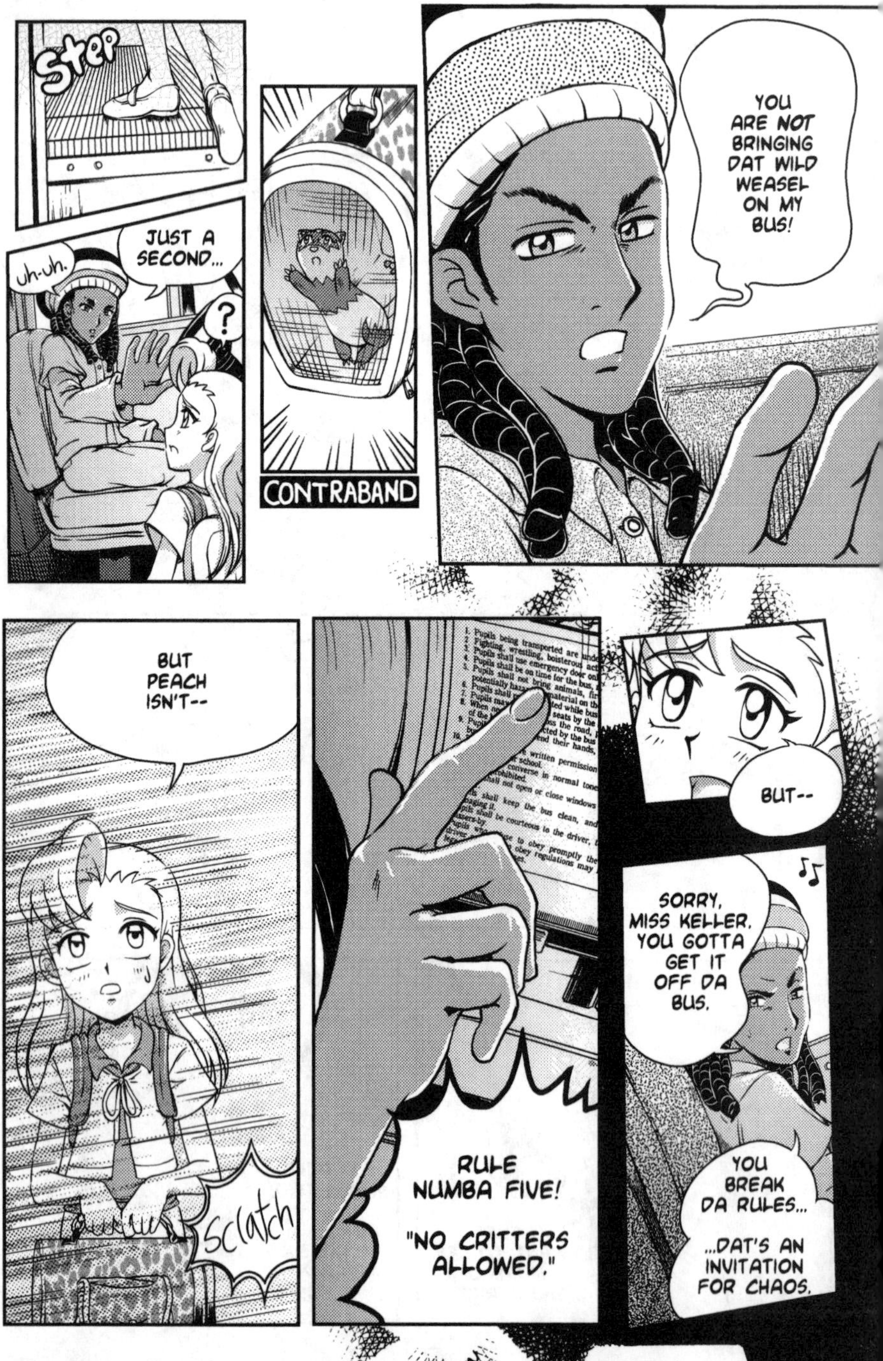

Step
CONTRABAND
YOU ARE NOT BRINGING DAT WILD WEASEL ON MY BUS!
uh-uh.
JUST A SECOND...
?
BUT PEACH ISN'T--
Sclatch
RULE NUMBA FIVE!
"NO CRITTERS ALLOWED."
BUT--
SORRY, MISS KELLER. YOU GOTTA GET IT OFF DA BUS.
YOU BREAK DA RULES...
...DAT'S AN INVITATION FOR CHAOS.

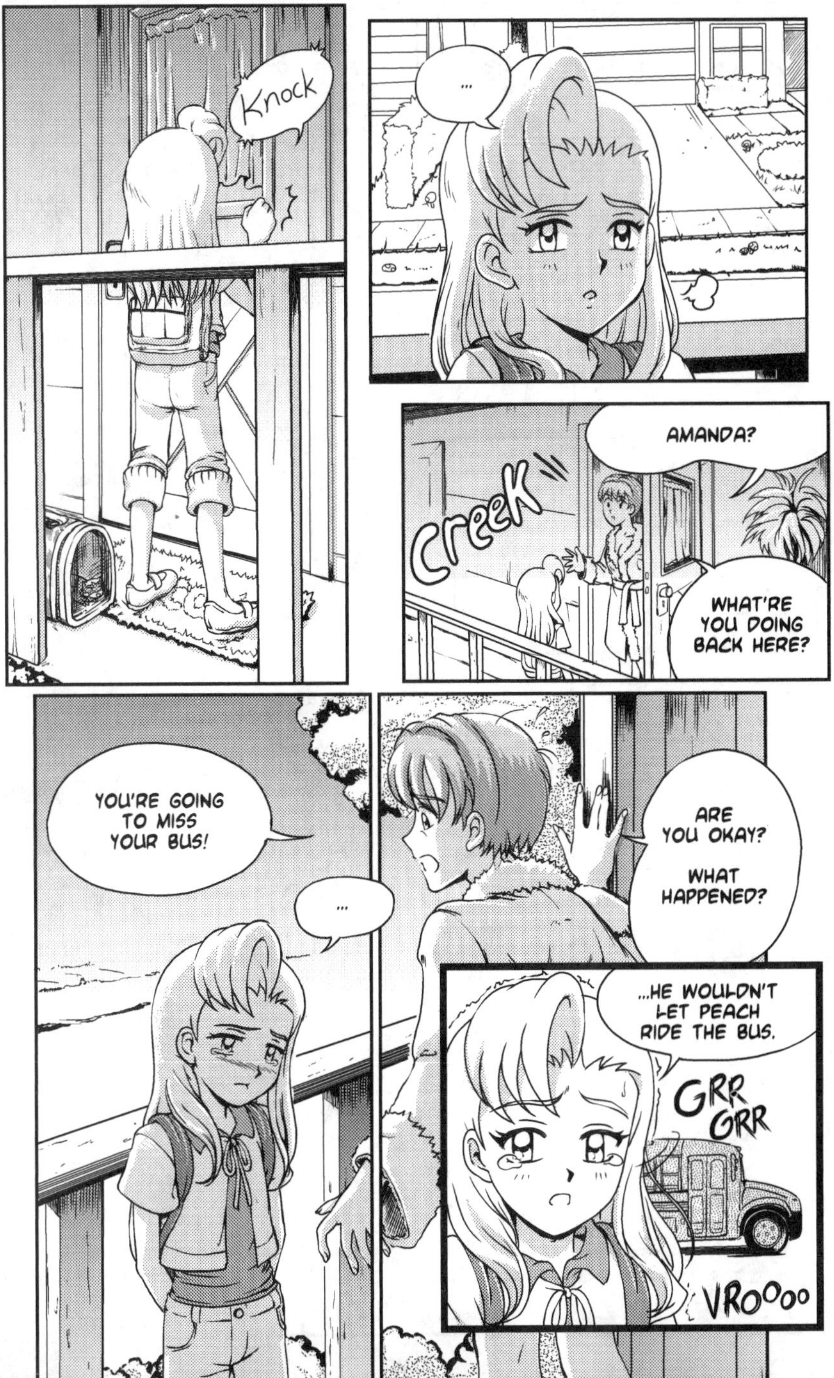
Knock
...
AMANDA?
CREEK
WHAT'RE YOU DOING BACK HERE?
YOU'RE GOING TO MISS YOUR BUS!
...
ARE YOU OKAY?
WHAT HAPPENED?
...HE WOULDN'T LET PEACH RIDE THE BUS.
GRR GRR
VROOOO

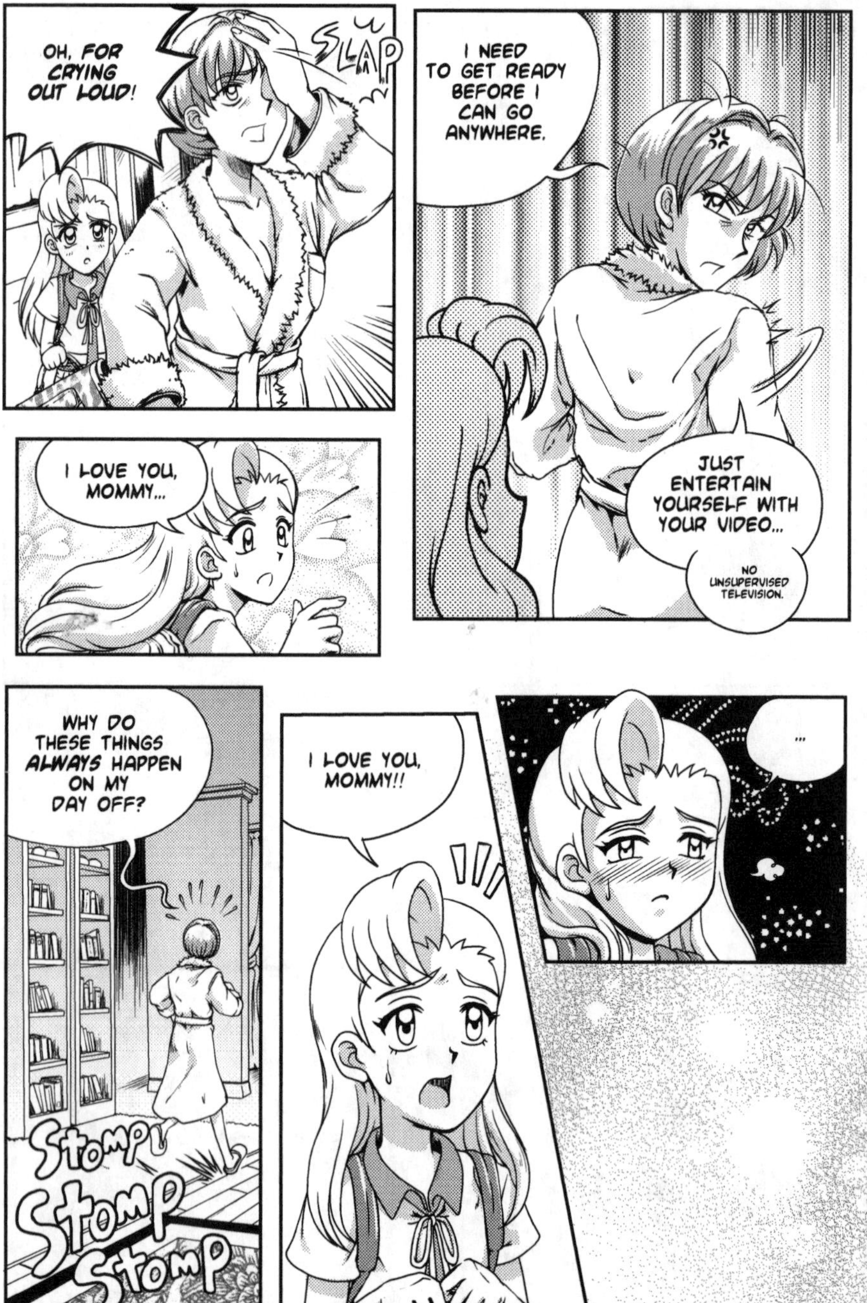

OH, FOR CRYING OUT LOUD!
SLAP
I NEED TO GET READY BEFORE I CAN GO ANYWHERE.
JUST ENTERTAIN YOURSELF WITH YOUR VIDEO...
NO UNSUPERVISED TELEVISION.
I LOVE YOU, MOMMY...
WHY DO THESE THINGS ALWAYS HAPPEN ON MY DAY OFF?
STOMP STOMP STOMP
I LOVE YOU, MOMMY!!
...

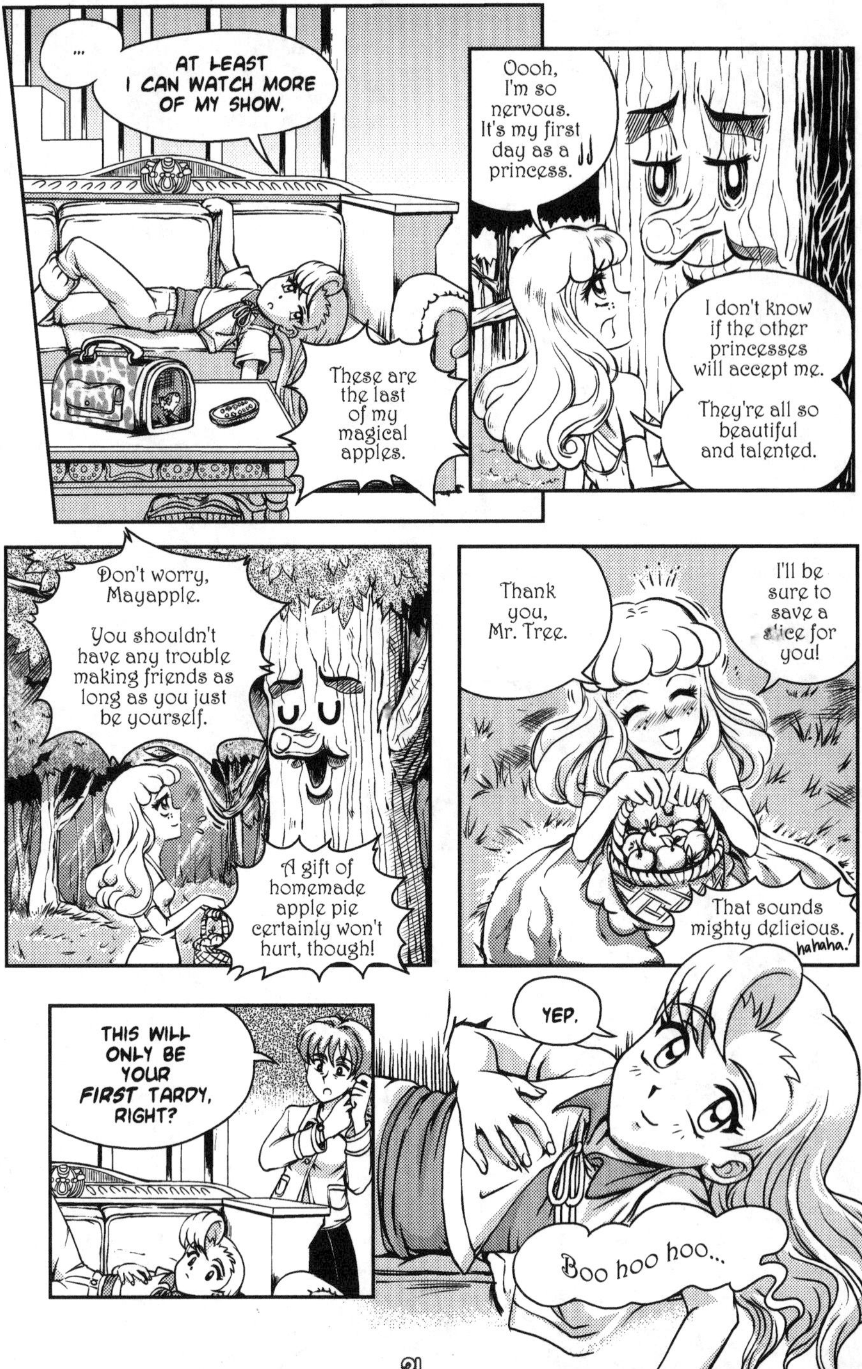
...
AT LEAST I CAN WATCH MORE OF MY SHOW.
These are the last of my magical apples.
Oooh, I'm so nervous. It's my first day as a princess.
I don't know if the other princesses will accept me.
They're all so beautiful and talented.
Don't worry, Mayapple.
You shouldn't have any trouble making friends as long as you just be yourself.
A gift of homemade apple pie certainly won't hurt, though!
Thank you, Mr. Tree.
I'll be sure to save a slice for you!
That sounds mighty delicious.
hahaha!
THIS WILL ONLY BE YOUR FIRST TARDY, RIGHT?
YEP.
Boo hoo hoo...

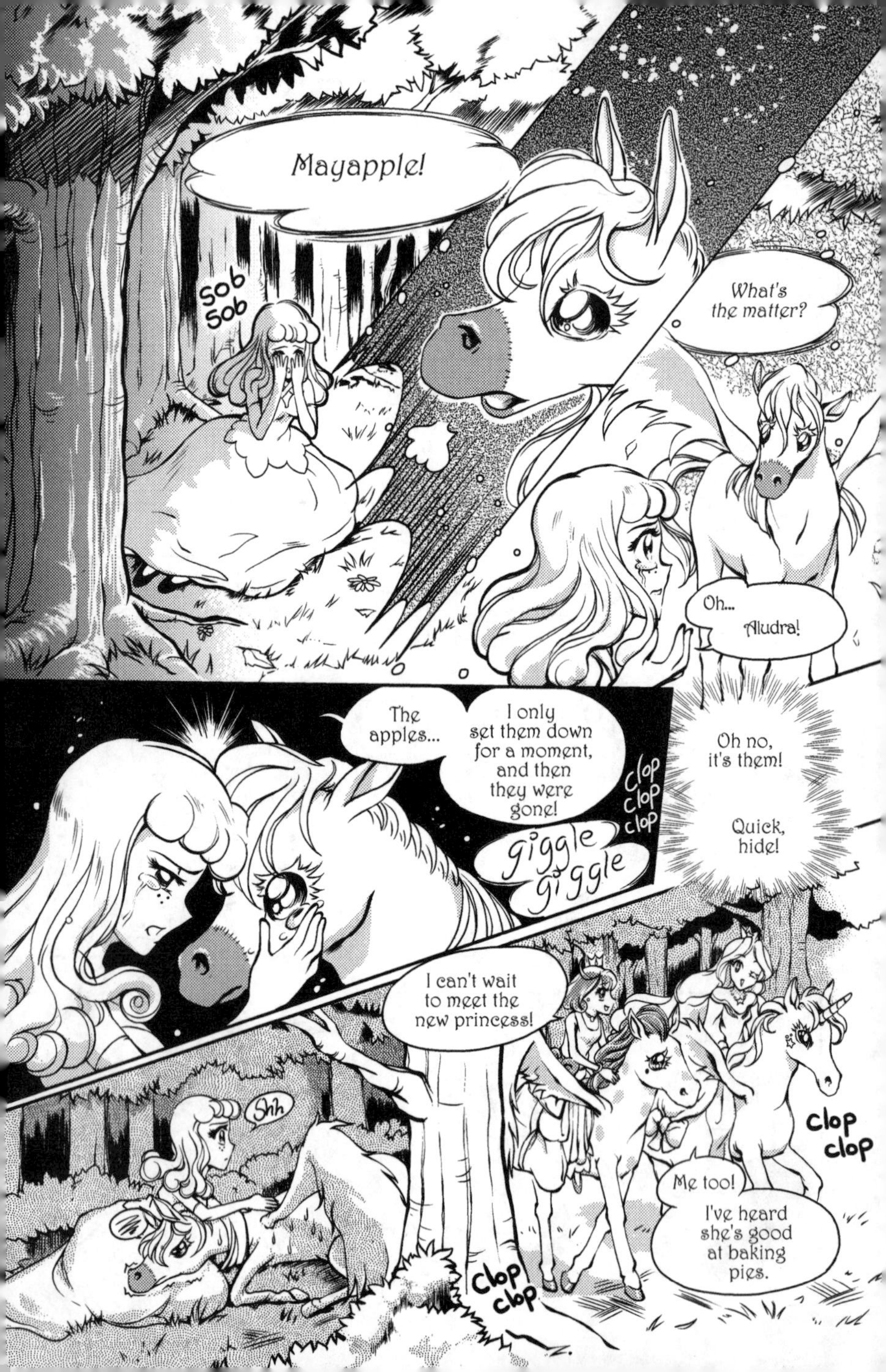

Mayapple!
Sob Sob
What's the matter?
Oh... Aludra!
The apples...
I only set them down for a moment, and then they were gone!
Clop clop clop
Giggle Giggle
Oh no, it's them!
Quick, hide!
I can't wait to meet the new princess!
Shh
Clop clop
Me too!
I've heard she's good at baking pies.
Clop clop

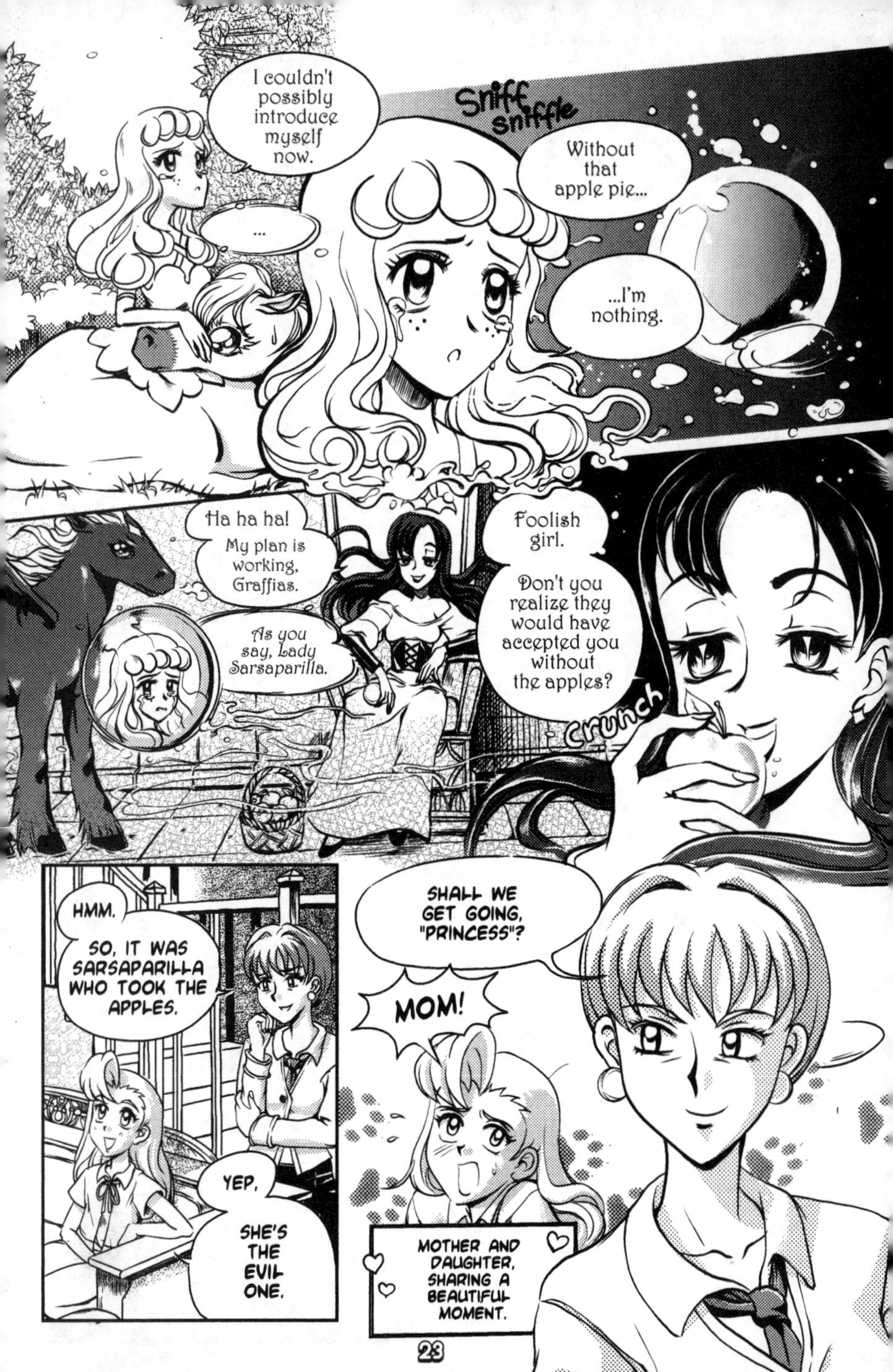
I couldn't possibly introduce myself now.
...
Sniff sniffle
Without that apple pie...
...I'm nothing.
Ha ha ha! My plan is working, Graffias.
As you say, Lady Sarsaparilla.
Foolish girl.
Don't you realize they would have accepted you without the apples?
Crunch
HMM.
SO, IT WAS SARSAPARILLA WHO TOOK THE APPLES.
YEP,
SHE'S THE EVIL ONE.
SHALL WE GET GOING, "PRINCESS"?
MOM!
MOTHER AND DAUGHTER, SHARING A BEAUTIFUL MOMENT.

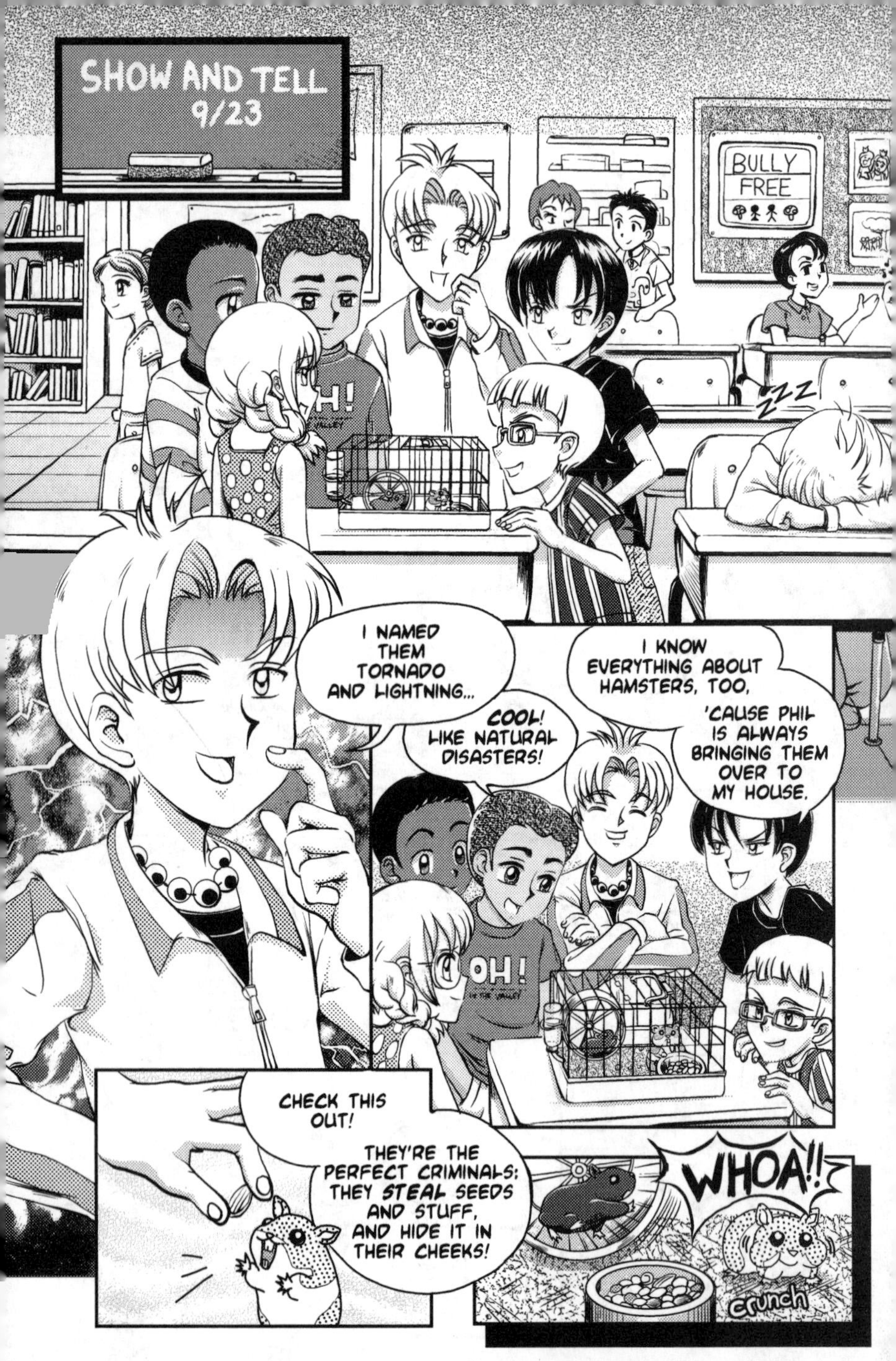
SHOW AND TELL 9/23
BULLY FREE
I NAMED THEM TORNADO AND LIGHTNING...
COOL! LIKE NATURAL DISASTERS!
I KNOW EVERYTHING ABOUT HAMSTERS, TOO,
'CAUSE PHIL IS ALWAYS BRINGING THEM OVER TO MY HOUSE.
CHECK THIS OUT!
THEY'RE THE PERFECT CRIMINALS: THEY STEAL SEEDS AND STUFF, AND HIDE IT IN THEIR CHEEKS!
WHOA!!
crunch

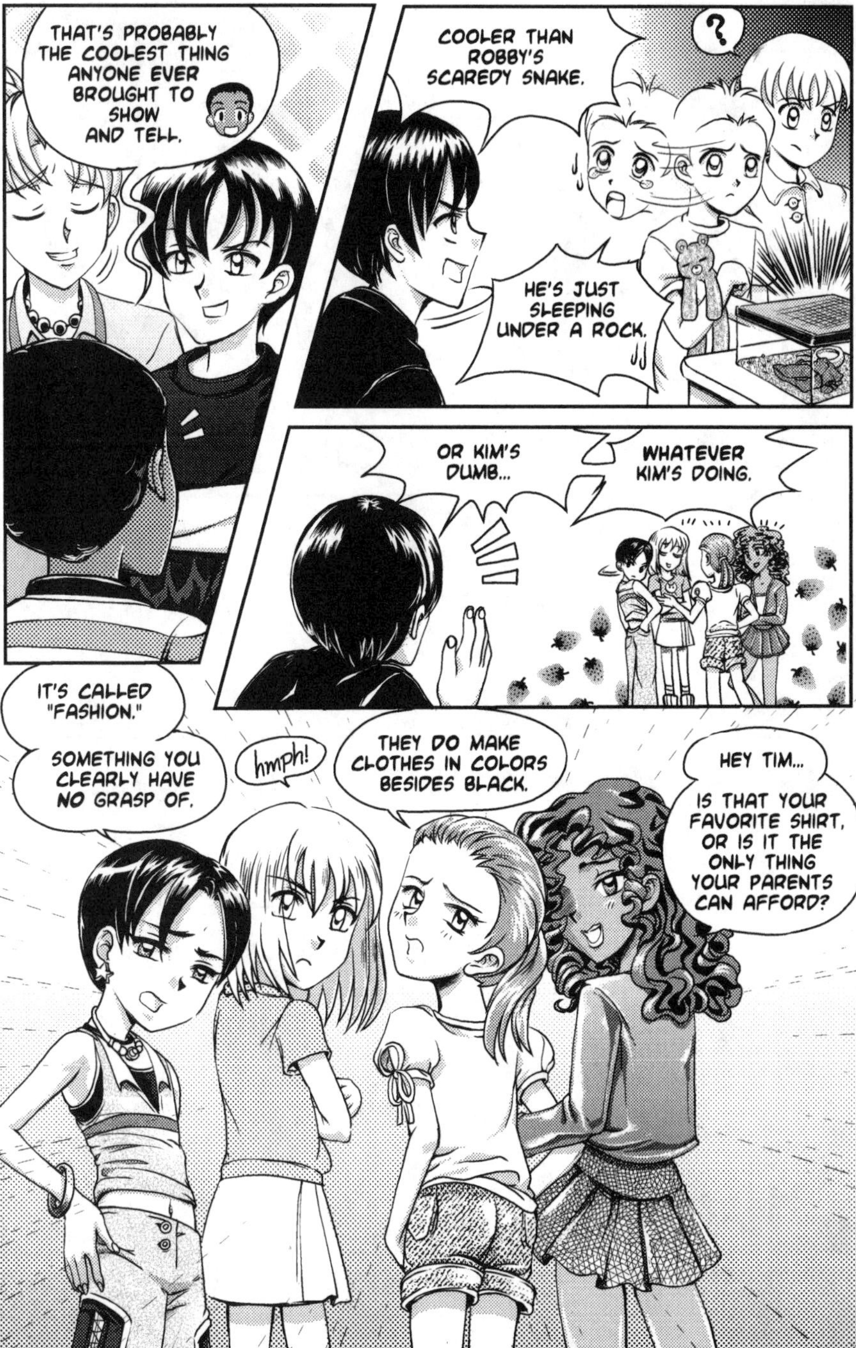
THAT'S PROBABLY THE COOLEST THING ANYONE EVER BROUGHT TO SHOW AND TELL.
COOLER THAN ROBBY'S SCAREDY SNAKE.
?
HE'S JUST SLEEPING UNDER A ROCK.
OR KIM'S DUMB...
WHATEVER KIM'S DOING.
IT'S CALLED "FASHION."
SOMETHING YOU CLEARLY HAVE NO GRASP OF.
hmph!
THEY DO MAKE CLOTHES IN COLORS BESIDES BLACK.
HEY TIM...
IS THAT YOUR FAVORITE SHIRT, OR IS IT THE ONLY THING YOUR PARENTS CAN AFFORD?

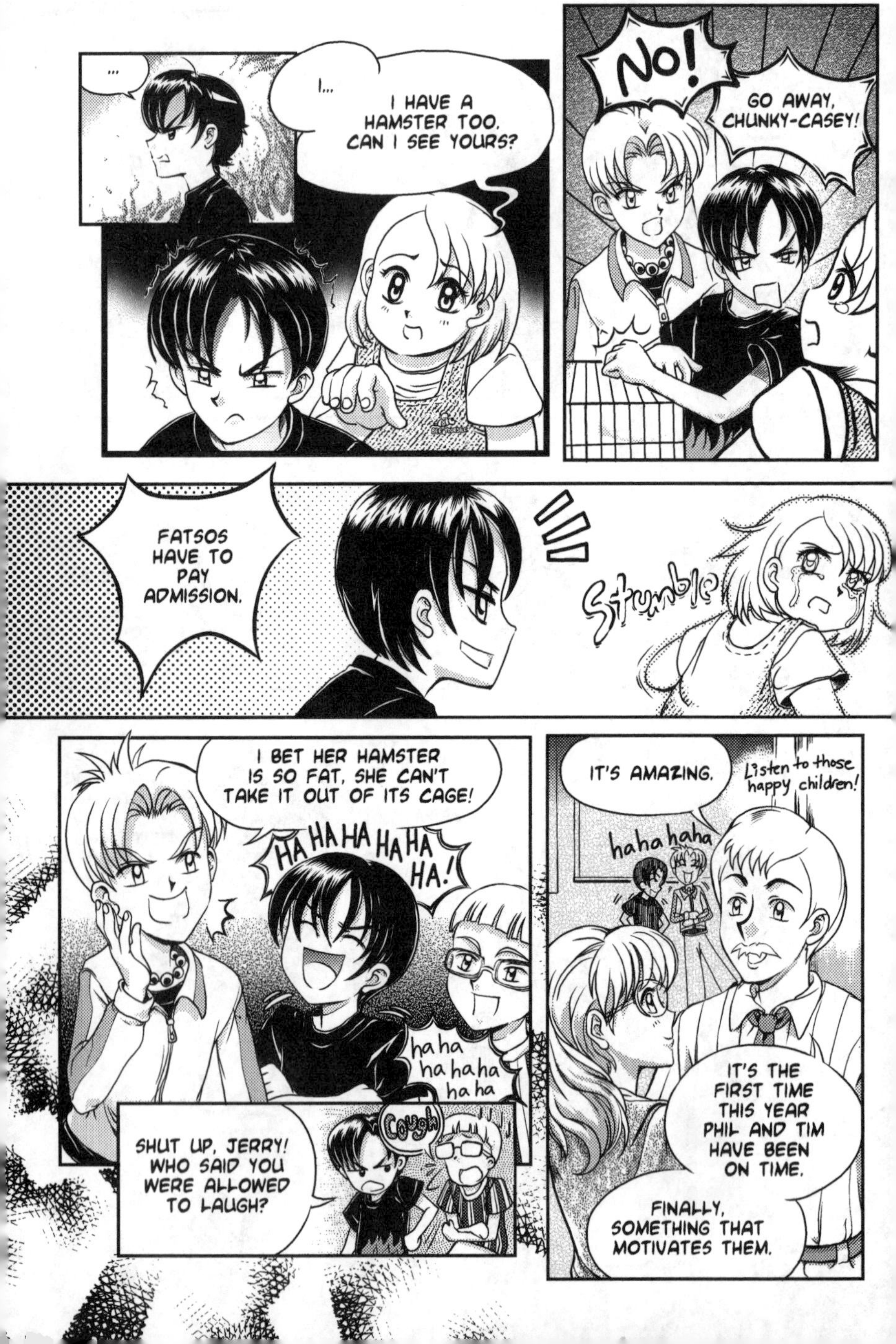
...
I...
I HAVE A HAMSTER TOO. CAN I SEE YOURS?
No!
GO AWAY, CHUNKY-CASEY!
FATSOS HAVE TO PAY ADMISSION.
Stumble
I BET HER HAMSTER IS SO FAT, SHE CAN'T TAKE IT OUT OF ITS CAGE!
HA HA HA HA HA HA HA!
ha ha ha ha ha ha ha
Cough
SHUT UP, JERRY! WHO SAID YOU WERE ALLOWED TO LAUGH?
IT'S AMAZING.
Listen to those happy children!
haha haha
IT'S THE FIRST TIME THIS YEAR PHIL AND TIM HAVE BEEN ON TIME.
FINALLY, SOMETHING THAT MOTIVATES THEM.

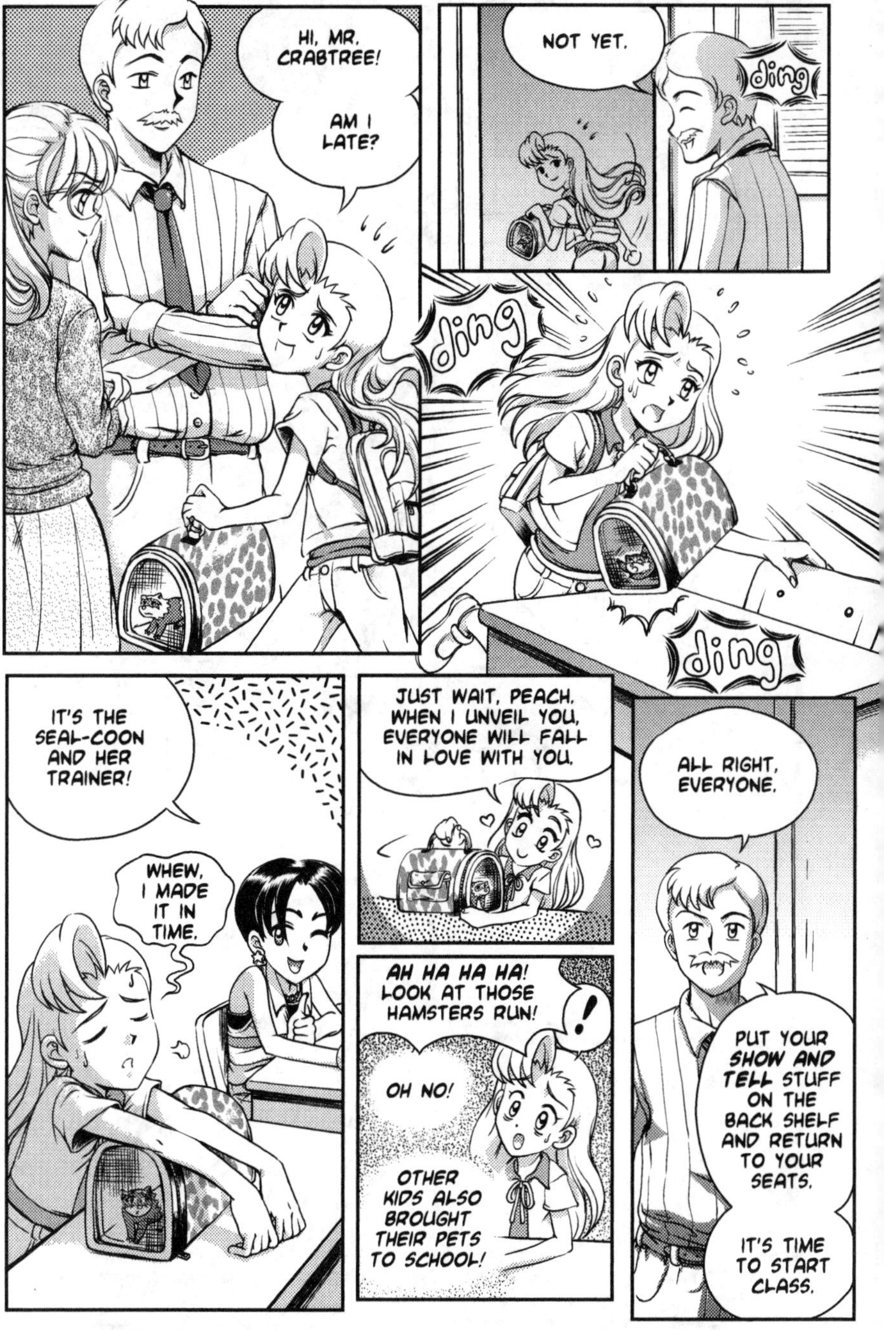
HI, MR. CRABTREE!
AM I LATE?
NOT YET.
ding
ding
ding
IT'S THE SEAL-COON AND HER TRAINER!
WHEW, I MADE IT IN TIME.
JUST WAIT, PEACH. WHEN I UNVEIL YOU, EVERYONE WILL FALL IN LOVE WITH YOU.
AH HA HA HA! LOOK AT THOSE HAMSTERS RUN!
!
OH NO!
OTHER KIDS ALSO BROUGHT THEIR PETS TO SCHOOL!
ALL RIGHT, EVERYONE.
PUT YOUR SHOW AND TELL STUFF ON THE BACK SHELF AND RETURN TO YOUR SEATS.
IT'S TIME TO START CLASS.

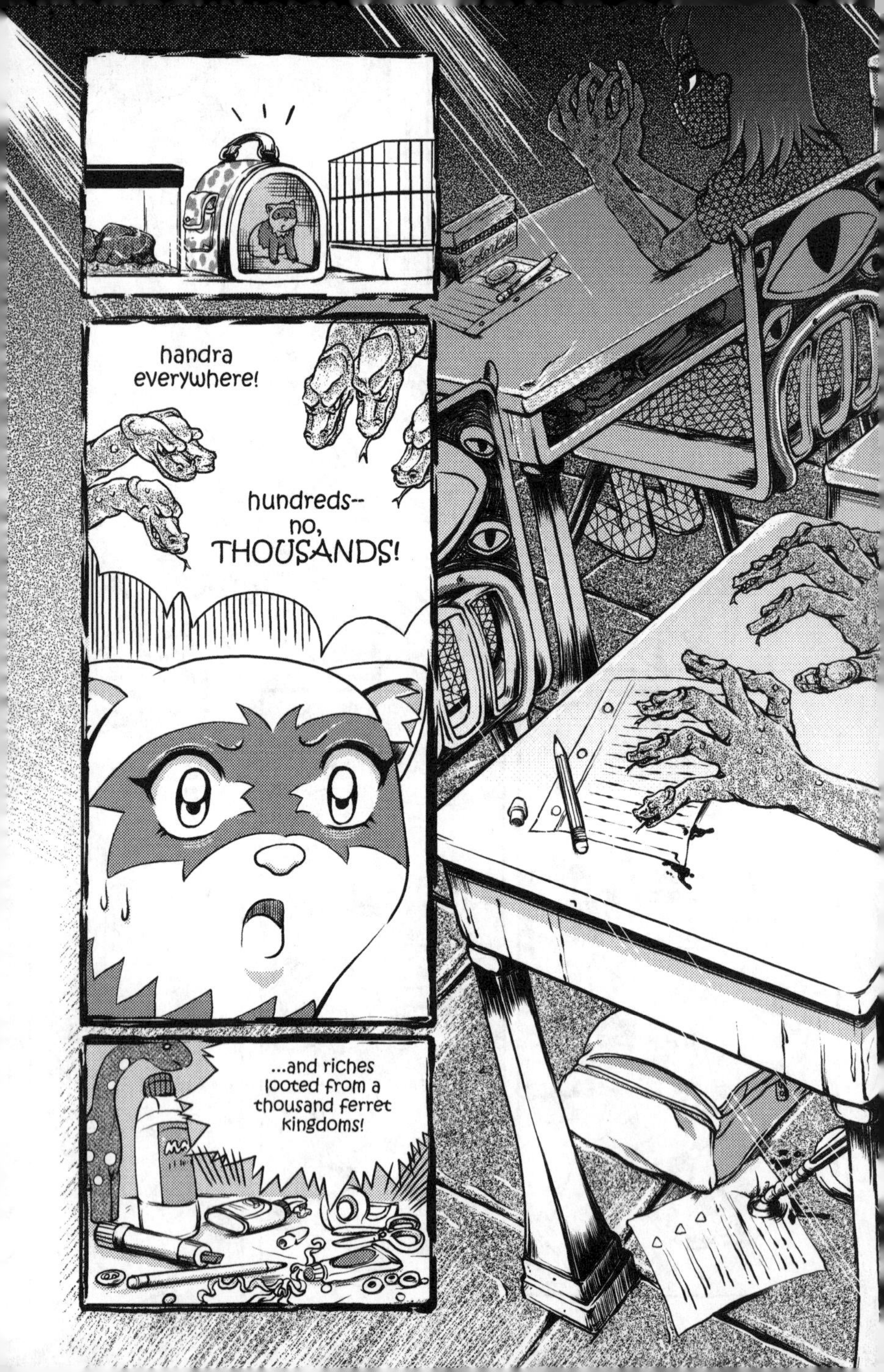
handra everywhere!
hundreds-- no, THOUSANDS!
...and riches looted from a thousand ferret kingdoms!

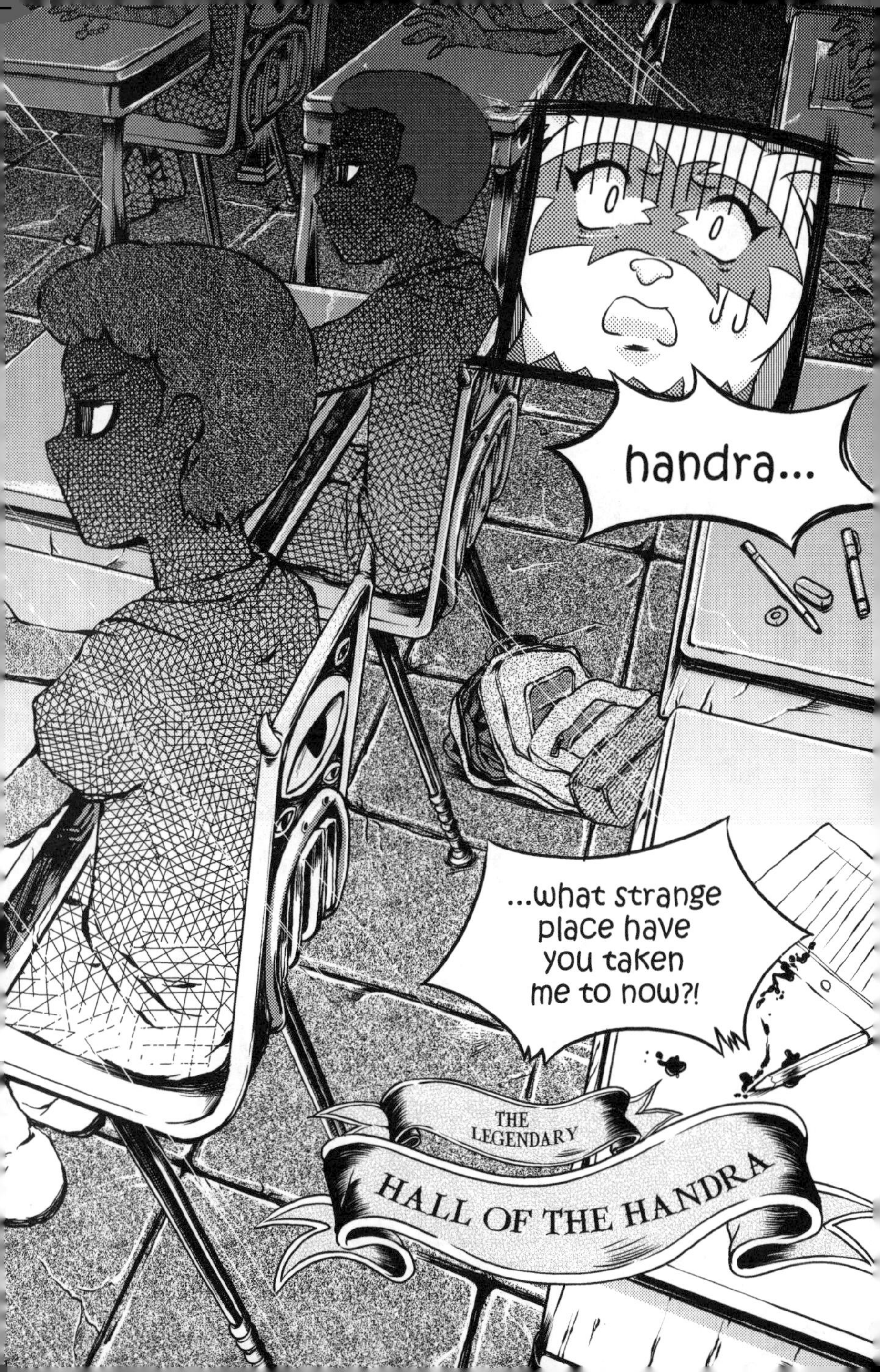
handra...
...what strange place have you taken me to now?!
THE LEGENDARY
HALL OF THE HANDRA

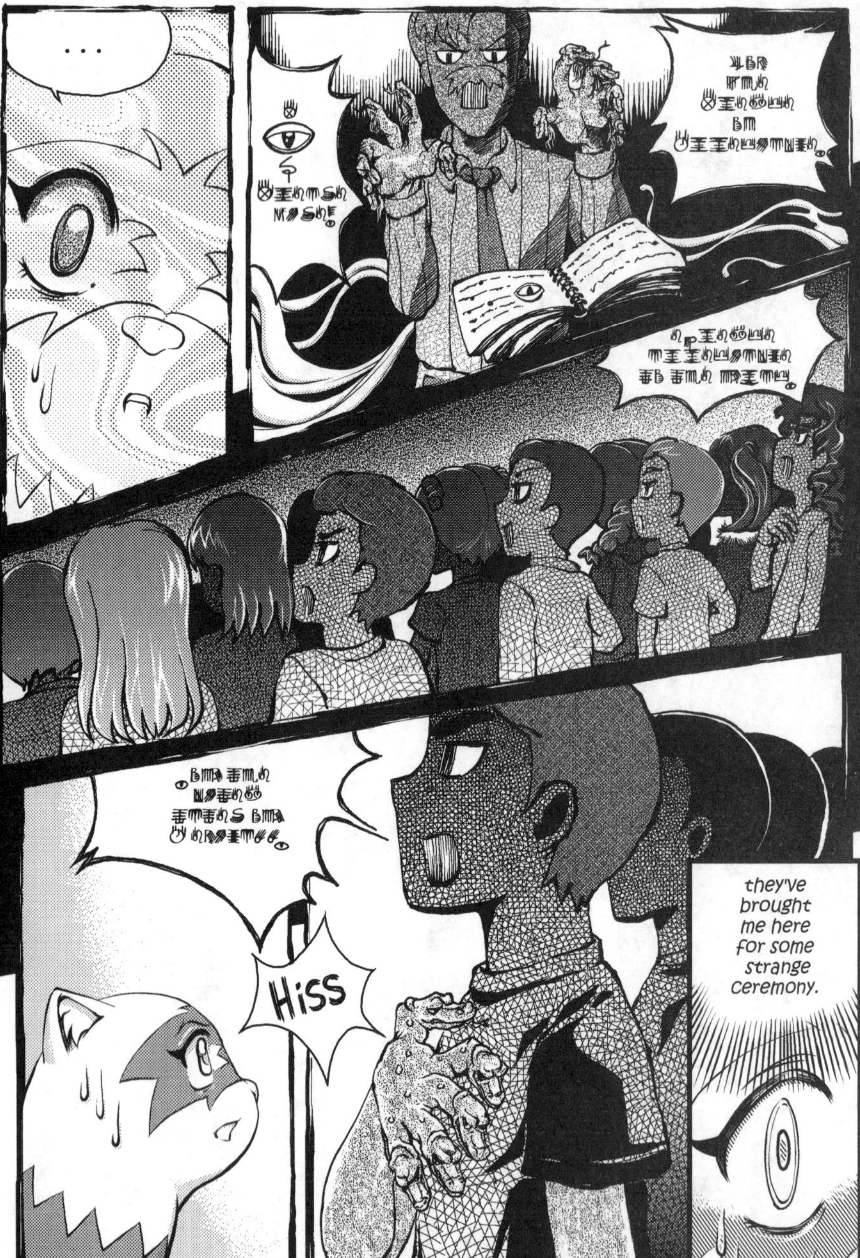

...
Hiss
they've brought me here for some strange ceremony.

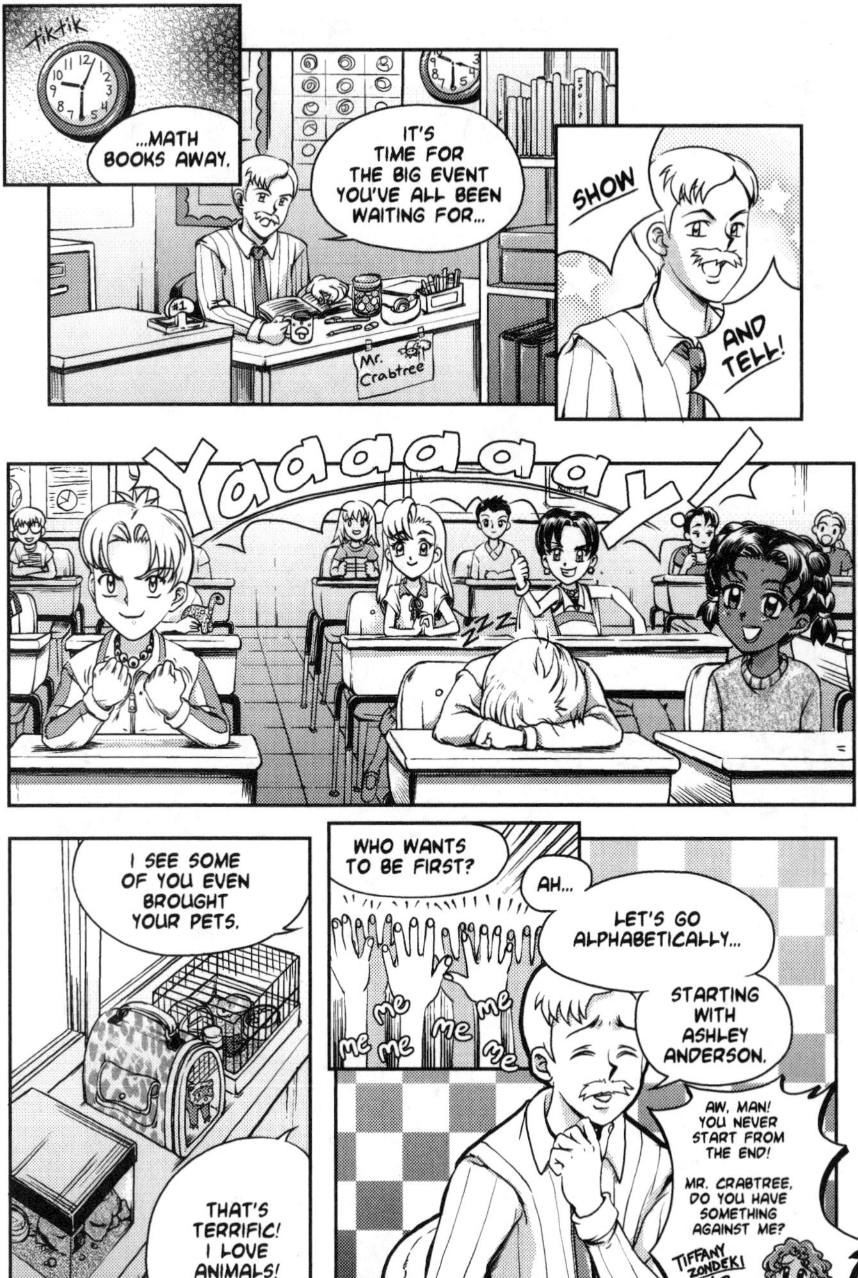
tiktik
...MATH BOOKS AWAY.
IT'S TIME FOR THE BIG EVENT YOU'VE ALL BEEN WAITING FOR...
#1
Mr. Crabtree
SHOW
AND TELL!
Yaaaaay!
I SEE SOME OF YOU EVEN BROUGHT YOUR PETS.
THAT'S TERRIFIC! I LOVE ANIMALS!
WHO WANTS TO BE FIRST?
me me me me me me
AH...
LET'S GO ALPHABETICALLY...
STARTING WITH ASHLEY ANDERSON.
AW, MAN! YOU NEVER START FROM THE END!
MR. CRABTREE, DO YOU HAVE SOMETHING AGAINST ME?
TIFFANY ZONDEKI

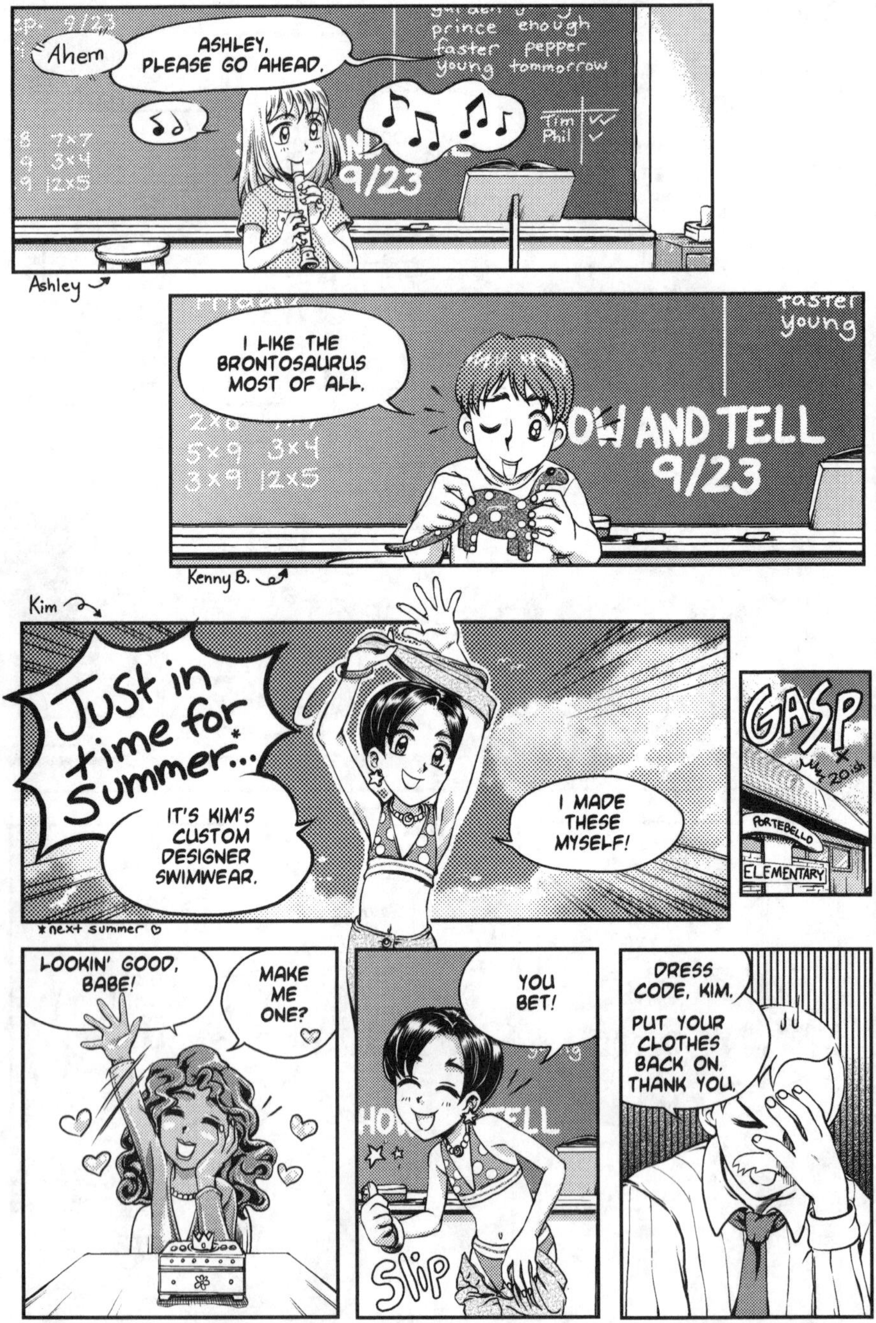
Ahem
ASHLEY, PLEASE GO AHEAD.
Ashley
I LIKE THE BRONTOSAURUS MOST OF ALL.
OW AND TELL 9/23
Kenny B.
Kim
Just in time for Summer...*
IT'S KIM'S CUSTOM DESIGNER SWIMWEAR.
I MADE THESE MYSELF!
*next summer
GASP
PORTEBELLO
ELEMENTARY
LOOKIN' GOOD, BABE!
MAKE ME ONE?
YOU BET!
Slip
DRESS CODE, KIM.
PUT YOUR CLOTHES BACK ON. THANK YOU.

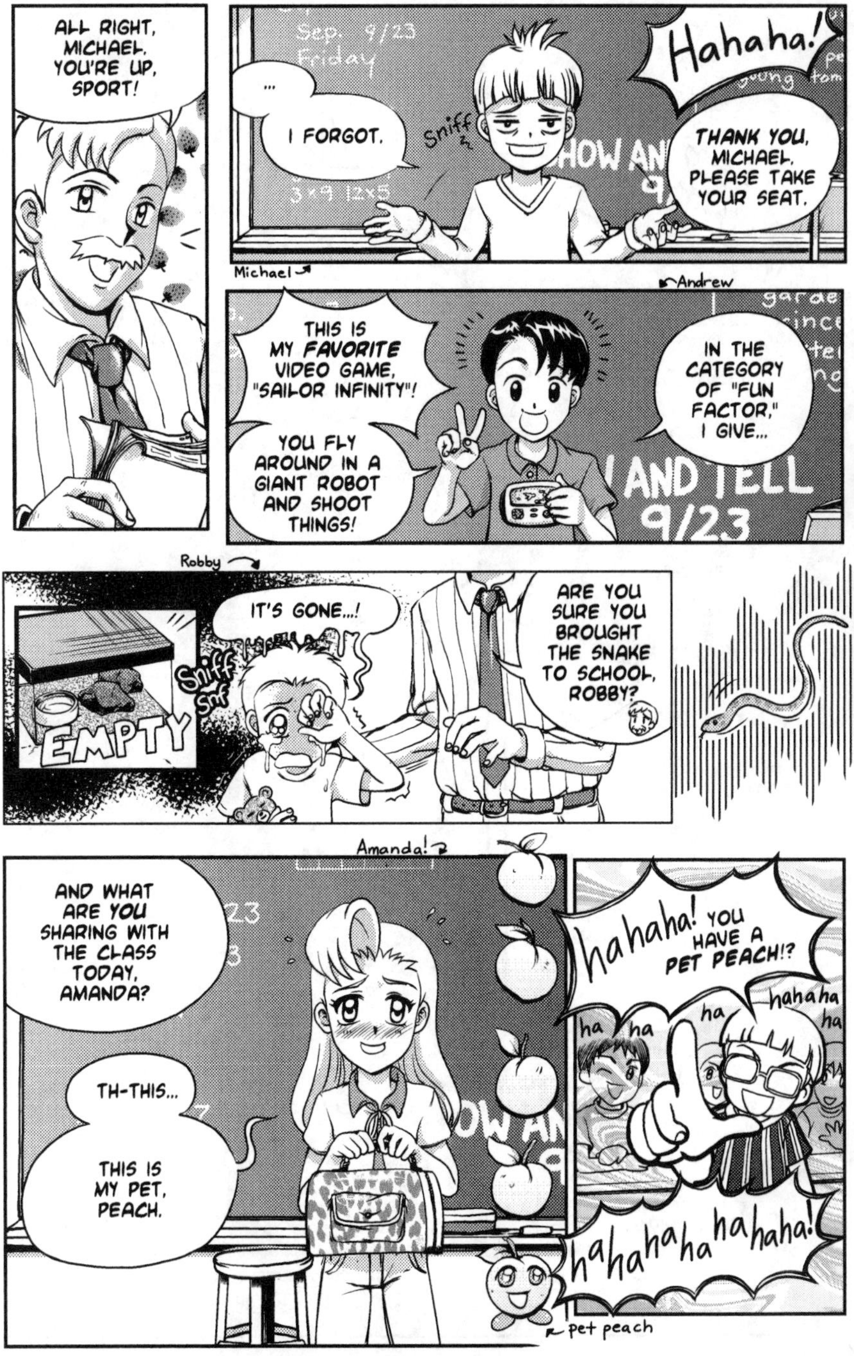
ALL RIGHT, MICHAEL, YOU'RE UP, SPORT!
...
I FORGOT.
Sniff
Hahaha!
THANK YOU, MICHAEL. PLEASE TAKE YOUR SEAT.
Michael
Andrew
THIS IS MY FAVORITE VIDEO GAME, "SAILOR INFINITY"!
YOU FLY AROUND IN A GIANT ROBOT AND SHOOT THINGS!
IN THE CATEGORY OF "FUN FACTOR," I GIVE...
Robby
IT'S GONE...!
Sniff Snf
EMPTY
ARE YOU SURE YOU BROUGHT THE SNAKE TO SCHOOL, ROBBY?
Amanda!
AND WHAT ARE YOU SHARING WITH THE CLASS TODAY, AMANDA?
TH-THIS...
THIS IS MY PET, PEACH.
hahaha! YOU HAVE A PET PEACH!?
ha ha ha hahaha ha
hahahahahahahaha!
pet peach

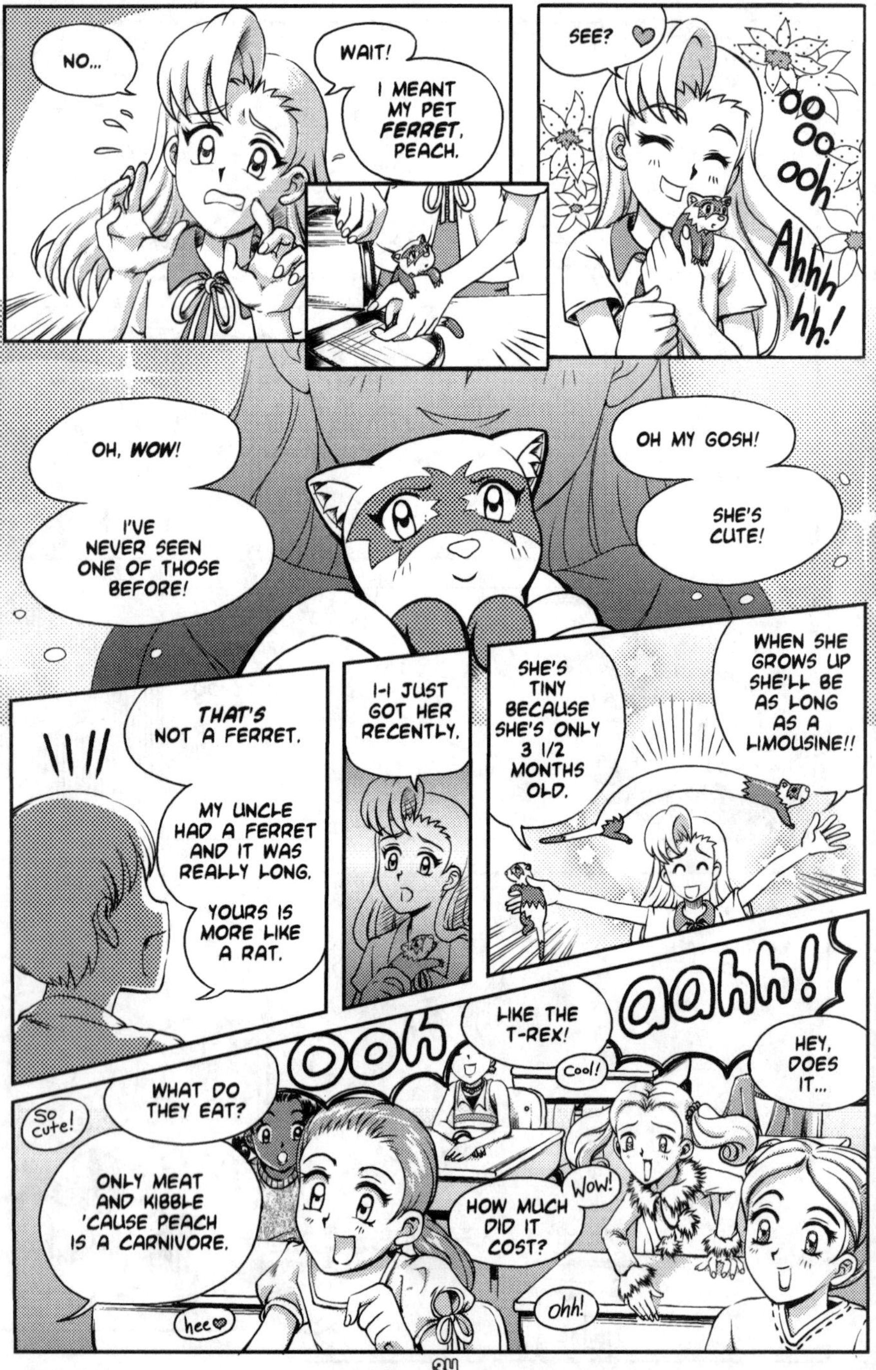
NO...
WAIT!
I MEANT MY PET FERRET, PEACH.
SEE?
OOOOooh
Ahhhhh!
OH, WOW!
I'VE NEVER SEEN ONE OF THOSE BEFORE!
OH MY GOSH!
SHE'S CUTE!
THAT'S NOT A FERRET.
MY UNCLE HAD A FERRET AND IT WAS REALLY LONG.
YOURS IS MORE LIKE A RAT.
I-I JUST GOT HER RECENTLY.
SHE'S TINY BECAUSE SHE'S ONLY 3 1/2 MONTHS OLD.
WHEN SHE GROWS UP SHE'LL BE AS LONG AS A LIMOUSINE!!
ooh
aahh!
LIKE THE T-REX!
Cool!
HEY, DOES IT...
WHAT DO THEY EAT?
So cute!
ONLY MEAT AND KIBBLE 'CAUSE PEACH IS A CARNIVORE.
Wow!
HOW MUCH DID IT COST?
ohh!
hee

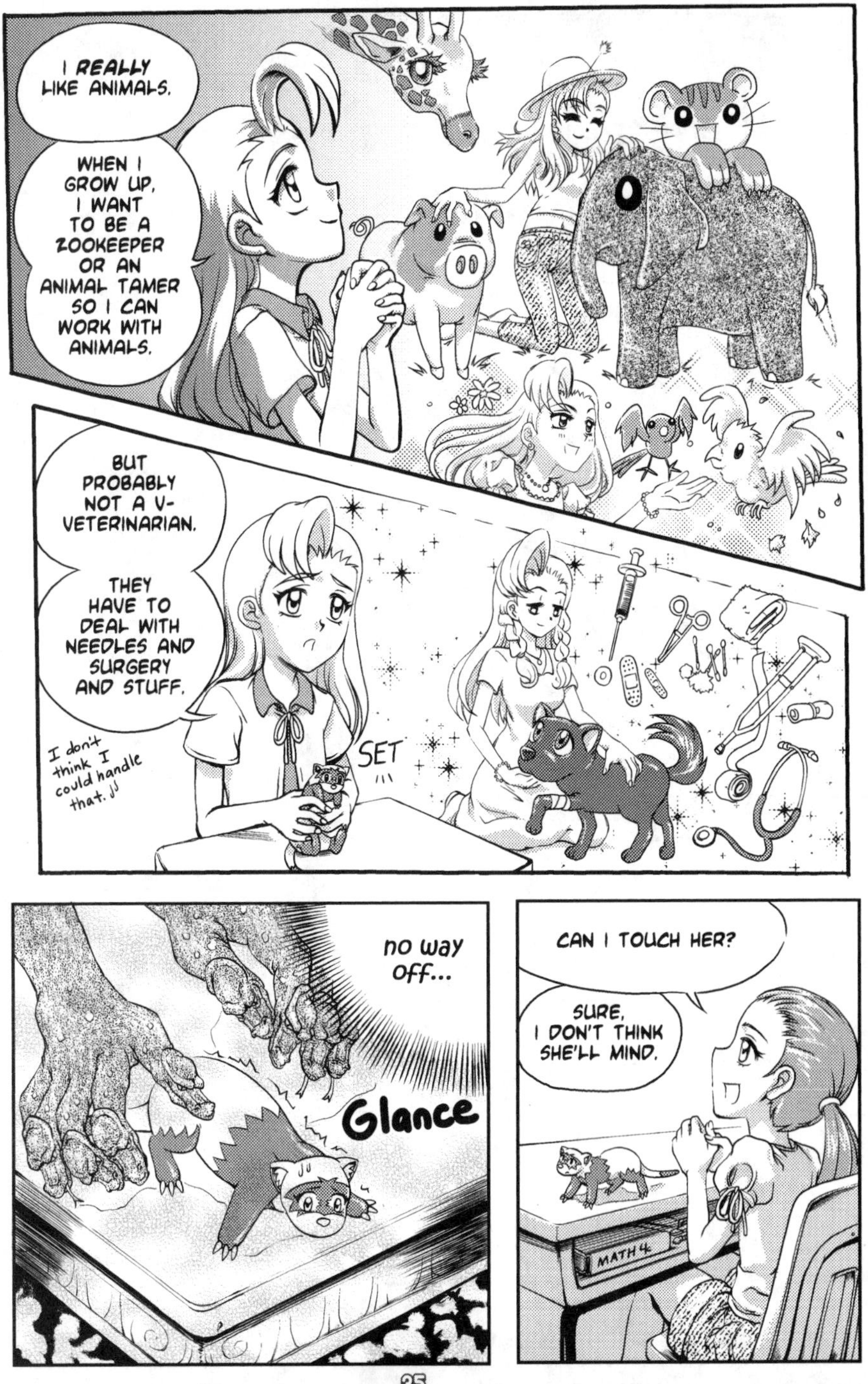
I REALLY LIKE ANIMALS.
WHEN I GROW UP, I WANT TO BE A ZOOKEEPER OR AN ANIMAL TAMER SO I CAN WORK WITH ANIMALS.
BUT PROBABLY NOT A V-VETERINARIAN.
THEY HAVE TO DEAL WITH NEEDLES AND SURGERY AND STUFF.
I don't think I could handle that.
SET
no way off...
Glance
CAN I TOUCH HER?
SURE, I DON'T THINK SHE'LL MIND.
MATH 4

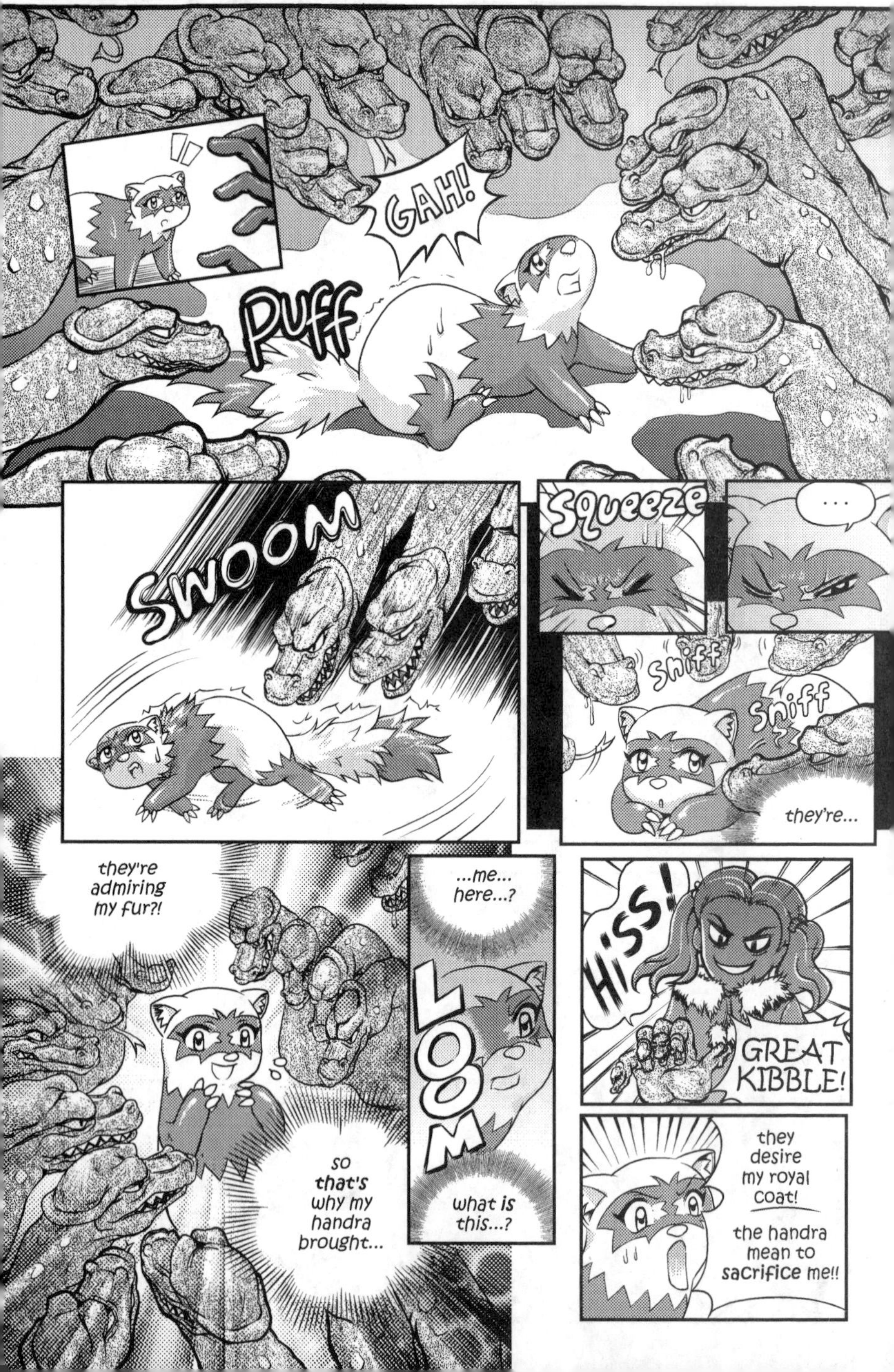
!!
GAH!
PUFF
SWOOM
Squeeze
...
sniff
sniff
they're...
they're admiring my fur?!
so that's why my handra brought...
...me... here...?
LOOM
what is this...?
HISS!
GREAT KIBBLE!
they desire my royal coat!
the handra mean to sacrifice me!!

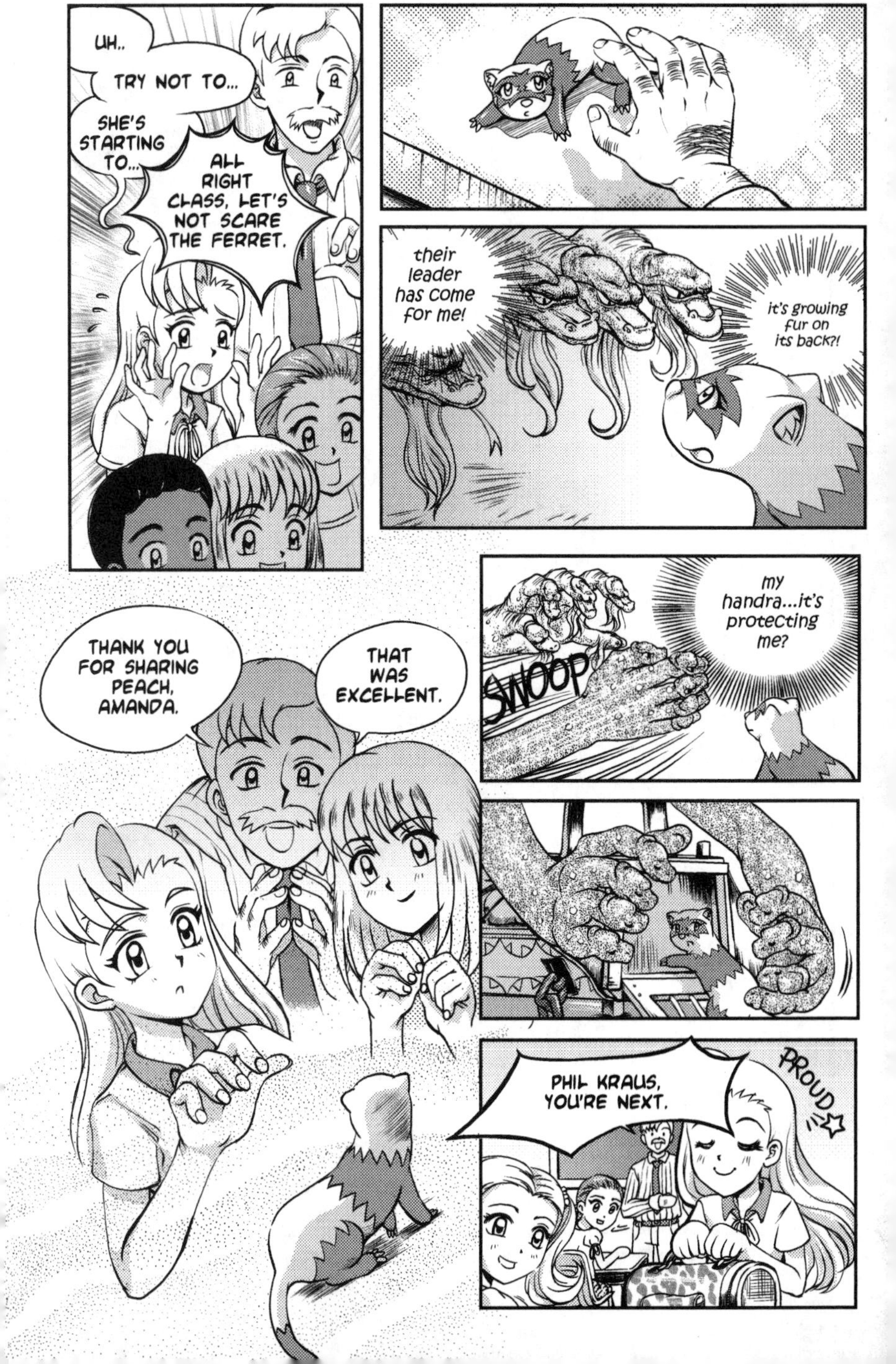
UH..
TRY NOT TO...
SHE'S STARTING TO...
ALL RIGHT CLASS, LET'S NOT SCARE THE FERRET.
their leader has come for me!
it's growing fur on its back?!
my handra...it's protecting me?
SWOOP
THANK YOU FOR SHARING PEACH, AMANDA.
THAT WAS EXCELLENT.
PHIL KRAUS, YOU'RE NEXT.
PROUD

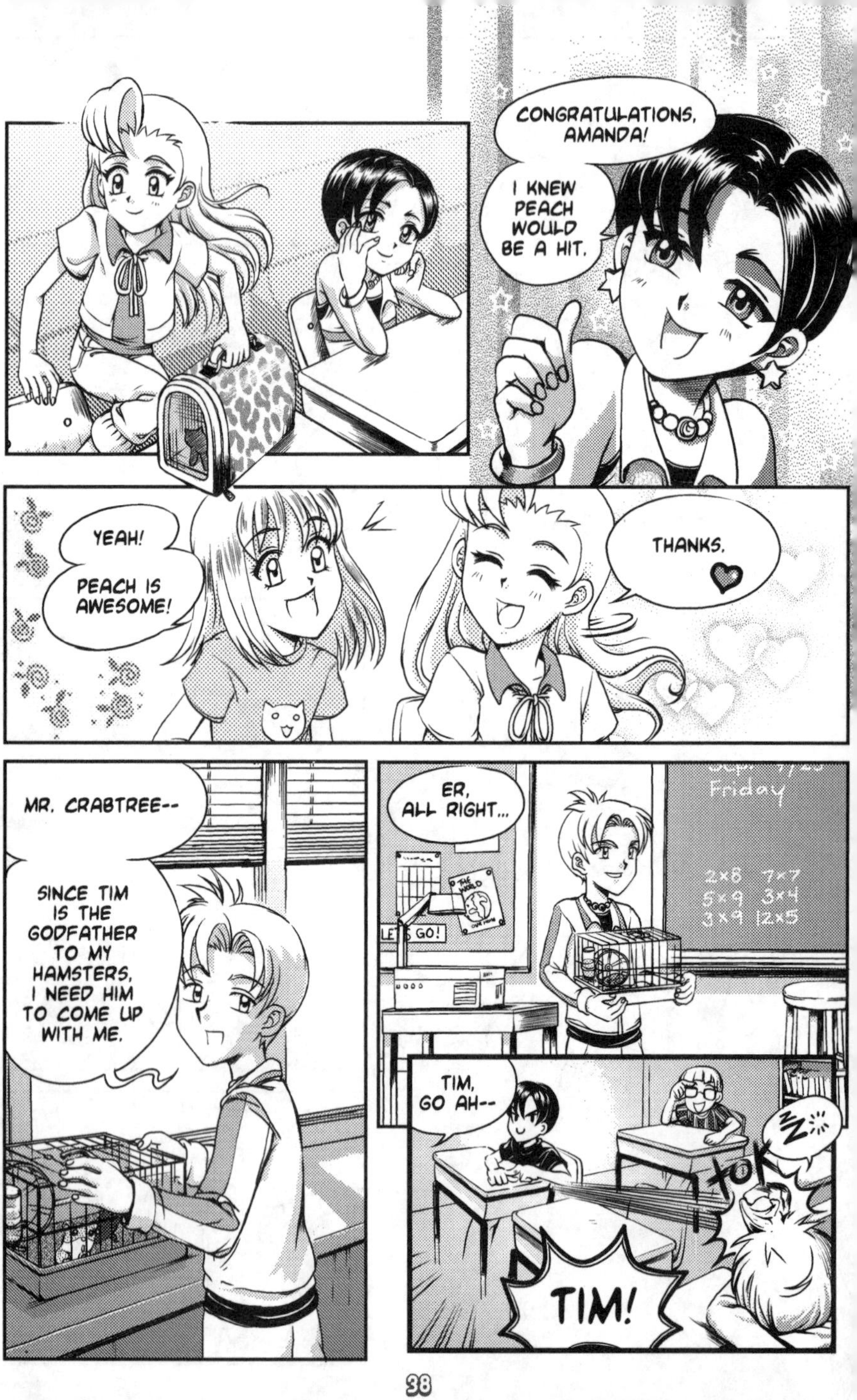
CONGRATULATIONS, AMANDA!
I KNEW PEACH WOULD BE A HIT.
YEAH!
PEACH IS MY AWESOME!
THANKS.
MR. CRABTREE--
SINCE TIM IS THE GODFATHER TO MY HAMSTERS, I NEED HIM TO COME UP WITH ME.
ER, ALL RIGHT...
Friday
2x8 7x7
5x9 3x4
3x9 12x5
TIM, GO AH--
TOK
TIM!

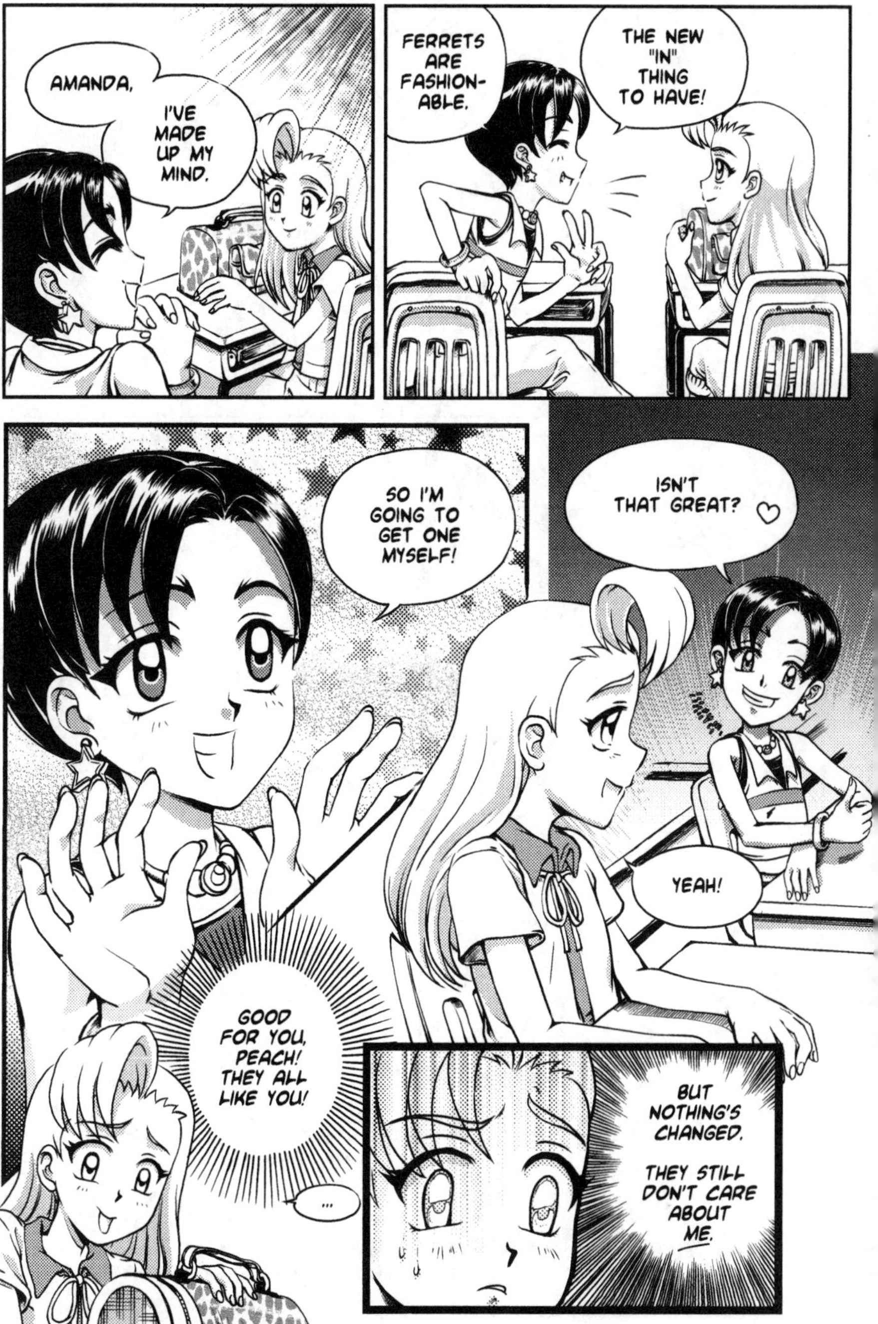
AMANDA,
I'VE MADE UP MY MIND.
FERRETS ARE FASHION-ABLE.
THE NEW "IN" THING TO HAVE!
SO I'M GOING TO GET ONE MYSELF!
ISN'T THAT GREAT? ♡
YEAH!
GOOD FOR YOU, PEACH! THEY ALL LIKE YOU!
...
BUT NOTHING'S CHANGED.
THEY STILL DON'T CARE ABOUT ME.

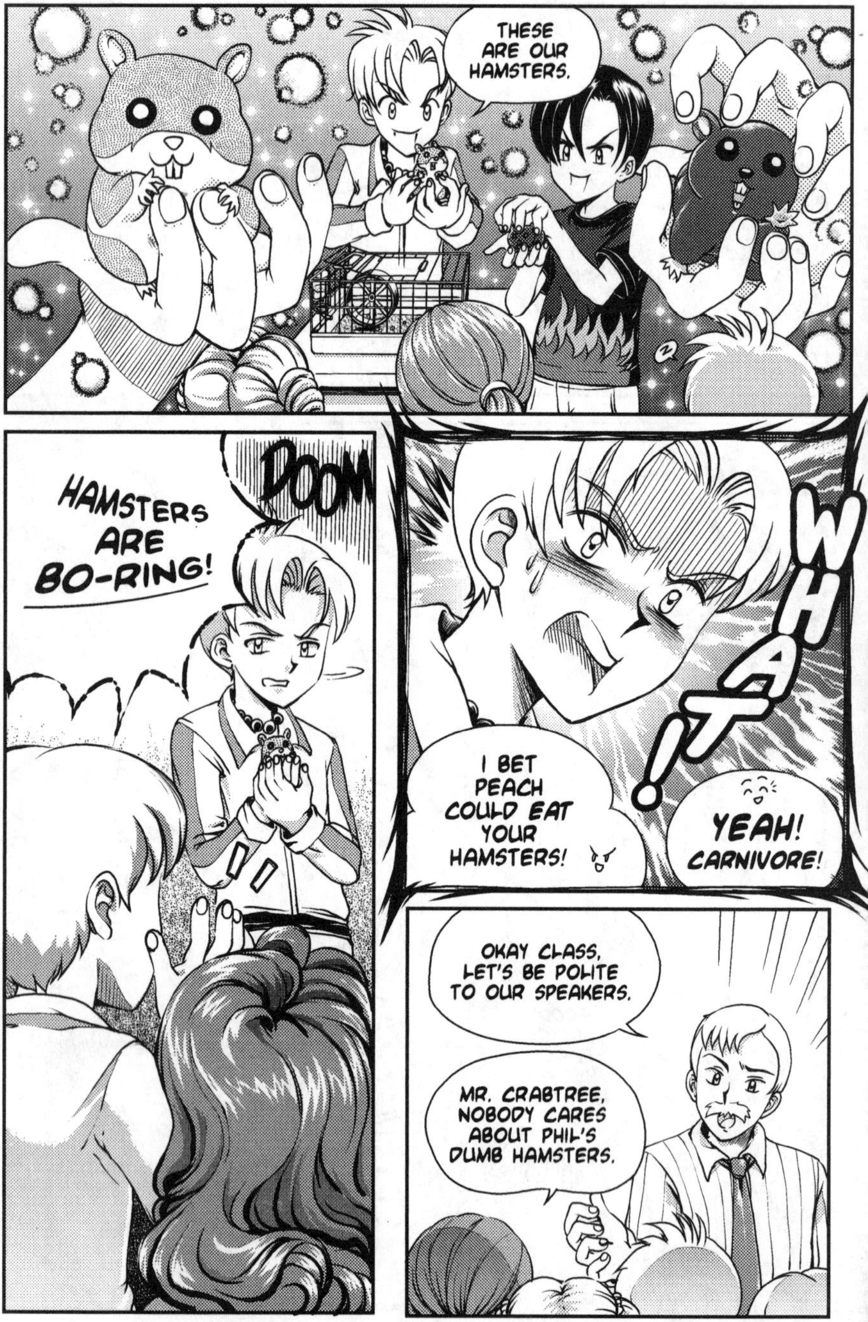
THESE ARE OUR HAMSTERS.
HAMSTERS ARE BO-RING!
DOOM
WHAT!?
I BET PEACH COULD EAT YOUR HAMSTERS!
YEAH! CARNIVORE!
OKAY CLASS, LET'S BE POLITE TO OUR SPEAKERS.
MR. CRABTREE, NOBODY CARES ABOUT PHIL'S DUMB HAMSTERS.

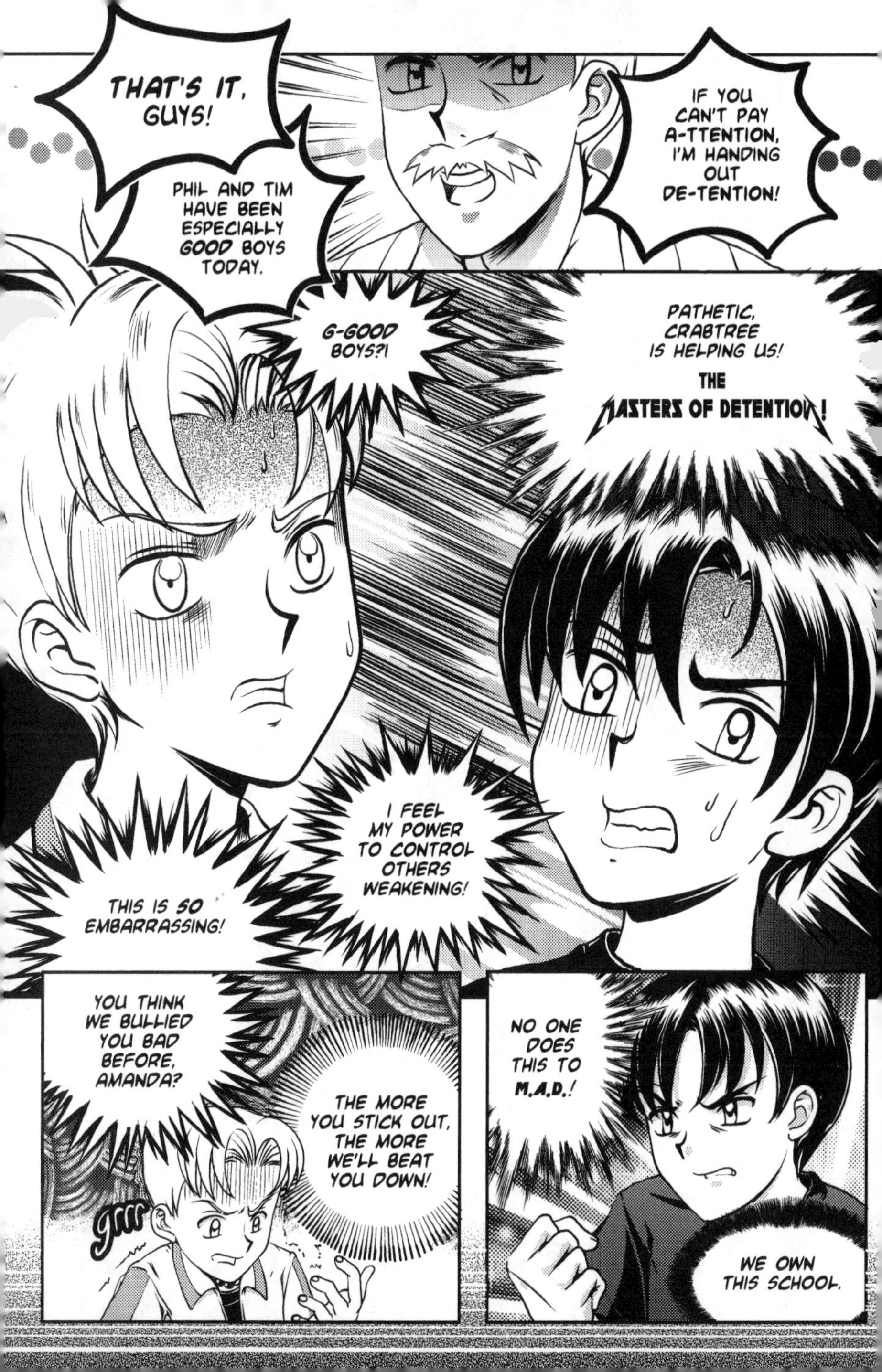
THAT'S IT, GUYS!
PHIL AND TIM HAVE BEEN ESPECIALLY GOOD BOYS TODAY.
IF YOU CAN'T PAY A-TTENTION, I'M HANDING OUT DE-TENTION!
G-GOOD BOYS?!
PATHETIC, CRABTREE IS HELPING US!
THE MASTERS OF DETENTION!
I FEEL MY POWER TO CONTROL OTHERS WEAKENING!
THIS IS SO EMBARRASSING!
YOU THINK WE BULLIED YOU BAD BEFORE, AMANDA?
THE MORE YOU STICK OUT, THE MORE WE'LL BEAT YOU DOWN!
grrr
NO ONE DOES THIS TO M.A.D.!
WE OWN THIS SCHOOL.

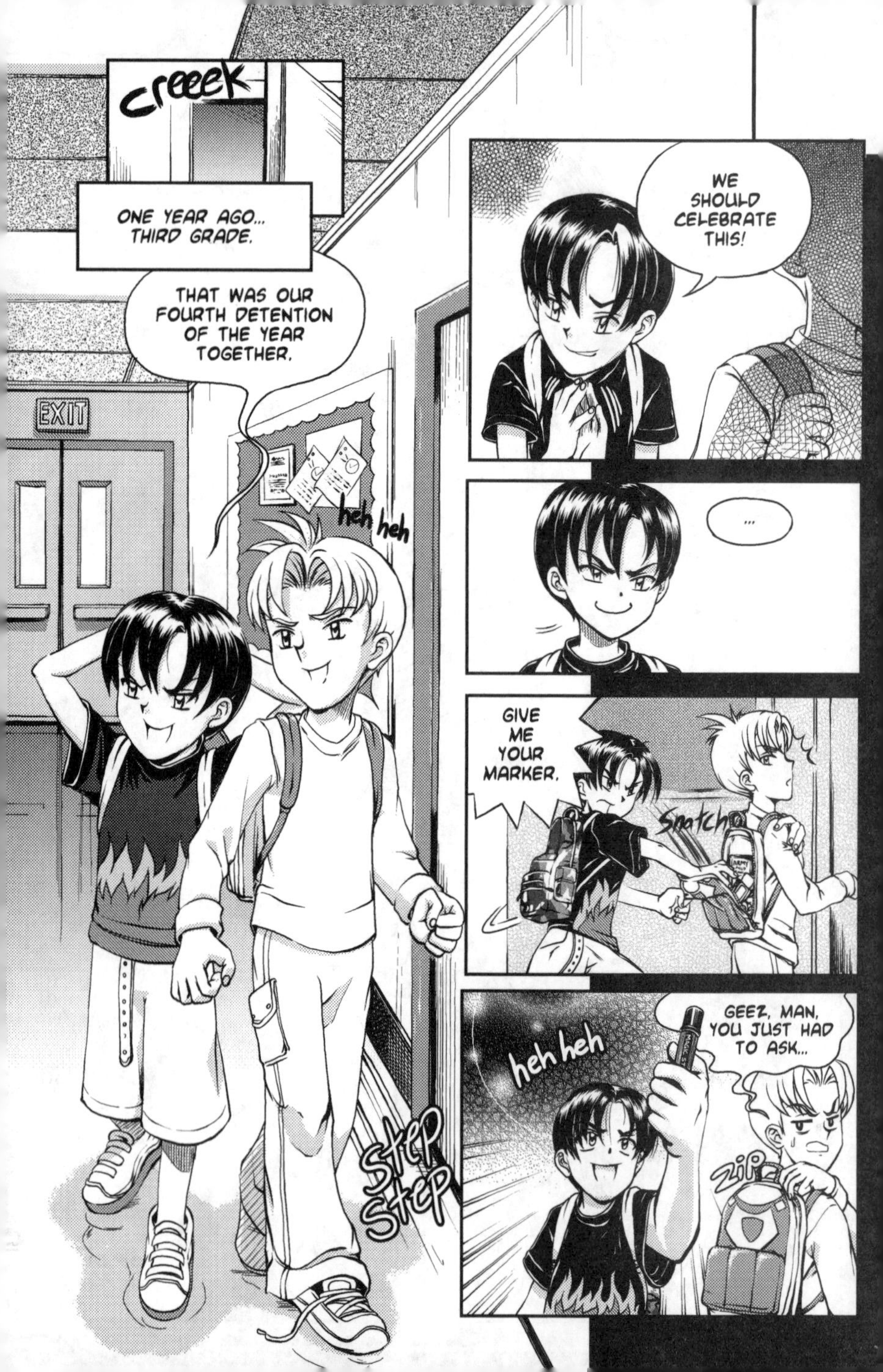
creeek
ONE YEAR AGO... THIRD GRADE.
THAT WAS OUR FOURTH DETENTION OF THE YEAR TOGETHER.
EXIT
heh heh
STEP STEP
WE SHOULD CELEBRATE THIS!
...
GIVE ME YOUR MARKER.
Snatch
heh heh
GEEZ, MAN, YOU JUST HAD TO ASK...
ZiP

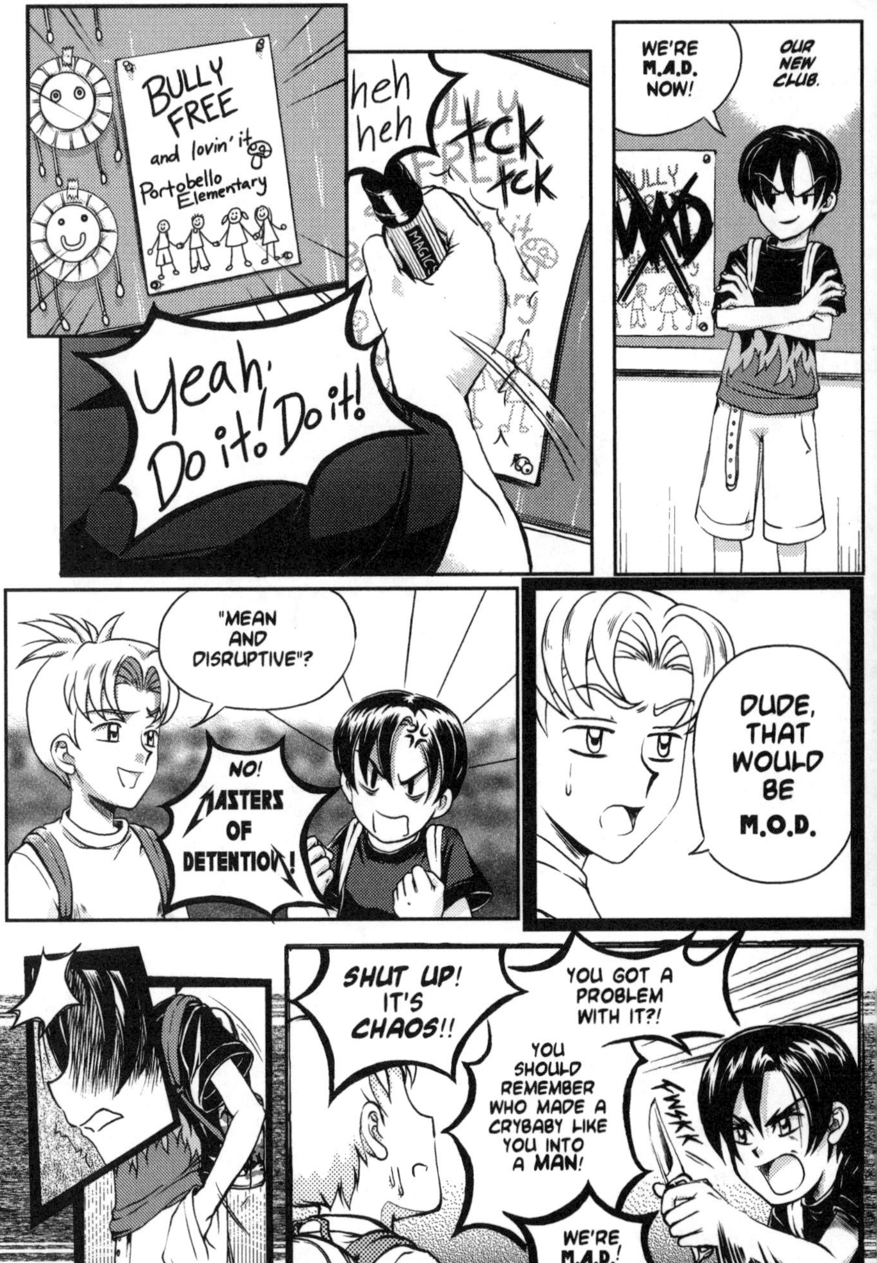
BULLY FREE and lovin' it Portobello Elementary
heh heh
tck tck
Yeah! Do it! Do it!
WE'RE M.A.D. NOW!
OUR NEW CLUB.
"MEAN AND DISRUPTIVE"?
NO! MASTERS OF DETENTION!
DUDE, THAT WOULD BE M.O.D.
SHUT UP! IT'S CHAOS!!
YOU GOT A PROBLEM WITH IT?!
YOU SHOULD REMEMBER WHO MADE A CRYBABY LIKE YOU INTO A MAN!
WE'RE M.A.D.! NOW AND FOREVER!

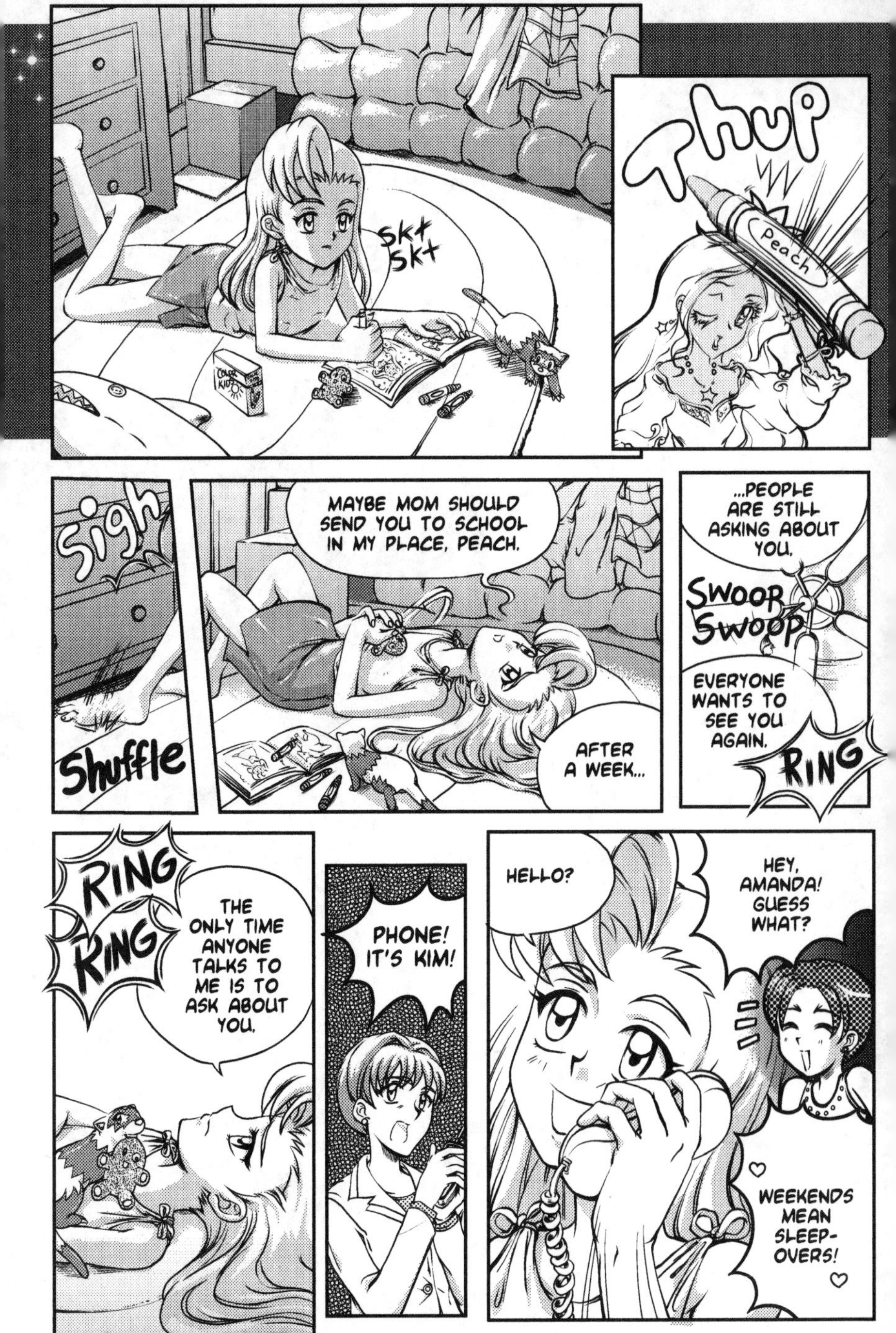
SKT SKT
THUP
Peach
SIGH
SHUFFLE
MAYBE MOM SHOULD SEND YOU TO SCHOOL IN MY PLACE, PEACH.
AFTER A WEEK...
...PEOPLE ARE STILL ASKING ABOUT YOU.
SWOOP SWOOP
EVERYONE WANTS TO SEE YOU AGAIN.
RING
RING RING
THE ONLY TIME ANYONE TALKS TO ME IS TO ASK ABOUT YOU.
PHONE! IT'S KIM!
HELLO?
HEY, AMANDA! GUESS WHAT?
WEEKENDS MEAN SLEEP-OVERS!

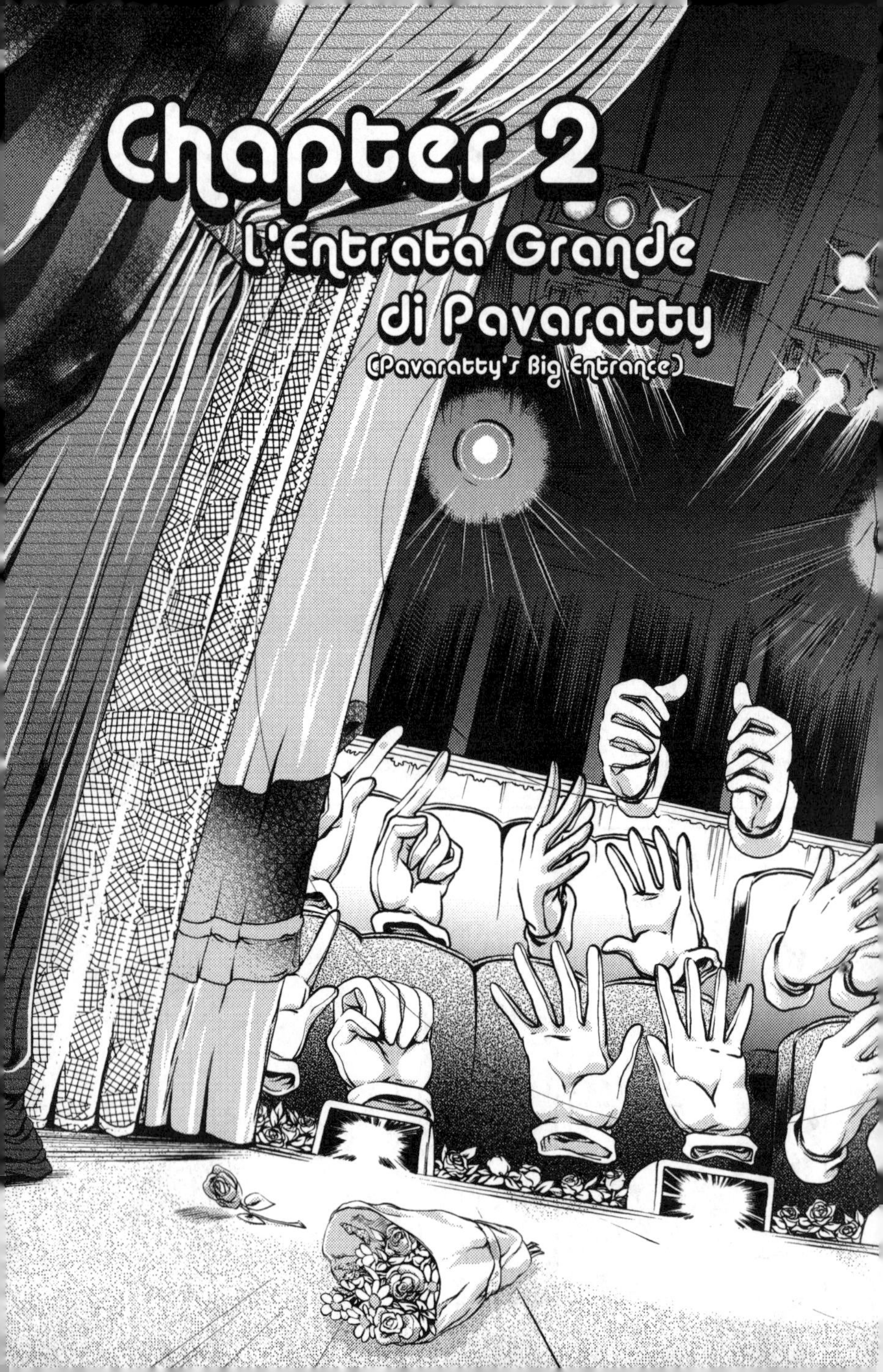
Chapter 2
l'Entrata Grande di Pavaratty
(Pavaratty's Big Entrance)

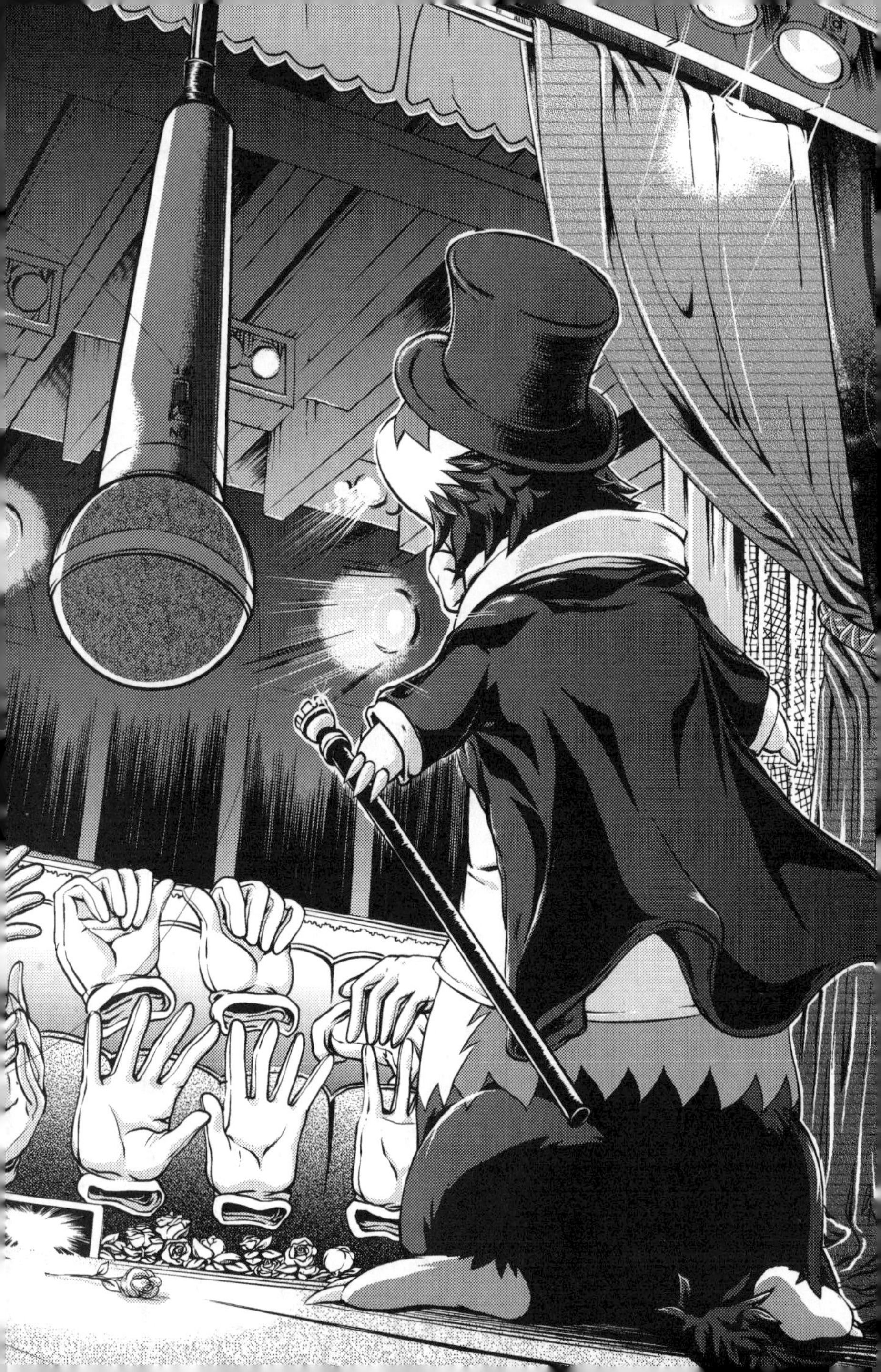

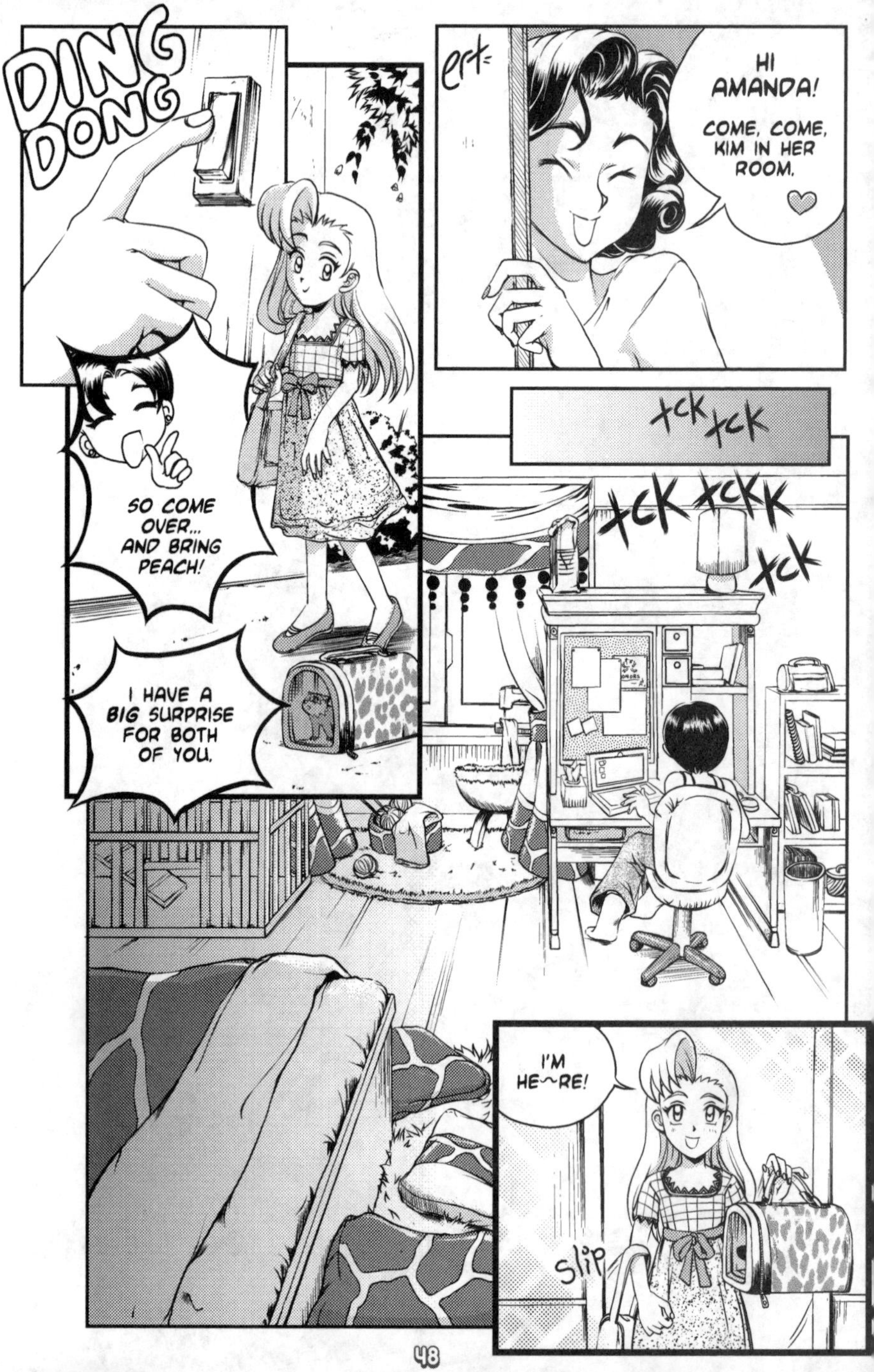
DING DONG
SO COME OVER... AND BRING PEACH!
I HAVE A BIG SURPRISE FOR BOTH OF YOU.
ert
HI AMANDA!
COME, COME, KIM IN HER ROOM.
tck tck
tck tckk tck
I'M HE~RE!
slip

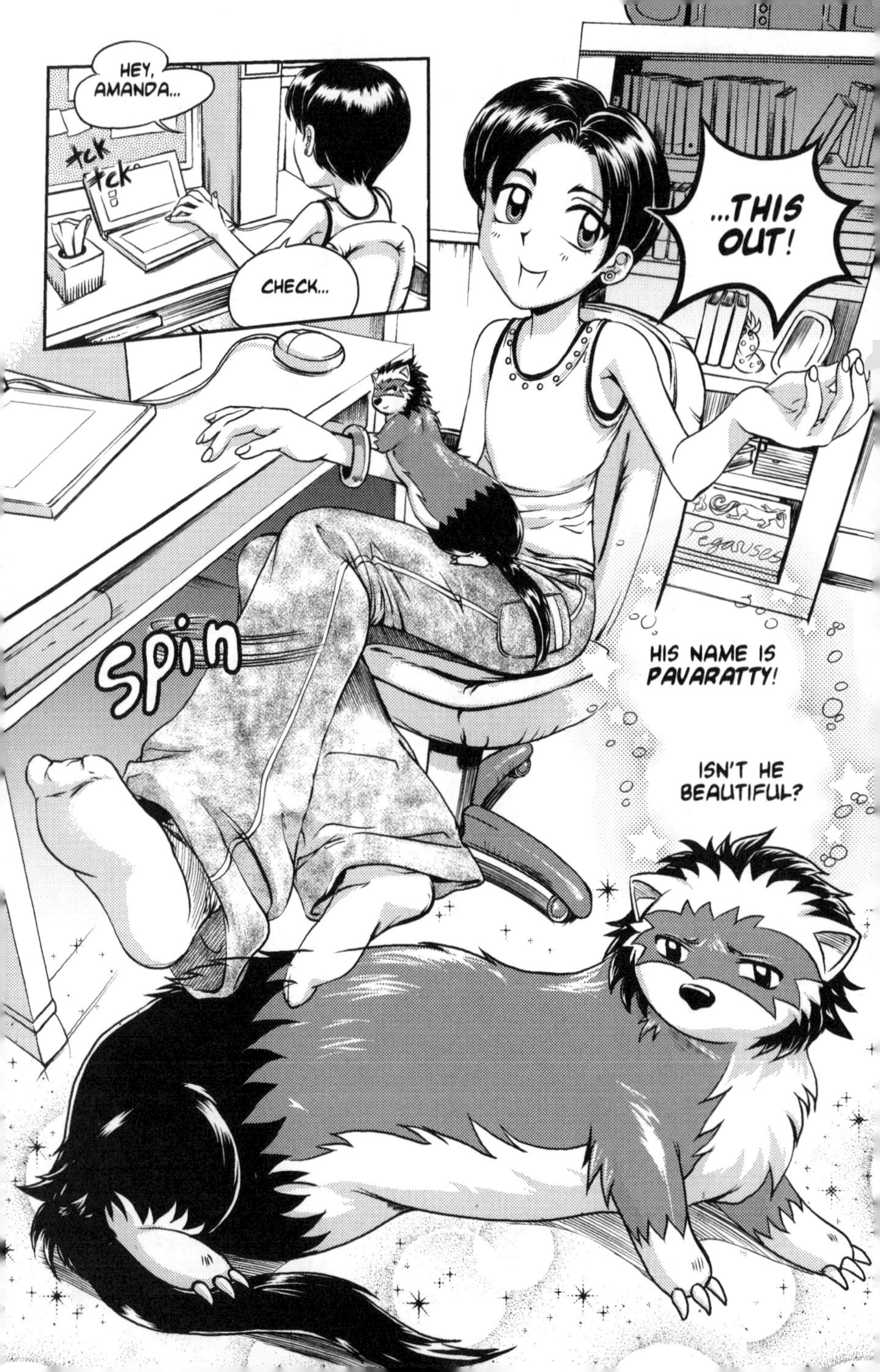

HEY, AMANDA...
tck tck
CHECK...
...THIS OUT!
Spin
Pegasuses
HIS NAME IS PAVARATTY!
ISN'T HE BEAUTIFUL?

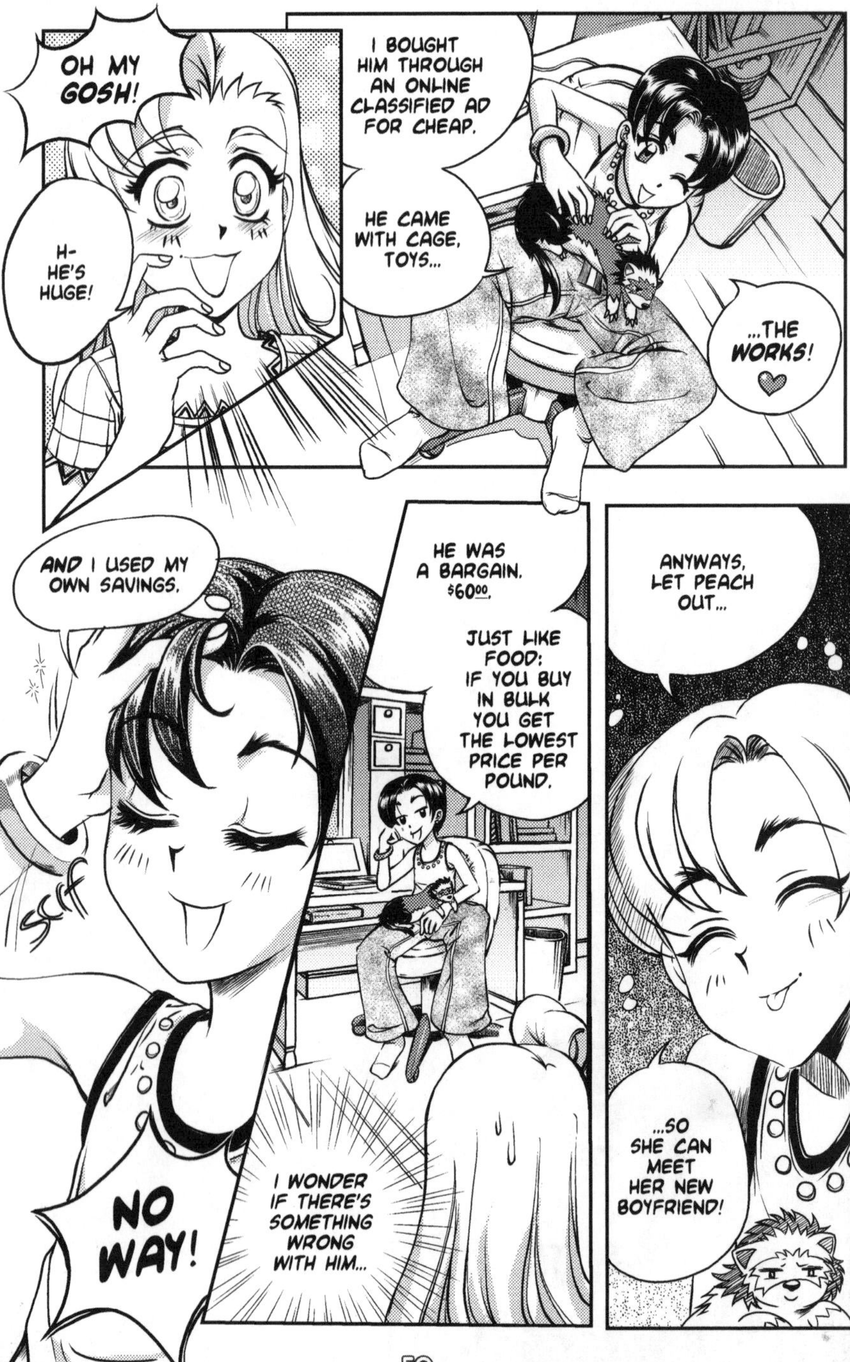

OH MY GOSH!
H- HE'S HUGE!
I BOUGHT HIM THROUGH AN ONLINE CLASSIFIED AD FOR CHEAP.
HE CAME WITH CAGE, TOYS...
...THE WORKS!
AND I USED MY OWN SAVINGS.
SCIFF
NO WAY!
HE WAS A BARGAIN. $60.00.
JUST LIKE FOOD: IF YOU BUY IN BULK YOU GET THE LOWEST PRICE PER POUND.
I WONDER IF THERE'S SOMETHING WRONG WITH HIM...
ANYWAYS, LET PEACH OUT...
...SO SHE CAN MEET HER NEW BOYFRIEND!

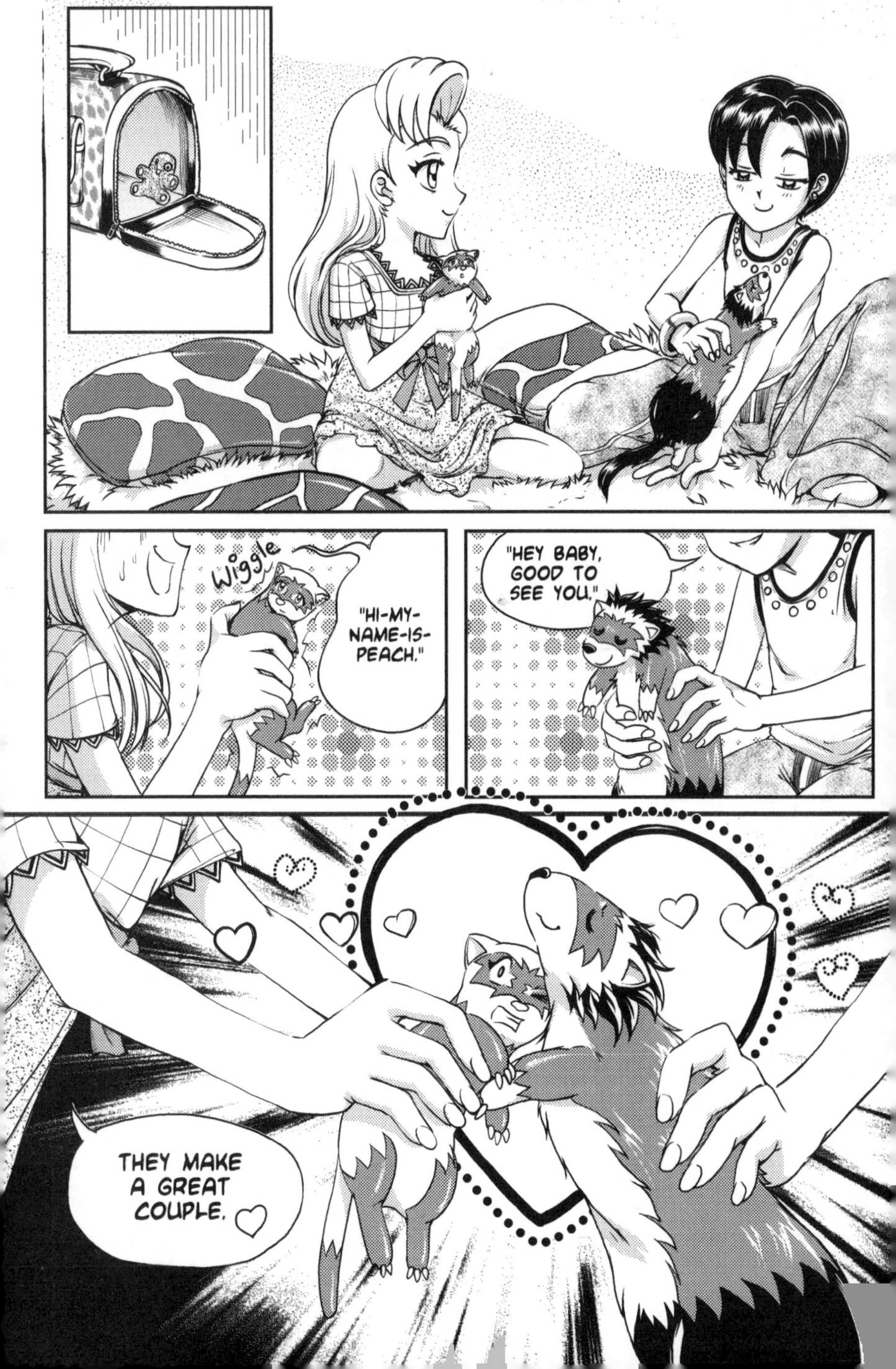

Wiggle
"HI-MY-NAME-IS-PEACH."
"HEY BABY, GOOD TO SEE YOU."
THEY MAKE A GREAT COUPLE.

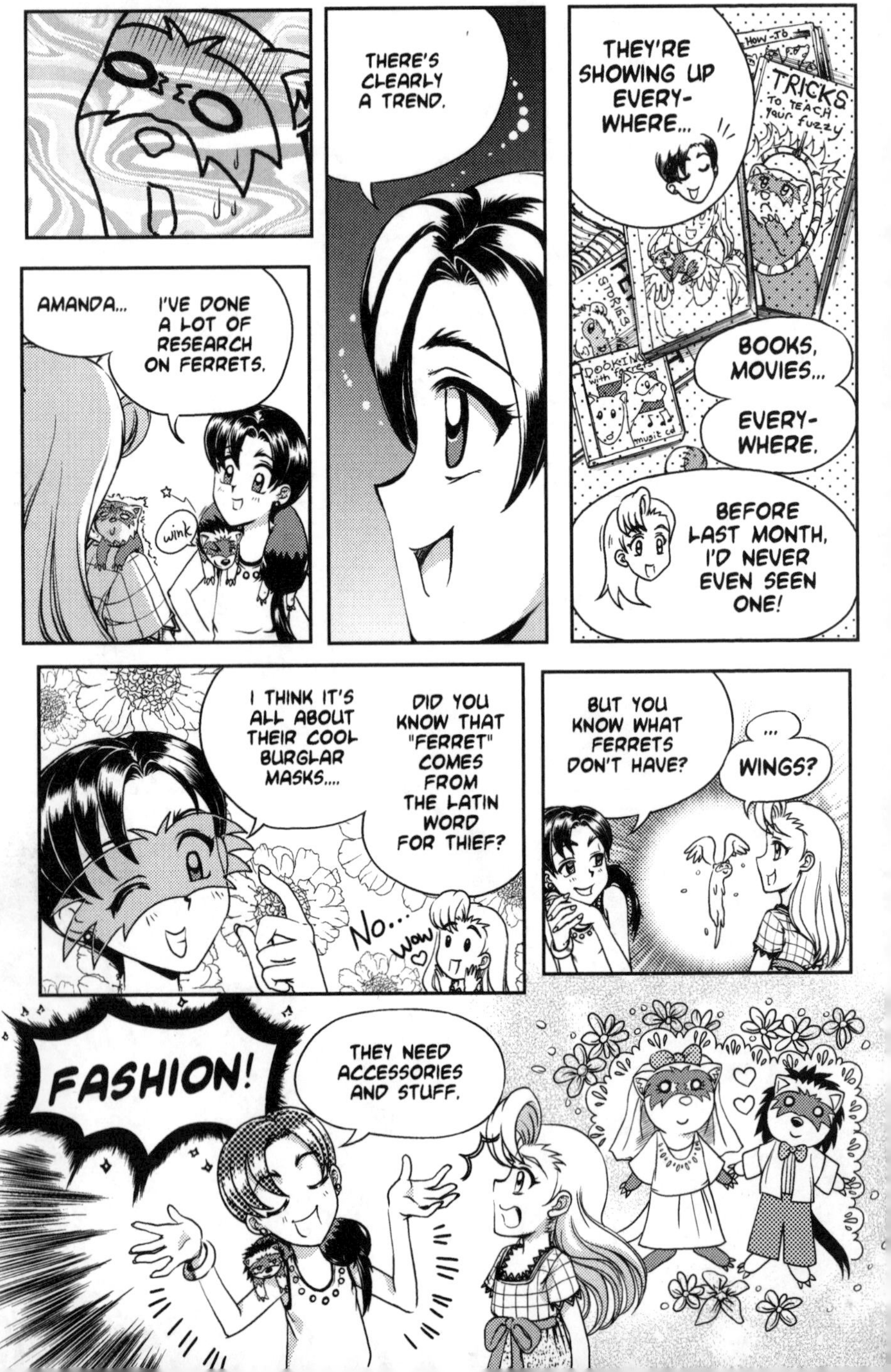
THERE'S CLEARLY A TREND.
THEY'RE SHOWING UP EVERY-WHERE...
TRICKS TO TEACH your fuzzy
AMANDA...
I'VE DONE A LOT OF RESEARCH ON FERRETS.
wink
BOOKS, MOVIES...
EVERY-WHERE.
BEFORE LAST MONTH, I'D NEVER EVEN SEEN ONE!
I THINK IT'S ALL ABOUT THEIR COOL BURGLAR MASKS....
DID YOU KNOW THAT "FERRET" COMES FROM THE LATIN WORD FOR THIEF?
No...
wow
BUT YOU KNOW WHAT FERRETS DON'T HAVE?
...
WINGS?
FASHION!
THEY NEED ACCESSORIES AND STUFF.

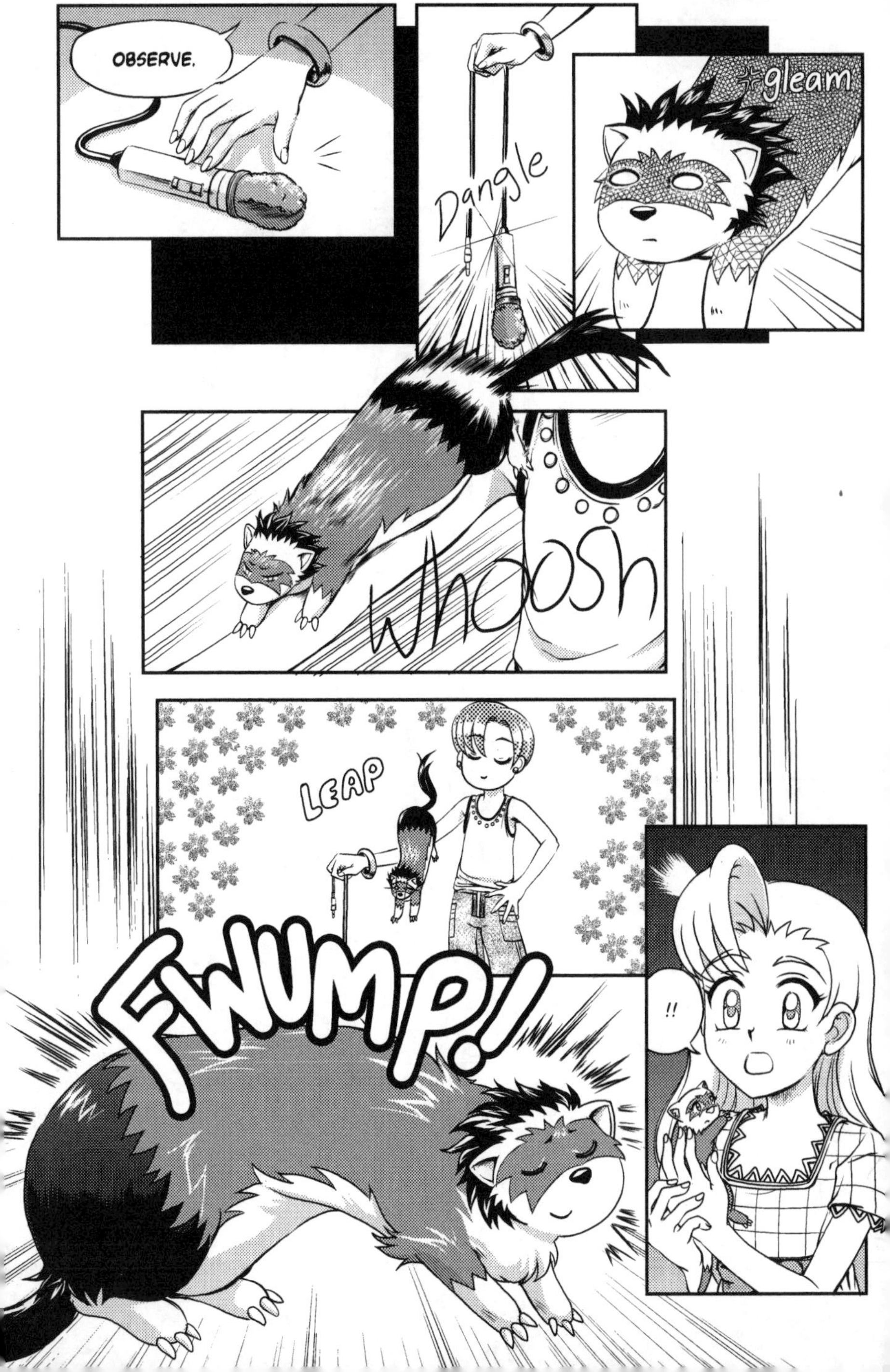
OBSERVE.
Dangle
gleam
Whoosh
LEAP
FWUMP!
!!

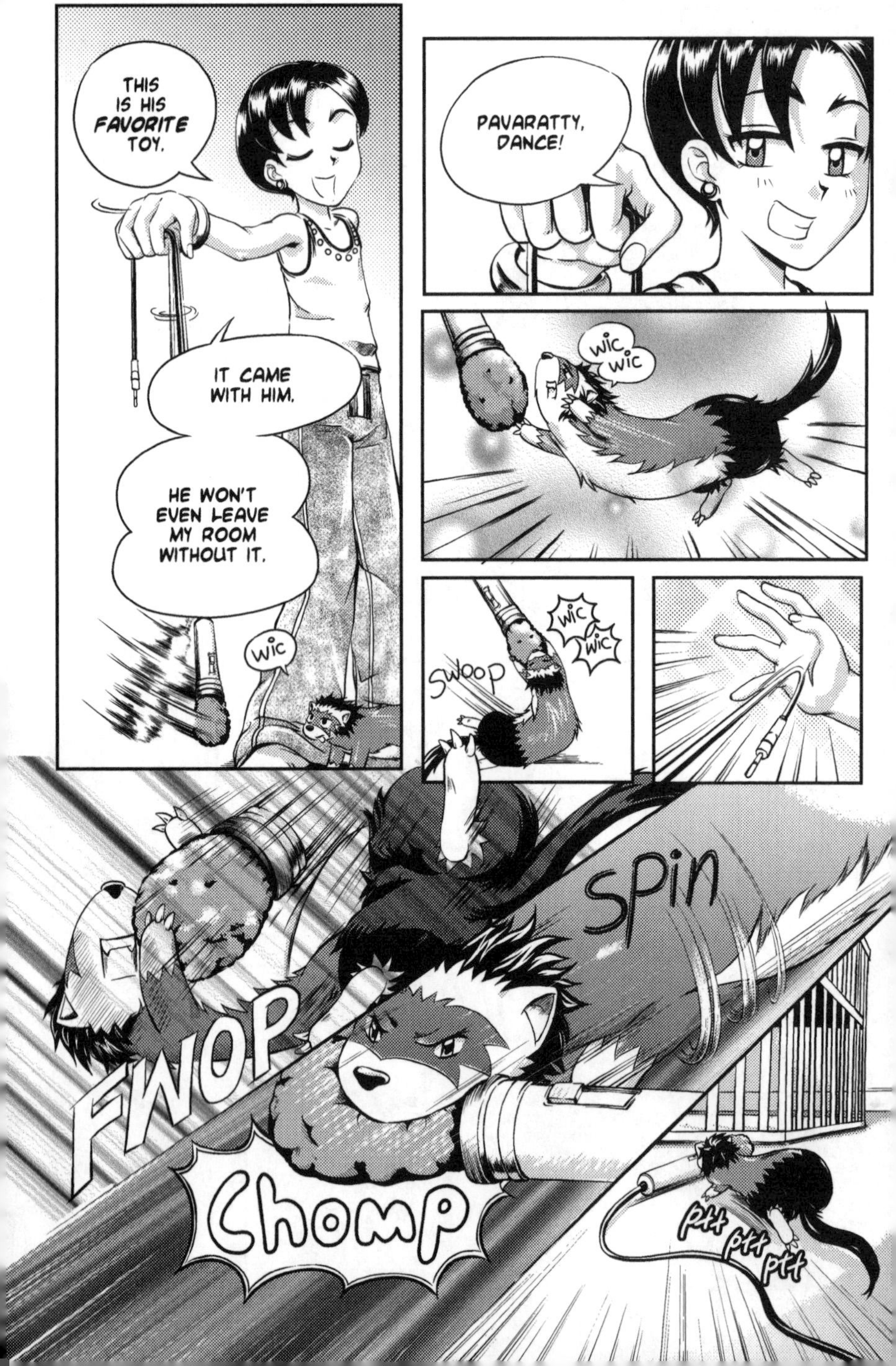

THIS IS HIS *FAVORITE* TOY.
IT CAME WITH HIM.
HE WON'T EVEN LEAVE MY ROOM WITHOUT IT.
wic
PAVARATTY, DANCE!
wic wic
SWOOP
wic
wic
SPIN
FWOP
Chomp
ptt ptt ptt

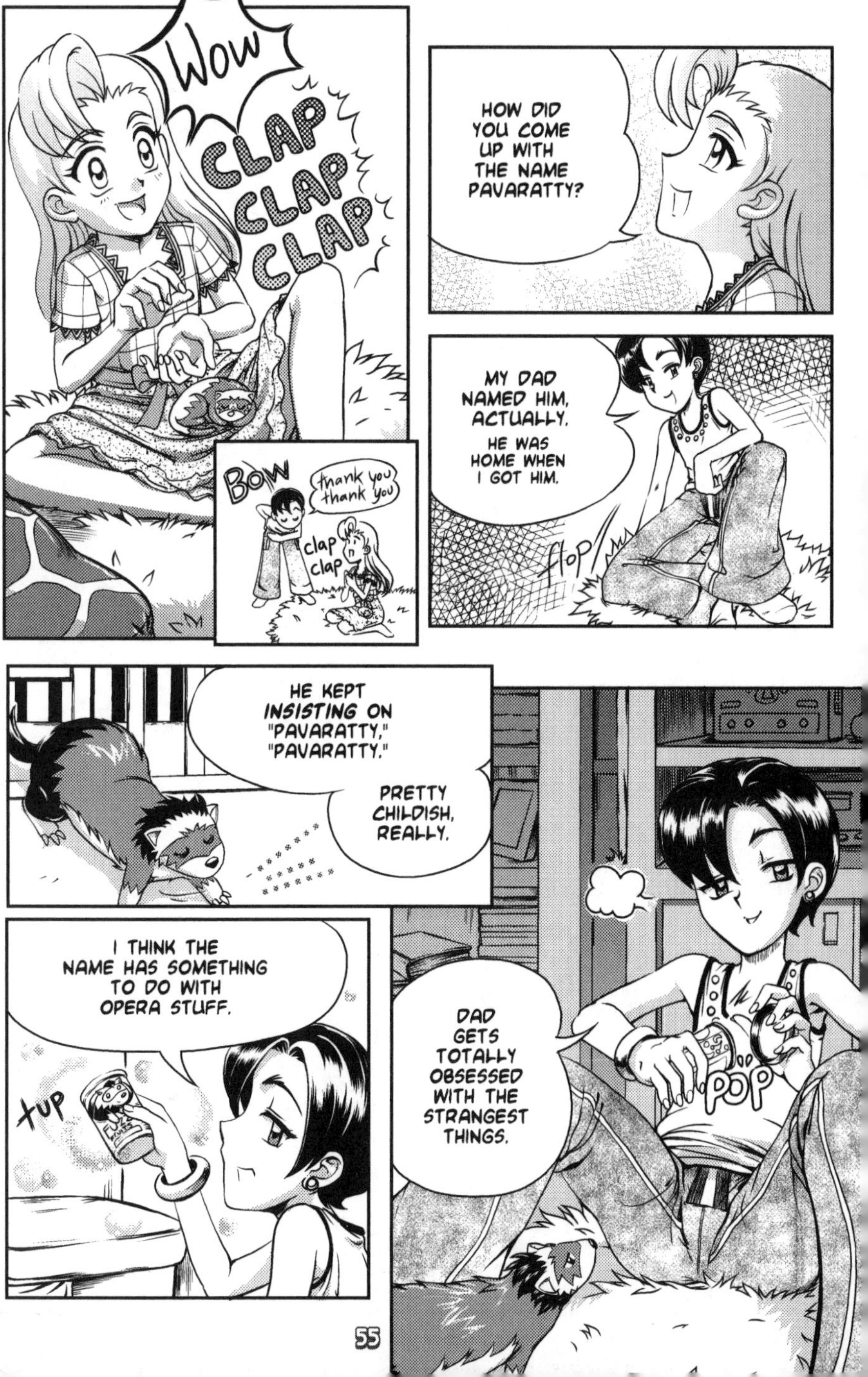
WOW
CLAP CLAP CLAP
HOW DID YOU COME UP WITH THE NAME PAVARATTY?
BOW
thank you thank you
clap clap
MY DAD NAMED HIM, ACTUALLY.
HE WAS HOME WHEN I GOT HIM.
flop
HE KEPT INSISTING ON "PAVARATTY," "PAVARATTY."
PRETTY CHILDISH, REALLY.
I THINK THE NAME HAS SOMETHING TO DO WITH OPERA STUFF.
tup
DAD GETS TOTALLY OBSESSED WITH THE STRANGEST THINGS.
POP

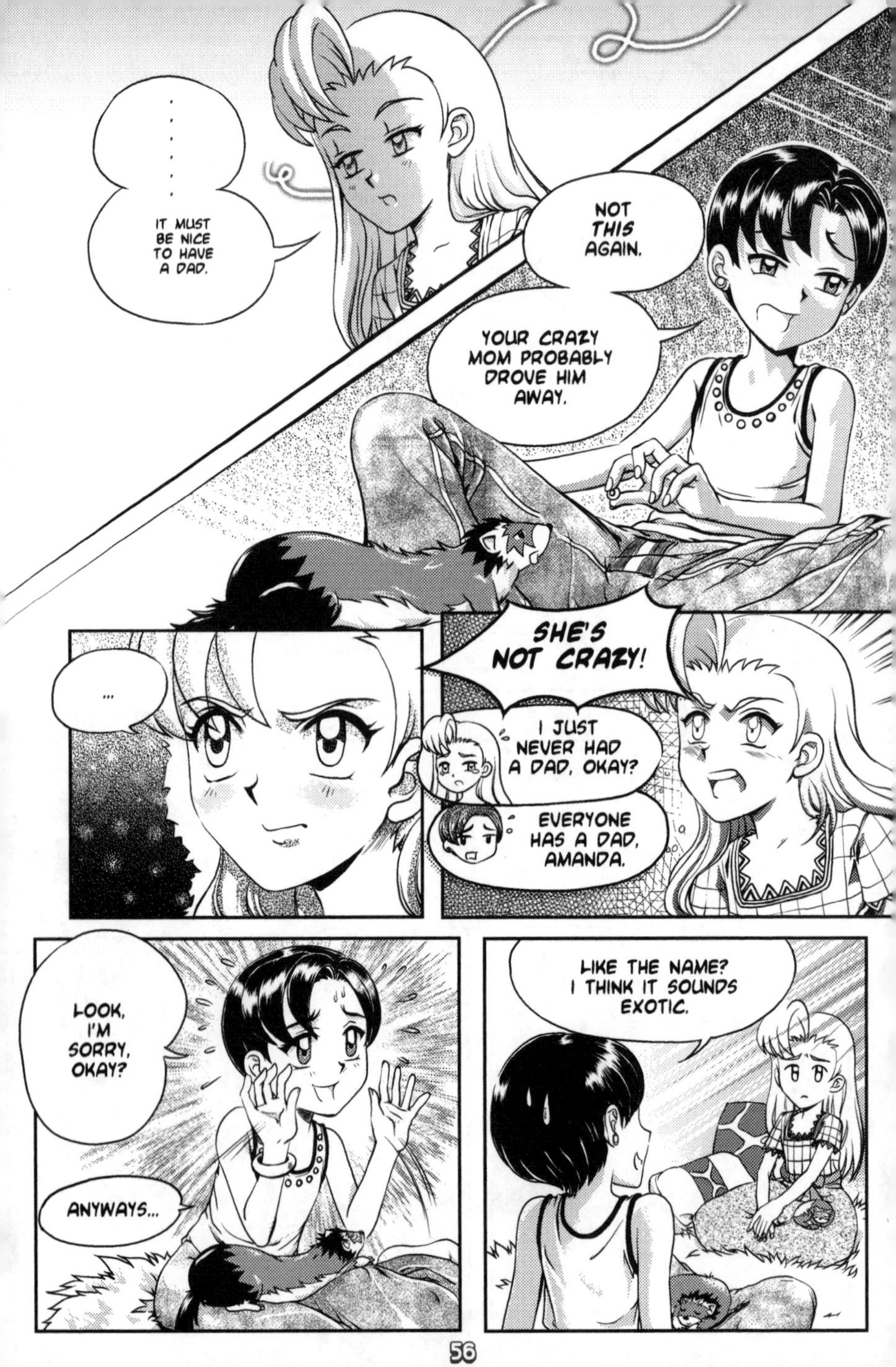
. . . . . .
IT MUST BE NICE TO HAVE A DAD.
NOT THIS AGAIN.
YOUR CRAZY MOM PROBABLY DROVE HIM AWAY.
SHE'S NOT CRAZY!
I JUST NEVER HAD A DAD, OKAY?
EVERYONE HAS A DAD, AMANDA.
...
LOOK, I'M SORRY, OKAY?
ANYWAYS...
LIKE THE NAME? I THINK IT SOUNDS EXOTIC.

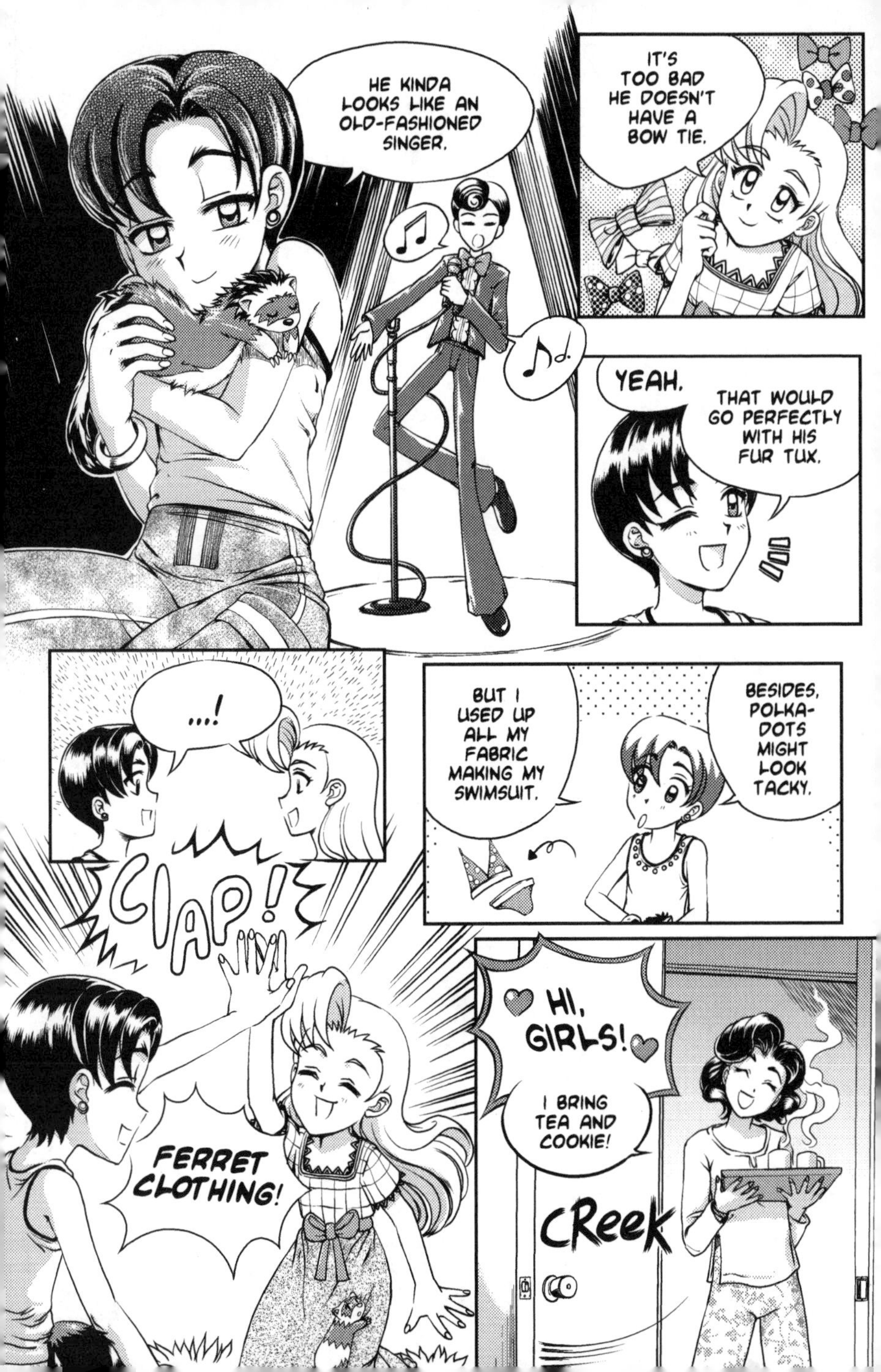

HE KINDA LOOKS LIKE AN OLD-FASHIONED SINGER.
IT'S TOO BAD HE DOESN'T HAVE A BOW TIE.
YEAH.
THAT WOULD GO PERFECTLY WITH HIS FUR TUX.
...!
BUT I USED UP ALL MY FABRIC MAKING MY SWIMSUIT.
BESIDES, POLKA-DOTS MIGHT LOOK TACKY.
CLAP!
FERRET CLOTHING!
HI, GIRLS!
I BRING TEA AND COOKIE!
CReek

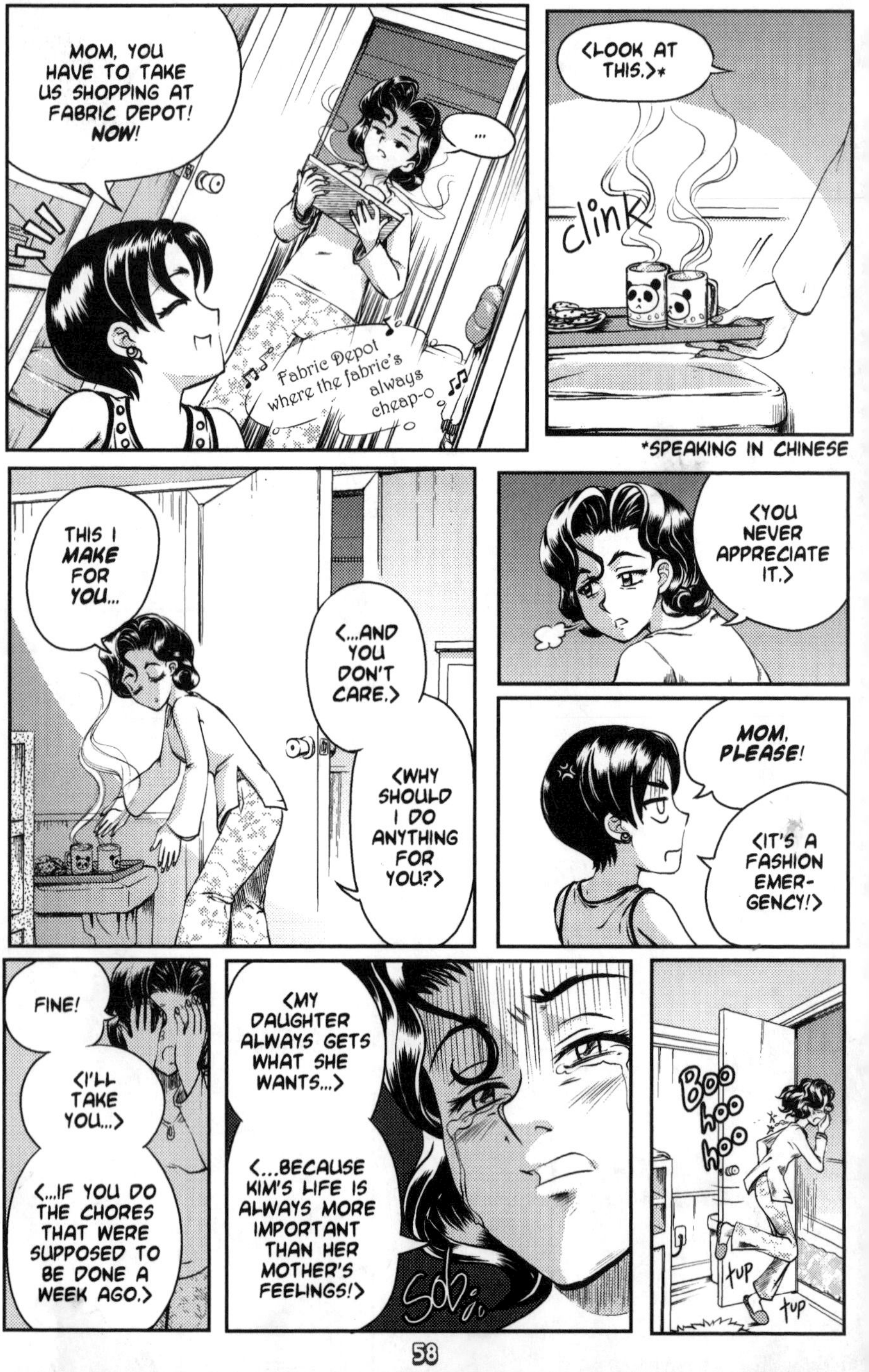
MOM, YOU HAVE TO TAKE US SHOPPING AT FABRIC DEPOT! NOW!
...
Fabric Depot where the fabric's always cheap-o
<LOOK AT THIS.>*
clink
*SPEAKING IN CHINESE
THIS I MAKE FOR YOU...
<...AND YOU DON'T CARE.>
<WHY SHOULD I DO ANYTHING FOR YOU?>
<YOU NEVER APPRECIATE IT.>
MOM, PLEASE!
<IT'S A FASHION EMER-GENCY!>
FINE!
<I'LL TAKE YOU...>
<...IF YOU DO THE CHORES THAT WERE SUPPOSED TO BE DONE A WEEK AGO.>
<MY DAUGHTER ALWAYS GETS WHAT SHE WANTS...>
<...BECAUSE KIM'S LIFE IS ALWAYS MORE IMPORTANT THAN HER MOTHER'S FEELINGS!>
SOB
Boo hoo hoo
tup
tup

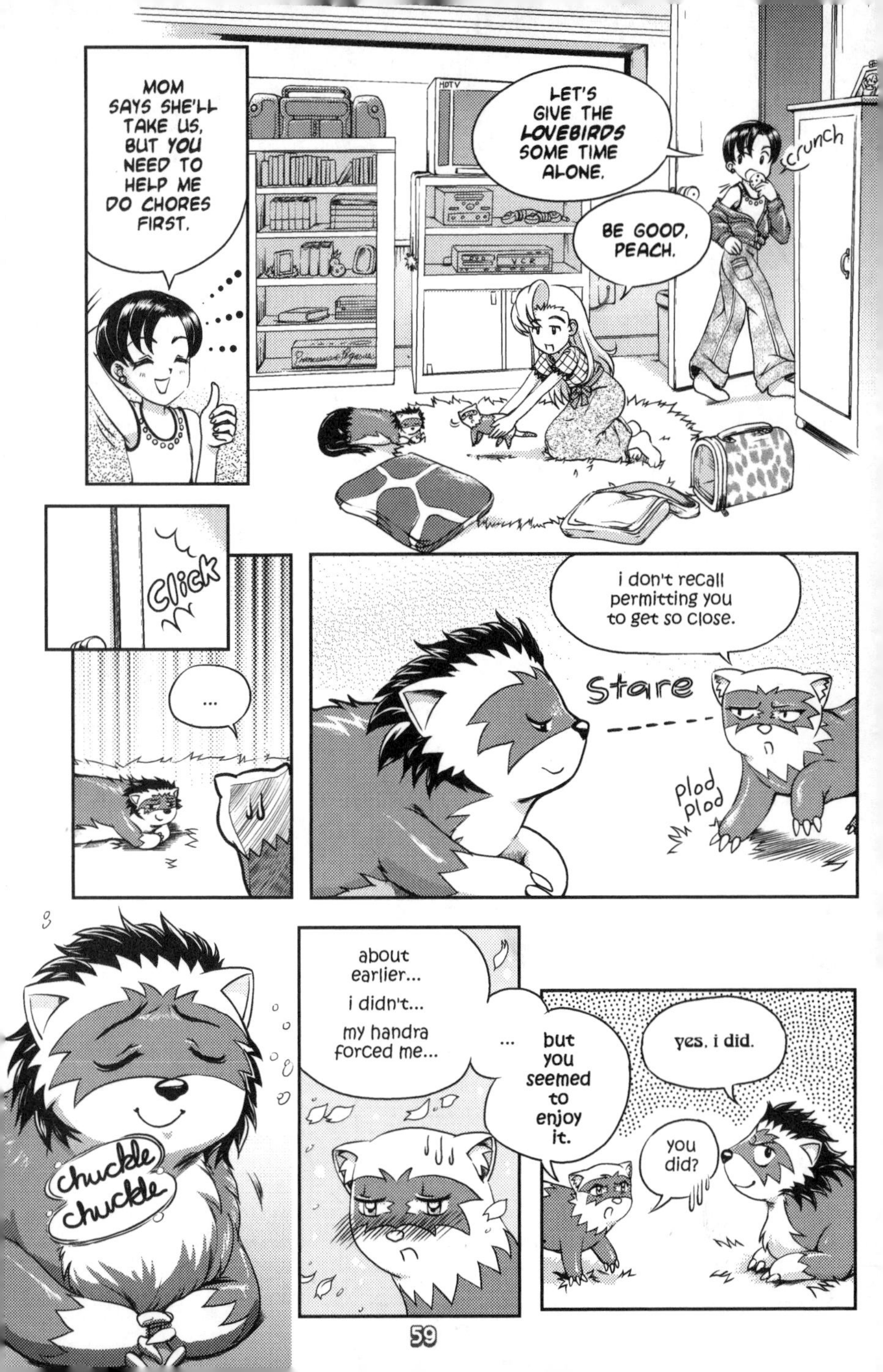
MOM SAYS SHE'LL TAKE US, BUT YOU NEED TO HELP ME DO CHORES FIRST.
LET'S GIVE THE LOVEBIRDS SOME TIME ALONE.
crunch
BE GOOD, PEACH.
Click
...
i don't recall permitting you to get so close.
Stare
plod plod
chuckle chuckle
about earlier...
i didn't...
my handra forced me...
...
but you seemed to enjoy it.
yes, i did.
you did?

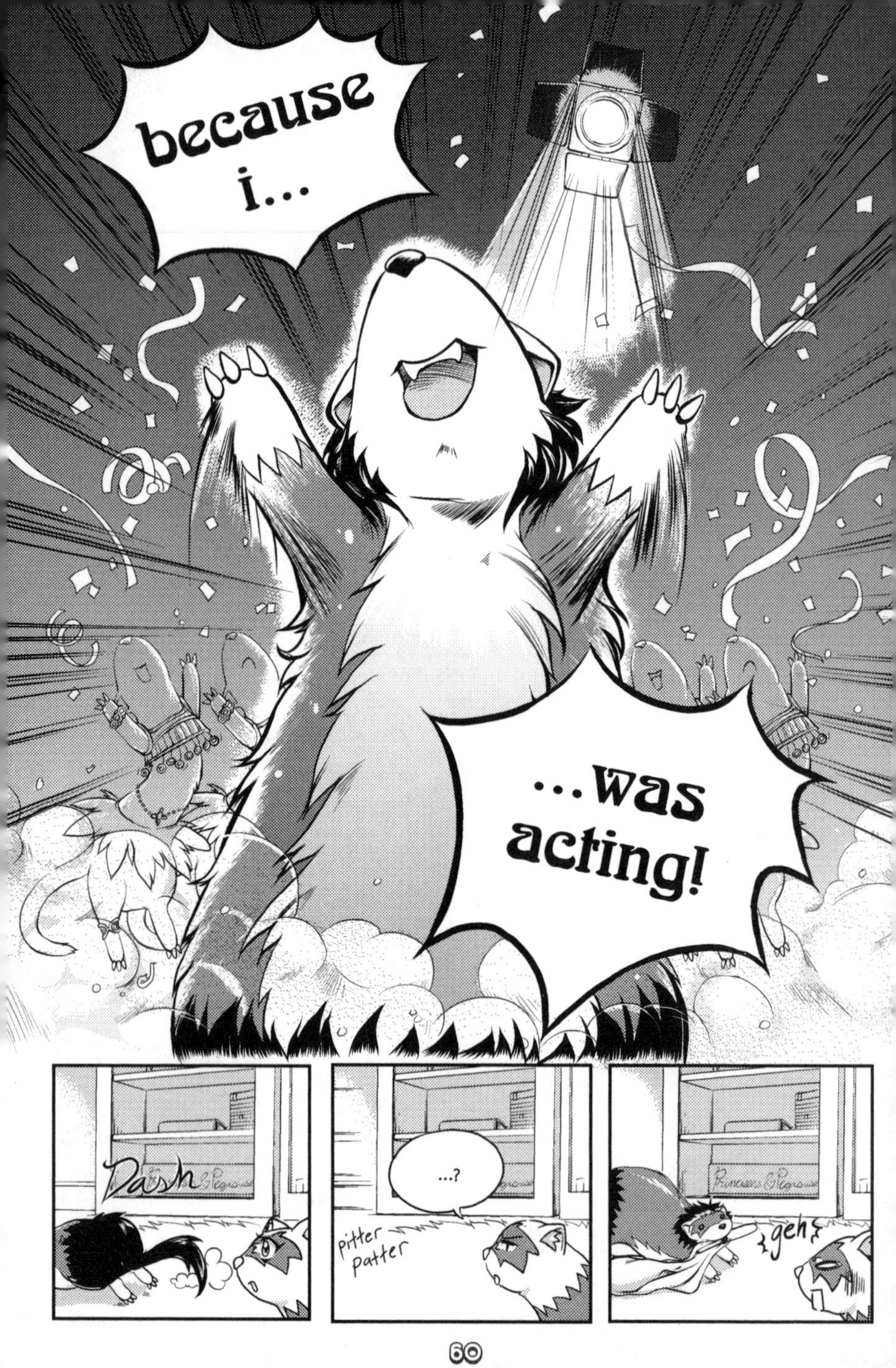
because i...
...was acting!
Dash
...?
pitter patter
geh

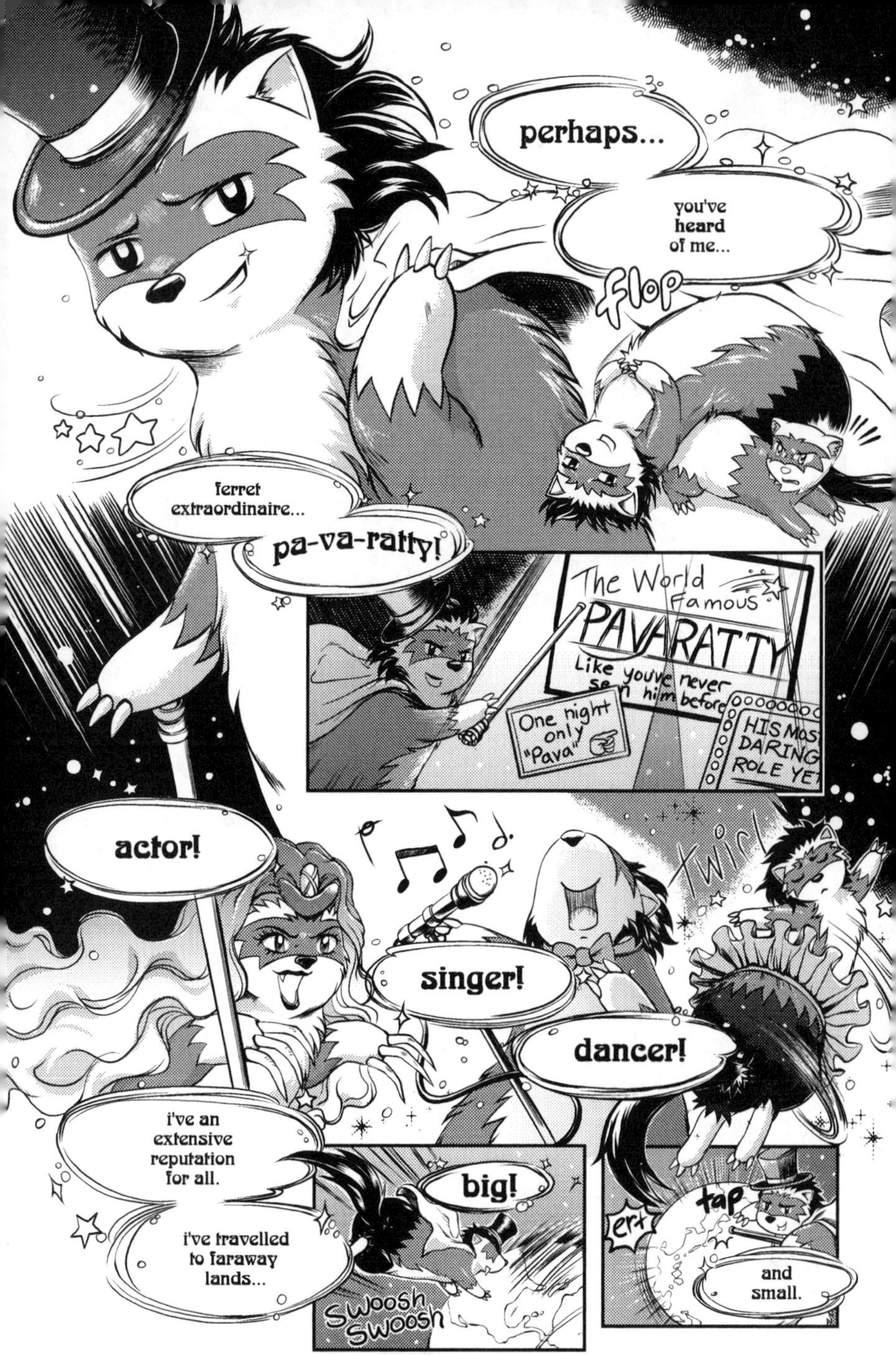
perhaps...
you've heard of me...
flop
ferret extraordinaire...
pa-va-ratty!
The World Famous PAVARATTY
Like you've never seen him before
One night only "Pava"
HIS MOST DARING ROLE YET
actor!
singer!
twirl
dancer!
i've an extensive reputation for all.
big!
i've travelled to faraway lands...
Swoosh Swoosh
ert
tap
and small.

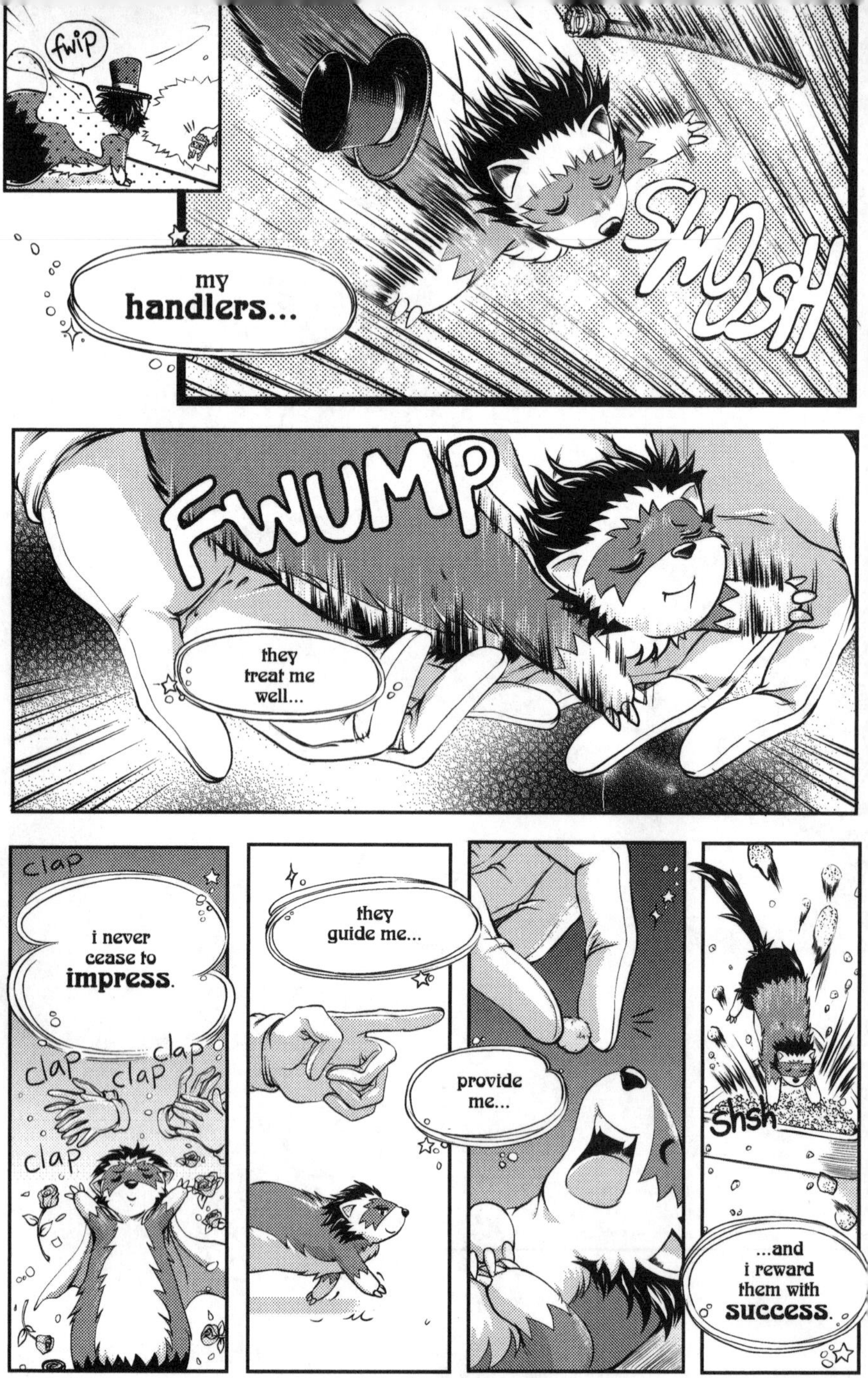
fwip
my handlers...
SWOOSH
FWUMP
they treat me well...
clap
i never cease to impress.
clap clap clap
clap
they guide me...
provide me...
Shsh
...and i reward them with success.

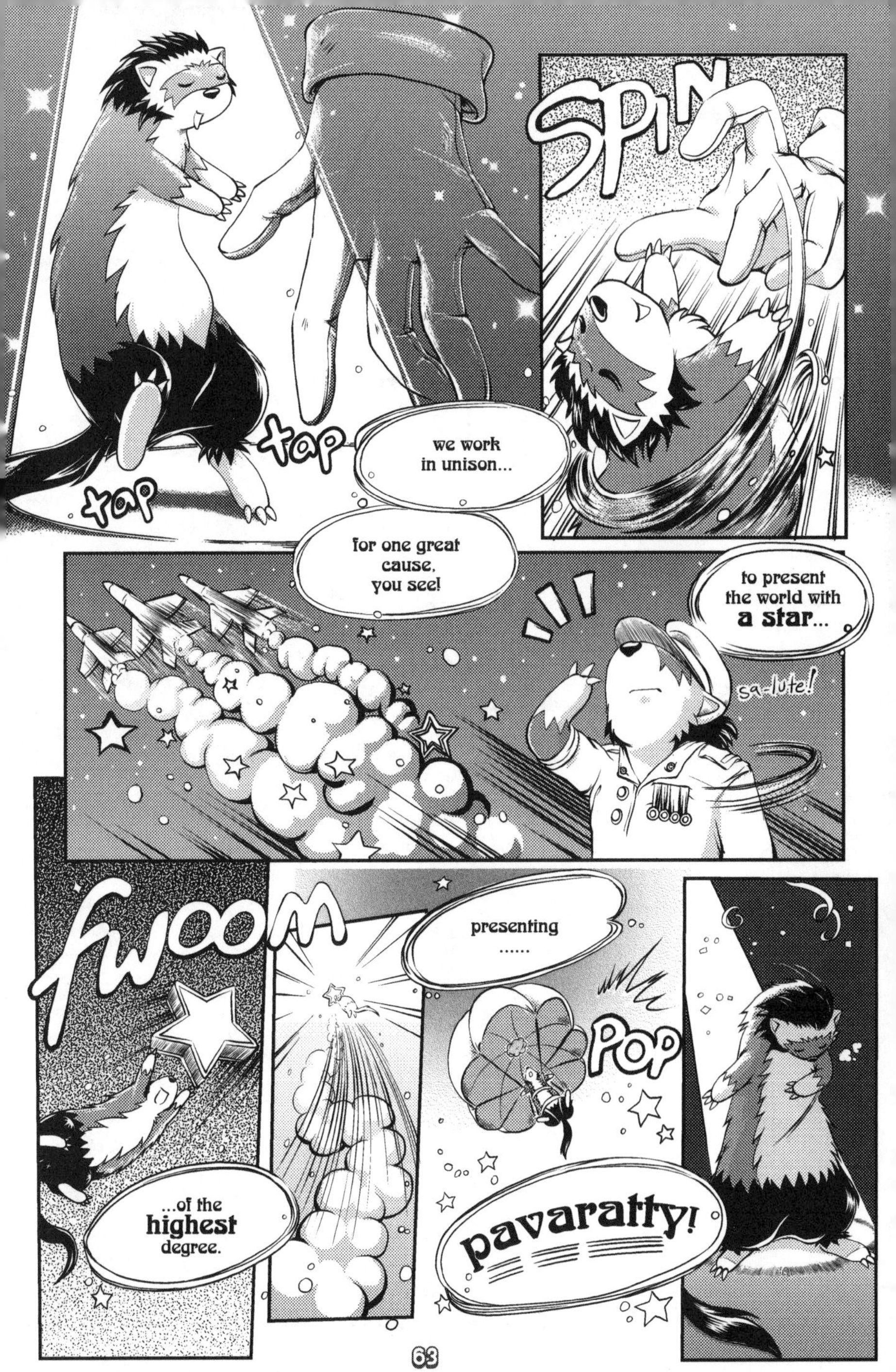

tap
tap
we work in unison...
SPIN
for one great cause, you see!
to present the world with a star...
sa-lute!
fwoom
presenting ......
POP
...of the highest degree.
pavaratty!

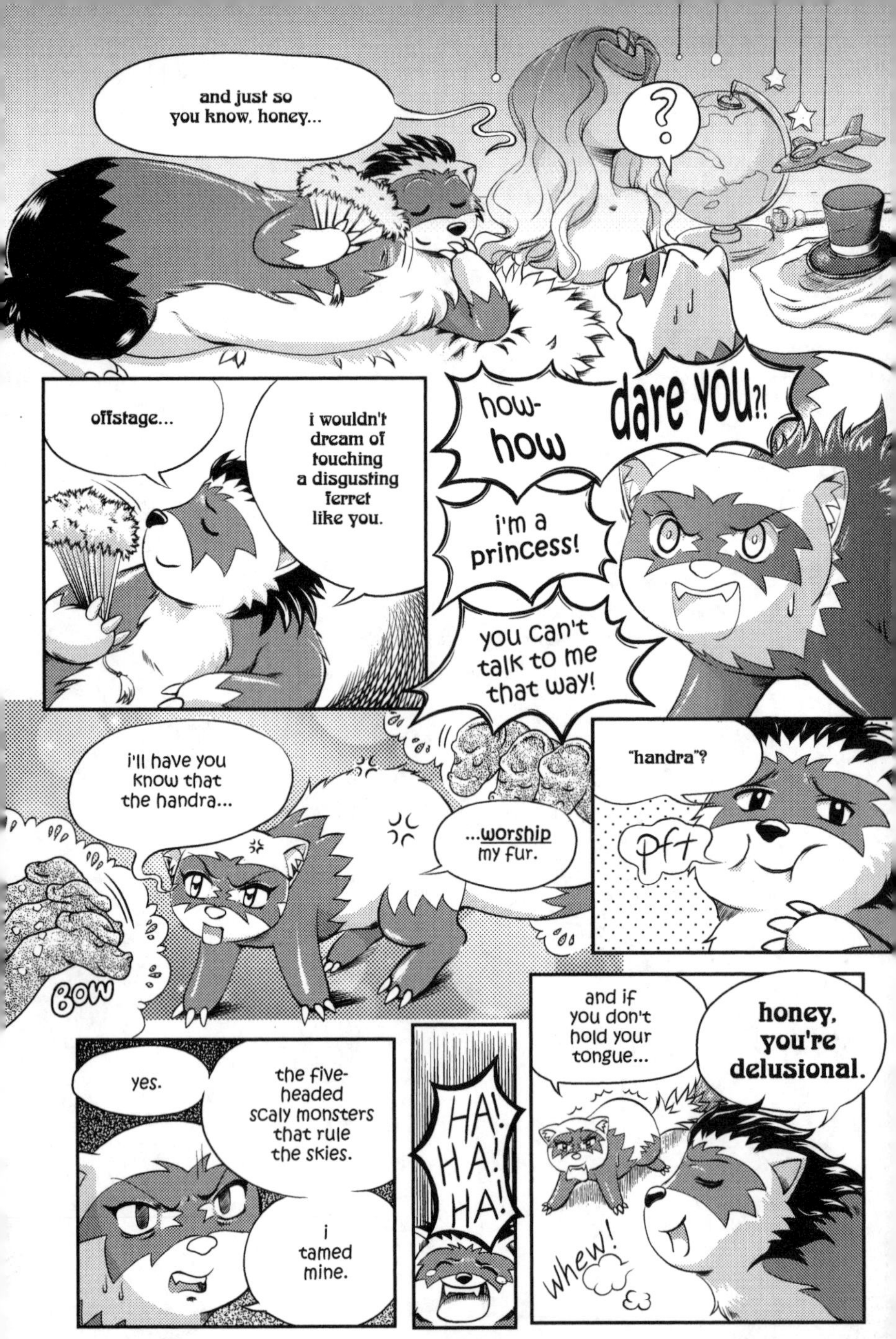
and just so you know, honey...
?
offstage...
i wouldn't dream of touching a disgusting ferret like you.
how-how
dare you?!
i'm a princess!
you can't talk to me that way!
i'll have you know that the handra...
...worship my fur.
BOW
"handra"?
pft
yes.
the five-headed scaly monsters that rule the skies.
i tamed mine.
HA! HA! HA!
and if you don't hold your tongue...
honey, you're delusional.
whew!

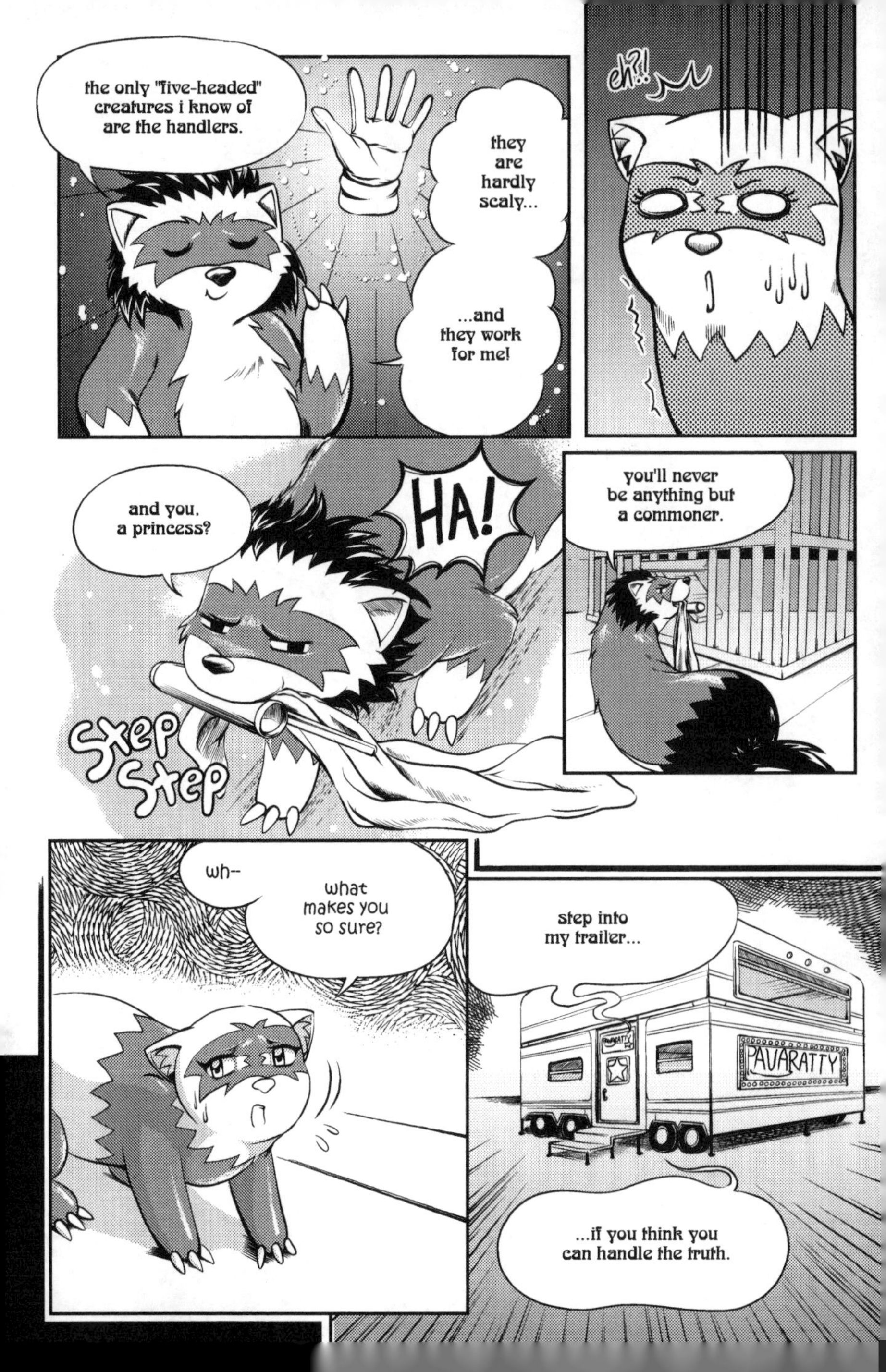

the only "five-headed" creatures i know of are the handlers.
they are hardly scaly...
...and they work for me!
eh?!
and you, a princess?
HA!
step step
you'll never be anything but a commoner.
wh--
what makes you so sure?
step into my trailer...
PAVARATTY
...if you think you can handle the truth.

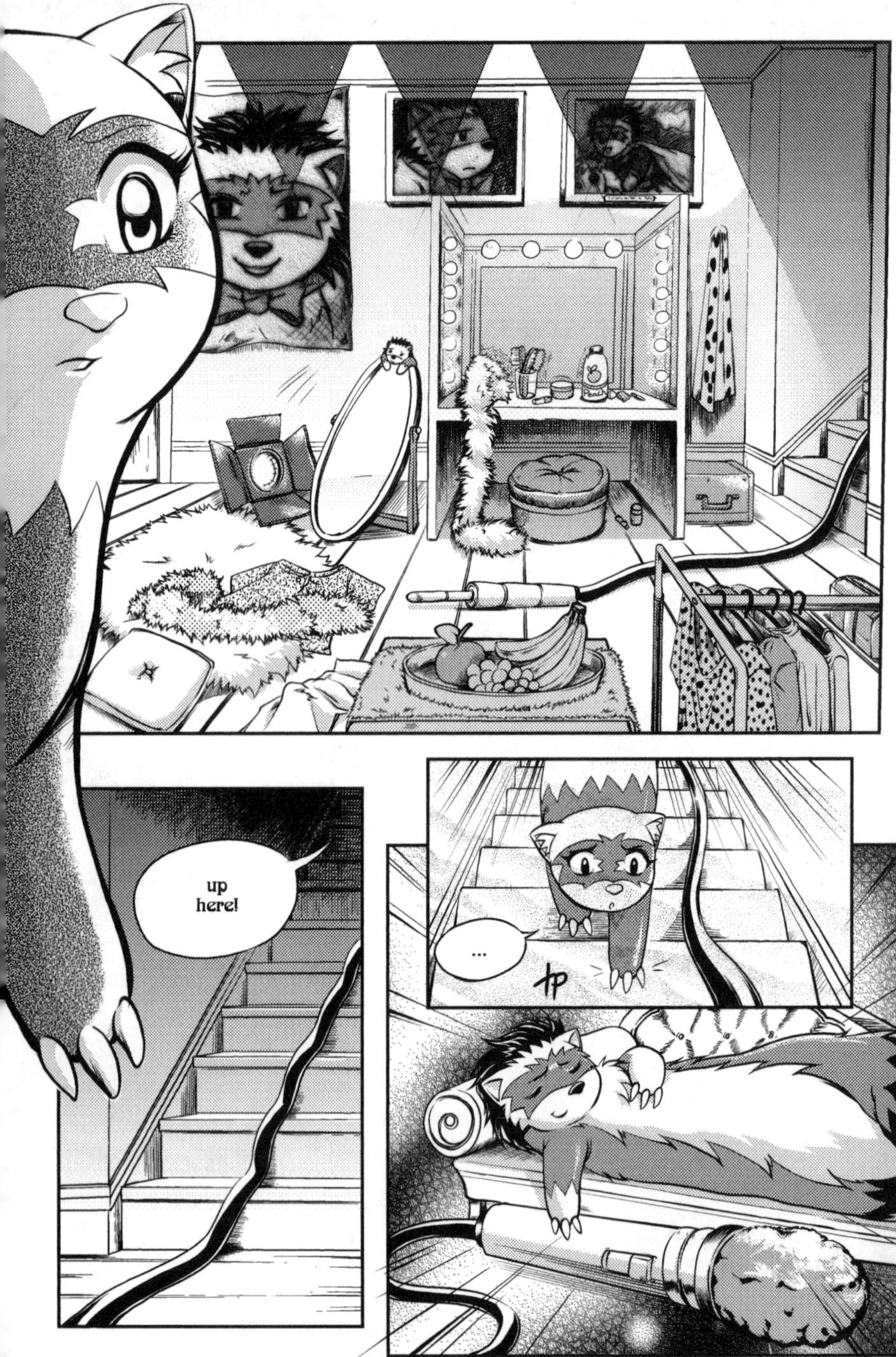
up here!
...
tp

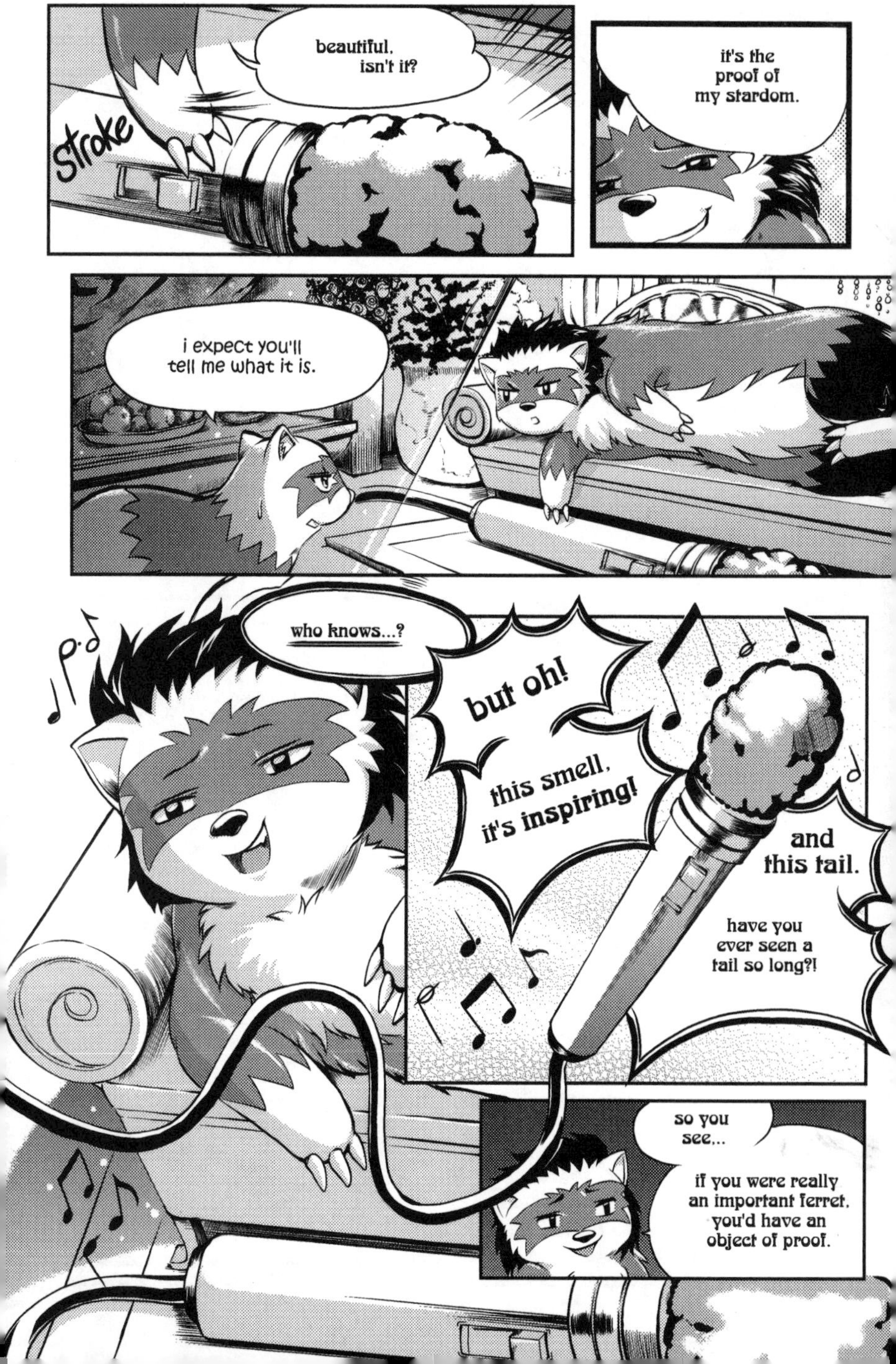
beautiful, isn't it?
stroke
it's the proof of my stardom.
i expect you'll tell me what it is.
who knows...?
but oh!
this smell, it's inspiring!
and this tail.
have you ever seen a tail so long?!
so you see,...
if you were really an important ferret, you'd have an object of proof.

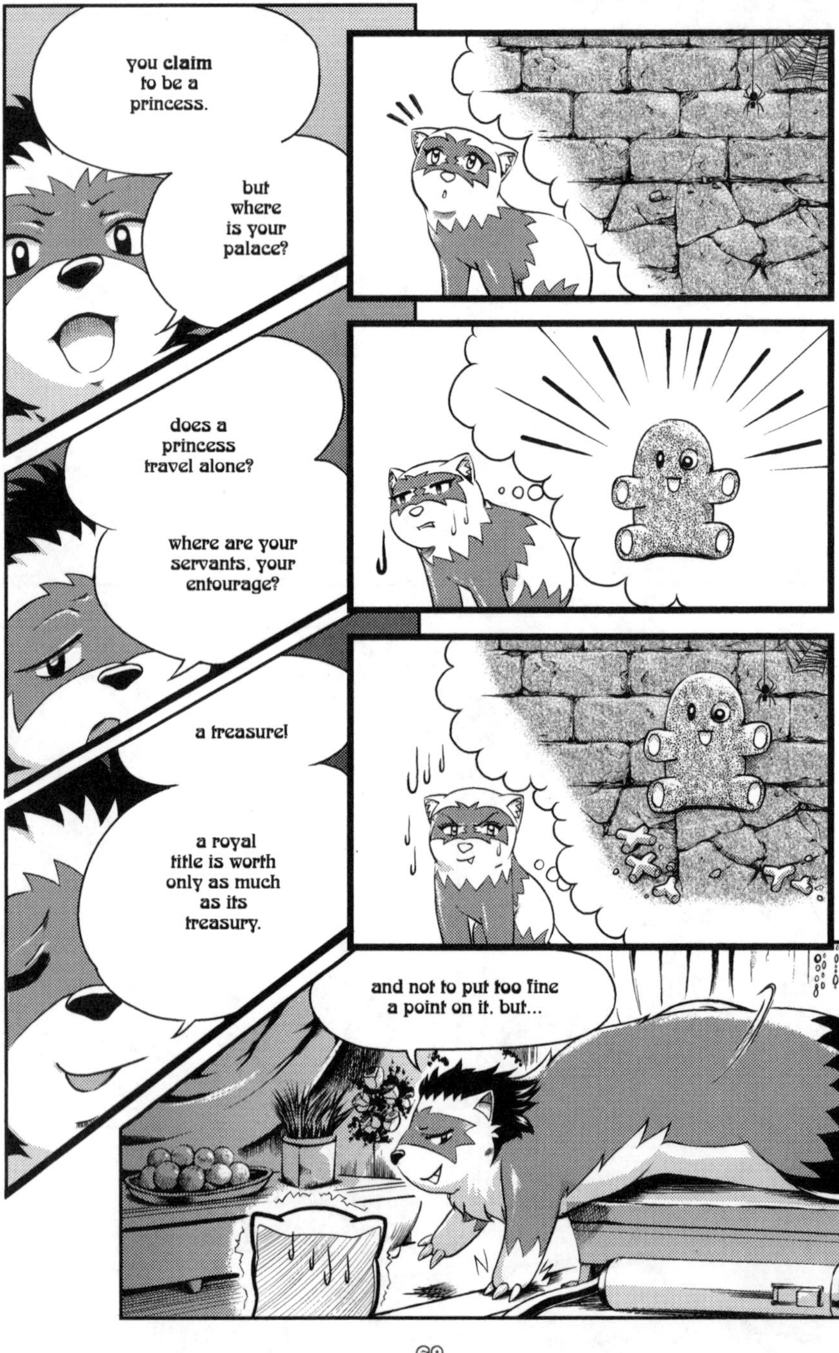

you claim to be a princess.
but where is your palace?
does a princess travel alone?
where are your servants, your entourage?
a treasure!
a royal title is worth only as much as its treasury.
and not to put too fine a point on it, but...

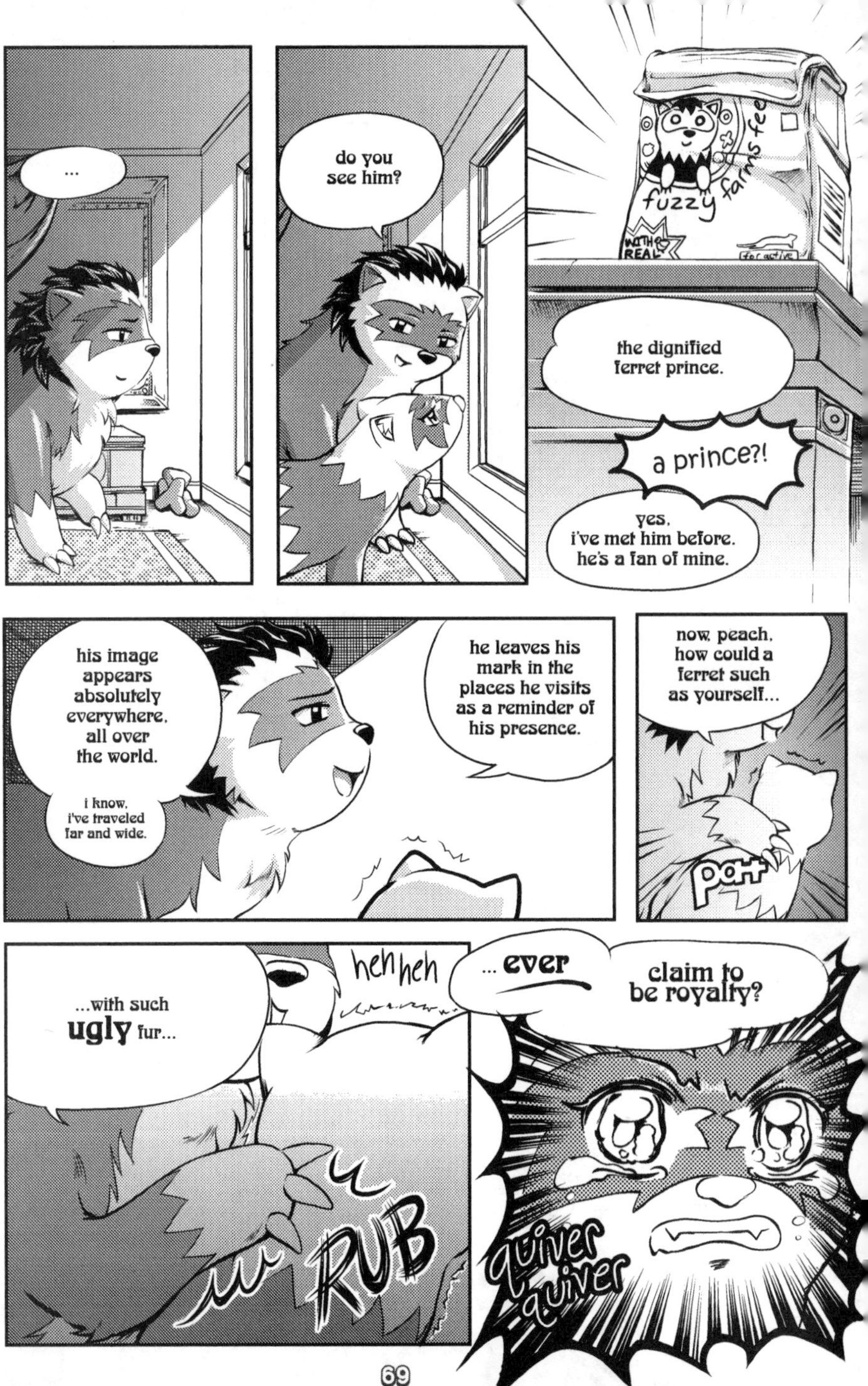

...
do you see him?
fuzzy farms fee
the dignified ferret prince.
a prince?!
yes, i've met him before. he's a fan of mine.
his image appears absolutely everywhere, all over the world.
i know, i've traveled far and wide.
he leaves his mark in the places he visits as a reminder of his presence.
now, peach, how could a ferret such as yourself...
pat
...with such **ugly** fur...
heh heh
RUB
... **ever**
claim to be royalty?
quiver quiver

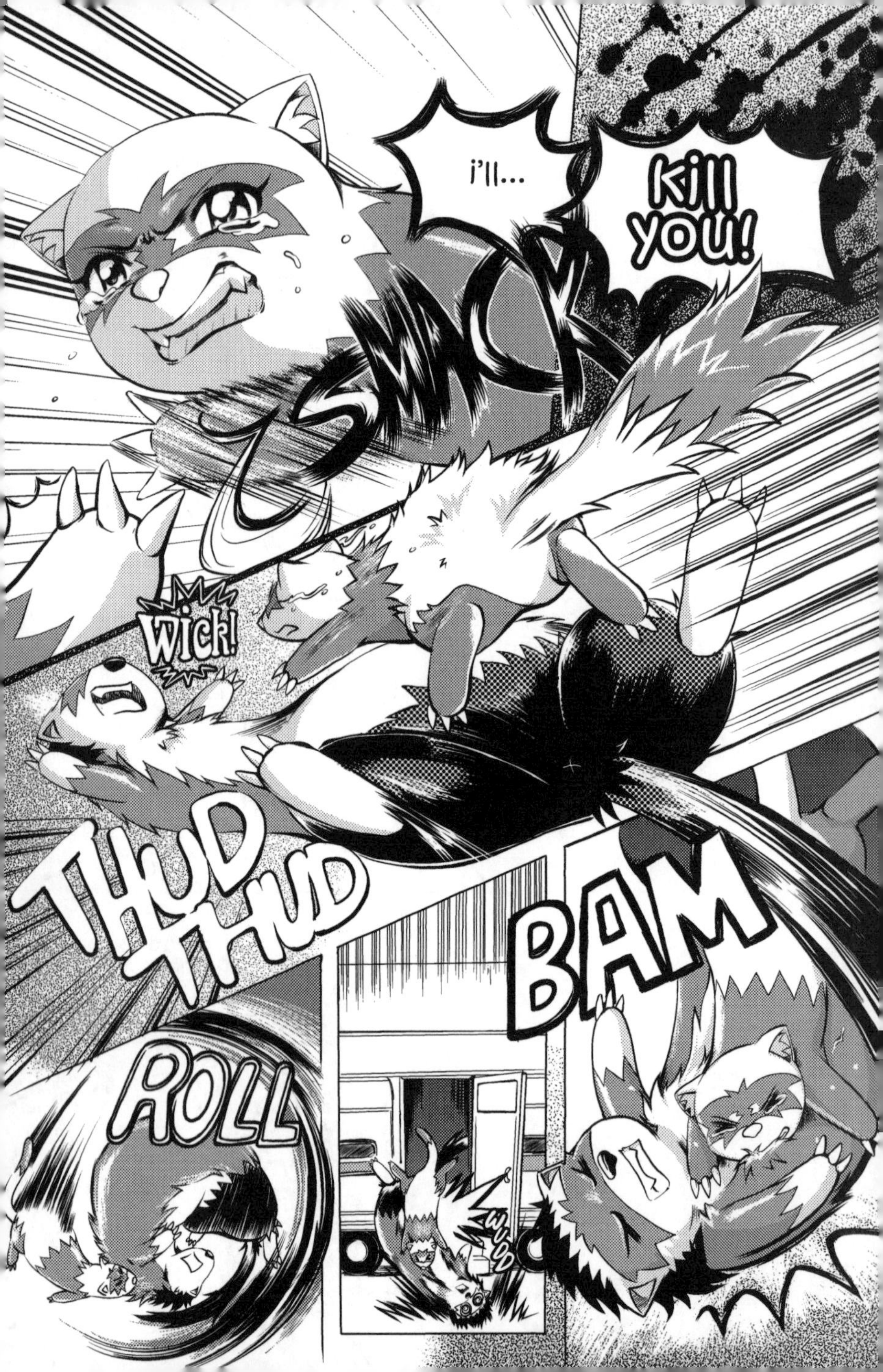
i'll...
kill you!
SMACK
Wick!
THUD THUD
BAM
ROLL

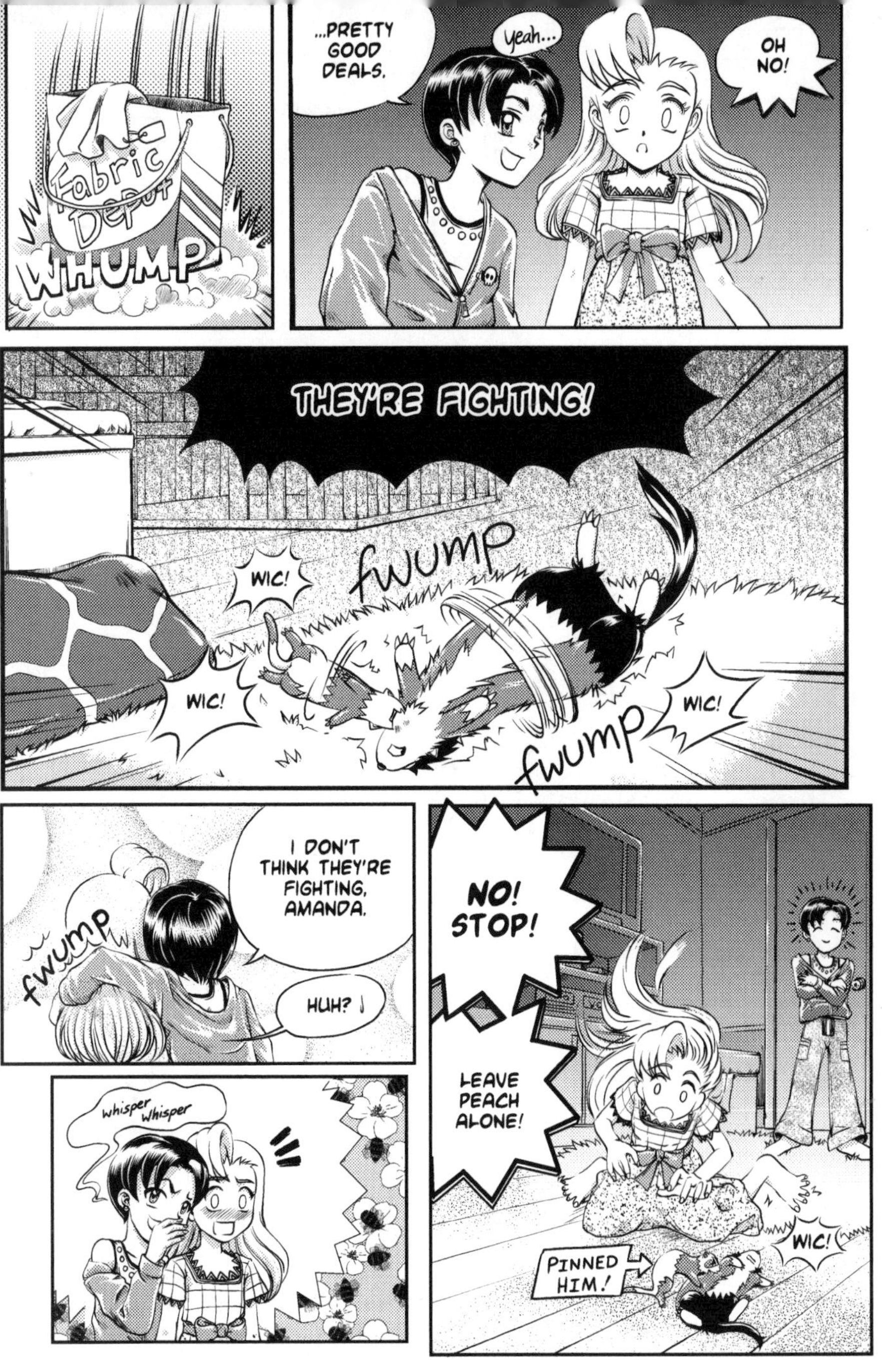

WHUMP
Fabric Depot
...PRETTY GOOD DEALS.
Yeah...
OH NO!
THEY'RE FIGHTING!
fwump
WIC!
WIC!
WIC!
fwump
I DON'T THINK THEY'RE FIGHTING, AMANDA.
fwump
HUH?
whisper whisper
NO! STOP!
LEAVE PEACH ALONE!
WIC!
PINNED HIM!

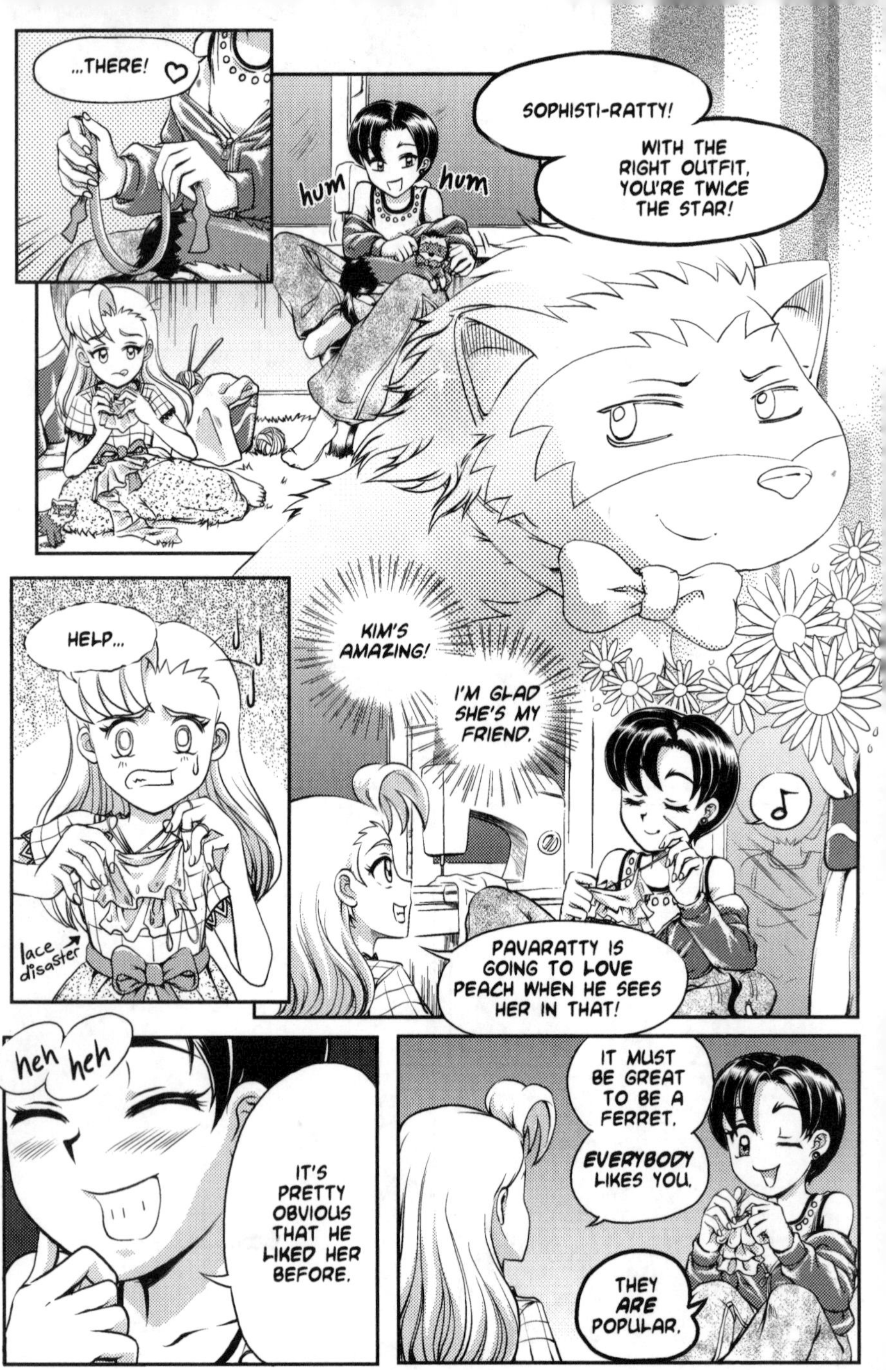
...THERE!
hum hum
SOPHISTI-RATTY!
WITH THE RIGHT OUTFIT, YOU'RE TWICE THE STAR!
HELP...
lace disaster
KIM'S AMAZING!
I'M GLAD SHE'S MY FRIEND.
PAVARATTY IS GOING TO LOVE PEACH WHEN HE SEES HER IN THAT!
heh heh
IT'S PRETTY OBVIOUS THAT HE LIKED HER BEFORE.
IT MUST BE GREAT TO BE A FERRET.
EVERYBODY LIKES YOU.
THEY ARE POPULAR.

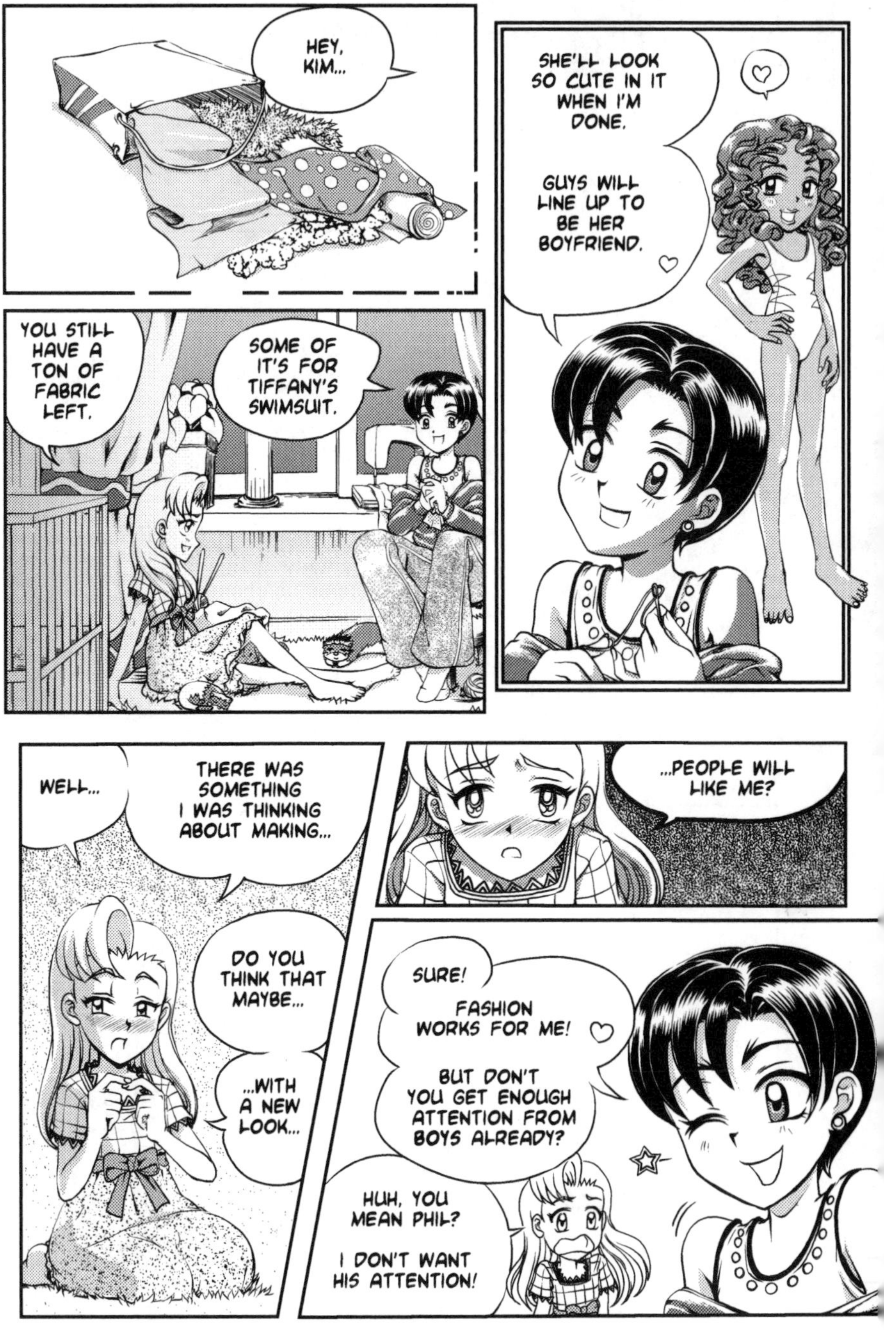

HEY, KIM...
YOU STILL HAVE A TON OF FABRIC LEFT.
SOME OF IT'S FOR TIFFANY'S SWIMSUIT.
SHE'LL LOOK SO CUTE IN IT WHEN I'M DONE.
GUYS WILL LINE UP TO BE HER BOYFRIEND.
WELL...
THERE WAS SOMETHING I WAS THINKING ABOUT MAKING...
DO YOU THINK THAT MAYBE...
...WITH A NEW LOOK...
...PEOPLE WILL LIKE ME?
SURE!
FASHION WORKS FOR ME!
BUT DON'T YOU GET ENOUGH ATTENTION FROM BOYS ALREADY?
HUH, YOU MEAN PHIL?
I DON'T WANT HIS ATTENTION!

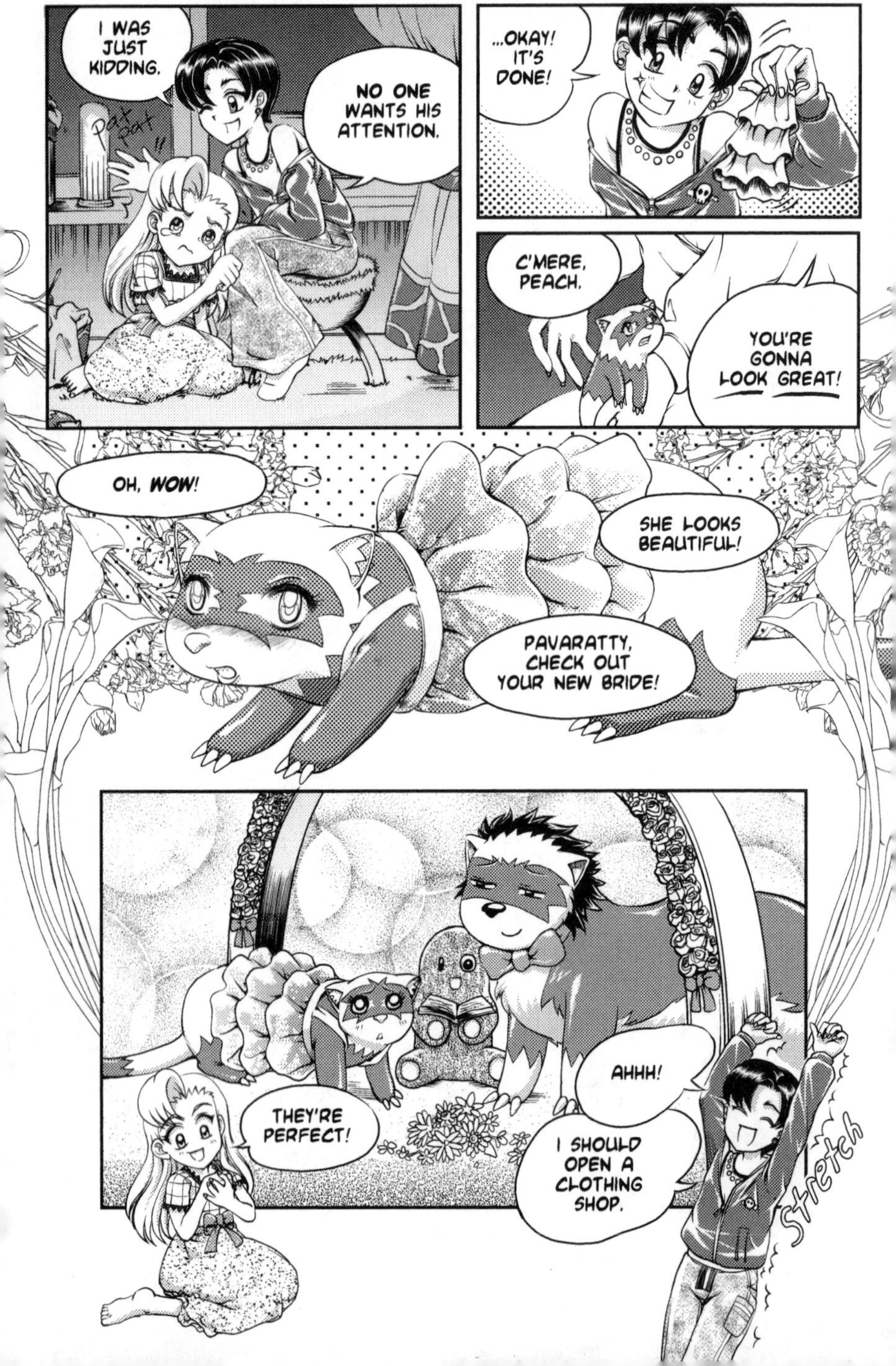
I WAS JUST KIDDING.
Pat pat !!
NO ONE WANTS HIS ATTENTION.
...OKAY! IT'S DONE!
C'MERE, PEACH.
YOU'RE GONNA LOOK GREAT!
OH, WOW!
SHE LOOKS BEAUTIFUL!
PAVARATTY, CHECK OUT YOUR NEW BRIDE!
THEY'RE PERFECT!
AHHH!
I SHOULD OPEN A CLOTHING SHOP.
Stretch

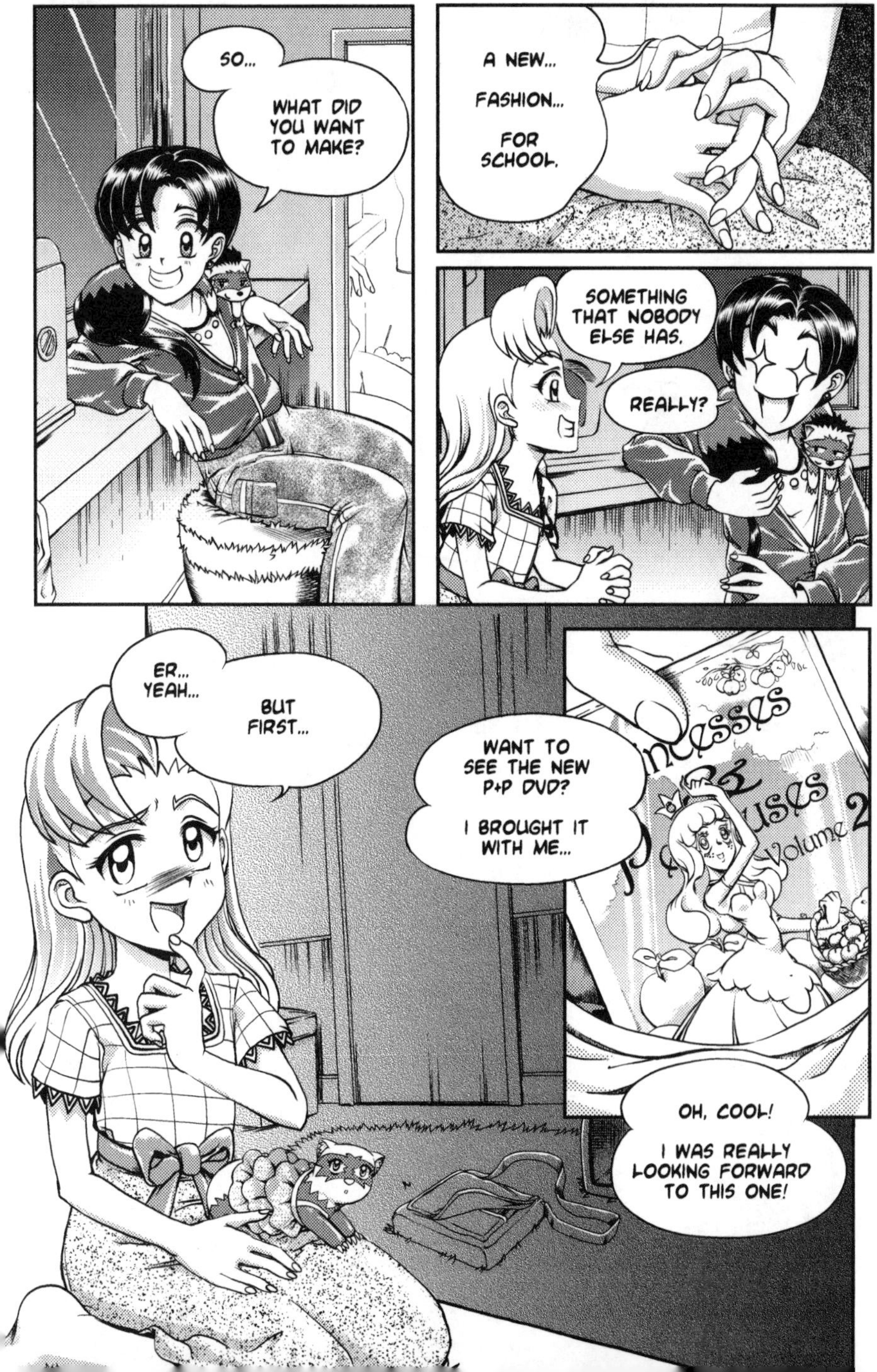
SO...
WHAT DID YOU WANT TO MAKE?
A NEW...
FASHION...
FOR SCHOOL.
SOMETHING THAT NOBODY ELSE HAS.
REALLY?
ER... YEAH...
BUT FIRST...
WANT TO SEE THE NEW P+P DVD?
I BROUGHT IT WITH ME...
OH, COOL!
I WAS REALLY LOOKING FORWARD TO THIS ONE!
Volume 2

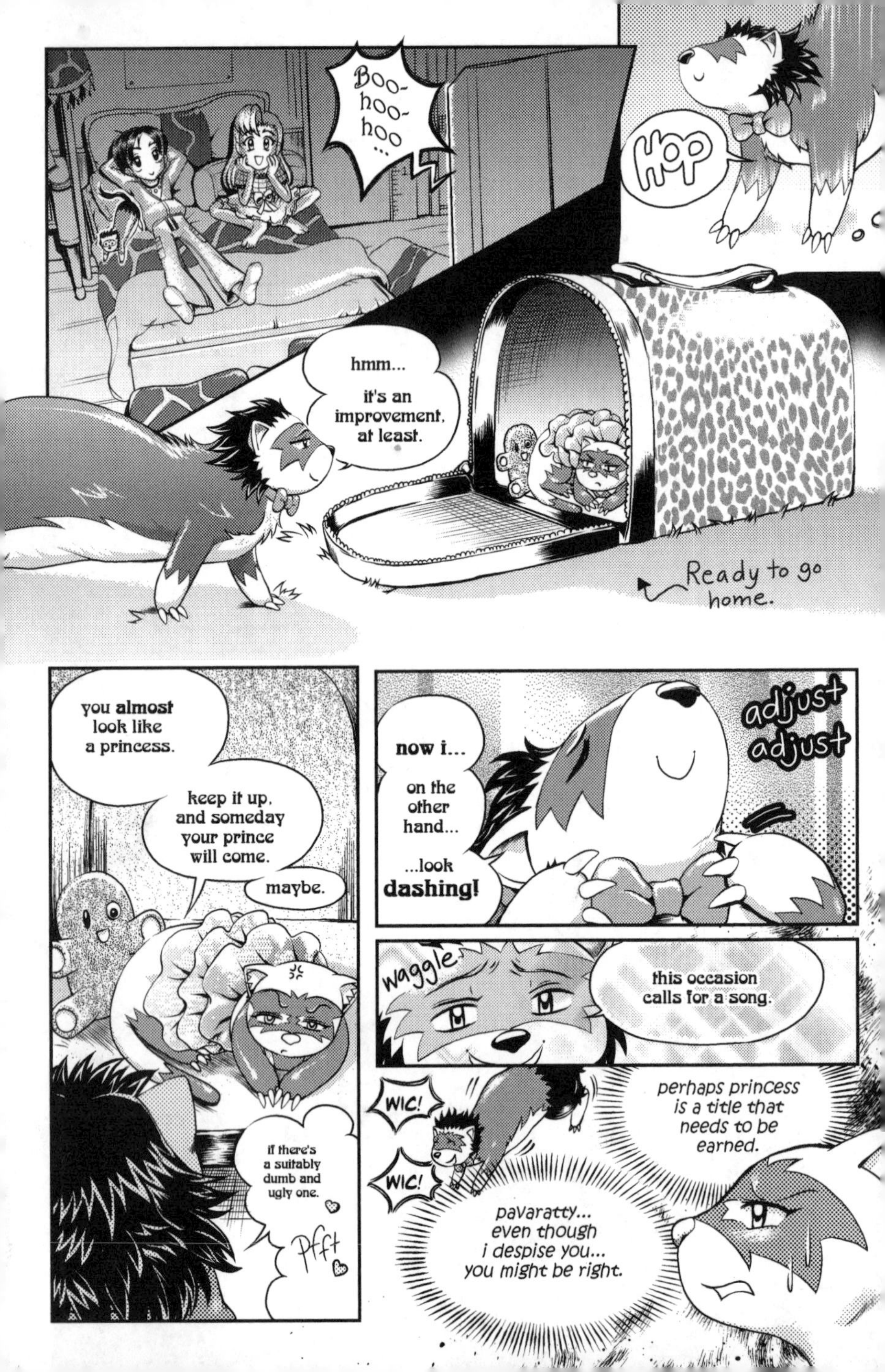
Boo-hoo-hoo...
Hop
hmm...
it's an improvement, at least.
Ready to go home.
you almost look like a princess.
keep it up, and someday your prince will come.
maybe.
if there's a suitably dumb and ugly one.
Pfft
now i...
on the other hand...
...look dashing!
adjust adjust
waggle
this occasion calls for a song.
WIC!
WIC!
perhaps princess is a title that needs to be earned.
pavaratty... even though i despise you... you might be right.

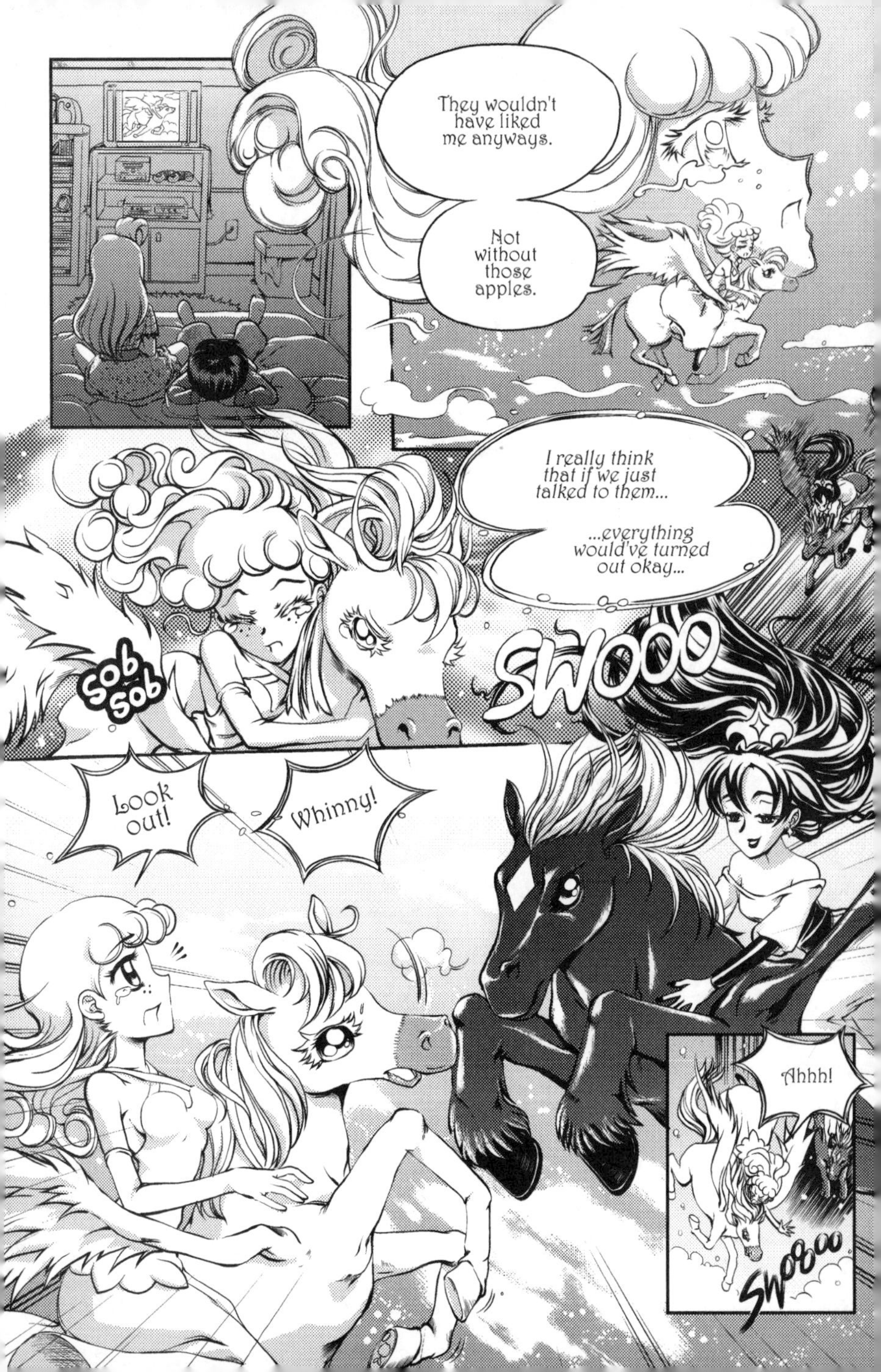
They wouldn't have liked me anyways.
Not without those apples.
I really think that if we just talked to them...
...everything would've turned out okay...
sob sob
SWOOO
Look out!
Whinny!
Ahhh!
SWOOO

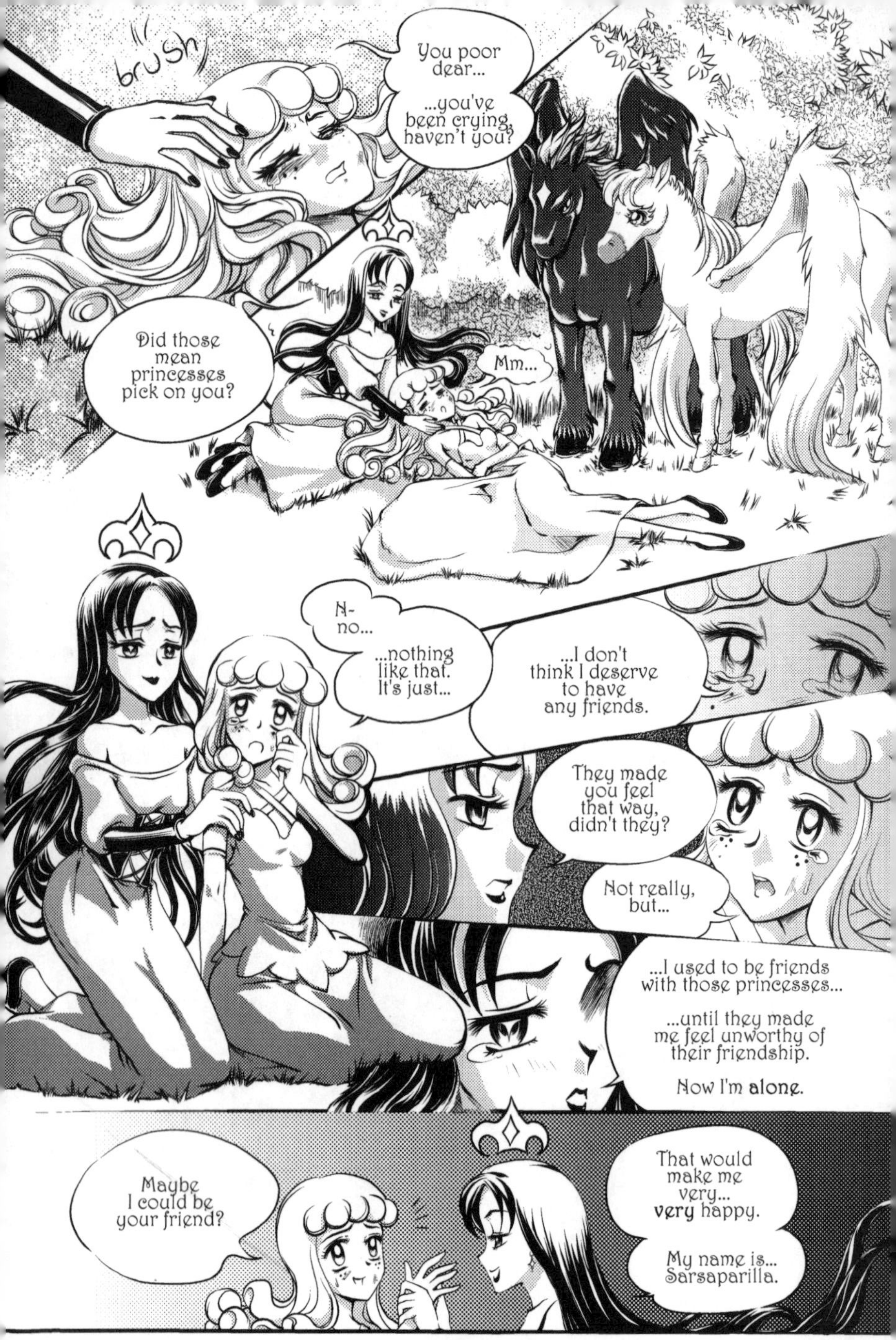
brush
You poor dear...
...you've been crying, haven't you?
Did those mean princesses pick on you?
Mm...
N- no...
...nothing like that. It's just...
...I don't think I deserve to have any friends.
They made you feel that way, didn't they?
Not really, but...
...I used to be friends with those princesses...
...until they made me feel unworthy of their friendship.
Now I'm **alone**.
Maybe I could be your friend?
That would make me very... **very** happy.
My name is... Sarsaparilla.

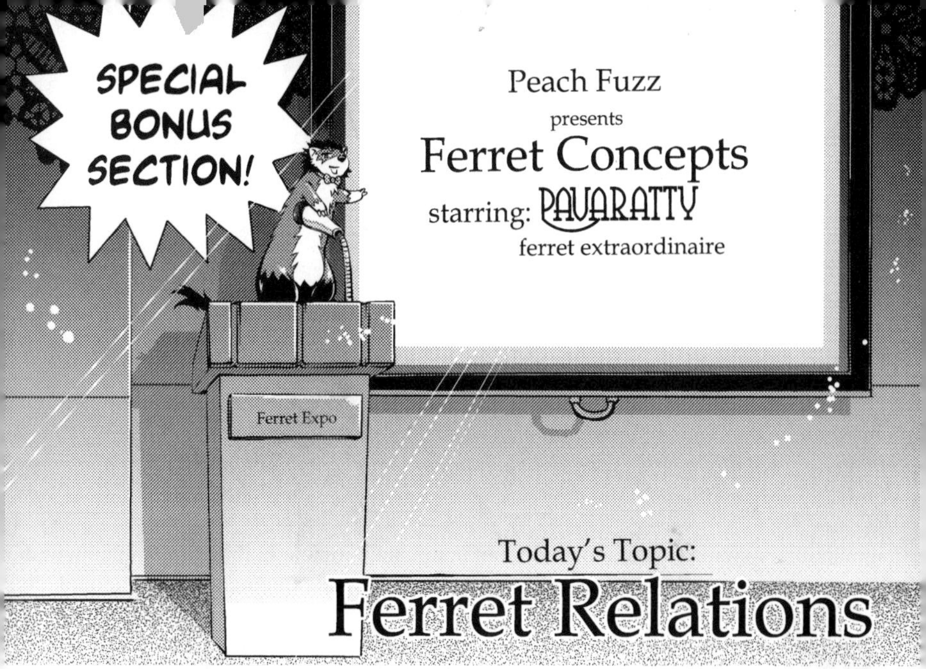
SPECIAL BONUS SECTION!
Peach Fuzz
presents
Ferret Concepts
starring: PAVARATTY
ferret extraordinaire
Ferret Expo
Today's Topic:
Ferret Relations

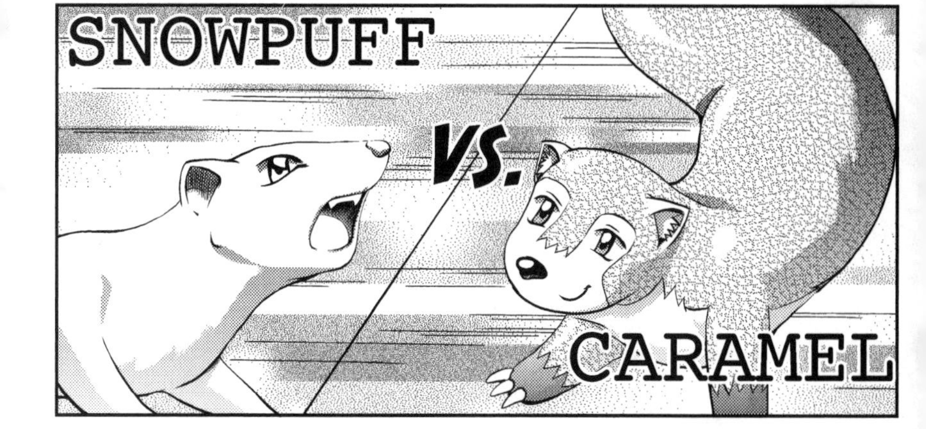
SNOWPUFF
VS.
CARAMEL

By nature, ferrets are solitary animals, but with the appropriate level of supervision and caution, they can usually be introduced to other ferrets with relatively little friction. In most cases, once an "alpha" ferret has been established, the ferrets will bond and become playmates.

As shown in my mock battle with Peach in Chapter 2, brute strength alone will not determine the dominant ferret in a group. Charisma, presence, and control are just as important when determining the true leaders, onstage and off.

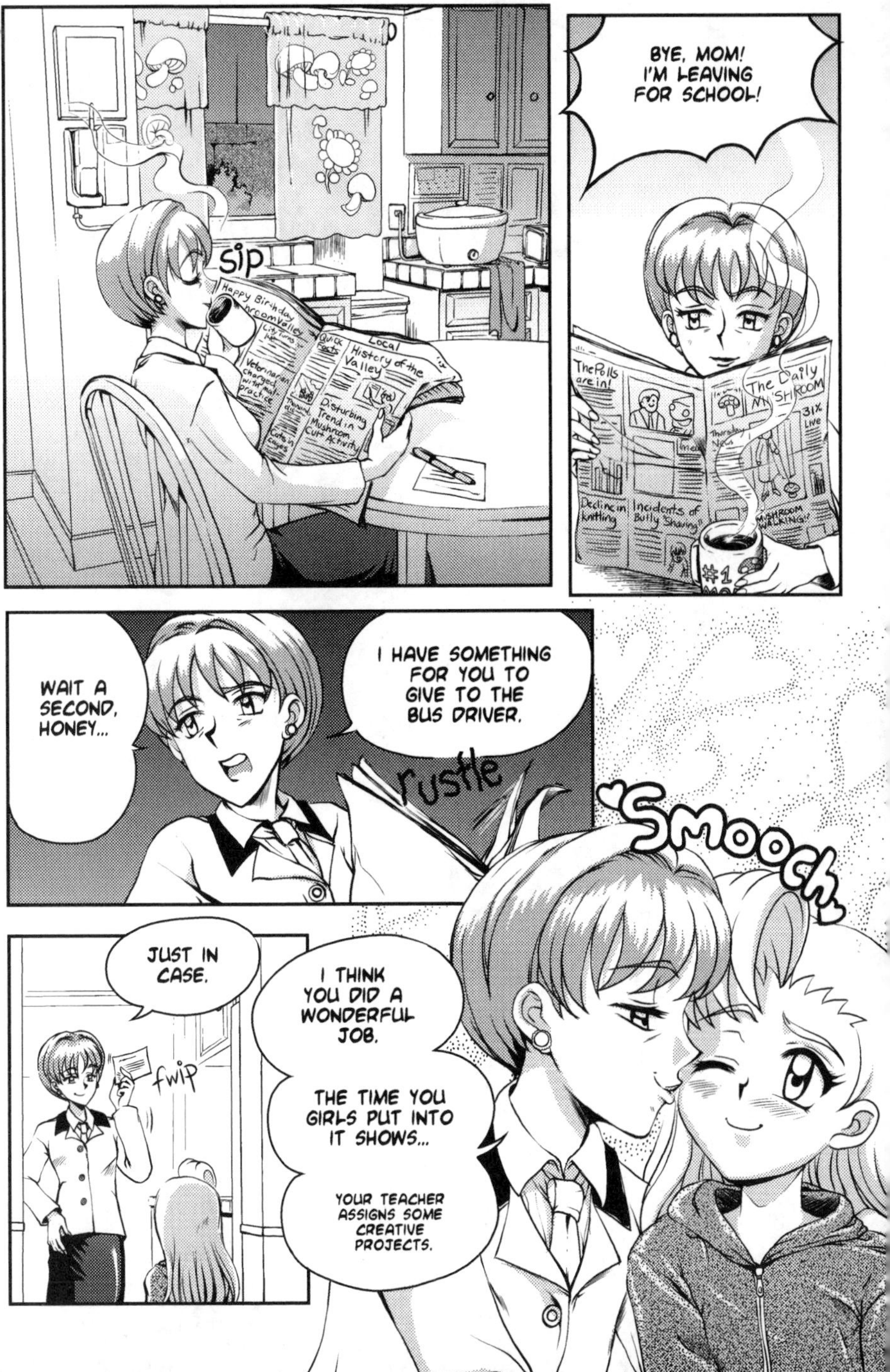
sip
Happy Birthday
Local History of the Valley
Quick Facts
Veterinarian charged with mal-practice
Disturbing Trend in Mushroom Cult Activity
BYE, MOM! I'M LEAVING FOR SCHOOL!
The Daily MUSHROOM
The Polls are in!
Decline in knitting
Incidents of Bully "Shaving"
MUSHROOM WALKING!?
#1
WAIT A SECOND, HONEY...
I HAVE SOMETHING FOR YOU TO GIVE TO THE BUS DRIVER.
rustle
JUST IN CASE.
fwip
Smooch
I THINK YOU DID A WONDERFUL JOB.
THE TIME YOU GIRLS PUT INTO IT SHOWS...
YOUR TEACHER ASSIGNS SOME CREATIVE PROJECTS.

Chapter 3
Changing Trends

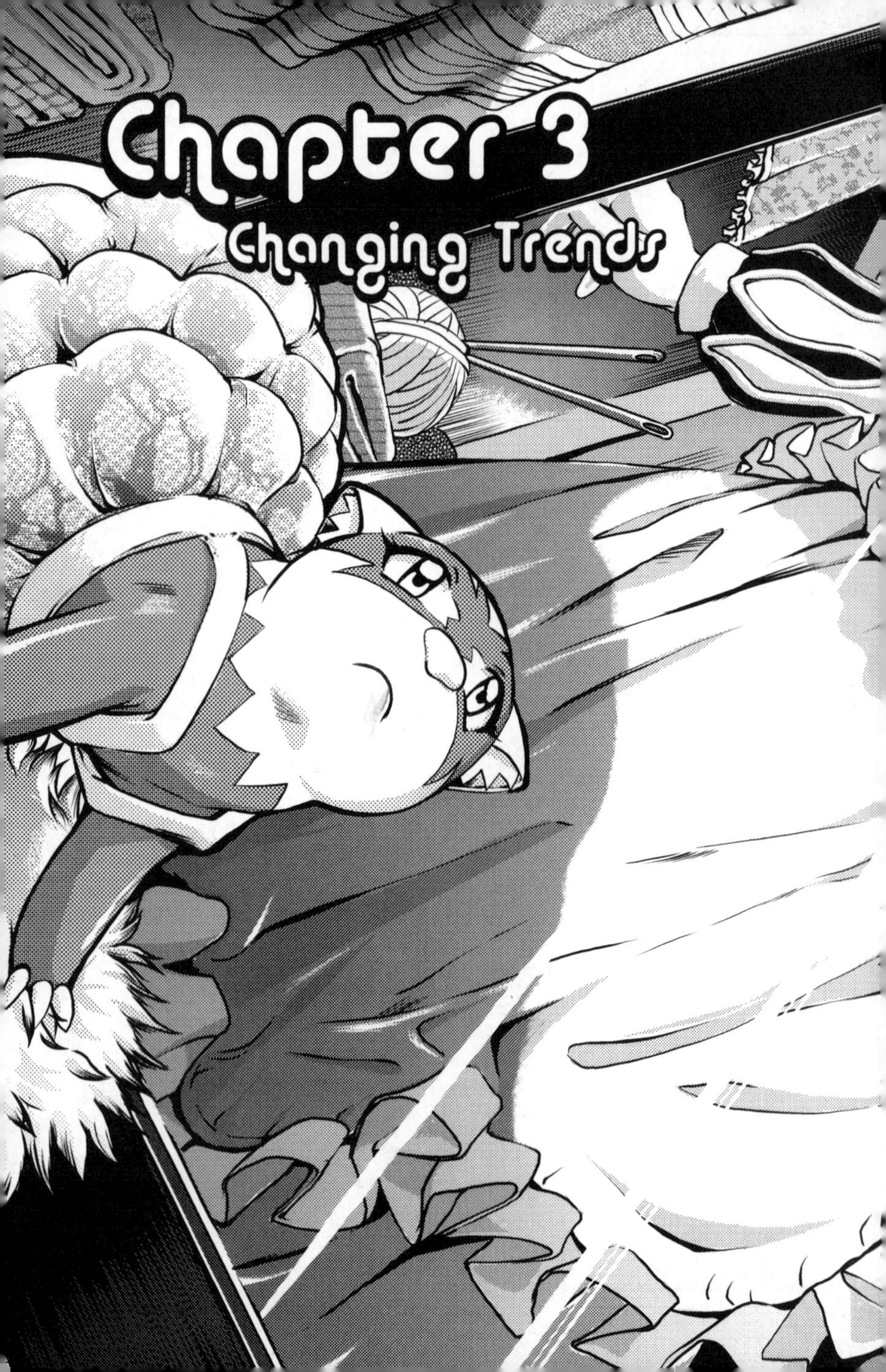

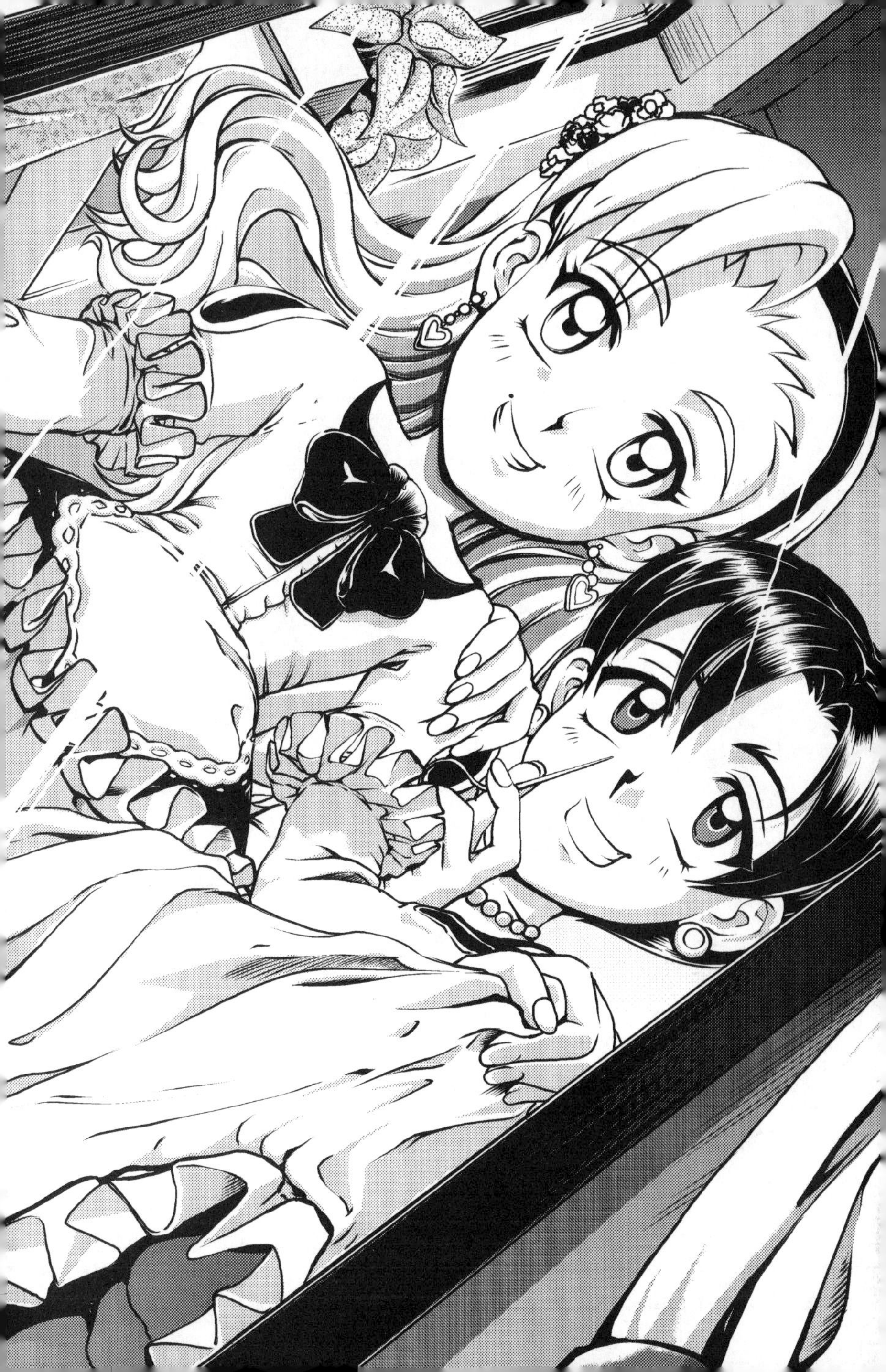

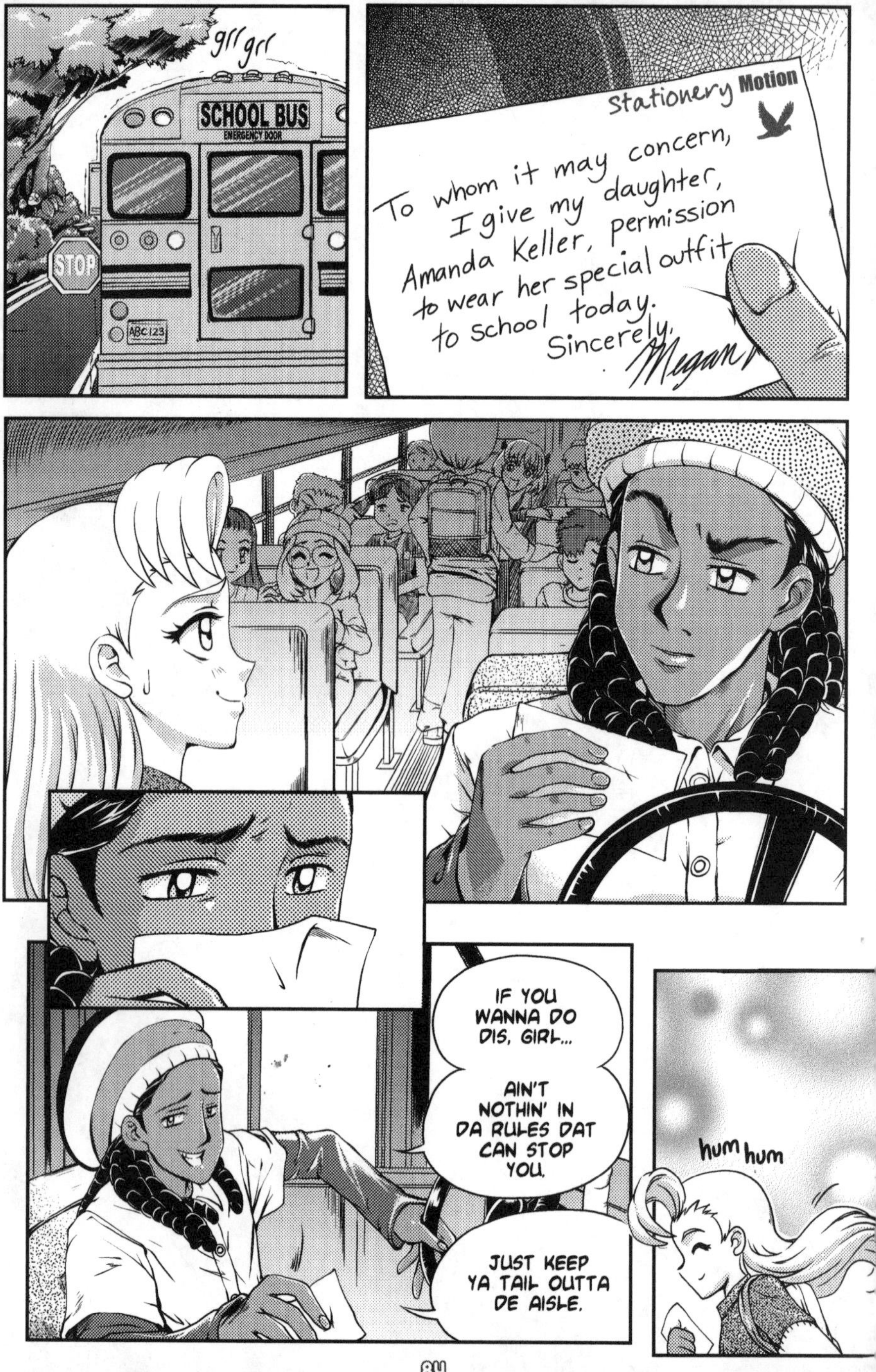
grr grr
SCHOOL BUS
EMERGENCY DOOR
STOP
ABC123
Stationery Motion
To whom it may concern,
I give my daughter,
Amanda Keller, permission
to wear her special outfit
to school today.
Sincerely,
Megan
IF YOU WANNA DO DIS, GIRL...
AIN'T NOTHIN' IN DA RULES DAT CAN STOP YOU.
JUST KEEP YA TAIL OUTTA DE AISLE.
hum hum

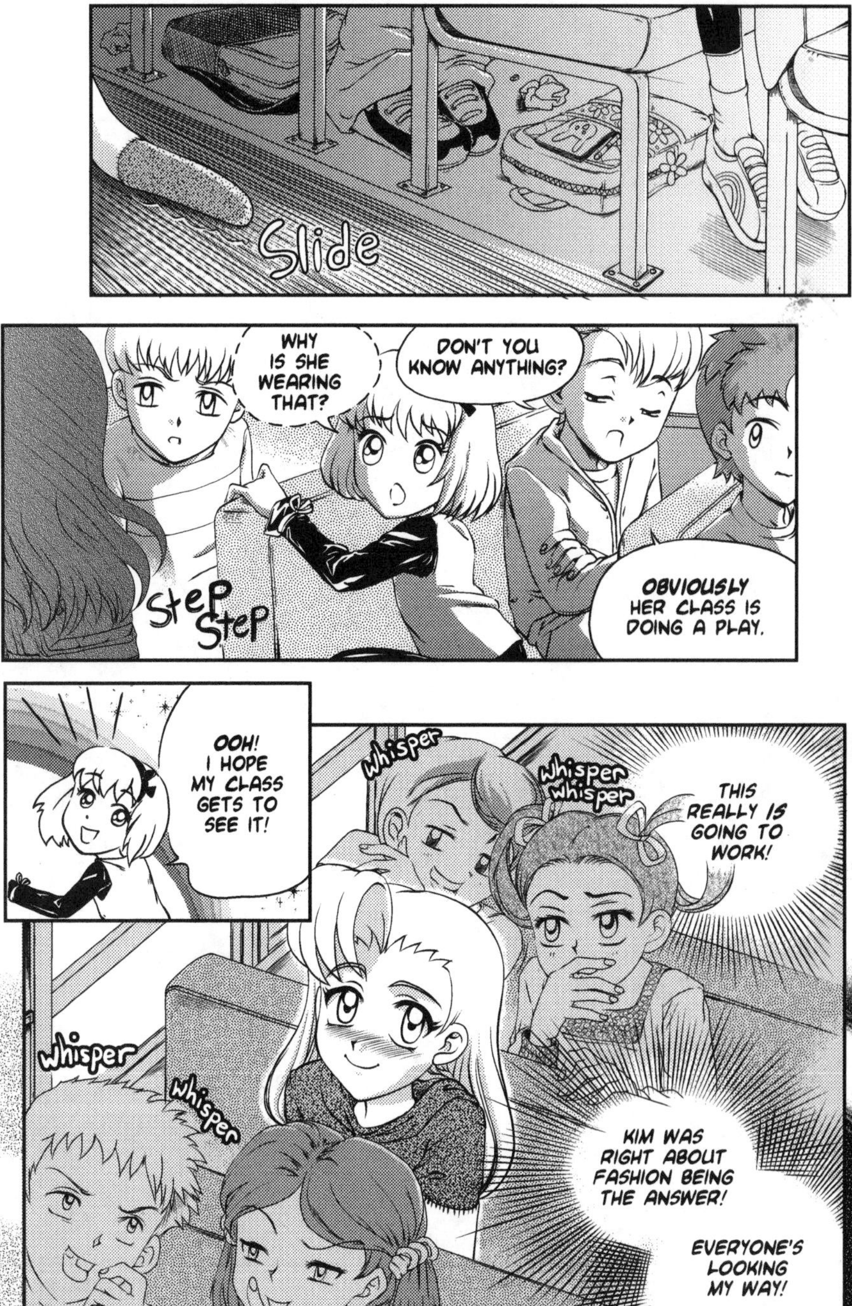
Slide
WHY IS SHE WEARING THAT?
DON'T YOU KNOW ANYTHING?
OBVIOUSLY HER CLASS IS DOING A PLAY.
Step Step
OOH! I HOPE MY CLASS GETS TO SEE IT!
whisper
whisper whisper
THIS REALLY IS GOING TO WORK!
whisper
whisper
KIM WAS RIGHT ABOUT FASHION BEING THE ANSWER!
EVERYONE'S LOOKING MY WAY!

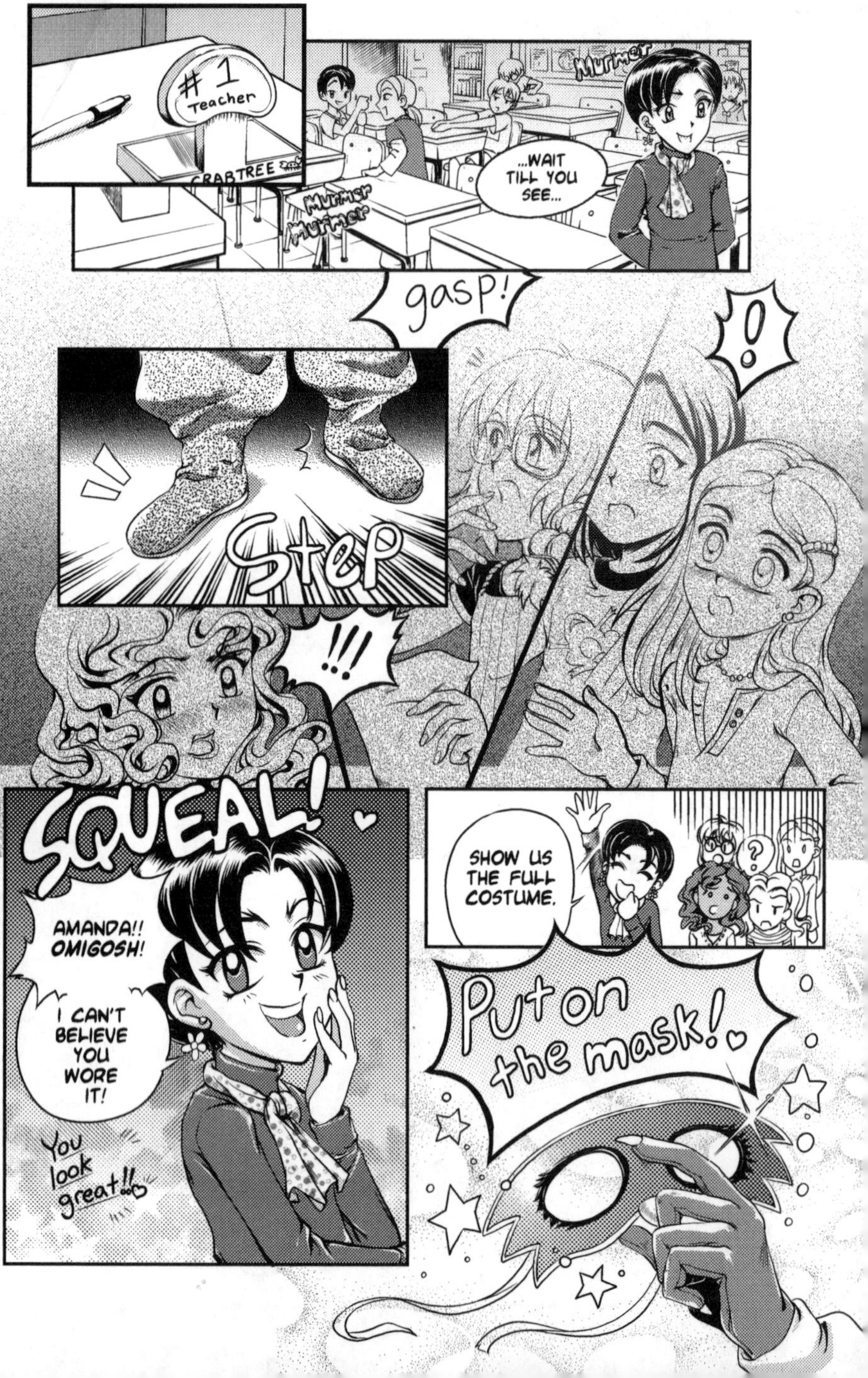

#1 Teacher
CRABTREE
Murmer
Murmer
Murmer
...WAIT TILL YOU SEE...
gasp!
!
Step
!!!
SQUEAL!
AMANDA!! OMIGOSH!
I CAN'T BELIEVE YOU WORE IT!
You look great!!
SHOW US THE FULL COSTUME.
?
Put on the mask!

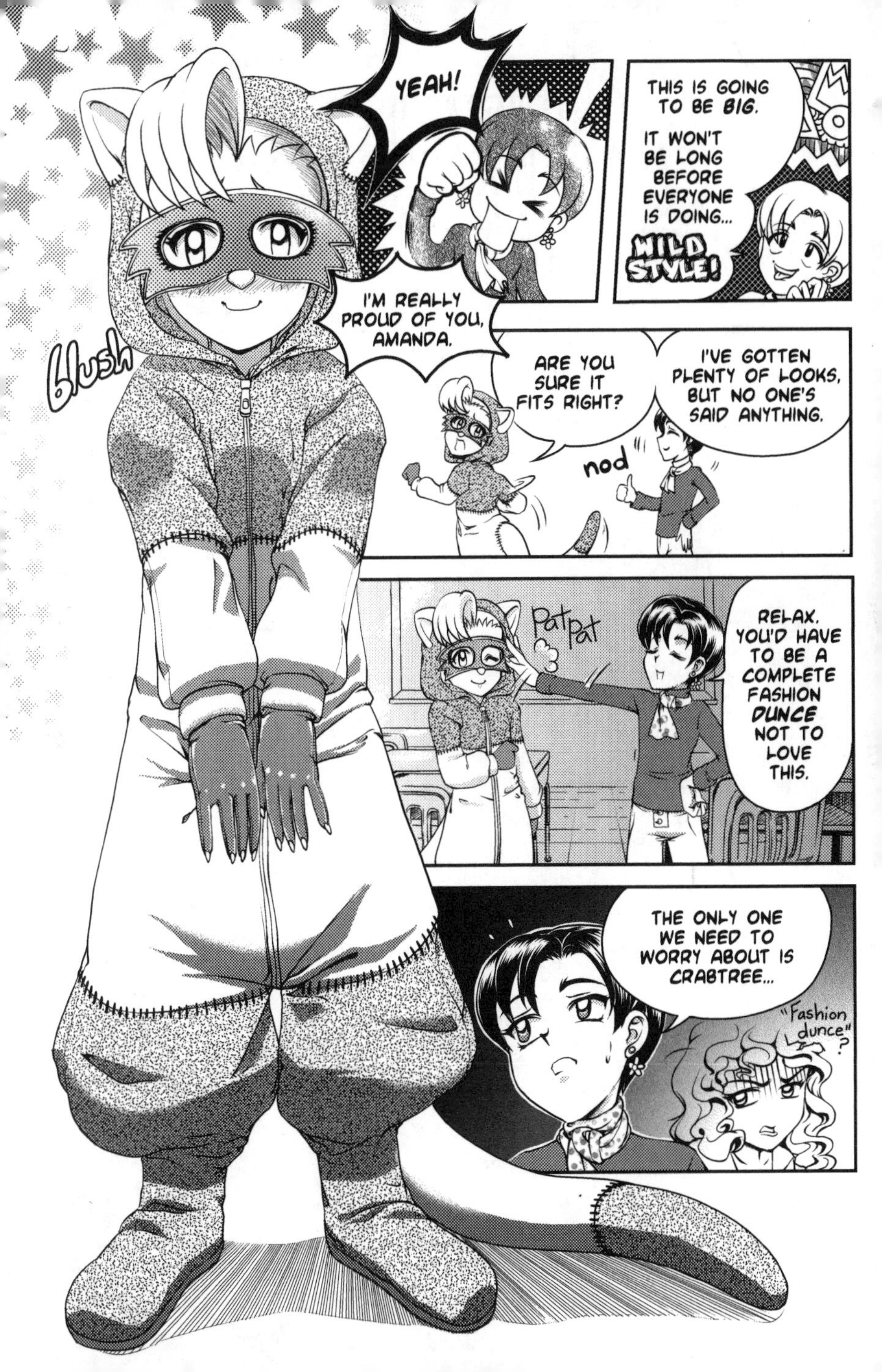

YEAH!
THIS IS GOING TO BE BIG.
IT WON'T BE LONG BEFORE EVERYONE IS DOING...
WILD STYLE!
I'M REALLY PROUD OF YOU, AMANDA.
blush
ARE YOU SURE IT FITS RIGHT?
I'VE GOTTEN PLENTY OF LOOKS, BUT NO ONE'S SAID ANYTHING.
nod
Pat Pat
RELAX. YOU'D HAVE TO BE A COMPLETE FASHION DUNCE NOT TO LOVE THIS.
THE ONLY ONE WE NEED TO WORRY ABOUT IS CRABTREE...
"Fashion dunce"?

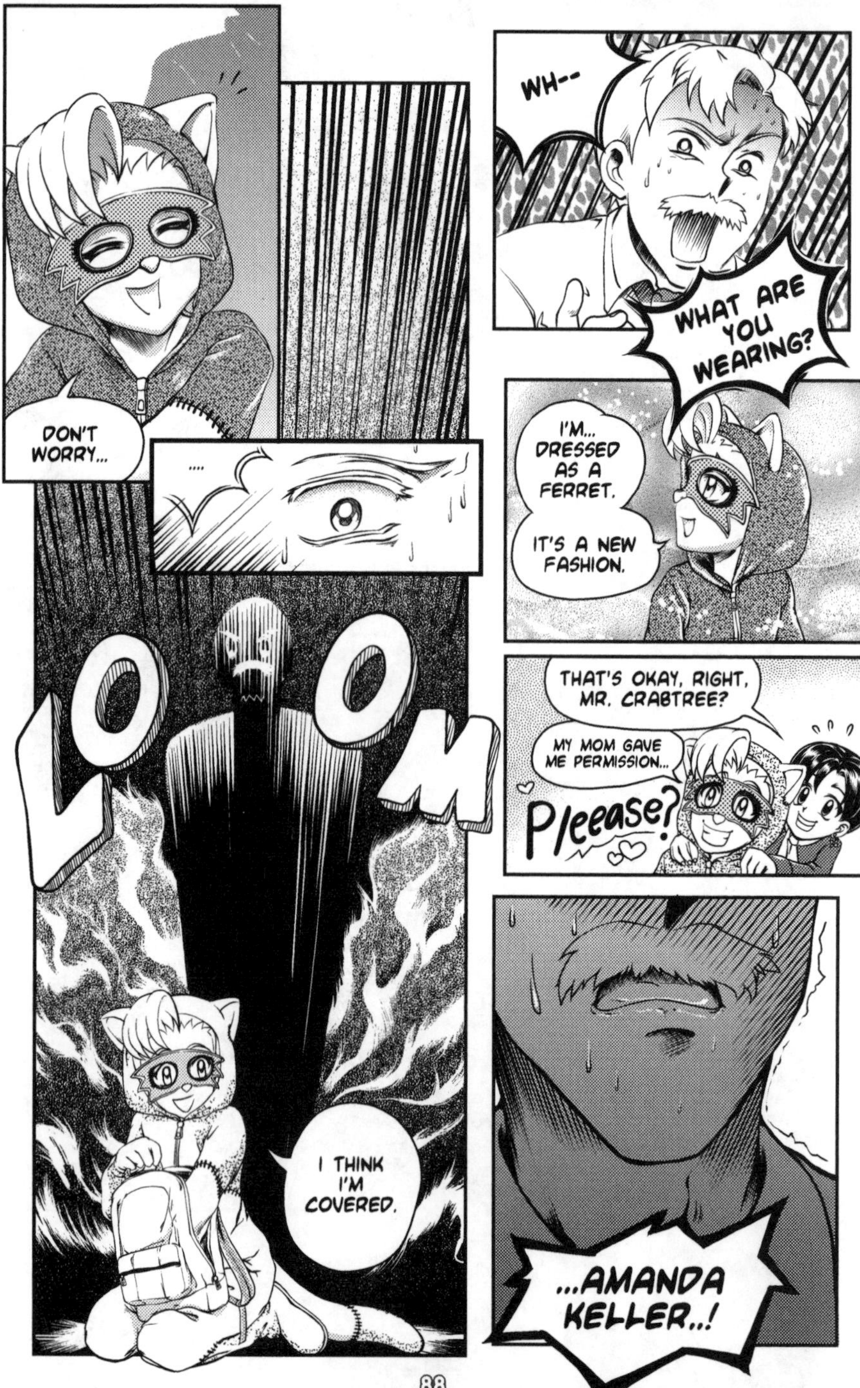
DON'T WORRY...
....
LOOM
I THINK I'M COVERED.
WH--
WHAT ARE YOU WEARING?
I'M... DRESSED AS A FERRET.
IT'S A NEW FASHION.
THAT'S OKAY, RIGHT, MR. CRABTREE?
MY MOM GAVE ME PERMISSION...
Pleease?
...AMANDA KELLER..!

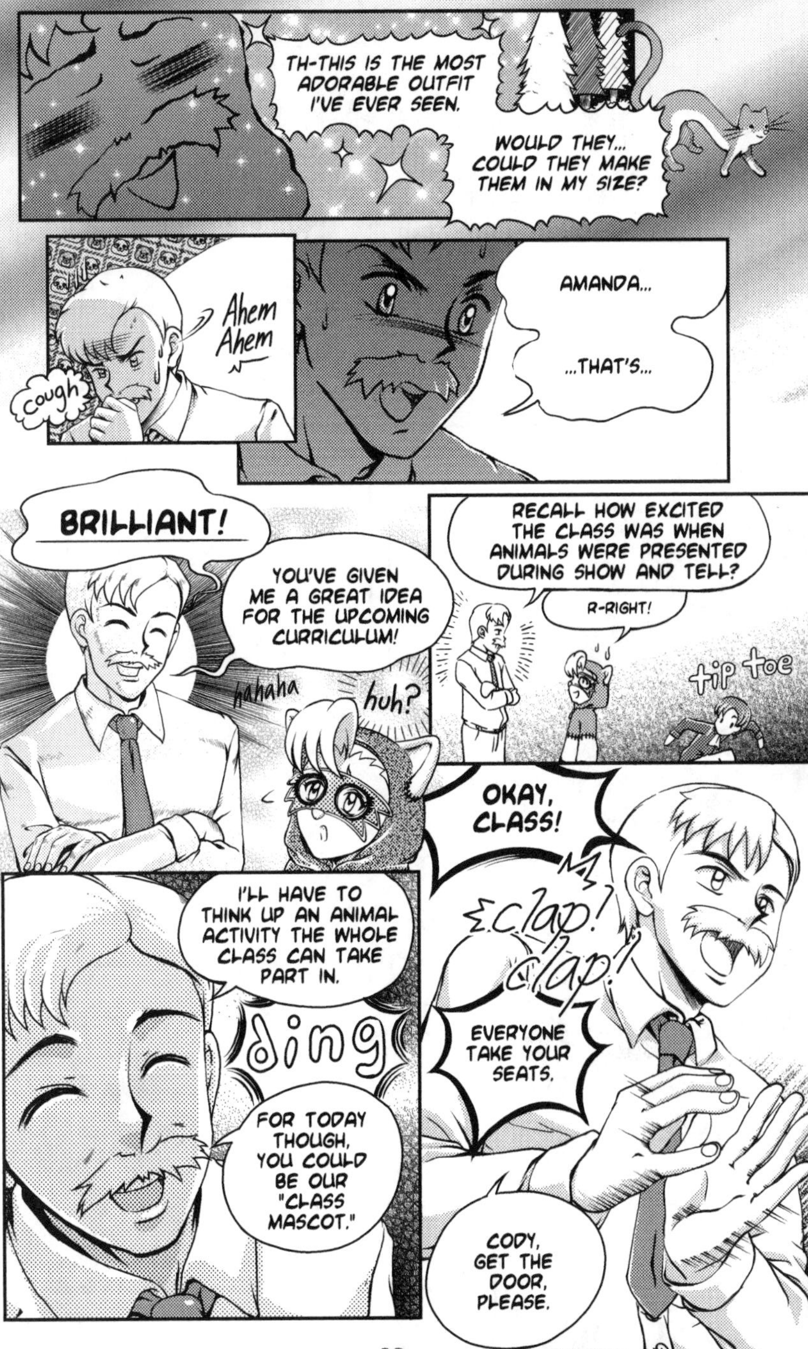

TH-THIS IS THE MOST ADORABLE OUTFIT I'VE EVER SEEN.
WOULD THEY... COULD THEY MAKE THEM IN MY SIZE?
Ahem Ahem
cough
AMANDA...
...THAT'S...
BRILLIANT!
YOU'VE GIVEN ME A GREAT IDEA FOR THE UPCOMING CURRICULUM!
hahaha
huh?
RECALL HOW EXCITED THE CLASS WAS WHEN ANIMALS WERE PRESENTED DURING SHOW AND TELL?
R-RIGHT!
tip toe
I'LL HAVE TO THINK UP AN ANIMAL ACTIVITY THE WHOLE CLASS CAN TAKE PART IN.
ding
FOR TODAY THOUGH, YOU COULD BE OUR "CLASS MASCOT."
OKAY, CLASS!
clap! clap!
EVERYONE TAKE YOUR SEATS.
CODY, GET THE DOOR, PLEASE.

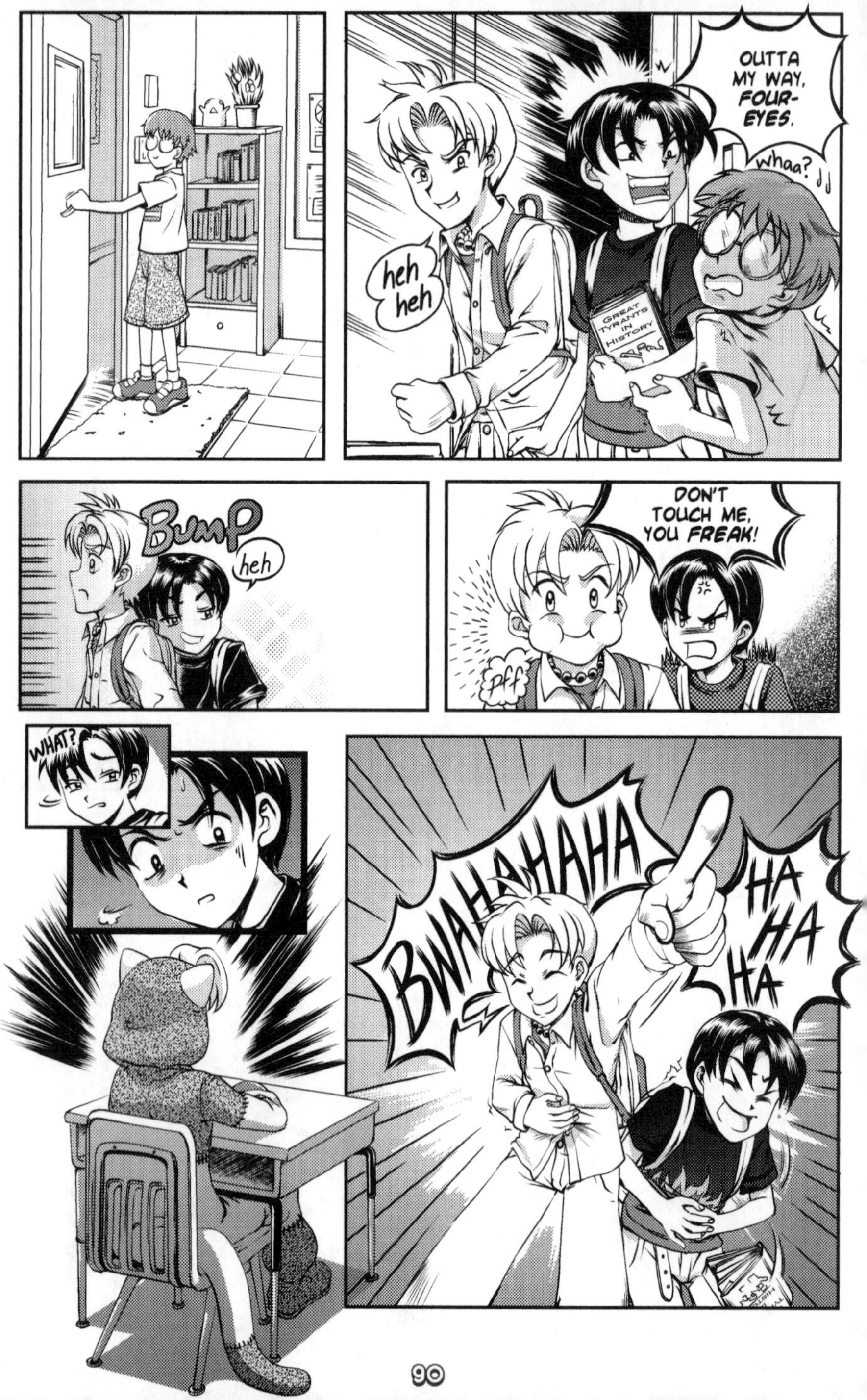
OUTTA MY WAY, FOUR-EYES.
whaa?
heh heh
GREAT TYRANTS IN HISTORY
BUMP
heh
DON'T TOUCH ME, YOU FREAK!
Pff
WHAT?
BWAHAHAHAHA
HA HA HA HA

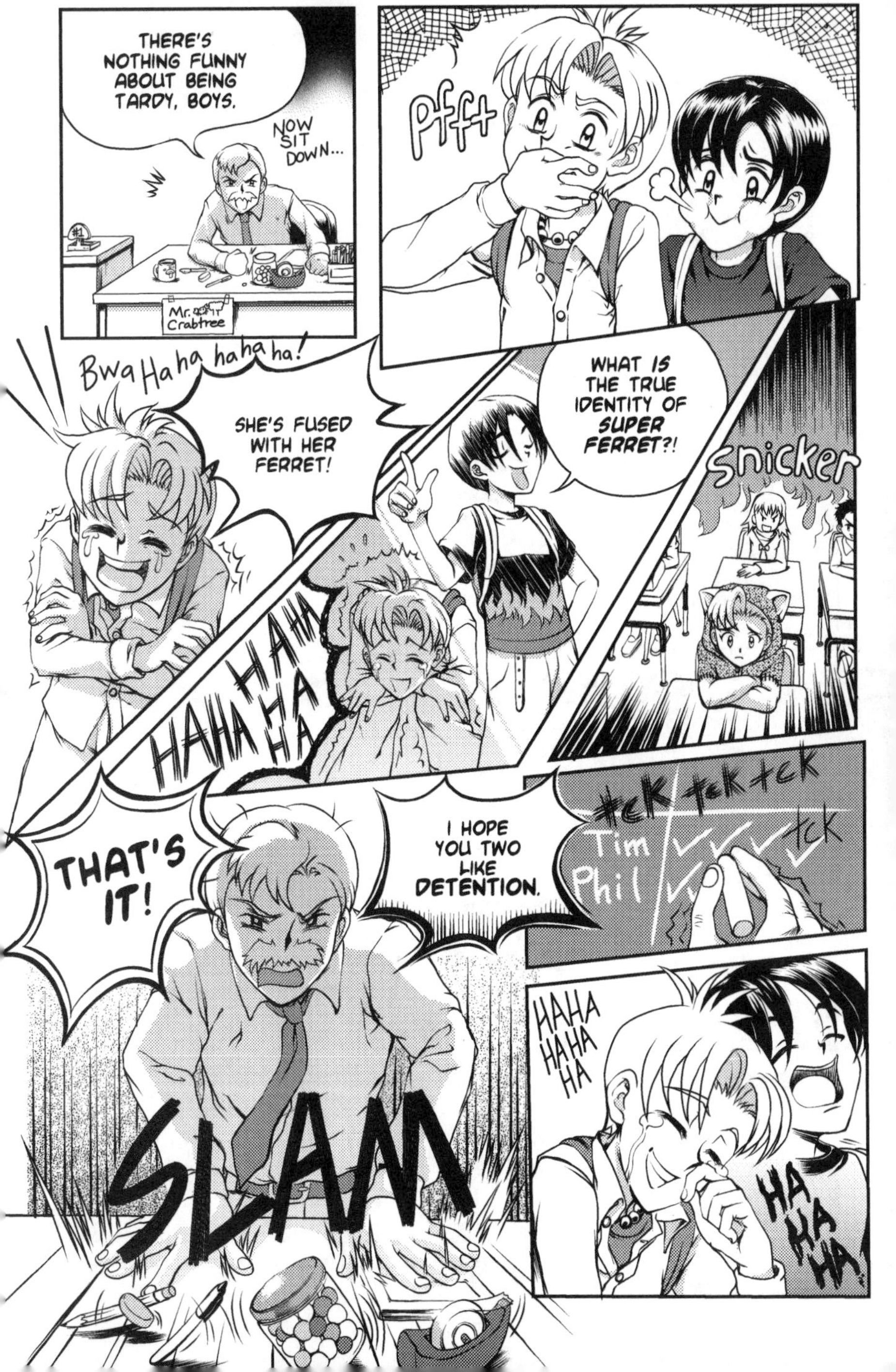
THERE'S NOTHING FUNNY ABOUT BEING TARDY, BOYS.
NOW SIT DOWN...
#1
Mr. Crabtree
Pfft
Bwa Ha ha ha ha ha!
SHE'S FUSED WITH HER FERRET!
WHAT IS THE TRUE IDENTITY OF SUPER FERRET?!
snicker
HAHA HA HAHA HA HA
THAT'S IT!
I HOPE YOU TWO LIKE DETENTION.
tck tck tck tck
Tim
Phil
tck
HAHA HAHA HA
HA HA HA HA
SLAM

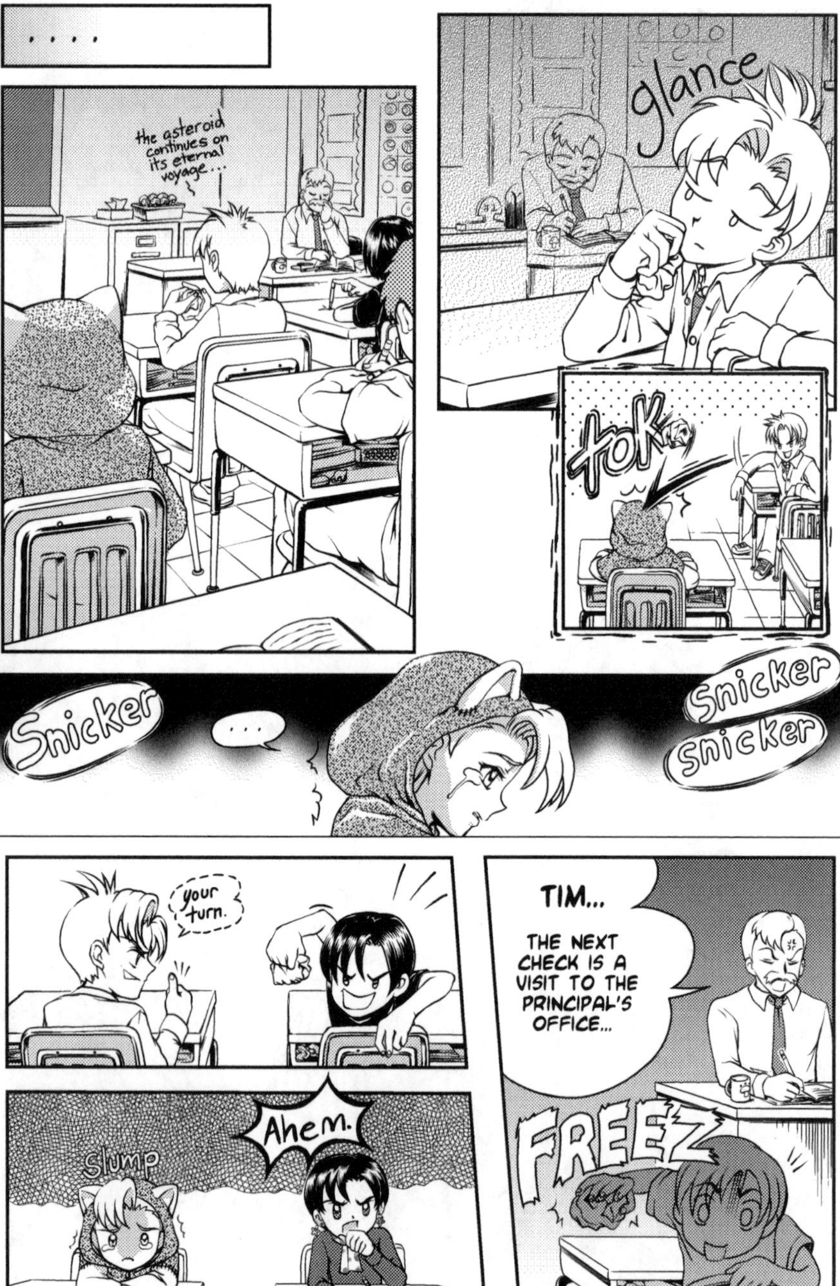
....
the asteroid continues on its eternal voyage...
glance
tok
Snicker
...
Snicker
snicker
your turn.
TIM...
THE NEXT CHECK IS A VISIT TO THE PRINCIPAL'S OFFICE...
slump
Ahem.
FREEZ

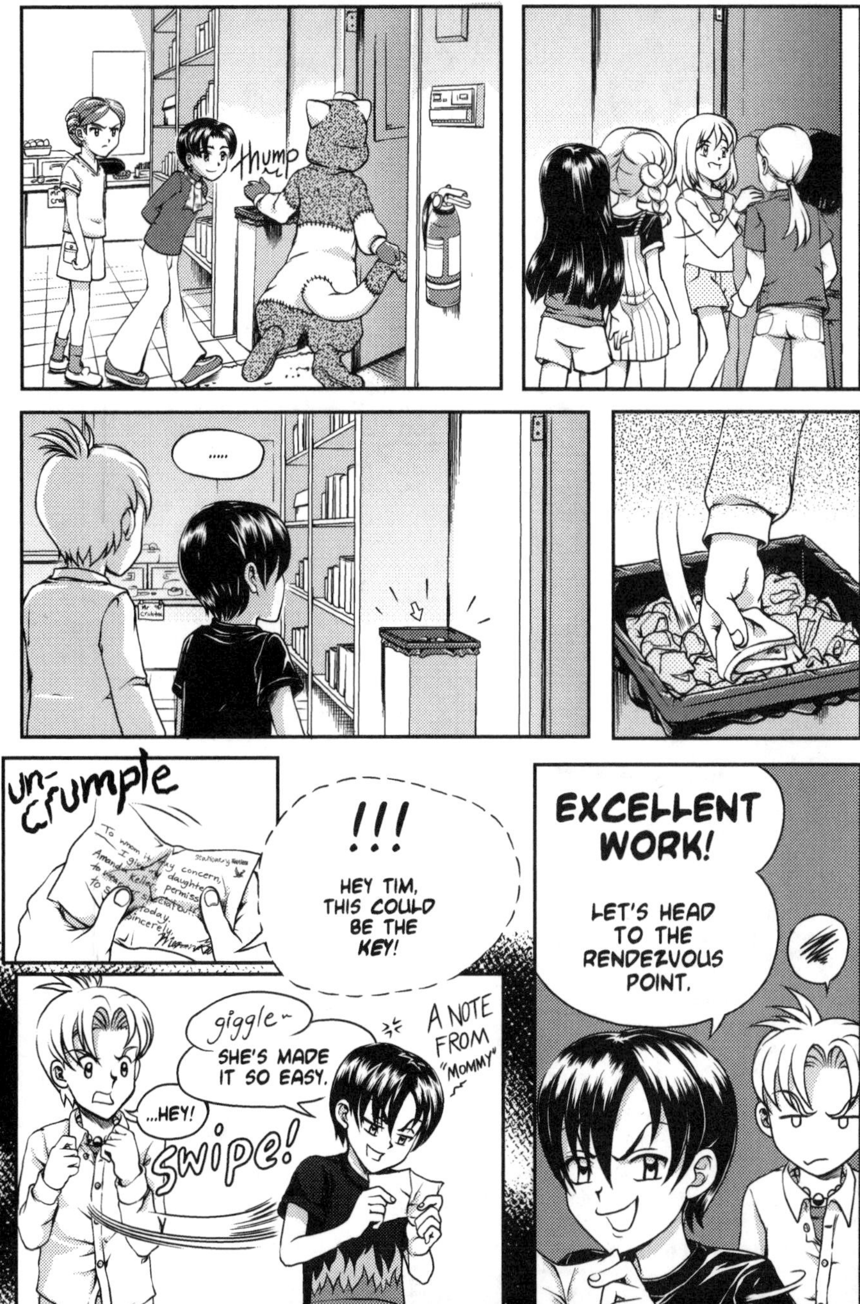
thump
.....
un-crumple
To whom it may concern,
I give my daughter,
Amanda Keller, permiss
today.
Sincerely,
Stationery
!!!
HEY TIM, THIS COULD BE THE KEY!
EXCELLENT WORK!
LET'S HEAD TO THE RENDEZVOUS POINT.
giggle~
SHE'S MADE IT SO EASY.
A NOTE FROM "MOMMY"
...HEY!
swipe!

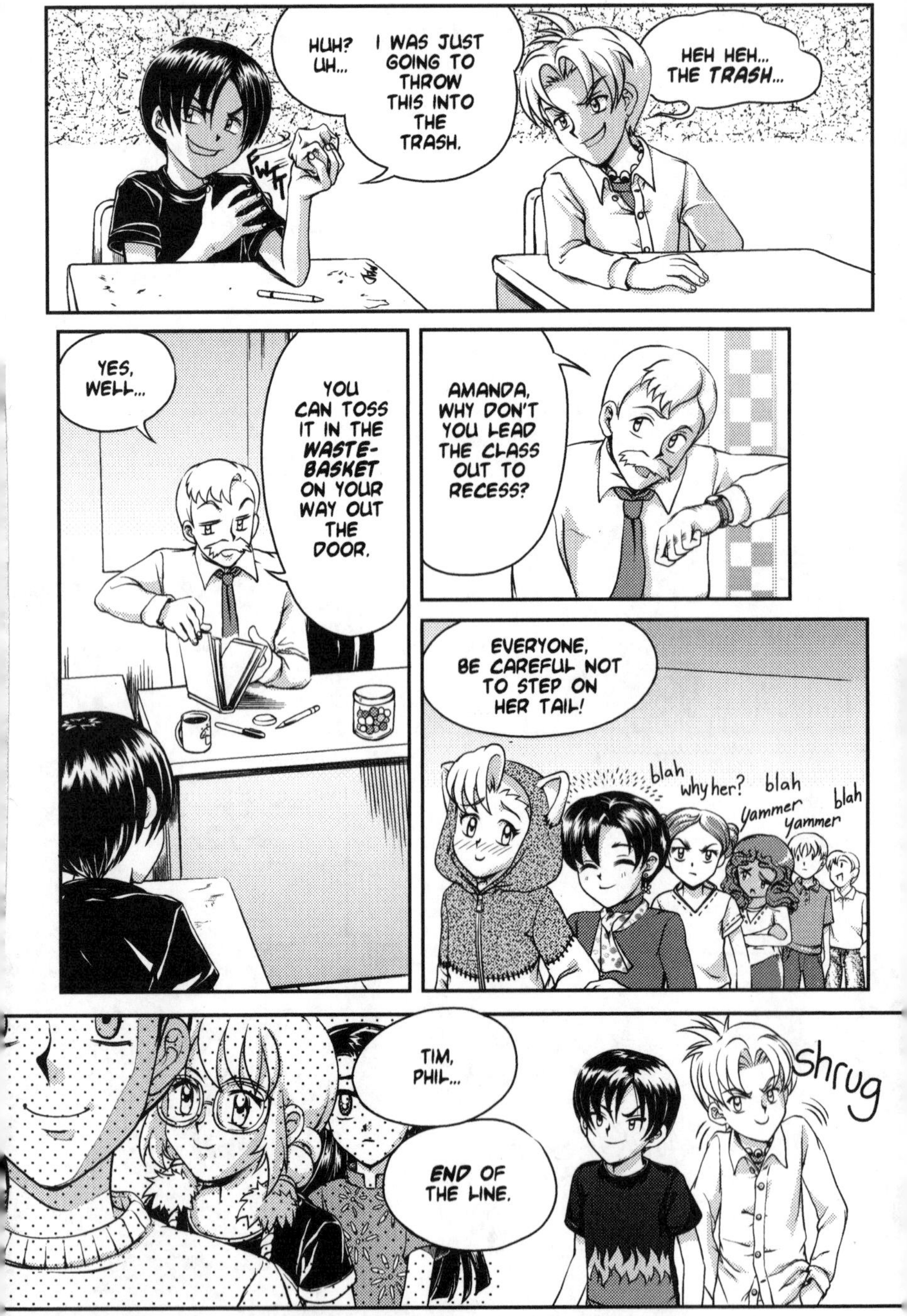
HUH? UH...
I WAS JUST GOING TO THROW THIS INTO THE TRASH.
HEH HEH... THE *TRASH*...
YES, WELL...
YOU CAN TOSS IT IN THE *WASTE-BASKET* ON YOUR WAY OUT THE DOOR.
AMANDA, WHY DON'T YOU LEAD THE CLASS OUT TO RECESS?
EVERYONE, BE CAREFUL NOT TO STEP ON HER TAIL!
blah
why her?
blah
yammer
yammer
blah
TIM, PHIL...
END OF THE LINE.
Shrug

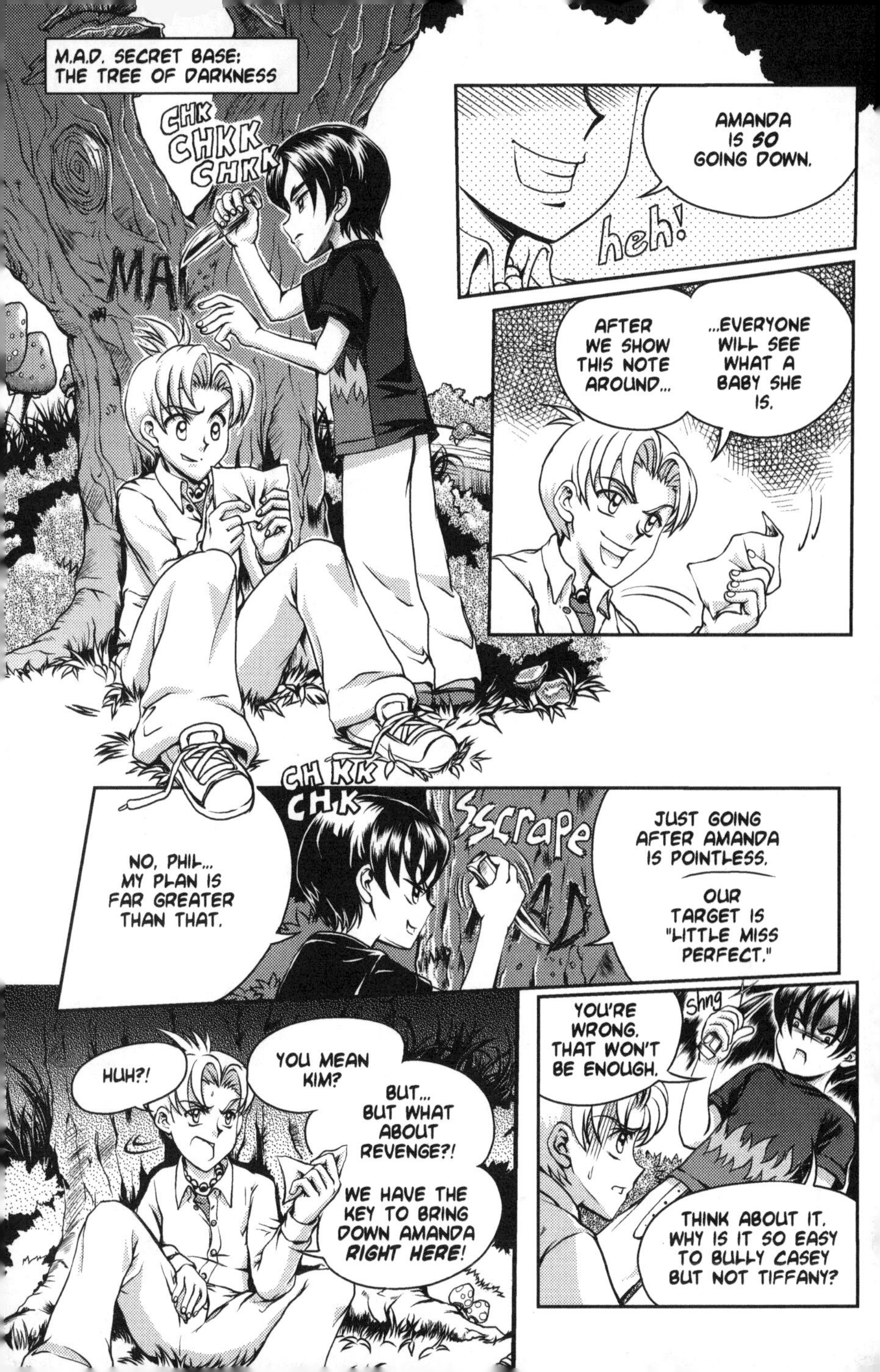
M.A.D. SECRET BASE: THE TREE OF DARKNESS
CHK CHKK CHKK
MA
AMANDA IS SO GOING DOWN.
heh!
AFTER WE SHOW THIS NOTE AROUND...
...EVERYONE WILL SEE WHAT A BABY SHE IS.
CHKK CHK
Sscrape
NO, PHIL... MY PLAN IS FAR GREATER THAN THAT.
JUST GOING AFTER AMANDA IS POINTLESS.
OUR TARGET IS "LITTLE MISS PERFECT."
HUH?!
YOU MEAN KIM?
BUT... BUT WHAT ABOUT REVENGE?!
WE HAVE THE KEY TO BRING DOWN AMANDA RIGHT HERE!
Shing
YOU'RE WRONG. THAT WON'T BE ENOUGH.
THINK ABOUT IT. WHY IS IT SO EASY TO BULLY CASEY BUT NOT TIFFANY?

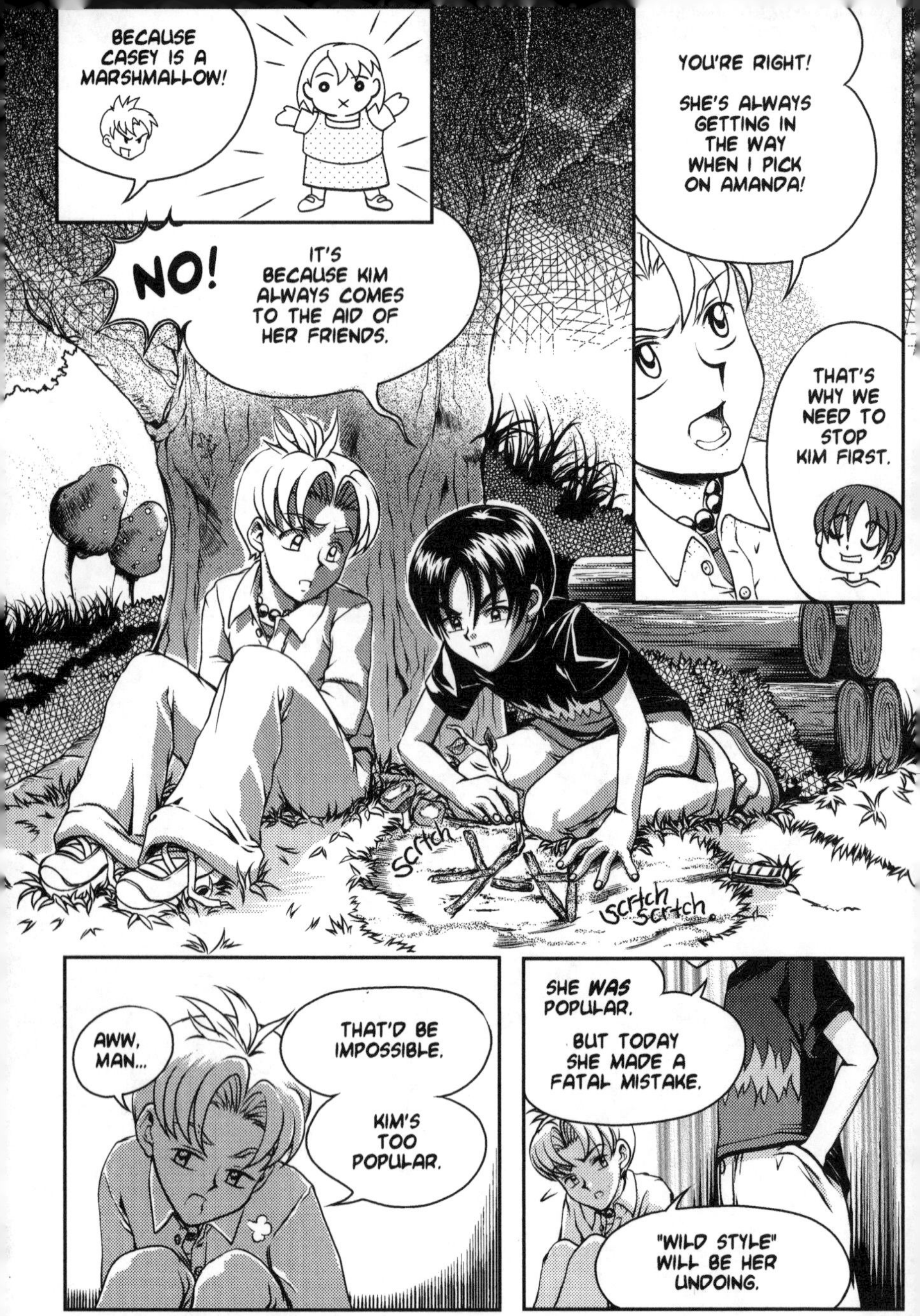
BECAUSE CASEY IS A MARSHMALLOW!
YOU'RE RIGHT!
SHE'S ALWAYS GETTING IN THE WAY WHEN I PICK ON AMANDA!
NO!
IT'S BECAUSE KIM ALWAYS COMES TO THE AID OF HER FRIENDS.
THAT'S WHY WE NEED TO STOP KIM FIRST.
SCRTCH
SCRTCH SCRTCH
AWW, MAN...
THAT'D BE IMPOSSIBLE.
KIM'S TOO POPULAR.
SHE *WAS* POPULAR.
BUT TODAY SHE MADE A FATAL MISTAKE.
"WILD STYLE" WILL BE HER UNDOING.

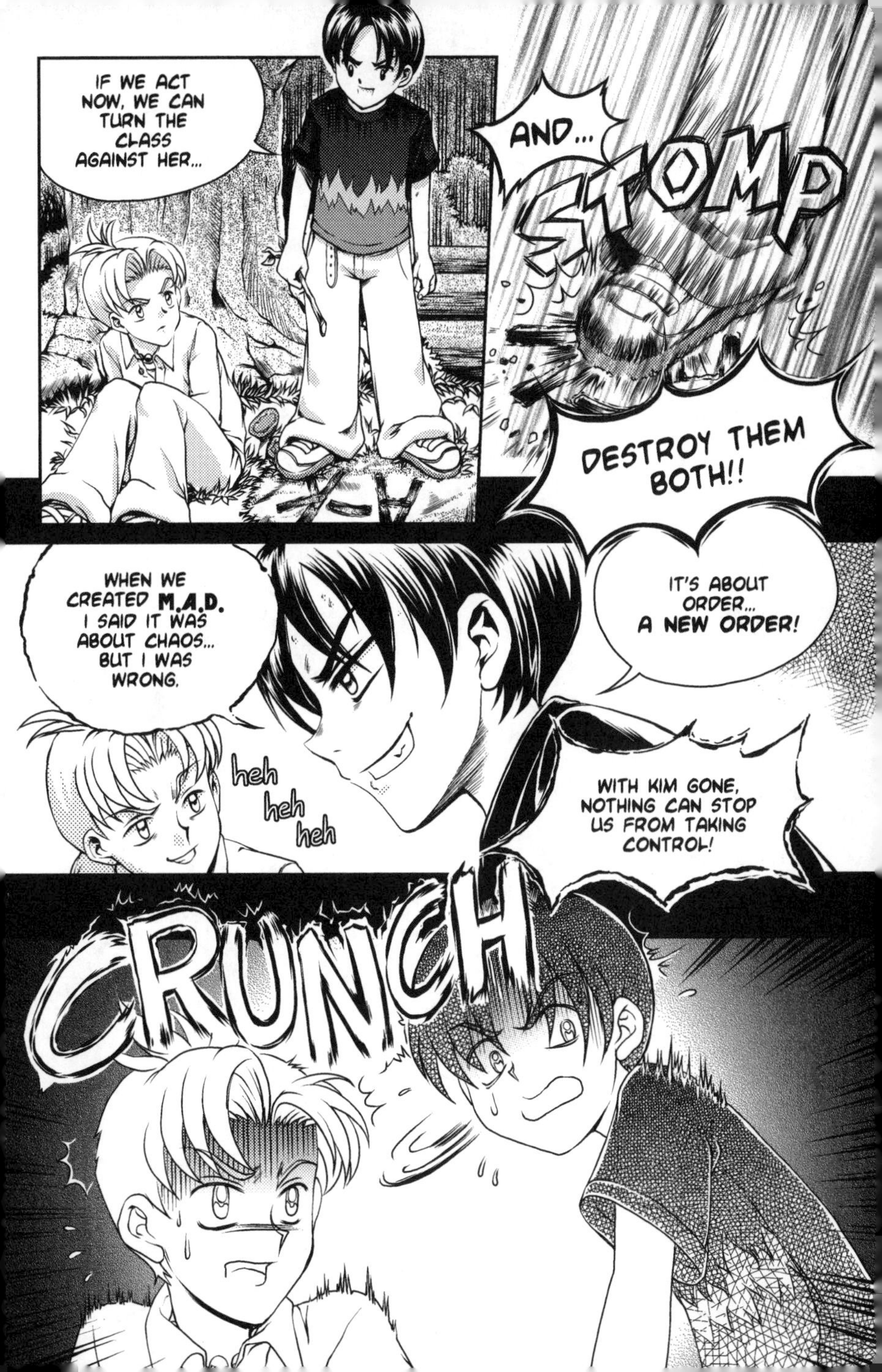

IF WE ACT NOW, WE CAN TURN THE CLASS AGAINST HER...
AND...
STOMP
DESTROY THEM BOTH!!
WHEN WE CREATED M.A.D. I SAID IT WAS ABOUT CHAOS... BUT I WAS WRONG.
IT'S ABOUT ORDER... A NEW ORDER!
heh heh heh
WITH KIM GONE, NOTHING CAN STOP US FROM TAKING CONTROL!
CRUNCH

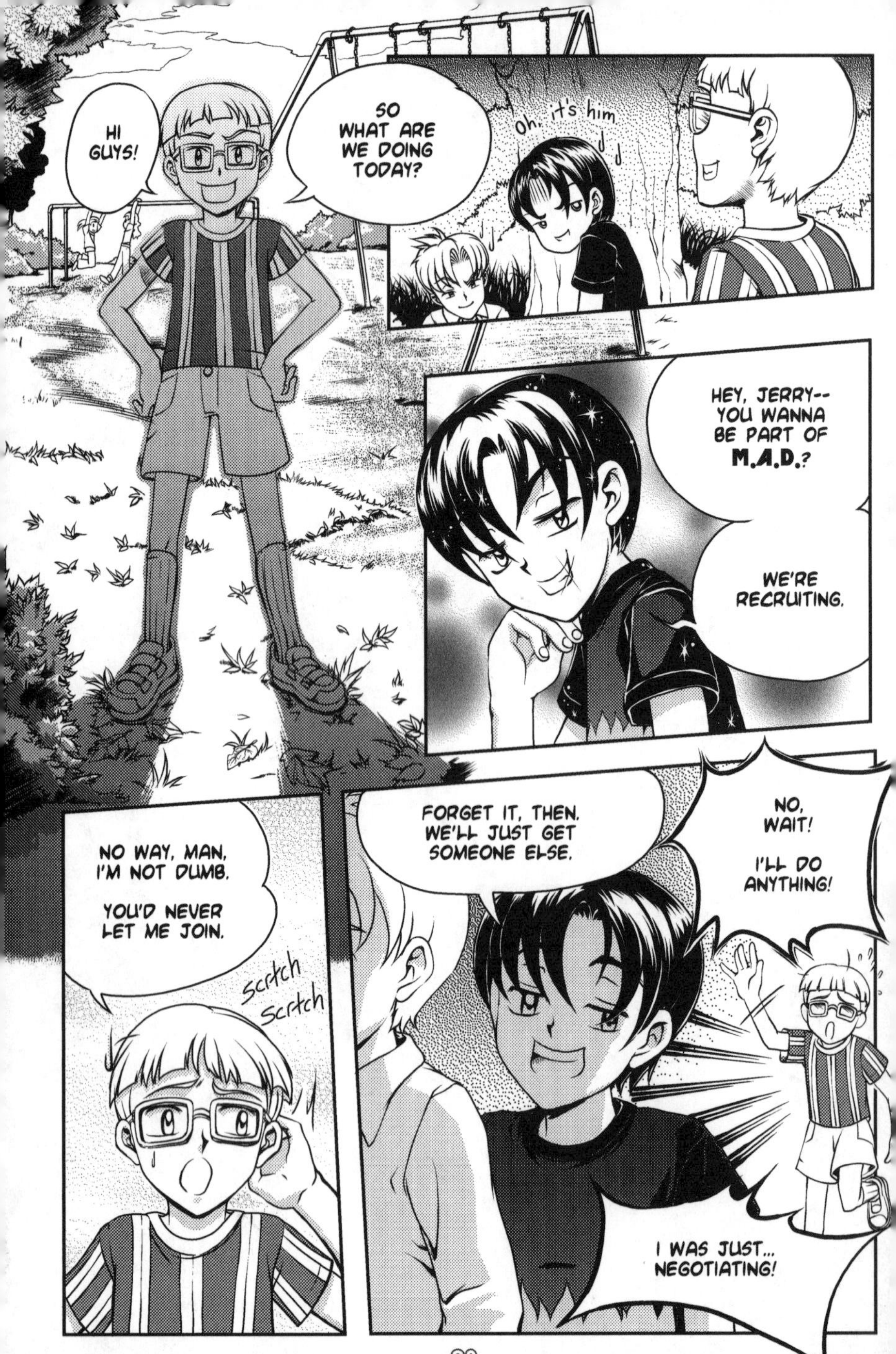
HI GUYS!
SO WHAT ARE WE DOING TODAY?
Oh, it's him.
HEY, JERRY-- YOU WANNA BE PART OF M.A.D.?
WE'RE RECRUITING.
NO WAY, MAN, I'M NOT DUMB.
YOU'D NEVER LET ME JOIN.
Scrtch Scrtch
FORGET IT, THEN. WE'LL JUST GET SOMEONE ELSE.
NO, WAIT!
I'LL DO ANYTHING!
I WAS JUST... NEGOTIATING!

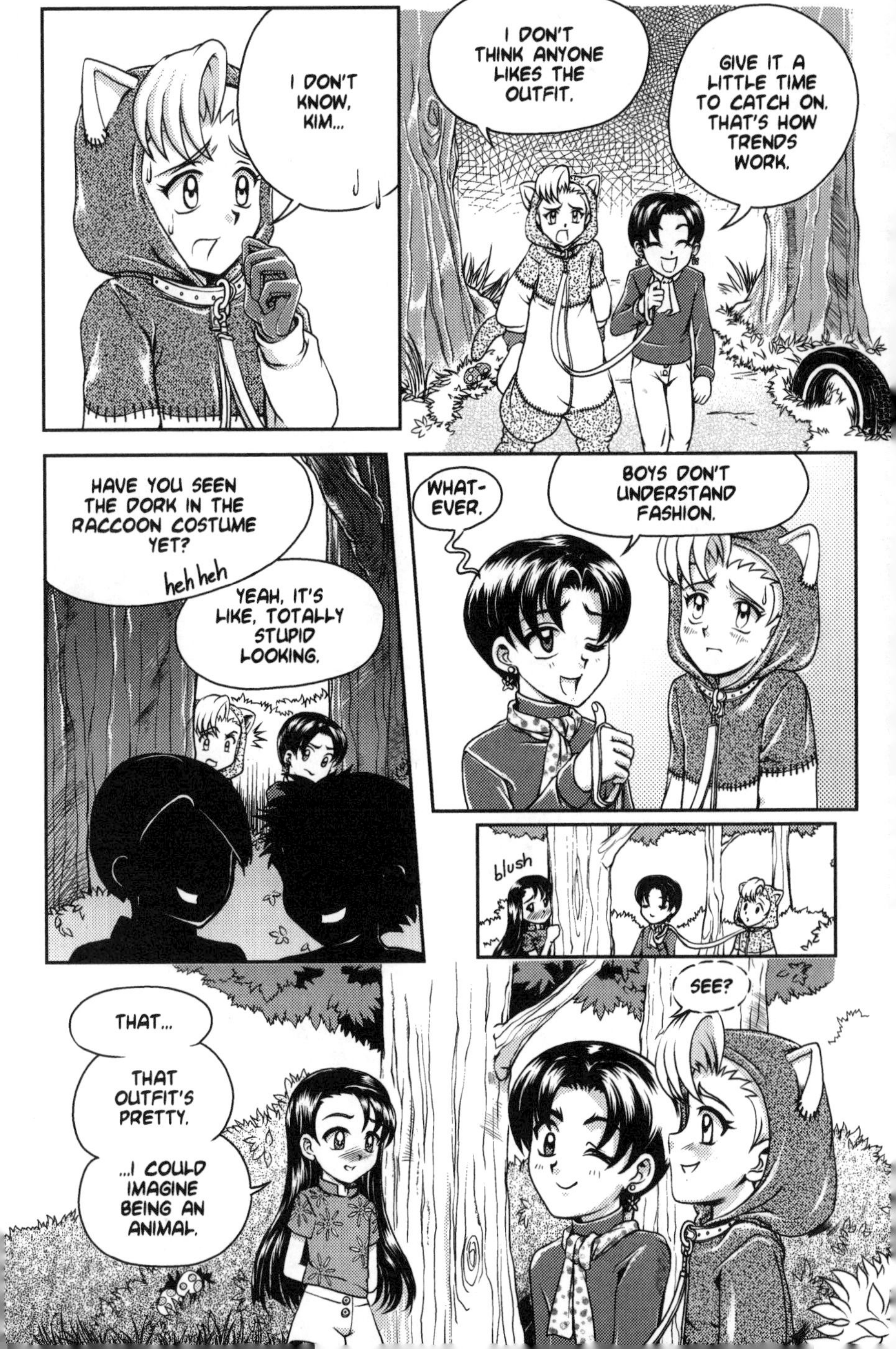
I DON'T KNOW, KIM...
I DON'T THINK ANYONE LIKES THE OUTFIT.
GIVE IT A LITTLE TIME TO CATCH ON. THAT'S HOW TRENDS WORK.
HAVE YOU SEEN THE DORK IN THE RACCOON COSTUME YET?
heh heh
YEAH, IT'S LIKE, TOTALLY STUPID LOOKING.
BOYS DON'T UNDERSTAND FASHION.
WHAT-EVER.
blush
THAT...
THAT OUTFIT'S PRETTY.
...I COULD IMAGINE BEING AN ANIMAL.
SEE?

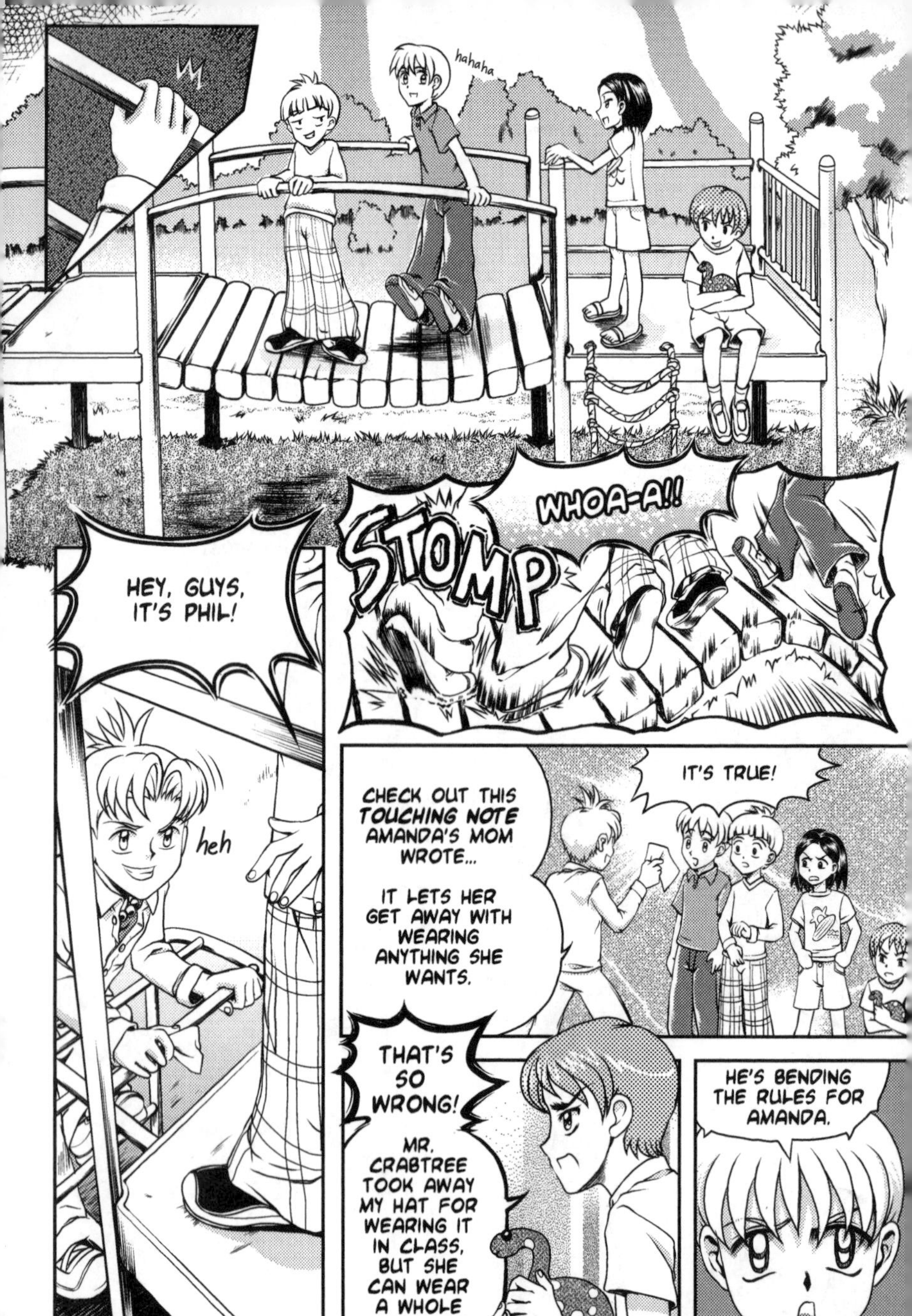
hahaha
HEY, GUYS, IT'S PHIL!
heh
STOMP
WHOA-A!!
CHECK OUT THIS TOUCHING NOTE AMANDA'S MOM WROTE...
IT LETS HER GET AWAY WITH WEARING ANYTHING SHE WANTS.
IT'S TRUE!
THAT'S SO WRONG!
MR. CRABTREE TOOK AWAY MY HAT FOR WEARING IT IN CLASS, BUT SHE CAN WEAR A WHOLE COSTUME?
HE'S BENDING THE RULES FOR AMANDA.

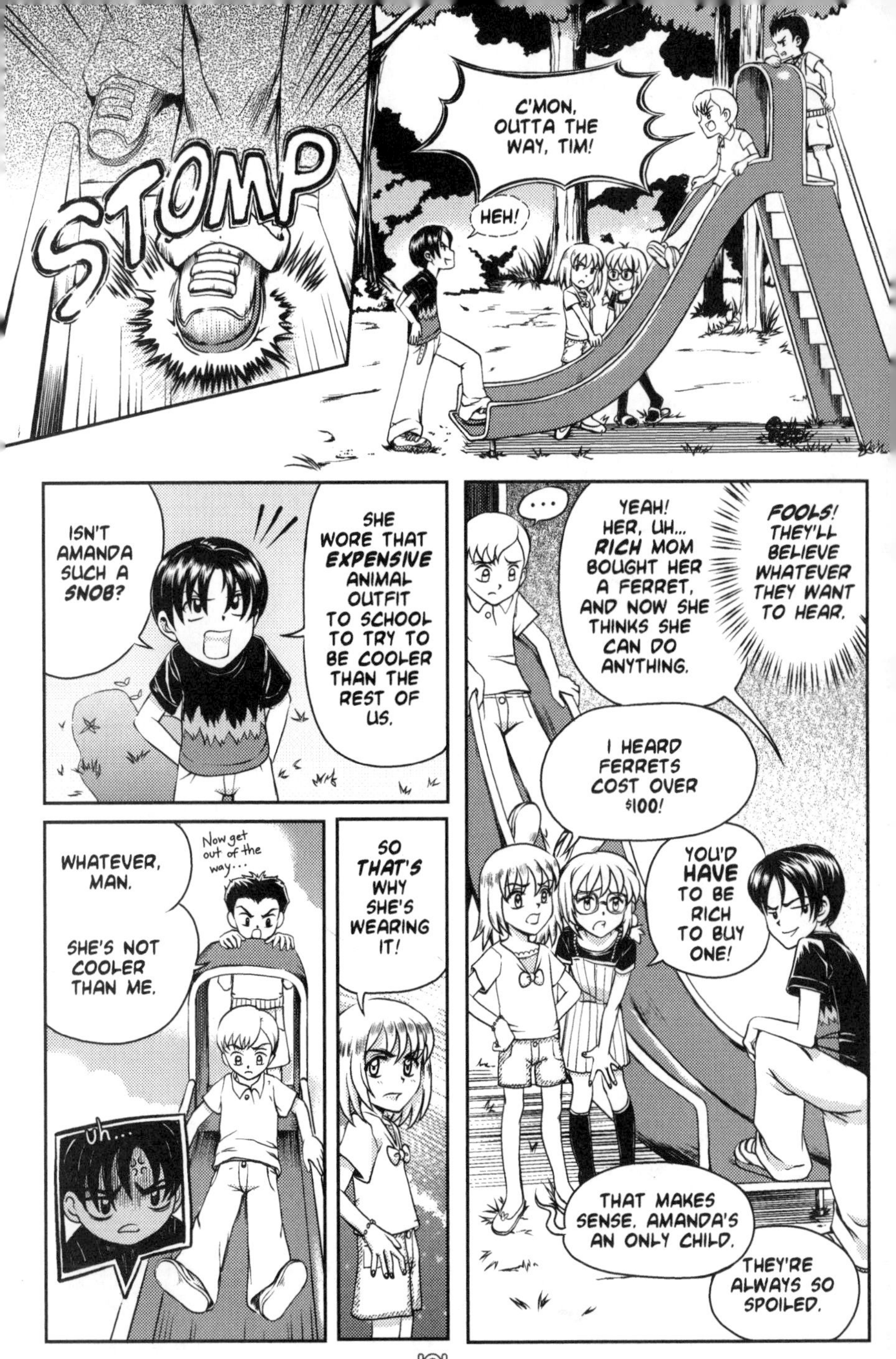
STOMP
C'MON, OUTTA THE WAY, TIM!
HEH!
ISN'T AMANDA SUCH A SNOB?
SHE WORE THAT EXPENSIVE ANIMAL OUTFIT TO SCHOOL TO TRY TO BE COOLER THAN THE REST OF US.
...
YEAH! HER, UH... RICH MOM BOUGHT HER A FERRET, AND NOW SHE THINKS SHE CAN DO ANYTHING.
FOOLS! THEY'LL BELIEVE WHATEVER THEY WANT TO HEAR.
I HEARD FERRETS COST OVER $100!
WHATEVER, MAN.
SHE'S NOT COOLER THAN ME.
Now get out of the way...
Uh...
SO THAT'S WHY SHE'S WEARING IT!
YOU'D HAVE TO BE RICH TO BUY ONE!
THAT MAKES SENSE. AMANDA'S AN ONLY CHILD.
THEY'RE ALWAYS SO SPOILED.

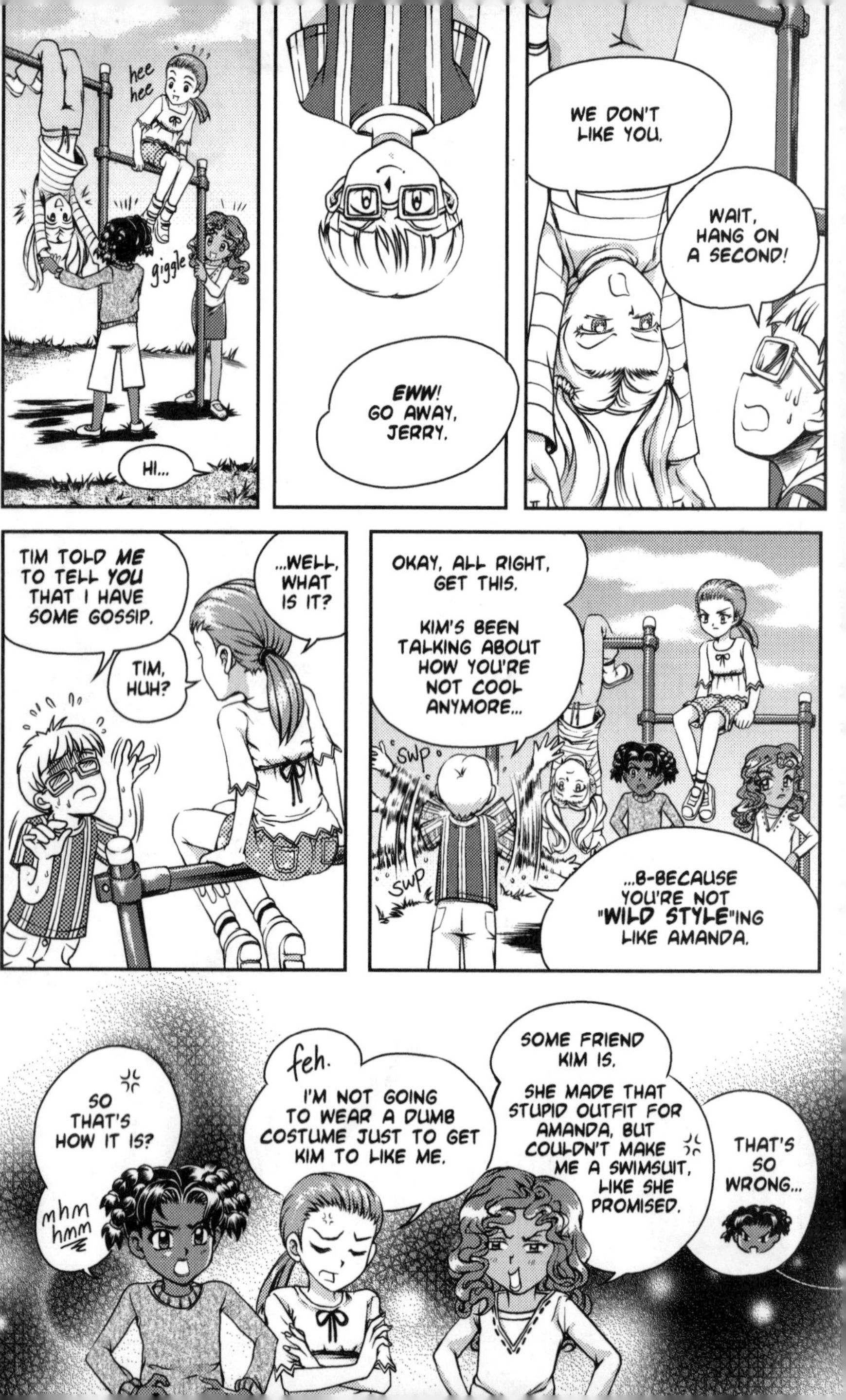

hee hee
giggle
HI...
EWW! GO AWAY, JERRY.
WE DON'T LIKE YOU.
WAIT, HANG ON A SECOND!
TIM TOLD ME TO TELL YOU THAT I HAVE SOME GOSSIP.
TIM, HUH?
...WELL, WHAT IS IT?
OKAY, ALL RIGHT, GET THIS.
KIM'S BEEN TALKING ABOUT HOW YOU'RE NOT COOL ANYMORE...
SWP
SWP
...B-BECAUSE YOU'RE NOT "WILD STYLE"ING LIKE AMANDA.
SO THAT'S HOW IT IS?
mhm hmm
feh.
I'M NOT GOING TO WEAR A DUMB COSTUME JUST TO GET KIM TO LIKE ME.
SOME FRIEND KIM IS.
SHE MADE THAT STUPID OUTFIT FOR AMANDA, BUT COULDN'T MAKE ME A SWIMSUIT, LIKE SHE PROMISED.
THAT'S SO WRONG...

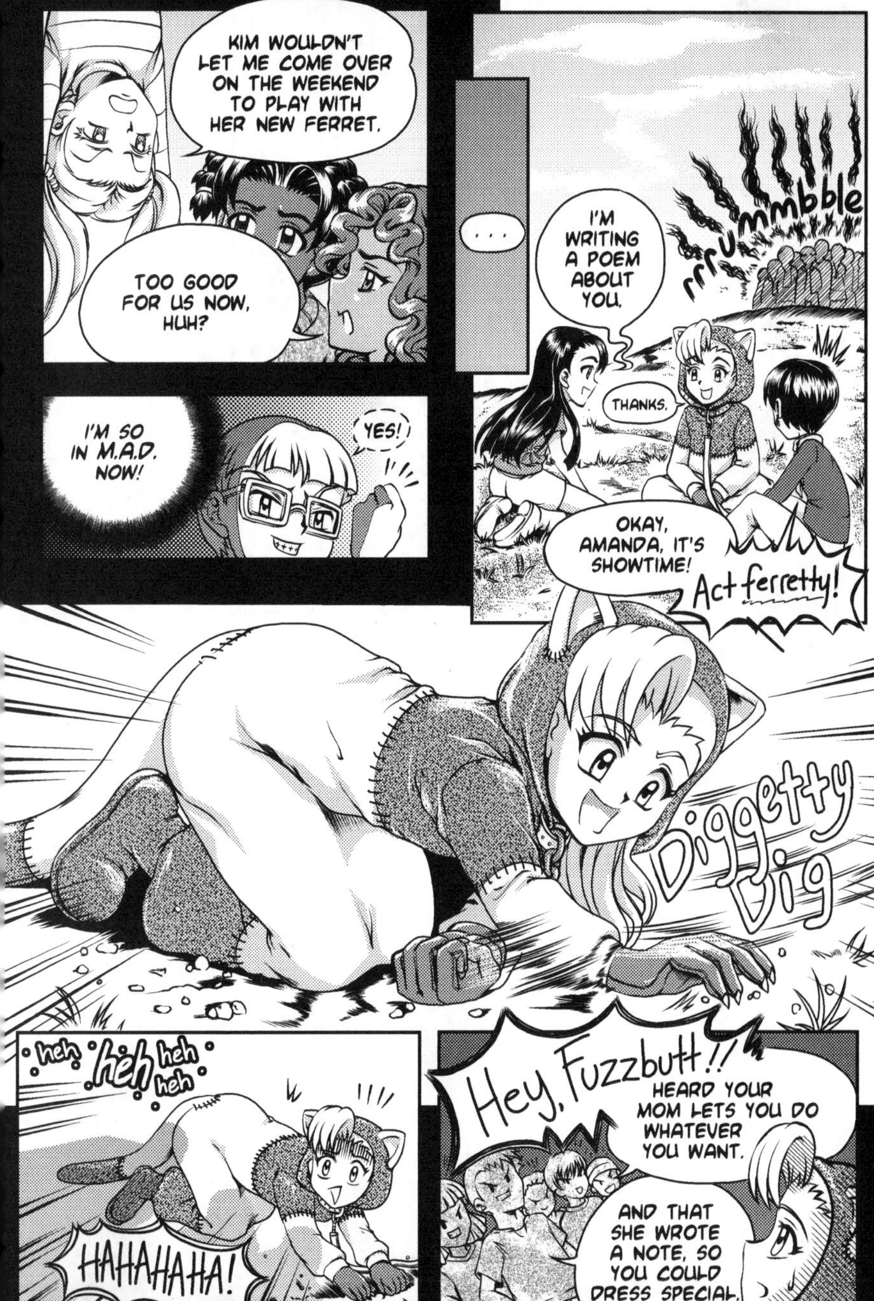
KIM WOULDN'T LET ME COME OVER ON THE WEEKEND TO PLAY WITH HER NEW FERRET.
TOO GOOD FOR US NOW, HUH?
I'M SO IN M.A.D. NOW!
YES!
. . .
rrrummmbble
I'M WRITING A POEM ABOUT YOU.
THANKS.
OKAY, AMANDA, IT'S SHOWTIME!
Act ferretty!
Diggetty Dig
heh heh heh heh
HAHAHAHA!
Hey, Fuzzbutt!!
HEARD YOUR MOM LETS YOU DO WHATEVER YOU WANT.
AND THAT SHE WROTE A NOTE, SO YOU COULD DRESS SPECIAL.

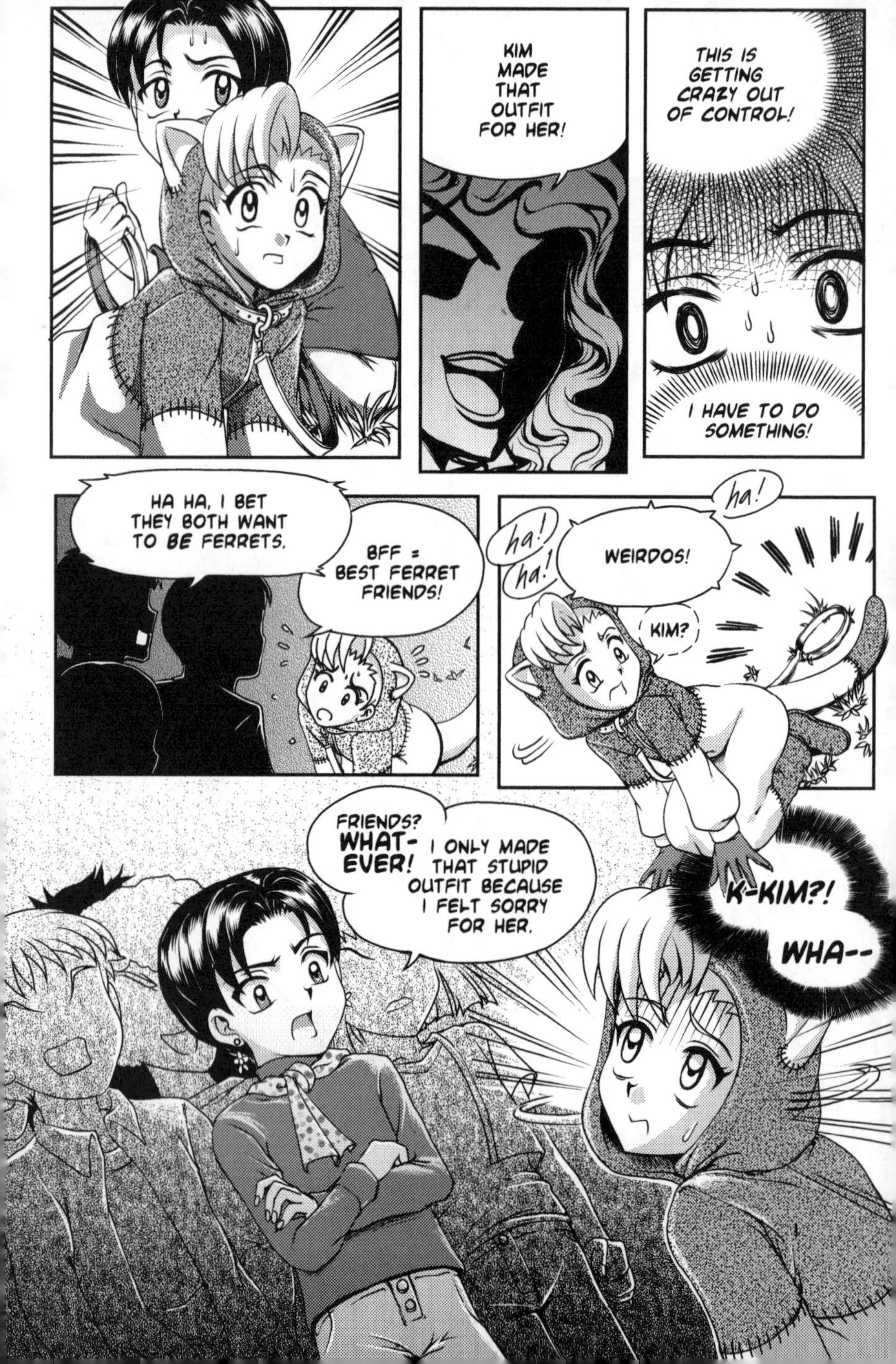
KIM MADE THAT OUTFIT FOR HER!
THIS IS GETTING CRAZY OUT OF CONTROL!
I HAVE TO DO SOMETHING!
HA HA, I BET THEY BOTH WANT TO BE FERRETS.
BFF = BEST FERRET FRIENDS!
ha! ha!
ha!
WEIRDOS!
KIM?
FRIENDS? WHAT-EVER!
I ONLY MADE THAT STUPID OUTFIT BECAUSE I FELT SORRY FOR HER.
K-KIM?!
WHA--

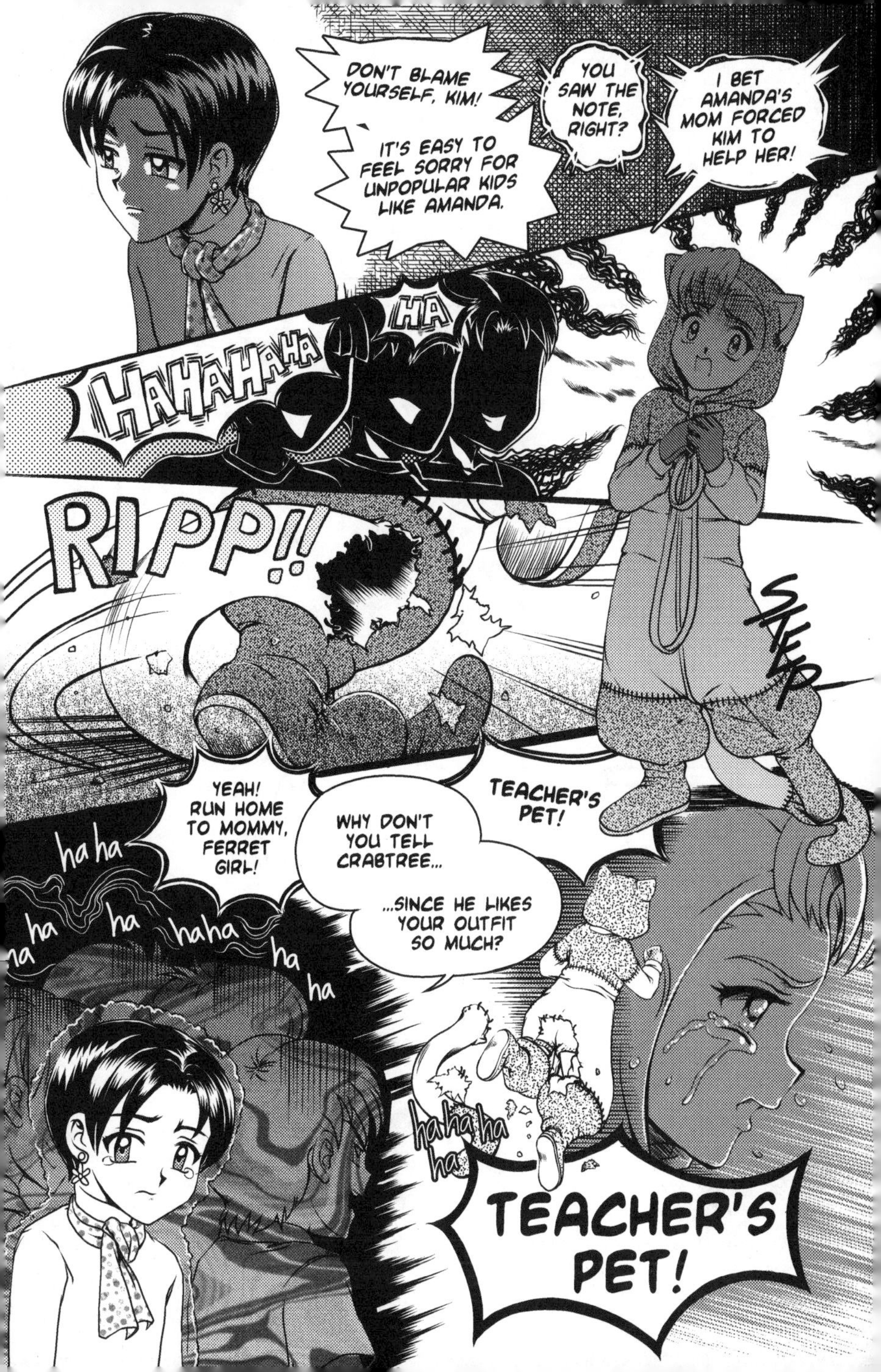
DON'T BLAME YOURSELF, KIM!
IT'S EASY TO FEEL SORRY FOR UNPOPULAR KIDS LIKE AMANDA.
YOU SAW THE NOTE, RIGHT?
I BET AMANDA'S MOM FORCED KIM TO HELP HER!
HA
HAHAHAHA
RIPP!!
SWEEP
YEAH! RUN HOME TO MOMMY, FERRET GIRL!
WHY DON'T YOU TELL CRABTREE...
...SINCE HE LIKES YOUR OUTFIT SO MUCH?
TEACHER'S PET!
ha ha
ha ha haha ha ha
haha ha ha
TEACHER'S PET!

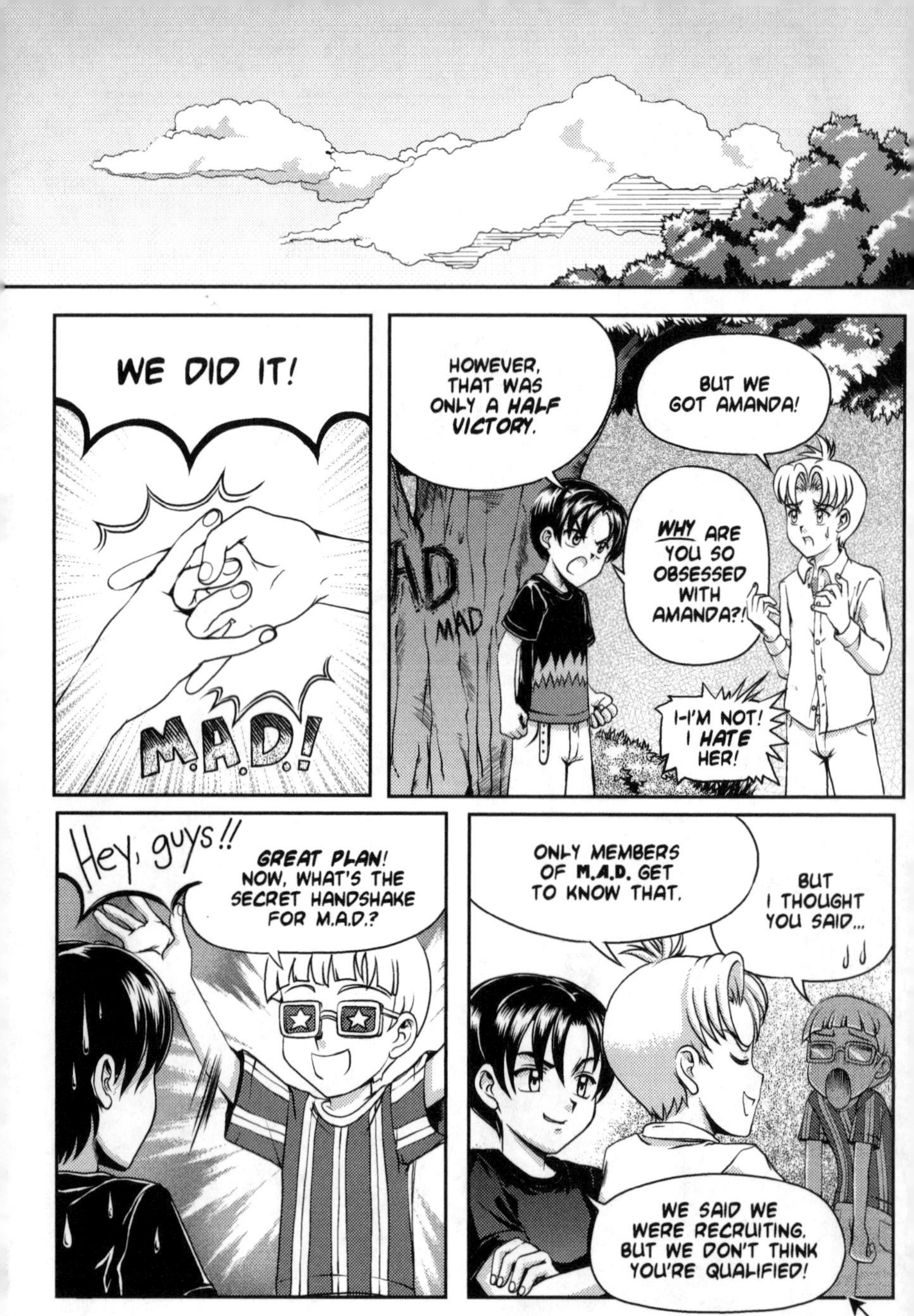

WE DID IT!
M.A.D.!
HOWEVER, THAT WAS ONLY A HALF VICTORY.
BUT WE GOT AMANDA!
WHY ARE YOU SO OBSESSED WITH AMANDA?!
I-I'M NOT! I HATE HER!
MAD
Hey, guys!!
GREAT PLAN! NOW, WHAT'S THE SECRET HANDSHAKE FOR M.A.D.?
ONLY MEMBERS OF M.A.D. GET TO KNOW THAT.
BUT I THOUGHT YOU SAID...
WE SAID WE WERE RECRUITING, BUT WE DON'T THINK YOU'RE QUALIFIED!
REASON #39 WHY YOU SHOULD NEVER MAKE ANY DEALS WITH THE BAD GUYS.

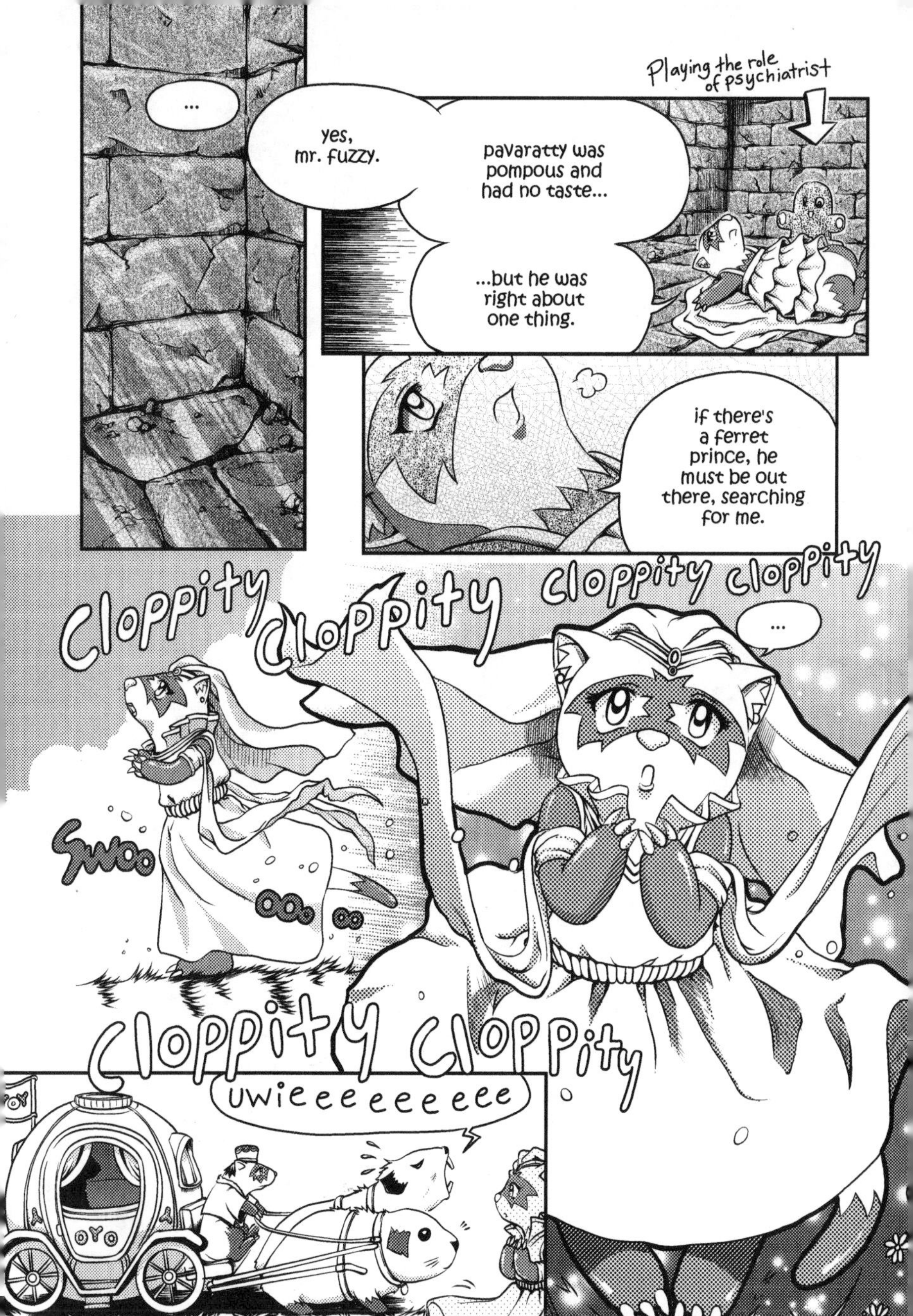

...
yes, mr. fuzzy.
pavaratty was pompous and had no taste...
...but he was right about one thing.
Playing the role of psychiatrist
if there's a ferret prince, he must be out there, searching for me.
Cloppity Cloppity cloppity cloppity
...
SWOo OOo oo
Cloppity Cloppity
UWieeeeeeeeee

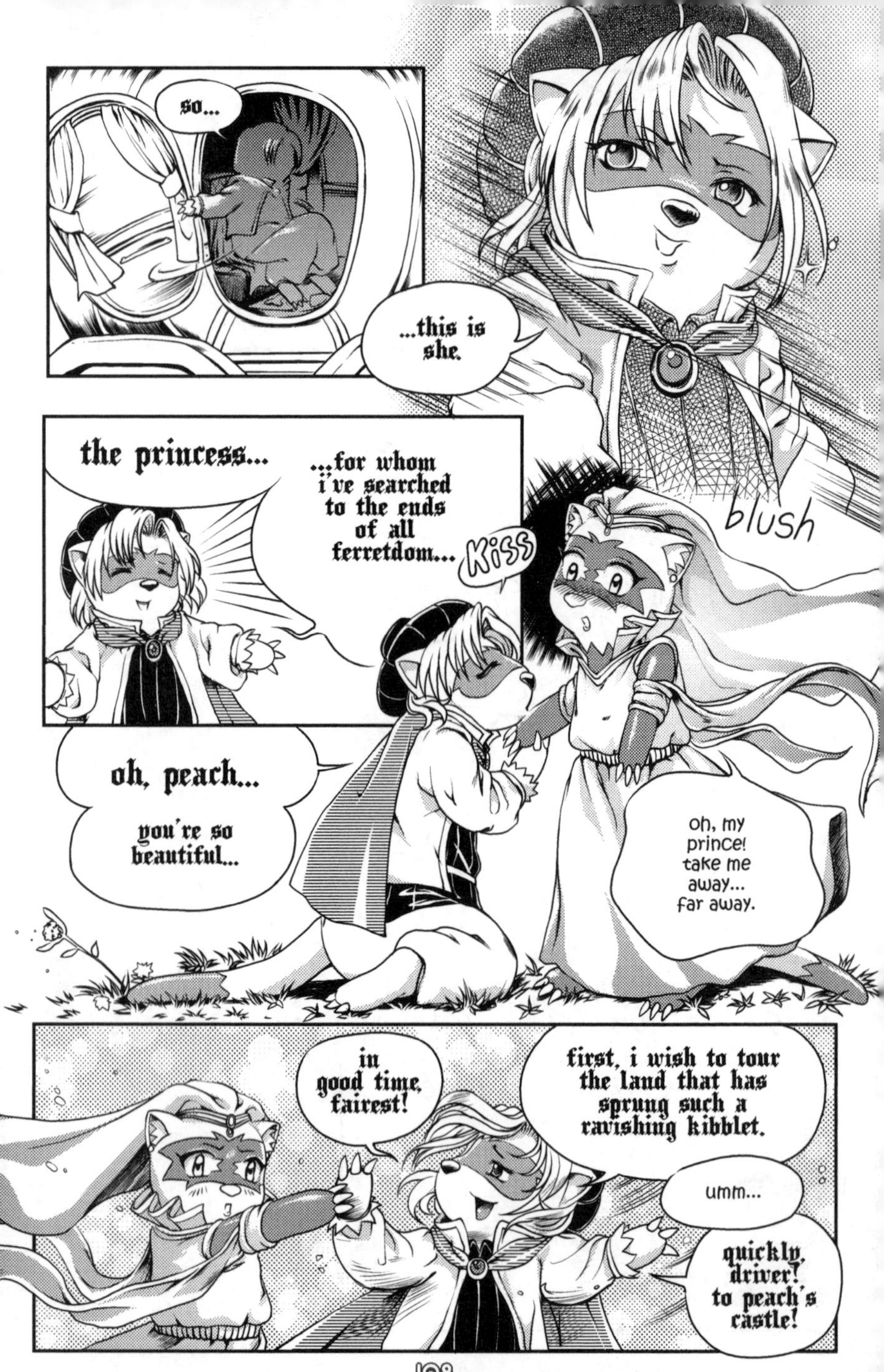
so...
...this is she.
blush
the princess...
...for whom i've searched to the ends of all ferretdom...
Kiss
oh, peach...
you're so beautiful...
oh, my prince! take me away... far away.
in good time, fairest!
first, i wish to tour the land that has sprung such a ravishing kibblet.
umm...
quickly, driver! to peach's castle!

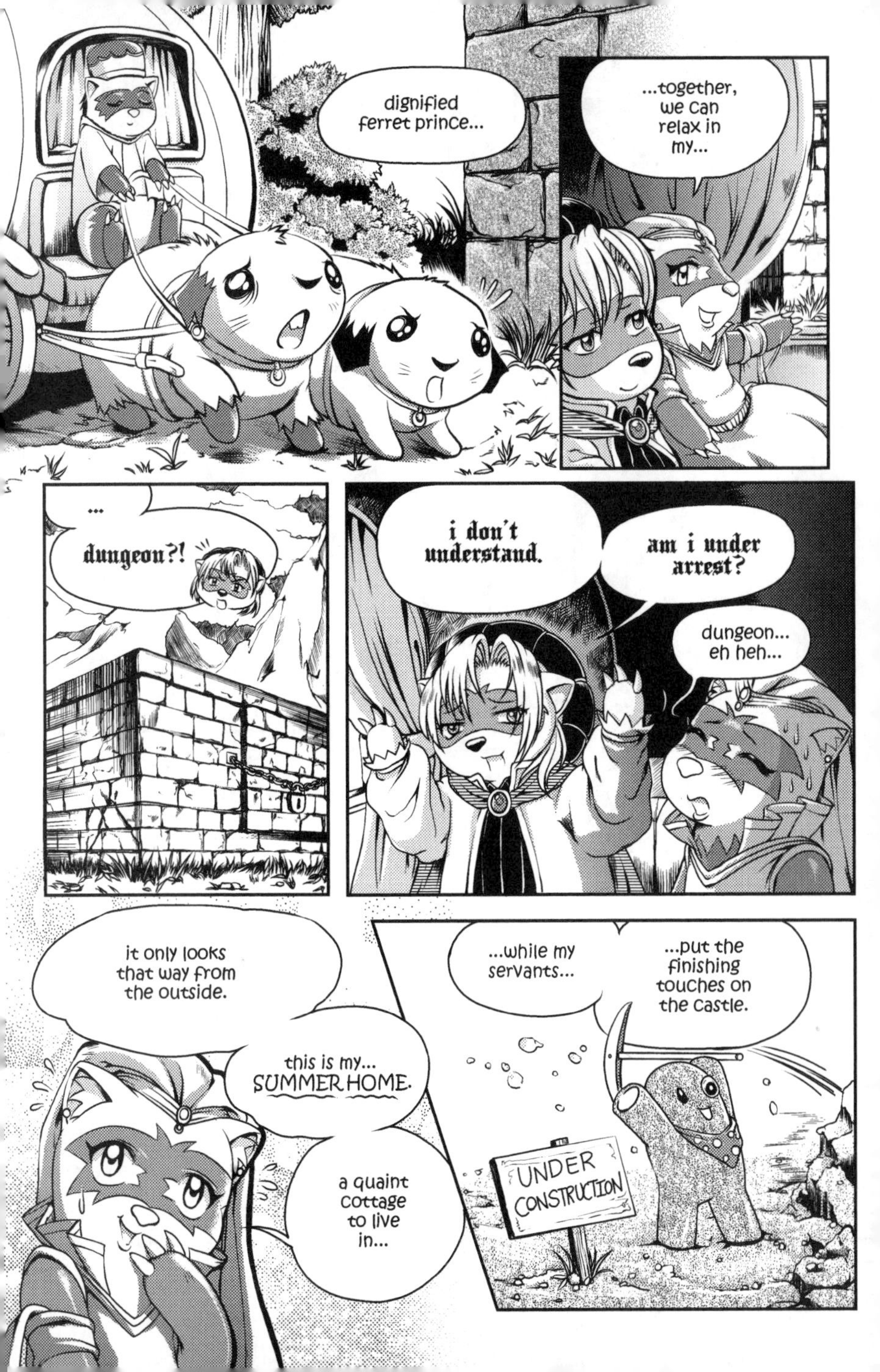
dignified ferret prince...
...together, we can relax in my...
...
dungeon?!
i don't understand.
am i under arrest?
dungeon... eh heh...
it only looks that way from the outside.
this is my... SUMMER HOME.
a quaint cottage to live in...
...while my servants...
...put the finishing touches on the castle.
UNDER CONSTRUCTION

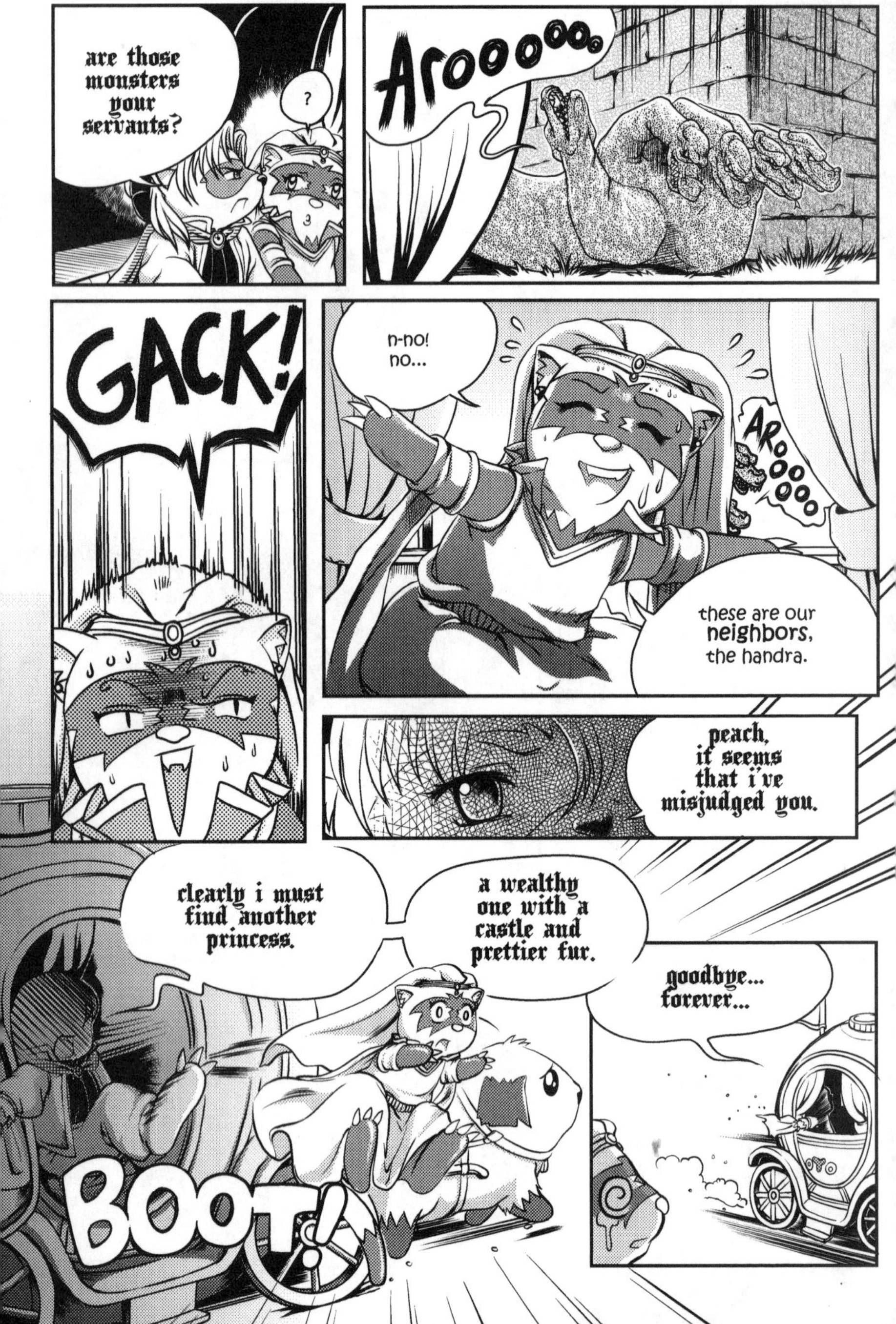

are those monsters your servants?
?
Arooooooo
GACK!
n-no! no...
AROOOOOOO
these are our neighbors, the handra.
peach, if seems that i've misjudged you.
clearly i must find another princess.
a wealthy one with a castle and prettier fur.
goodbye... forever...
BOOT!

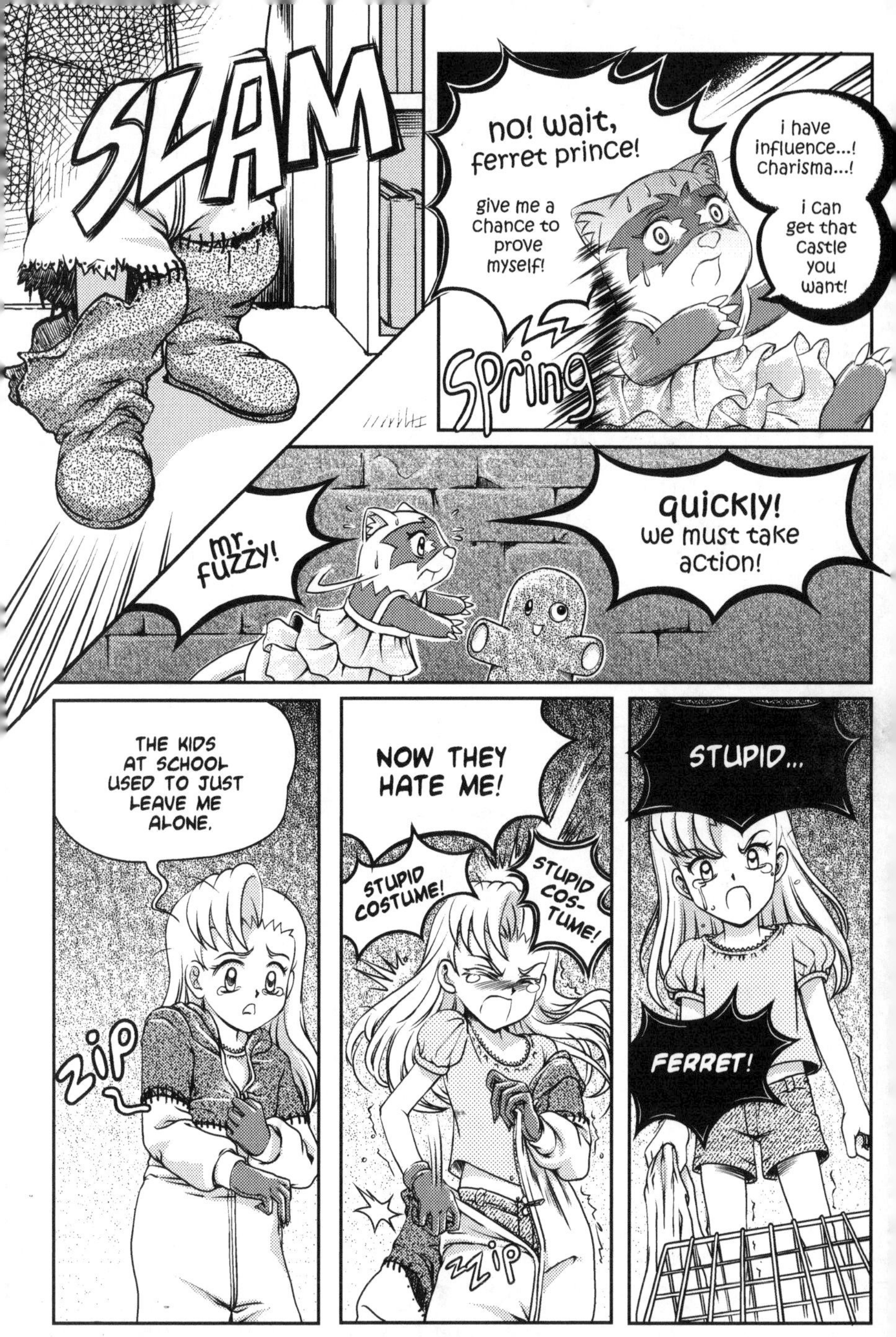
SLAM
no! wait, ferret prince!
give me a chance to prove myself!
i have influence...! charisma...!
i can get that castle you want!
Spring
mr. FUZZY!
quickly! we must take action!
THE KIDS AT SCHOOL USED TO JUST LEAVE ME ALONE.
ZIP
NOW THEY HATE ME!
STUPID COSTUME!
STUPID COS-TUME!
ZZIP
STUPID...
FERRET!

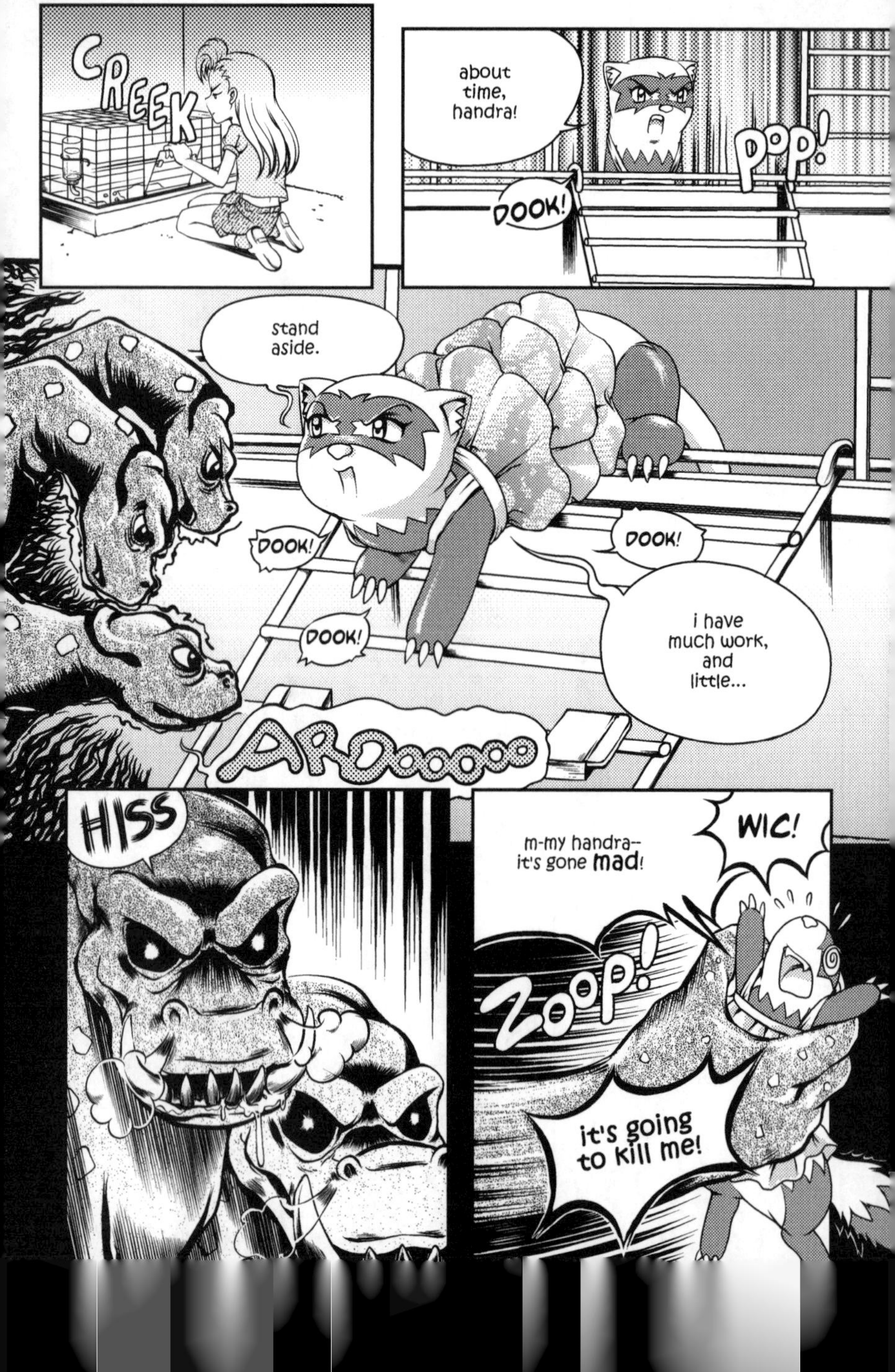
CREEK
about time, handra!
POP!
DOOK!
stand aside.
DOOK!
DOOK!
DOOK!
i have much work, and little...
ARDoooooo
HISS
m-my handra-- it's gone mad!
WIC!
ZOOP!
it's going to kill me!

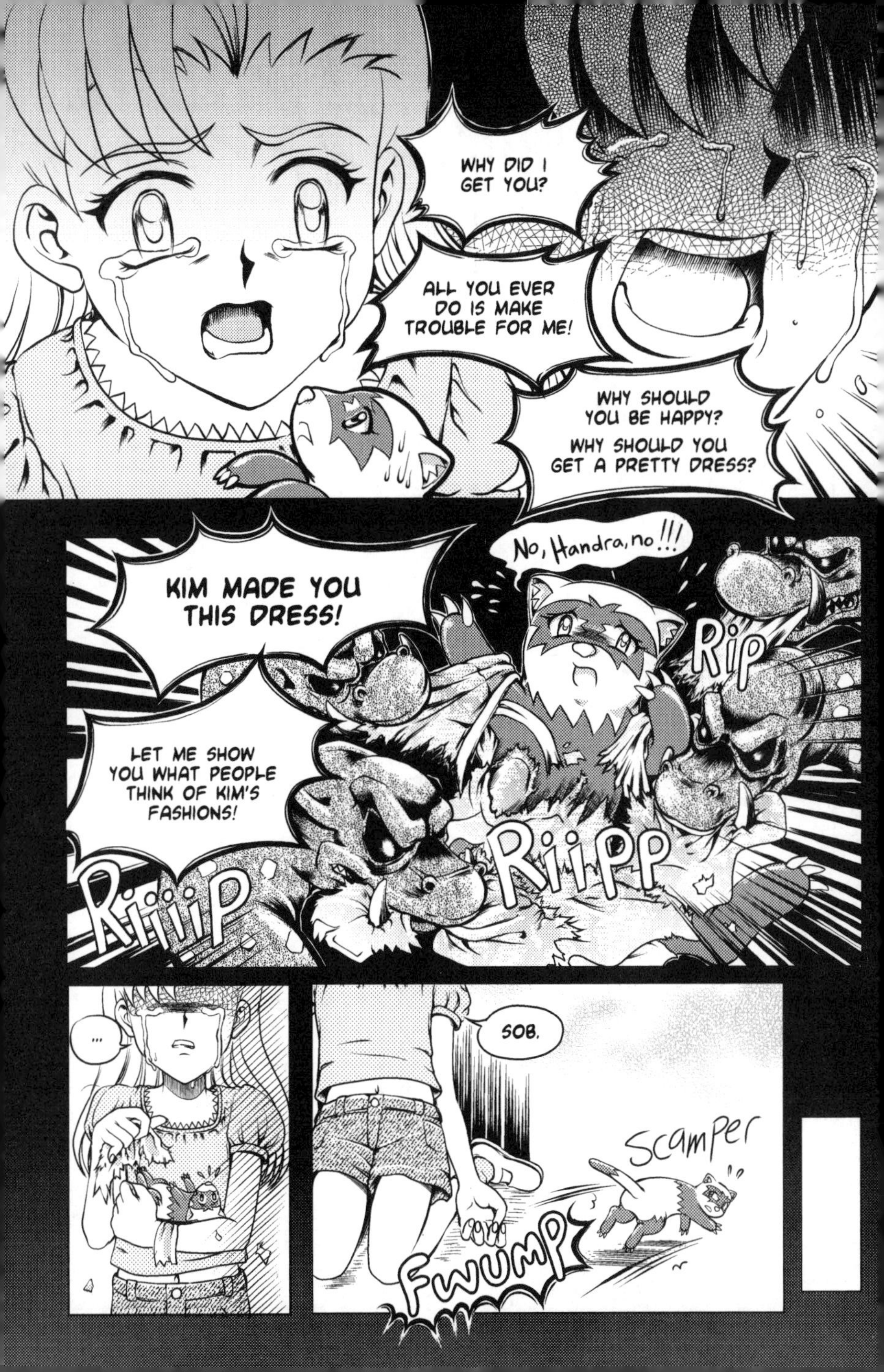
WHY DID I GET YOU?
ALL YOU EVER DO IS MAKE TROUBLE FOR ME!
WHY SHOULD YOU BE HAPPY?
WHY SHOULD YOU GET A PRETTY DRESS?
KIM MADE YOU THIS DRESS!
No, Handra, no!!!
Rip
LET ME SHOW YOU WHAT PEOPLE THINK OF KIM'S FASHIONS!
Riiipp
Riiiip
...
SOB.
Scamper
Fwump

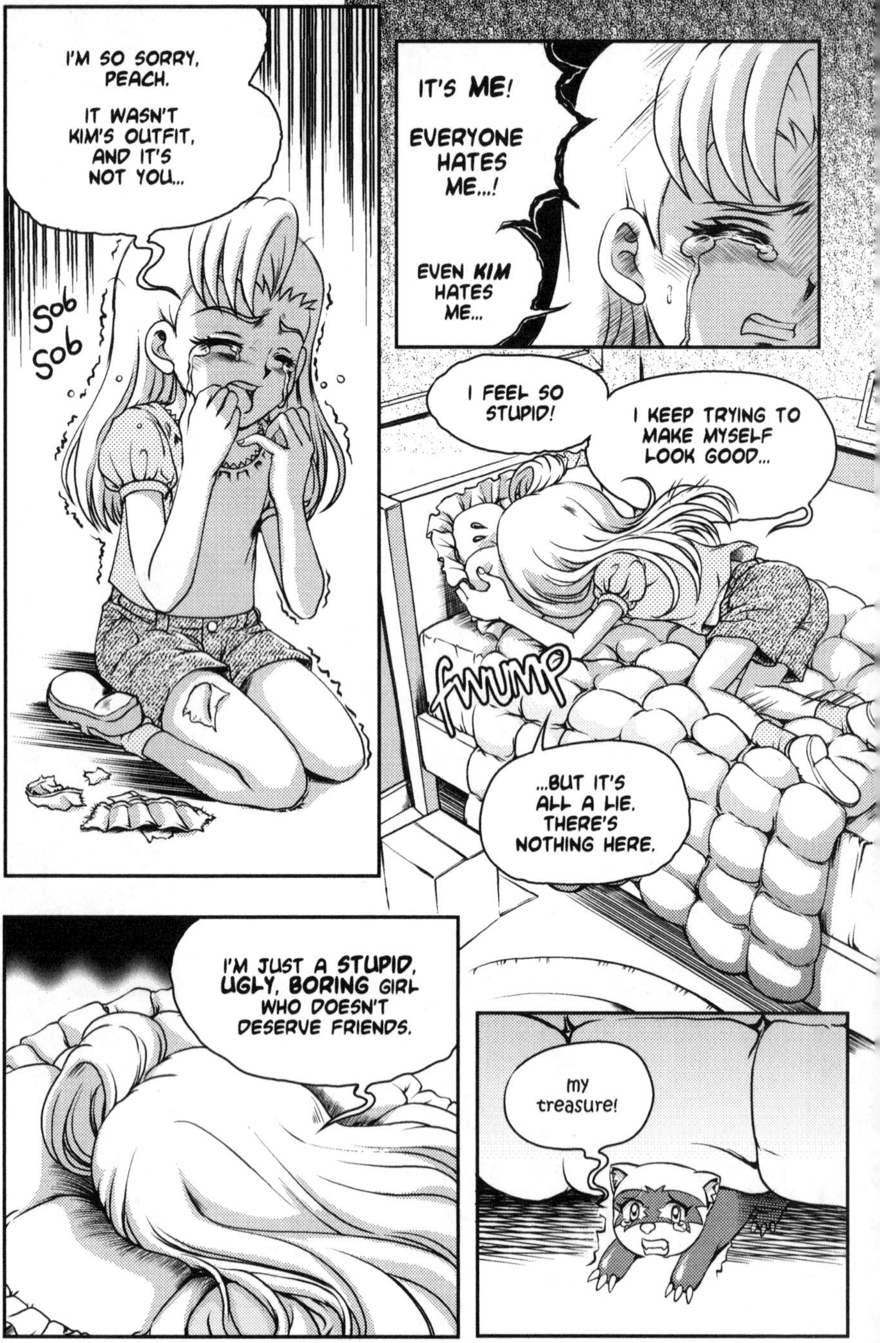
I'M SO SORRY, PEACH.
IT WASN'T KIM'S OUTFIT, AND IT'S NOT YOU...
Sob Sob
IT'S ME!
EVERYONE HATES ME...!
EVEN KIM HATES ME...
I FEEL SO STUPID!
I KEEP TRYING TO MAKE MYSELF LOOK GOOD...
FWUMP
...BUT IT'S ALL A LIE. THERE'S NOTHING HERE.
I'M JUST A STUPID, UGLY, BORING GIRL WHO DOESN'T DESERVE FRIENDS.
my treasure!

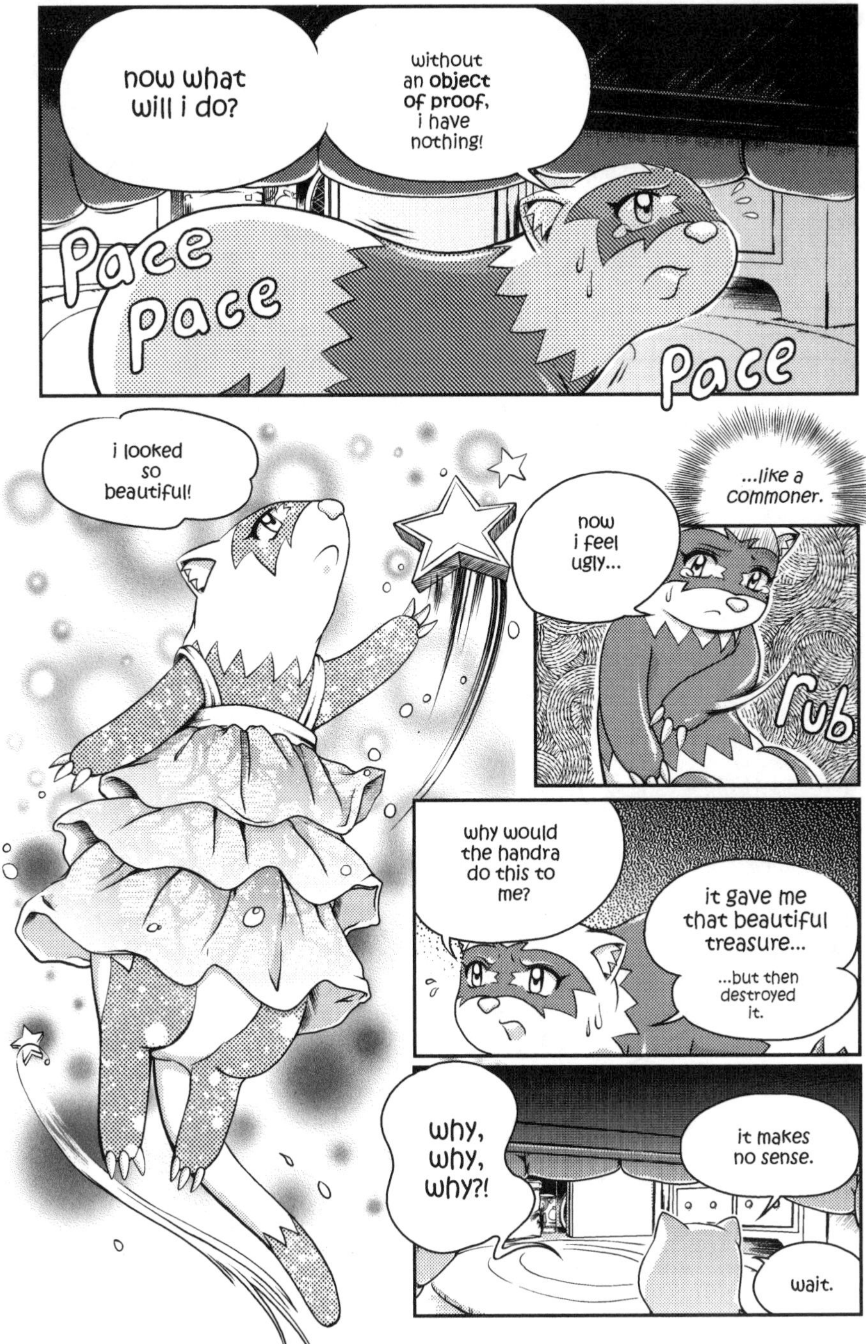

now what will i do?
without an object of proof, i have nothing!
Pace pace
Pace
i looked so beautiful!
now i feel ugly...
...like a commoner.
rub
why would the handra do this to me?
it gave me that beautiful treasure...
...but then destroyed it.
why, why, why?!
it makes no sense.
wait.

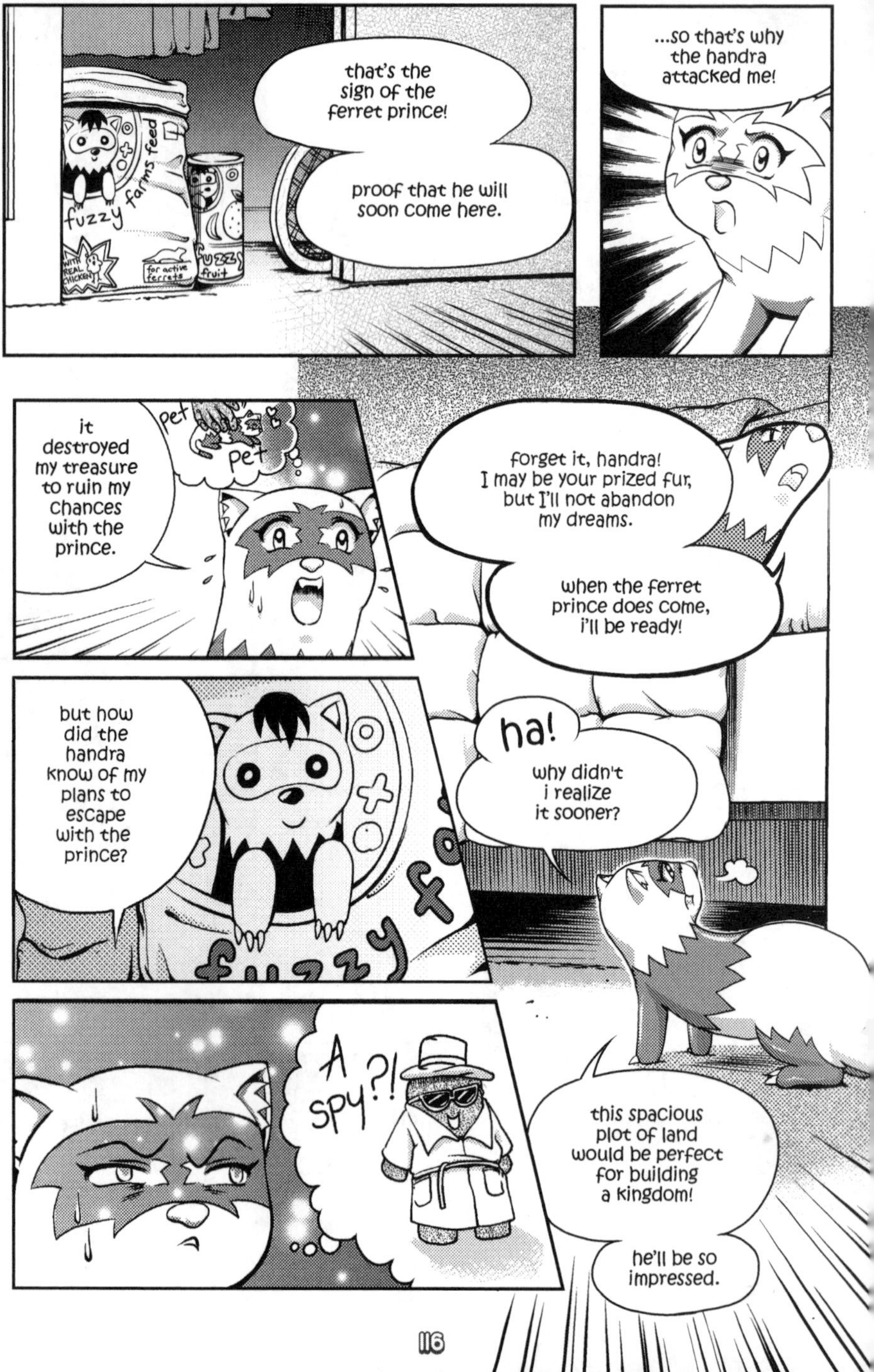
that's the sign of the ferret prince!
proof that he will soon come here.
fuzzy farms feed
for active ferrets
WITH REAL CHICKEN
fuzzy fruit
...so that's why the handra attacked me!
it destroyed my treasure to ruin my chances with the prince.
pet pet
forget it, handra! I may be your prized fur, but I'll not abandon my dreams.
when the ferret prince does come, i'll be ready!
but how did the handra know of my plans to escape with the prince?
ha!
why didn't i realize it sooner?
A spy?!
this spacious plot of land would be perfect for building a kingdom!
he'll be so impressed.

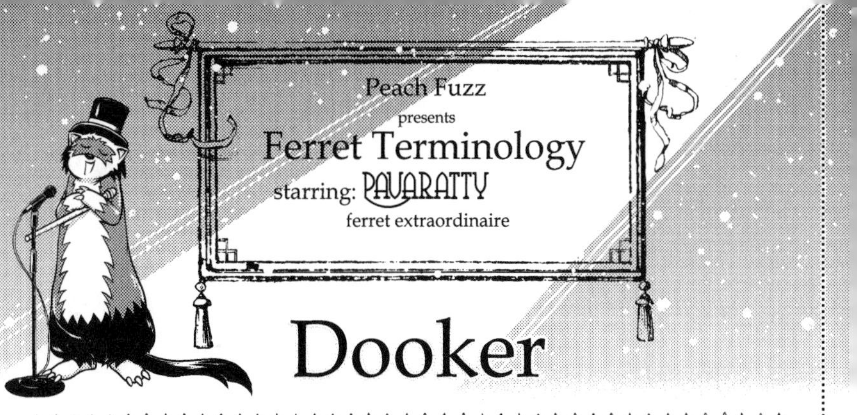

Peach Fuzz

presents

Ferret Terminology

starring: PAVARATTY

ferret extraordinaire

Dooker

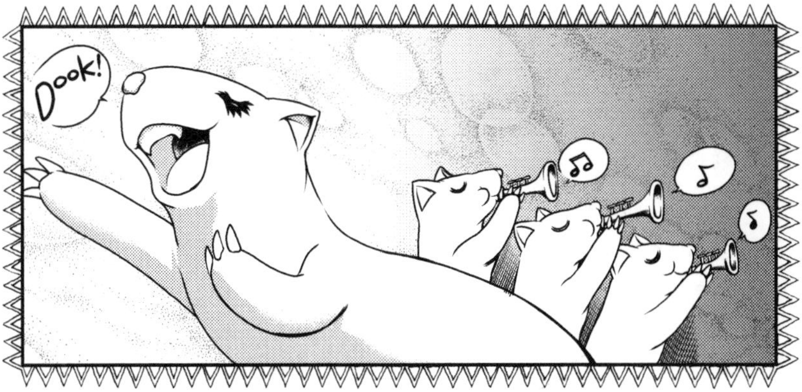

Dook!

It's not often necessary for ferrets to make noise. We are usually quiet by nature, letting our body language do the talking for us. But when our emotions become too great, body language alone cannot express what a ferret feels deep inside. In those instances...we ***dook!***

The dook of a ferret can emanate as any of several beautiful chittering sounds. Now, not all ferrets are created equal. Some ferrets make a high-pitched dook that sounds like ***"wick!"*** Others, low grunting noises. As a Professional Dooker, I have an excellent range and can reproduce all of these sounds.

Not all dooks are meant to express excitement, though. A dook can mean many things, depending on the situation. Sudden dooking in a non-dooker can signal a problem. It could mean, "I'm in pain--help me, Handlers." Then again, it could also mean, "Listen to me--I'm starting my amateur career." Handlers should be mindful of our little noises, especially screams or hisses. These are definite signs of distress.

Now, a song...

"Dook! Dook!" *"Wick! Dook! Dook!"*

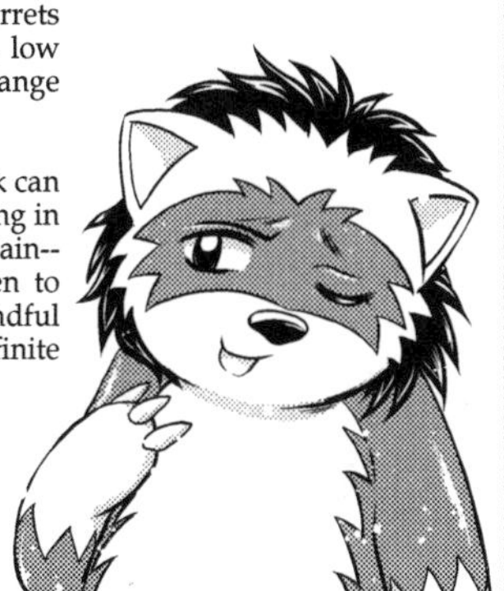

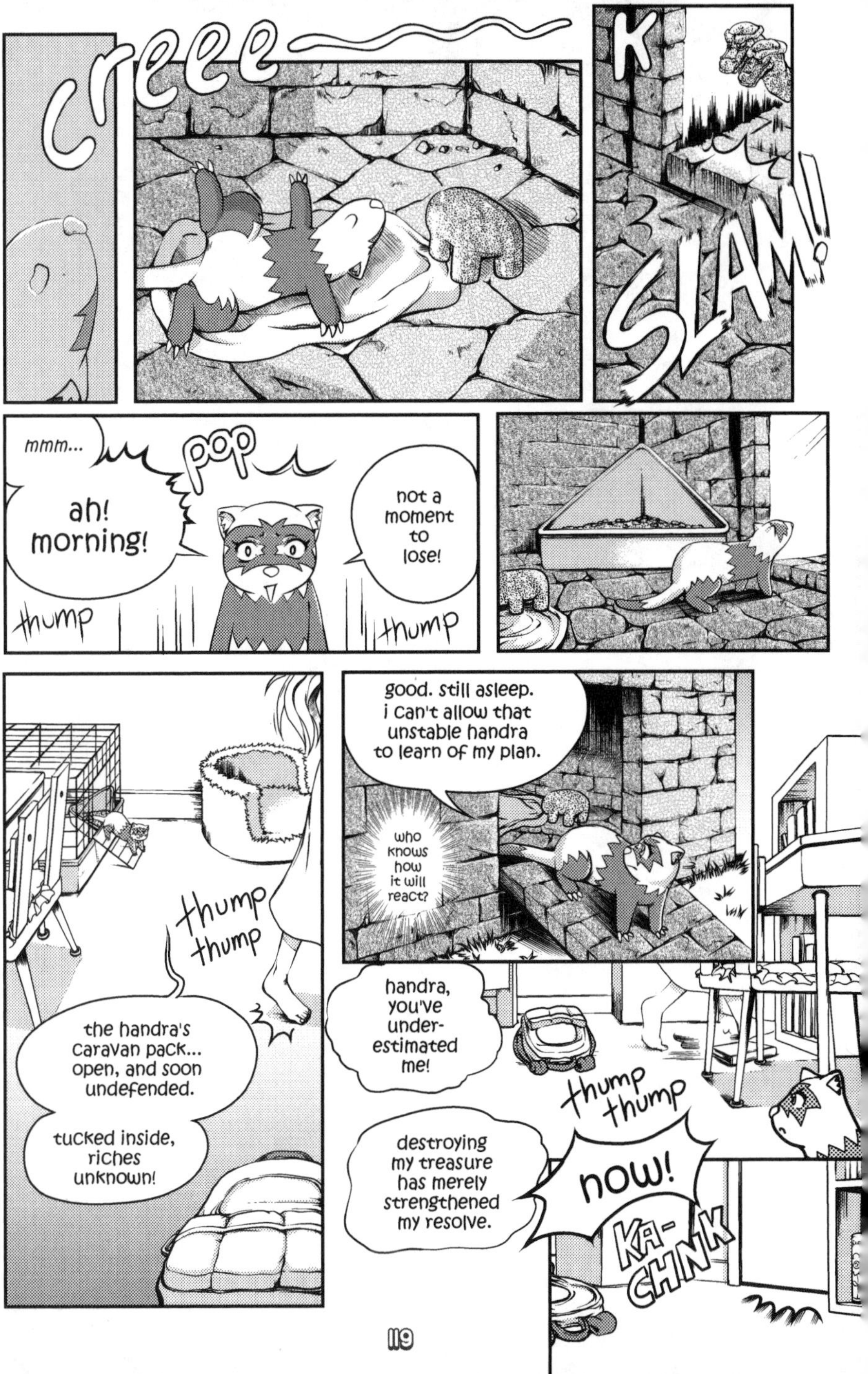
creeee
K
SLAM!
mmm...
ah! morning!
pop
not a moment to lose!
thump
thump
thump thump
good. still asleep. i can't allow that unstable handra to learn of my plan.
who knows how it will react?
the handra's caravan pack... open, and soon undefended.
tucked inside, riches unknown!
handra, you've under-estimated me!
destroying my treasure has merely strengthened my resolve.
thump thump
now!
KA-CHNK

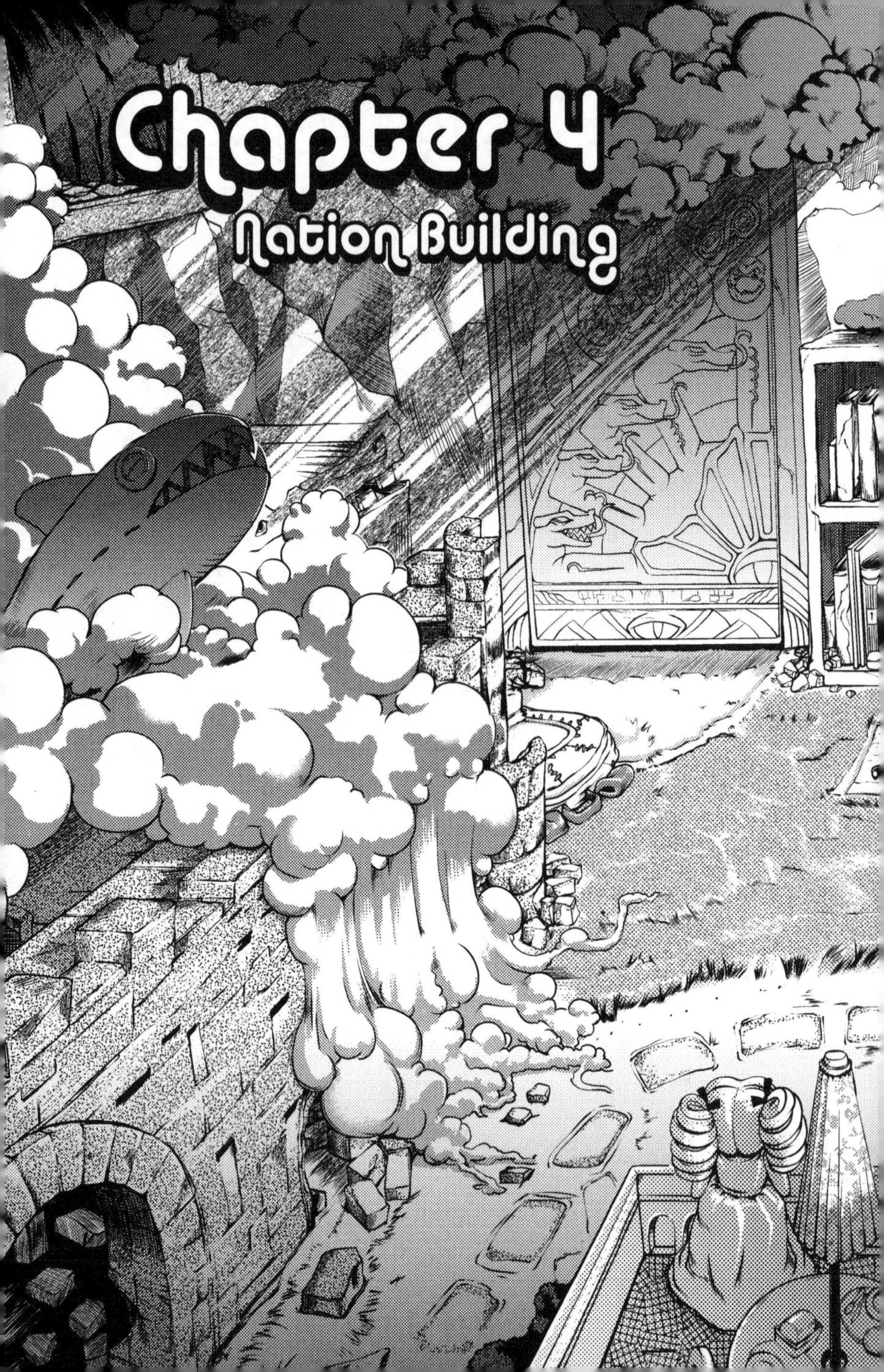
Chapter 4
Nation Building

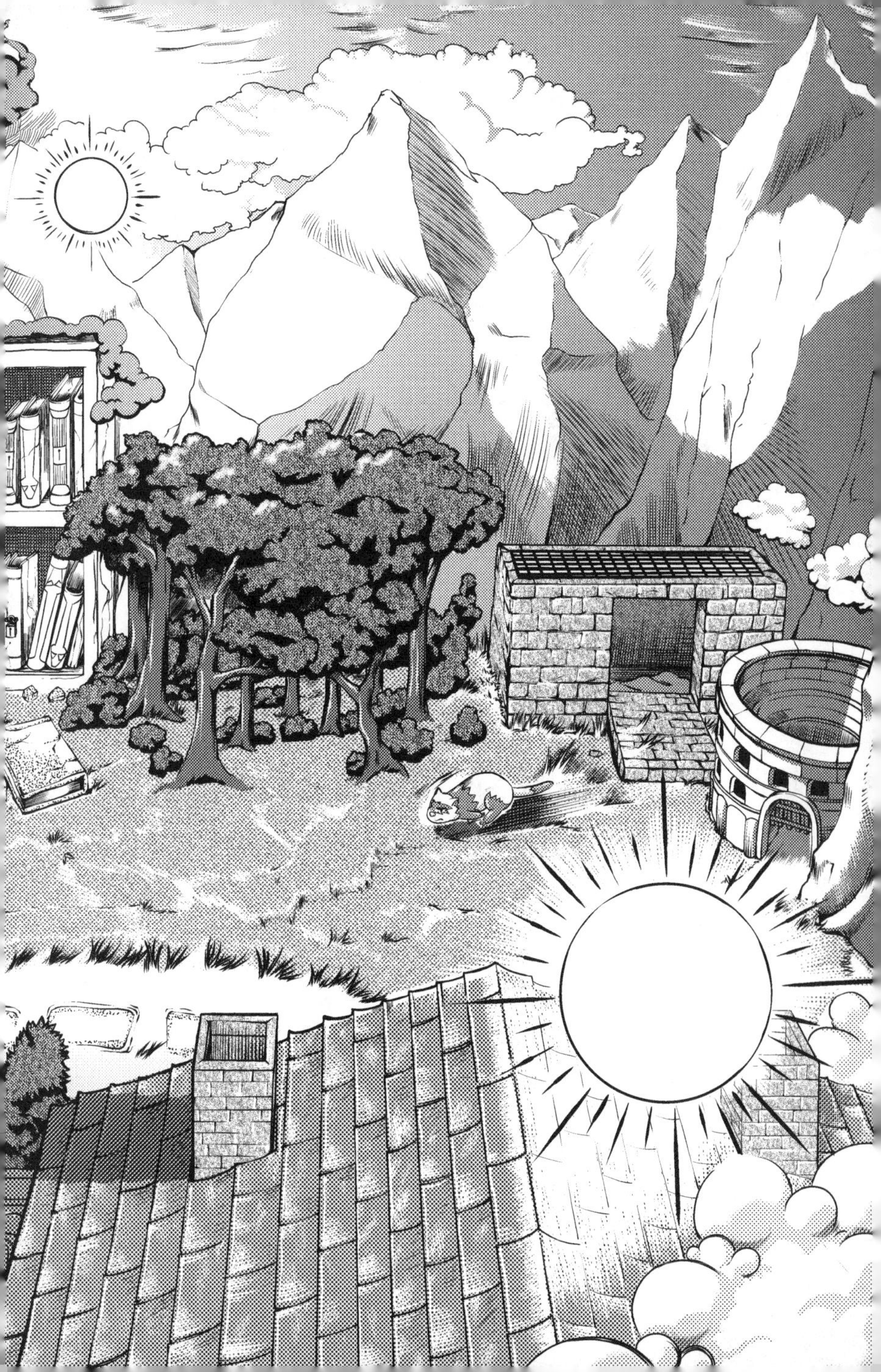

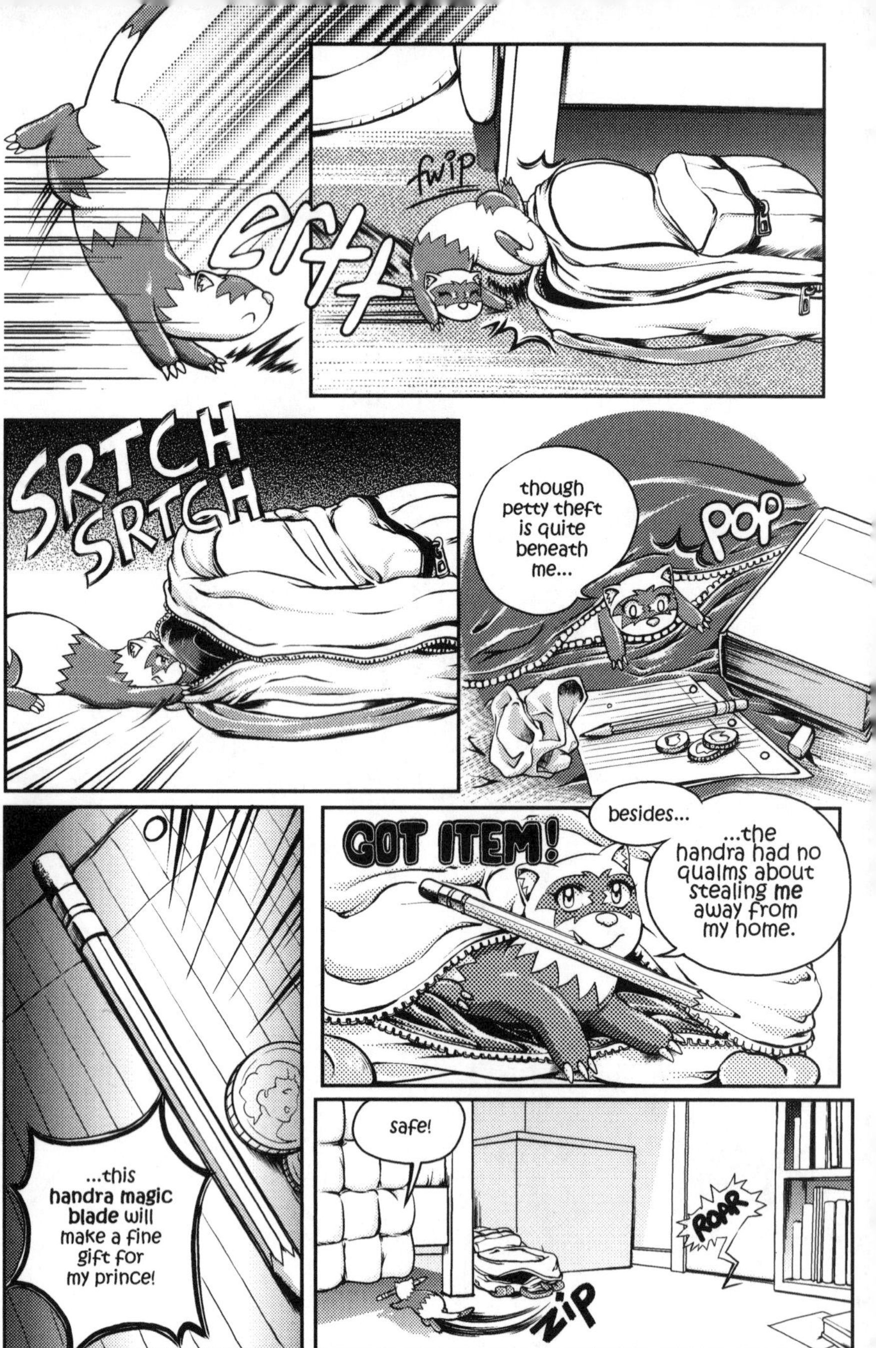
erff
fwip
SRTCH SRTCH
though petty theft is quite beneath me...
POP
GOT ITEM!
besides...
...the handra had no qualms about stealing me away from my home.
...this handra magic blade will make a fine gift for my prince!
safe!
ROAR
ZIP

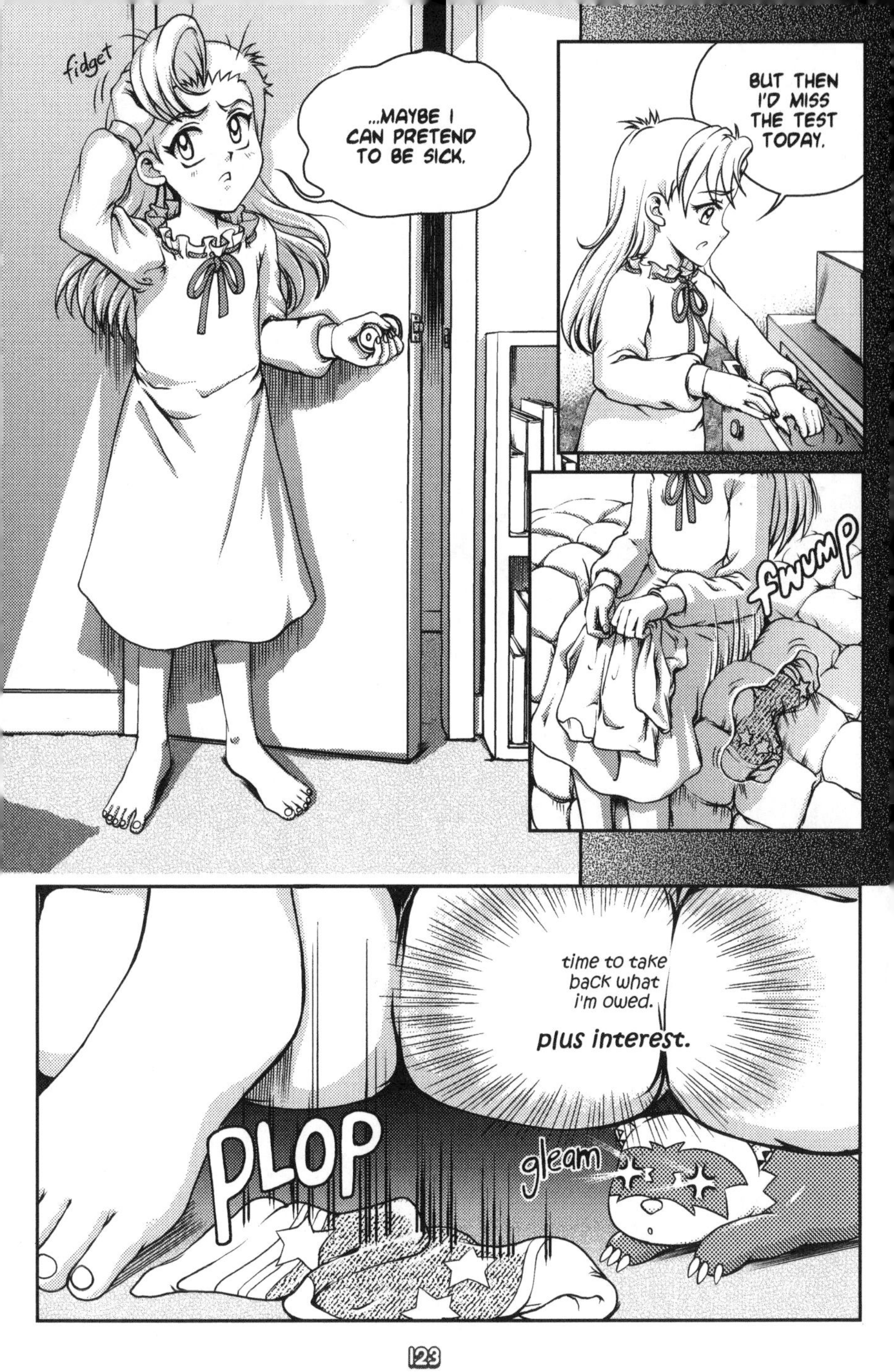
fidget
...MAYBE I CAN PRETEND TO BE SICK.
BUT THEN I'D MISS THE TEST TODAY.
fwump
time to take back what i'm owed.
plus interest.
PLOP
gleam

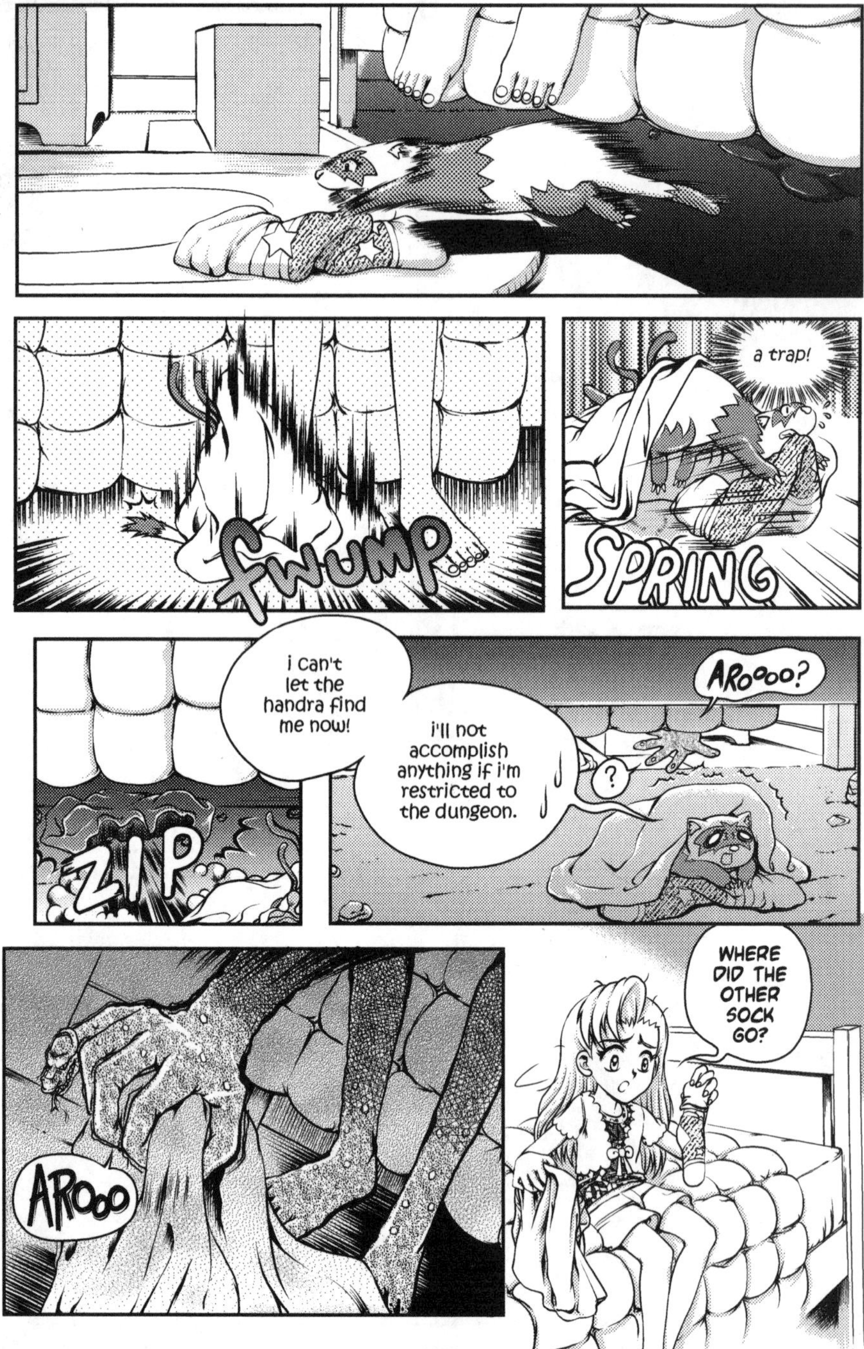
fwump
a trap!
SPRING
i can't let the handra find me now!
i'll not accomplish anything if i'm restricted to the dungeon.
ZIP
AROooo?
?
AROoo
WHERE DID THE OTHER SOCK GO?

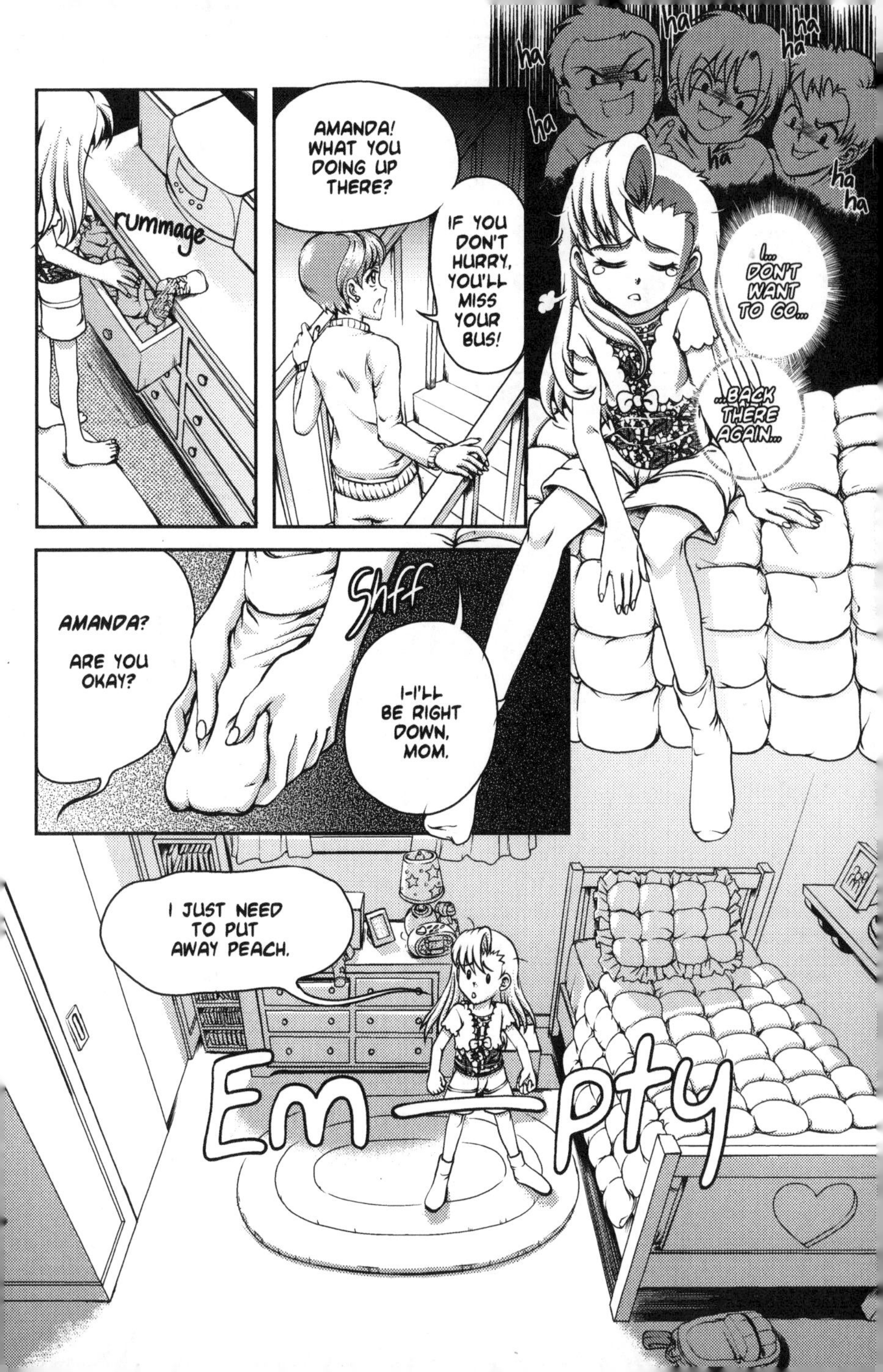
ha
ha
ha
ha
ha
ha
ha
ha
rummage
AMANDA! WHAT YOU DOING UP THERE?
IF YOU DON'T HURRY, YOU'LL MISS YOUR BUS!
I... DON'T WANT TO GO...
...BACK THERE AGAIN...
AMANDA?
ARE YOU OKAY?
Shff
I-I'LL BE RIGHT DOWN, MOM.
I JUST NEED TO PUT AWAY PEACH.
Em—pty

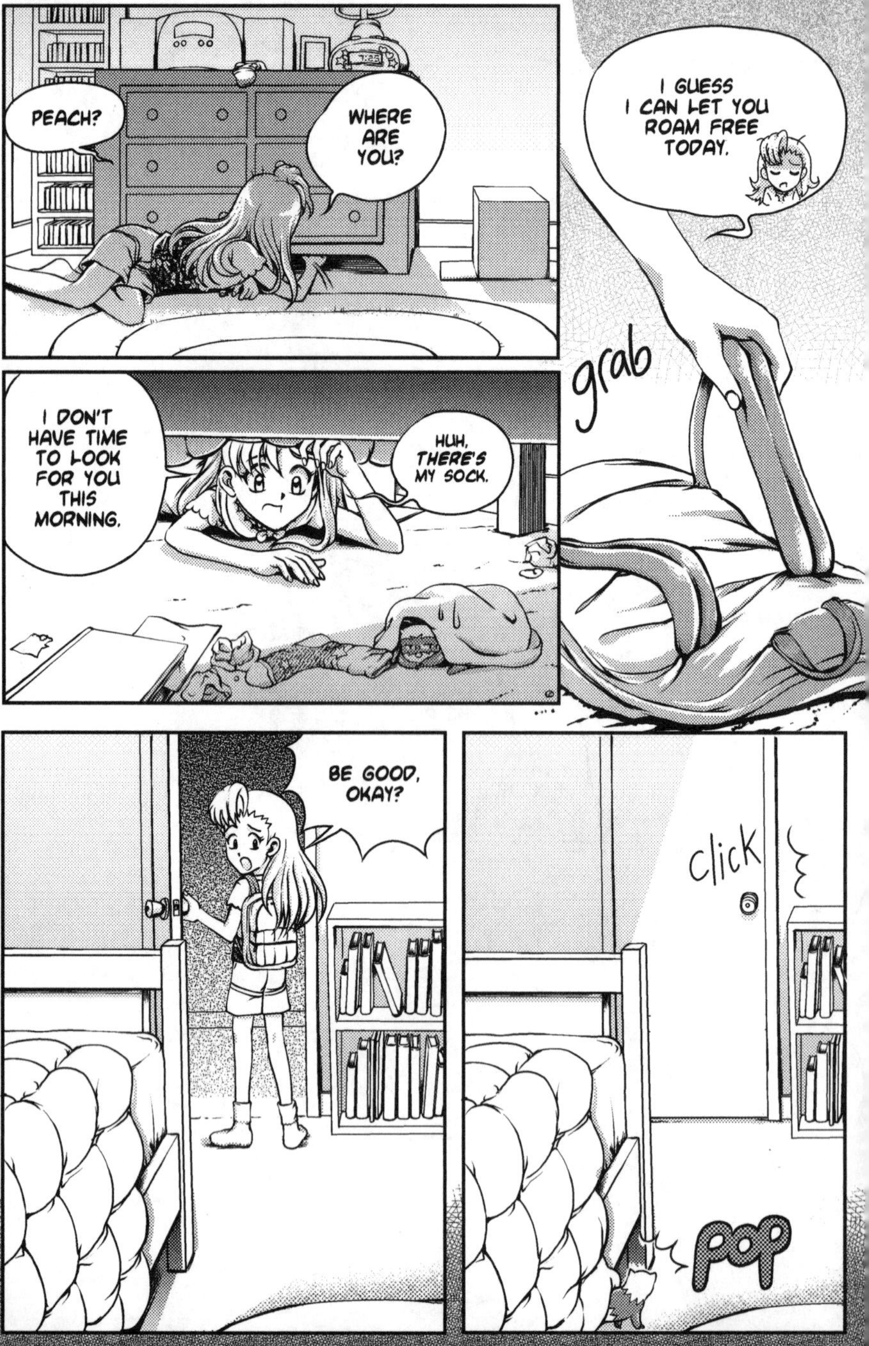
PEACH?
WHERE ARE YOU?
I DON'T HAVE TIME TO LOOK FOR YOU THIS MORNING.
HUH, THERE'S MY SOCK.
I GUESS I CAN LET YOU ROAM FREE TODAY.
grab
BE GOOD, OKAY?
click
POP

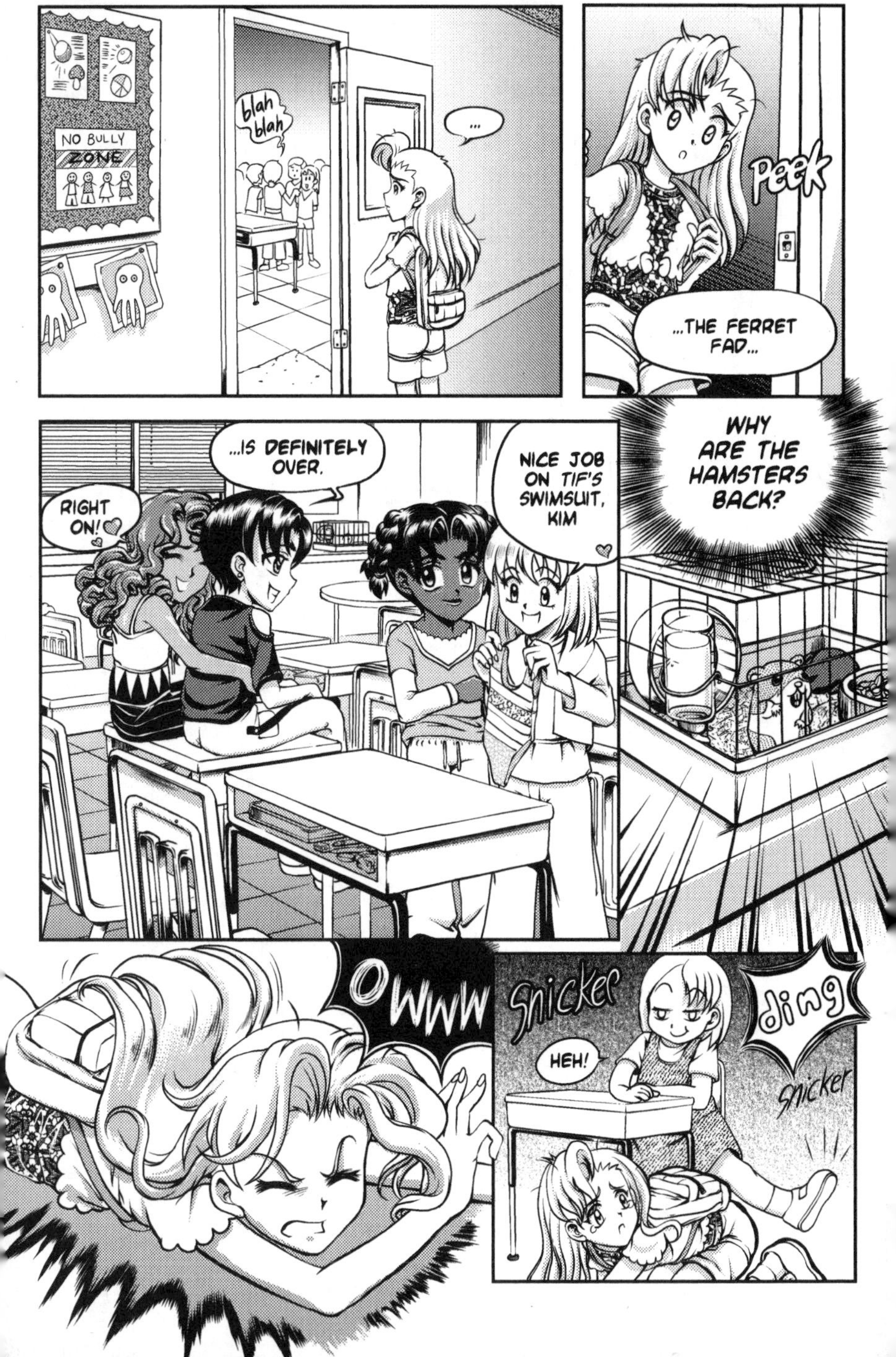
NO BULLY
ZONE
blah blah
...
Peek
...THE FERRET FAD...
...IS DEFINITELY OVER.
RIGHT ON!
NICE JOB ON TIF'S SWIMSUIT, KIM
WHY ARE THE HAMSTERS BACK?
OWWW
snicker
HEH!
ding
snicker

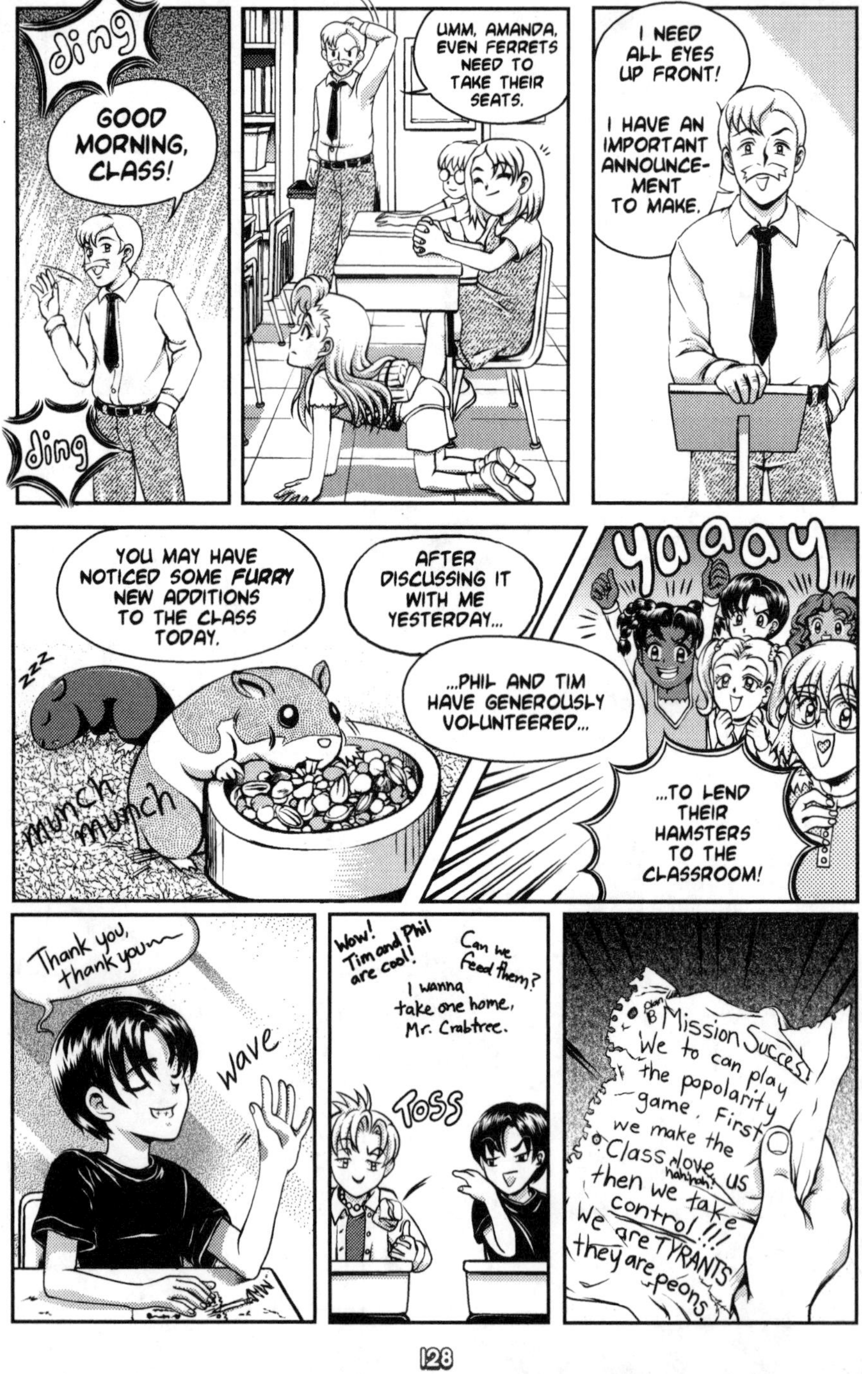
ding
GOOD MORNING, CLASS!
ding
UMM, AMANDA, EVEN FERRETS NEED TO TAKE THEIR SEATS.
I NEED ALL EYES UP FRONT!
I HAVE AN IMPORTANT ANNOUNCE-MENT TO MAKE.
YOU MAY HAVE NOTICED SOME **FURRY** NEW ADDITIONS TO THE CLASS TODAY.
zzz
munch munch
AFTER DISCUSSING IT WITH ME YESTERDAY...
...PHIL AND TIM HAVE GENEROUSLY VOLUNTEERED...
yaaay
...TO LEND THEIR HAMSTERS TO THE CLASSROOM!
Thank you, thank you~
wave
Wow! Tim and Phil are cool!
Can we feed them?
I wanna take one home, Mr. Crabtree.
TOSS
plan B Mission Succes! We to can play the popolarity game. First we make the Class love us
hah hah!
then we take control!!! We are TYRANTS they are peons

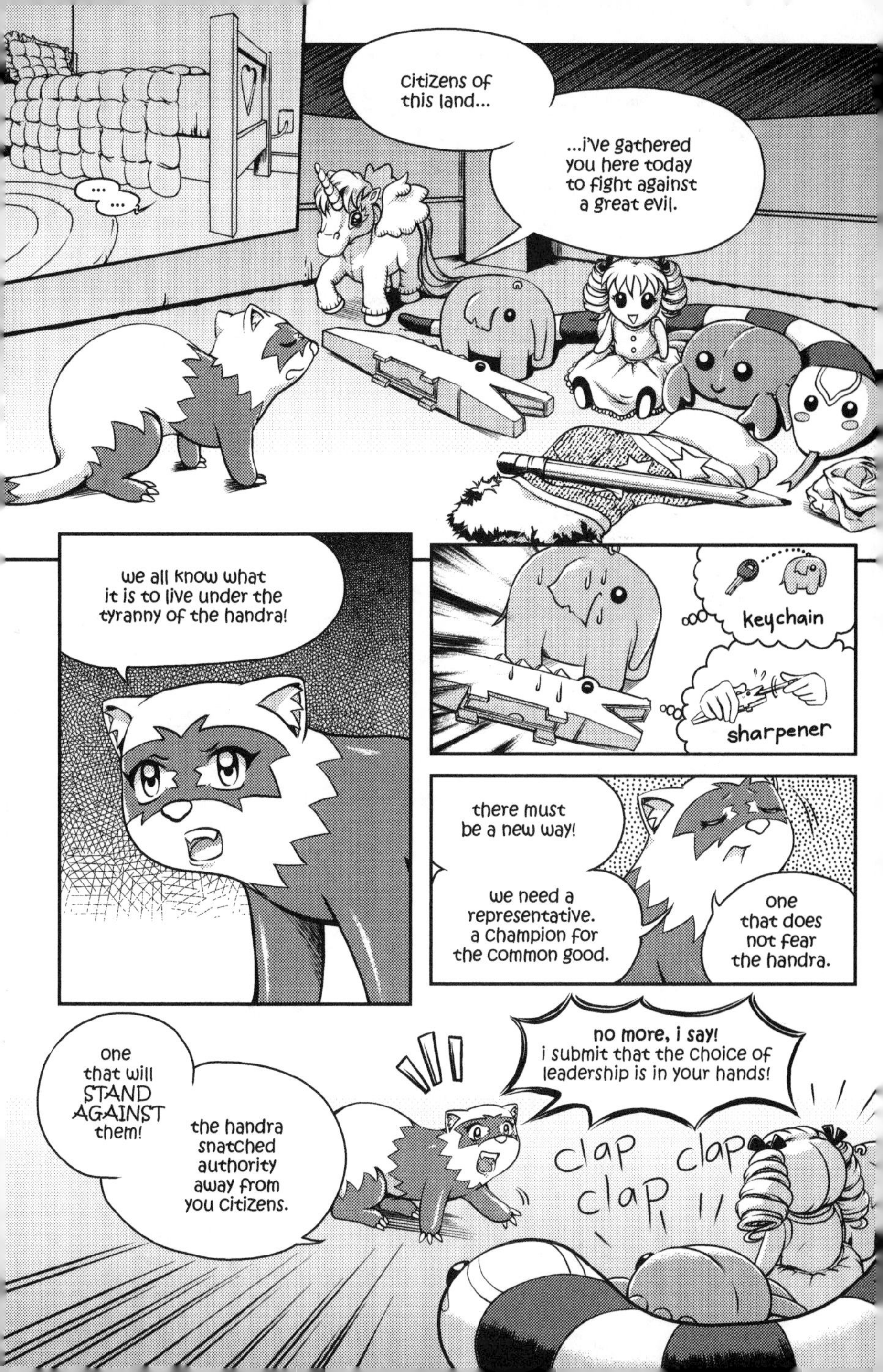

citizens of this land...
...i've gathered you here today to fight against a great evil.
...
...
we all know what it is to live under the tyranny of the handra!
keychain
sharpener
there must be a new way!
we need a representative. a champion for the common good.
one that does not fear the handra.
one that will STAND AGAINST them!
the handra snatched authority away from you citizens.
no more, i say! i submit that the choice of leadership is in your hands!
clap clap clap

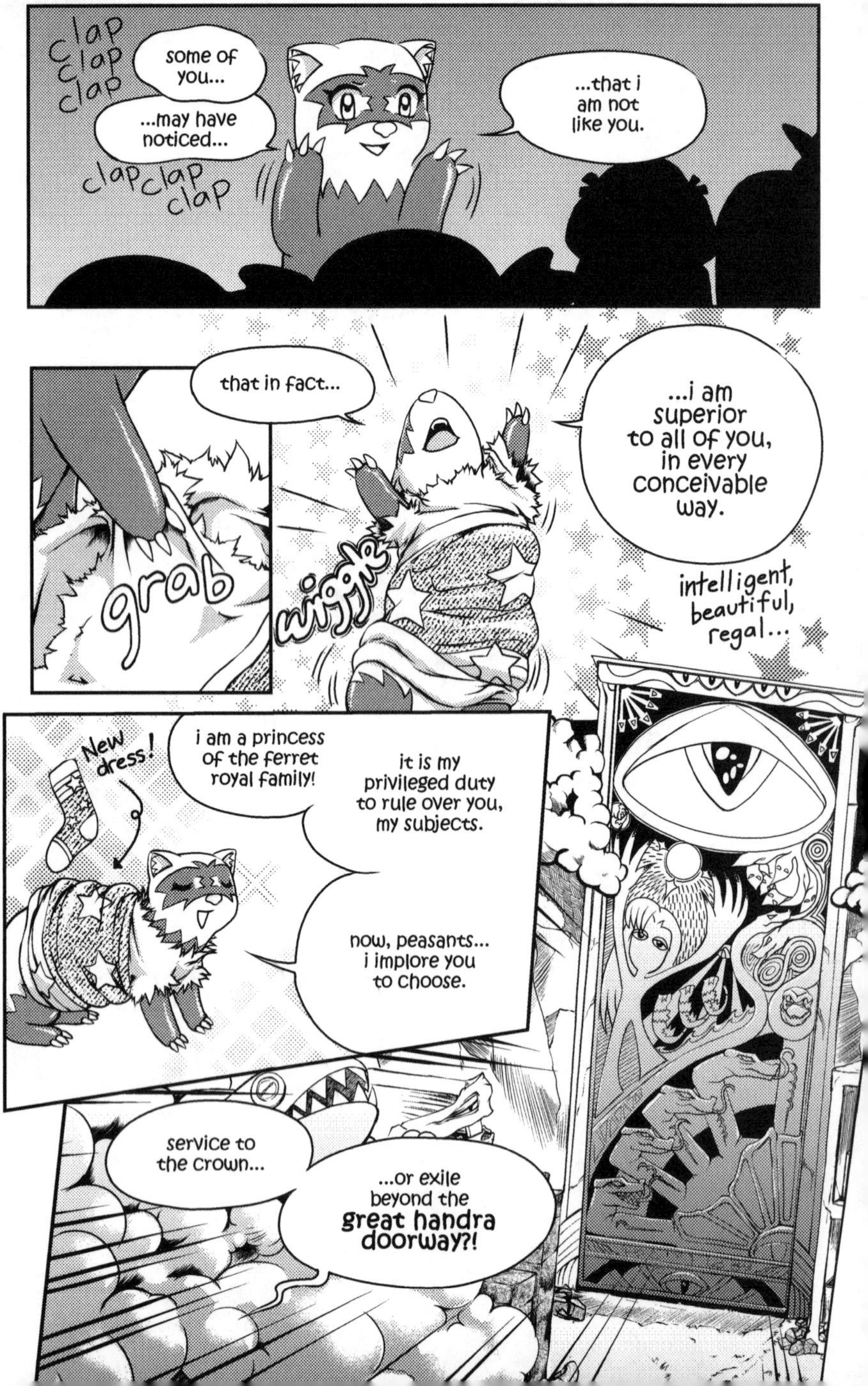
clap clap clap
some of you...
...may have noticed...
clap clap clap
...that i am not like you.
that in fact...
...i am superior to all of you, in every conceivable way.
grab
wiggle
intelligent, beautiful, regal...
New dress!
i am a princess of the ferret royal family!
it is my privileged duty to rule over you, my subjects.
now, peasants... i implore you to choose.
service to the crown...
...or exile beyond the great handra doorway?!

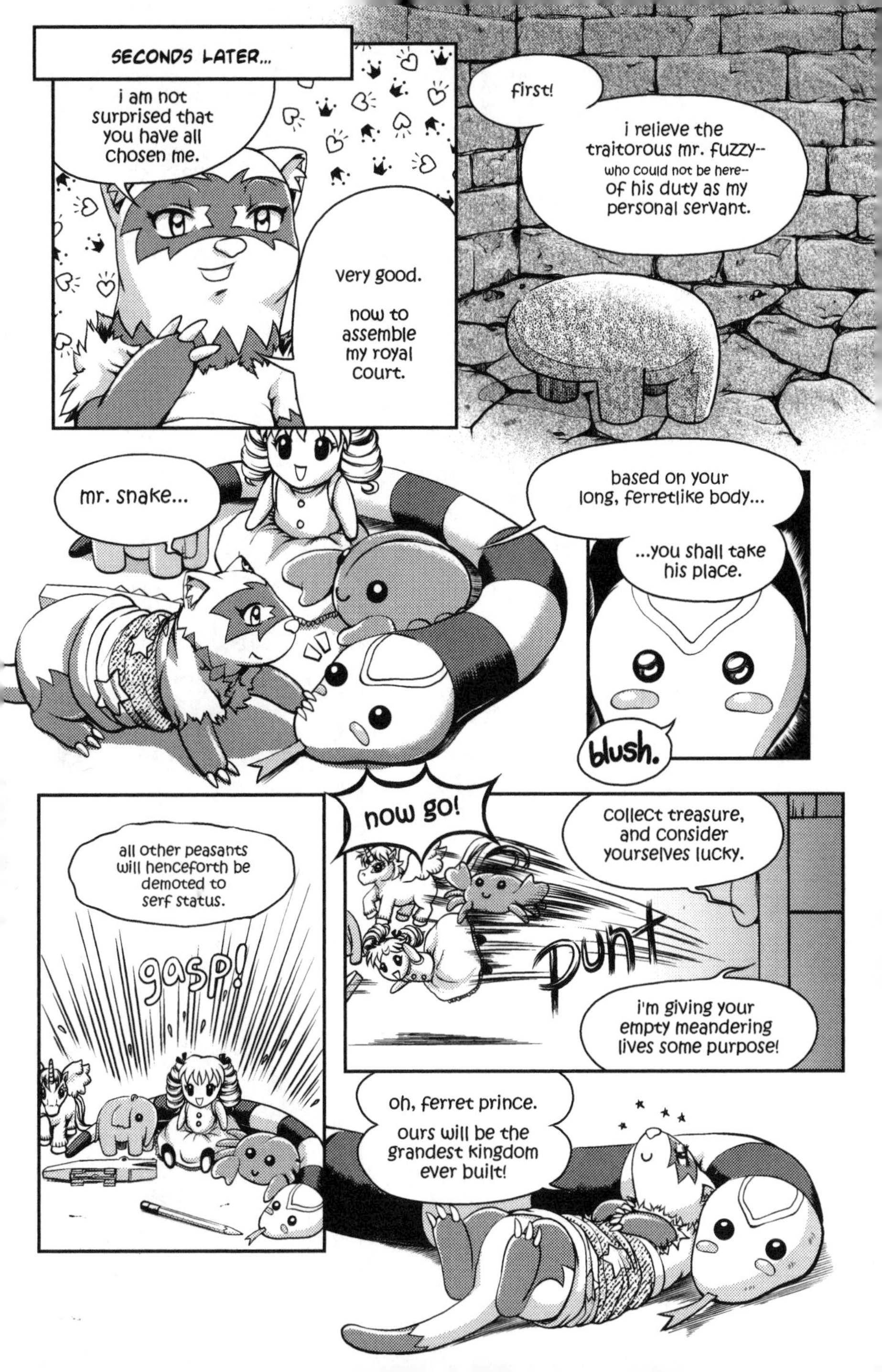
seconds later...
i am not surprised that you have all chosen me.
very good.
now to assemble my royal court.
first!
i relieve the traitorous mr. fuzzy-- who could not be here-- of his duty as my personal servant.
mr. snake...
based on your long, ferretlike body...
...you shall take his place.
blush.
all other peasants will henceforth be demoted to serf status.
gasp!
now go!
collect treasure, and consider yourselves lucky.
punt
i'm giving your empty meandering lives some purpose!
oh, ferret prince.
ours will be the grandest kingdom ever built!

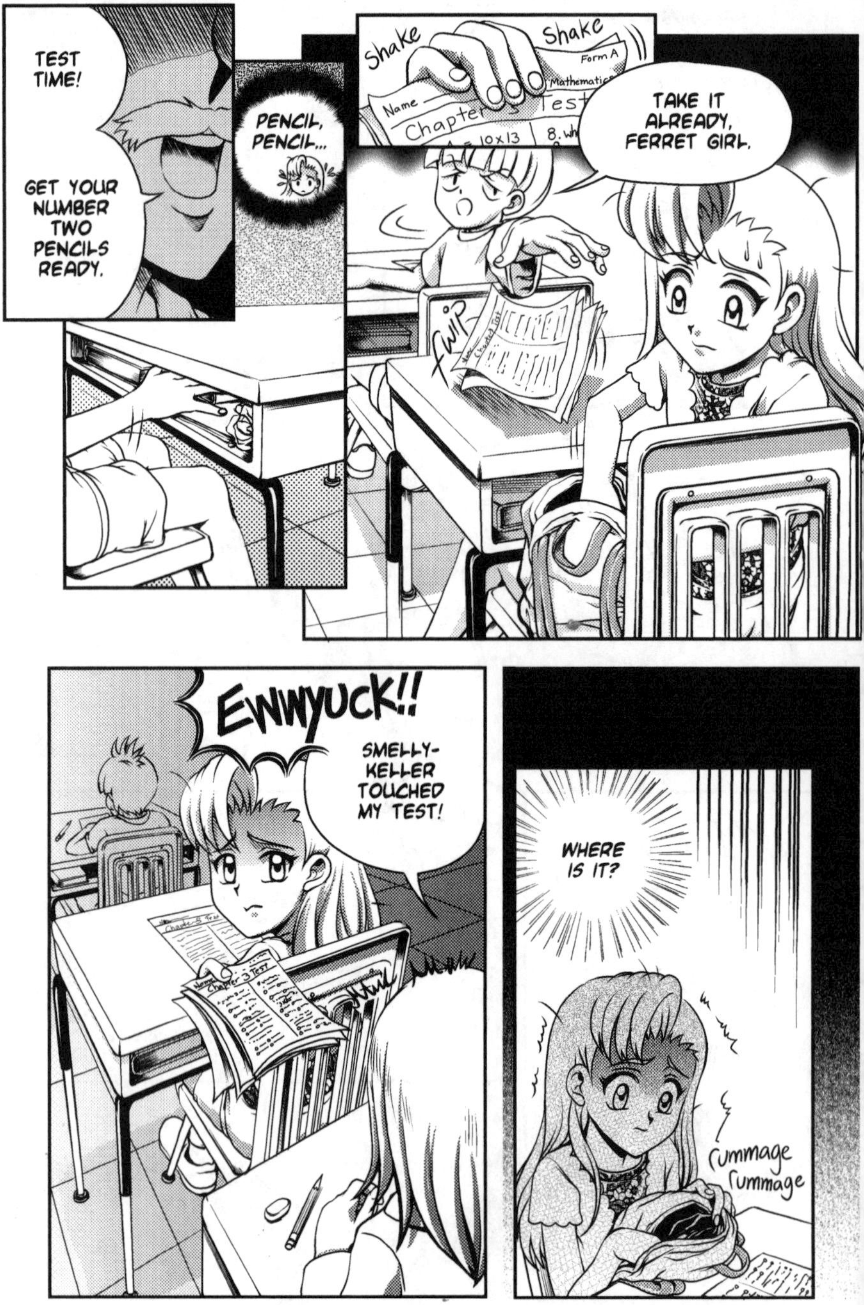
TEST TIME!
GET YOUR NUMBER TWO PENCILS READY.
PENCIL, PENCIL...
Shake Shake
Form A
Mathematics
Name
Chapter 3 Test
TAKE IT ALREADY, FERRET GIRL.
fwip
EWWYUCK!!
SMELLY-KELLER TOUCHED MY TEST!
Chapter 3 Test
WHERE IS IT?
rummage rummage

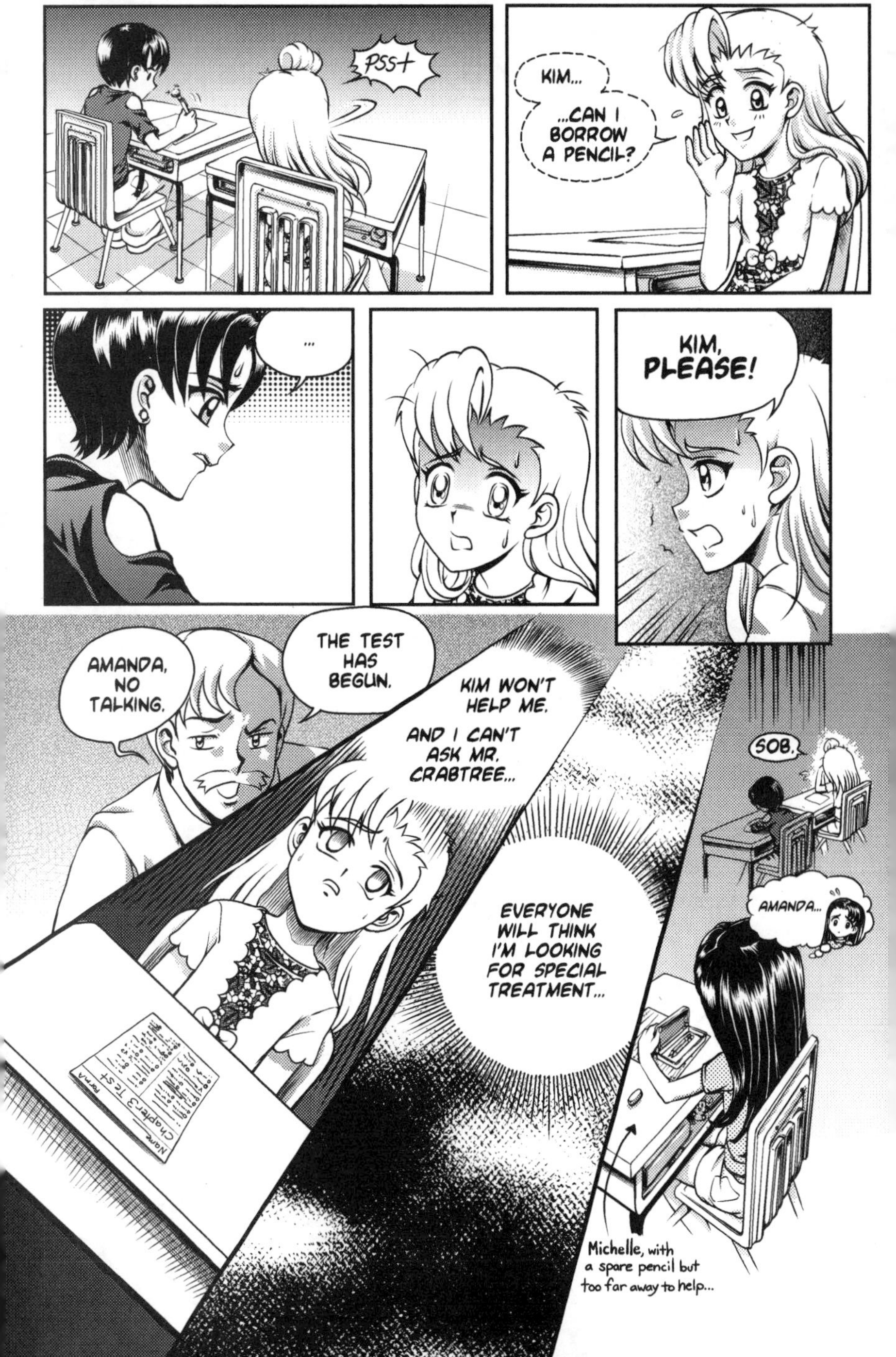
PSST
KIM...
...CAN I BORROW A PENCIL?
...
KIM, PLEASE!
AMANDA, NO TALKING.
THE TEST HAS BEGUN.
KIM WON'T HELP ME.
AND I CAN'T ASK MR. CRABTREE...
EVERYONE WILL THINK I'M LOOKING FOR SPECIAL TREATMENT...
SOB.
AMANDA...
Chapter 3 Test
Michelle, with a spare pencil but too far away to help...

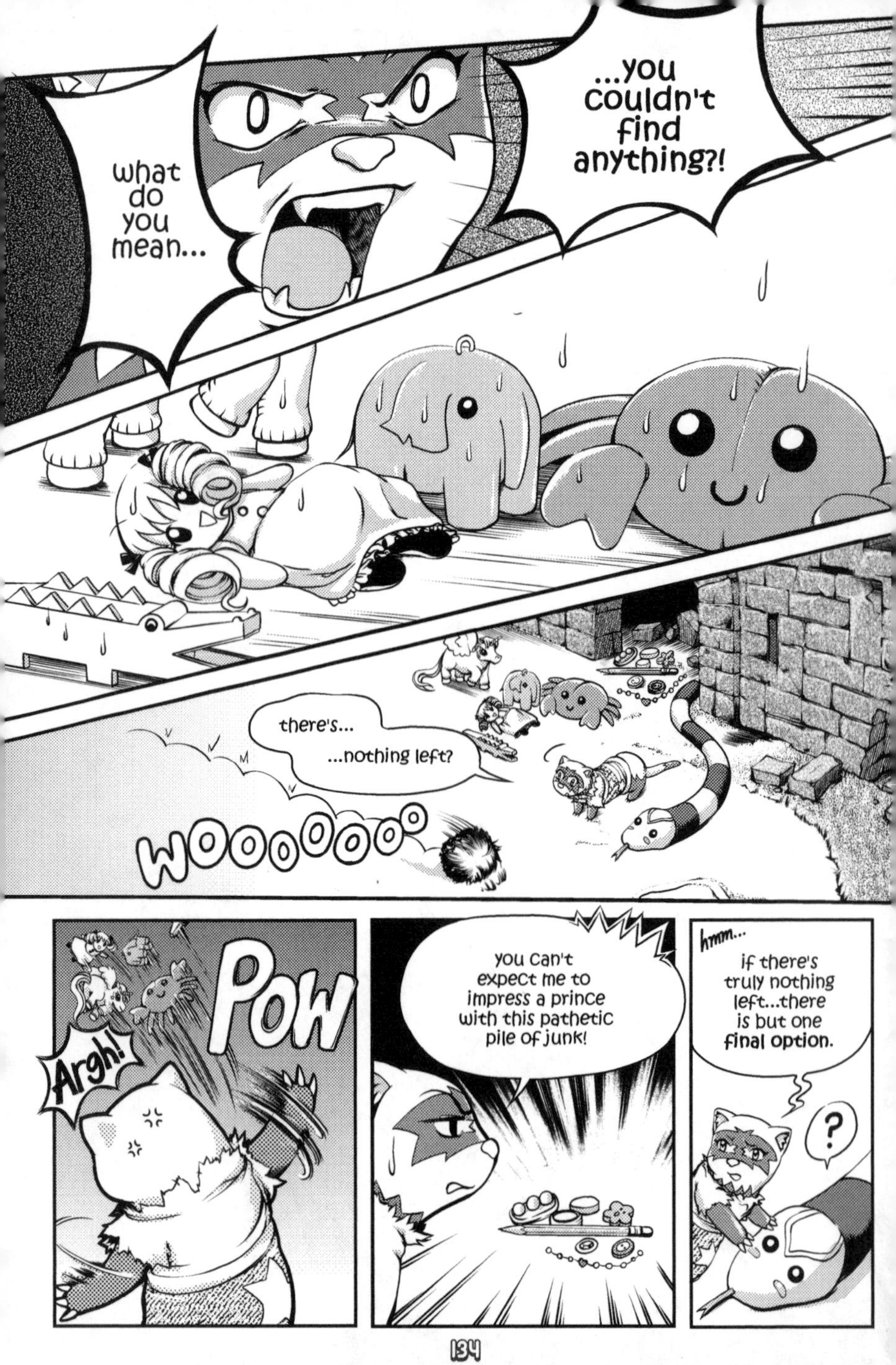

what do you mean...
...you couldn't find anything?!
there's... ...nothing left?
WOOOOOOO
POW
Argh!
you can't expect me to impress a prince with this pathetic pile of junk!
hmm...
if there's truly nothing left...there is but one final option.
?

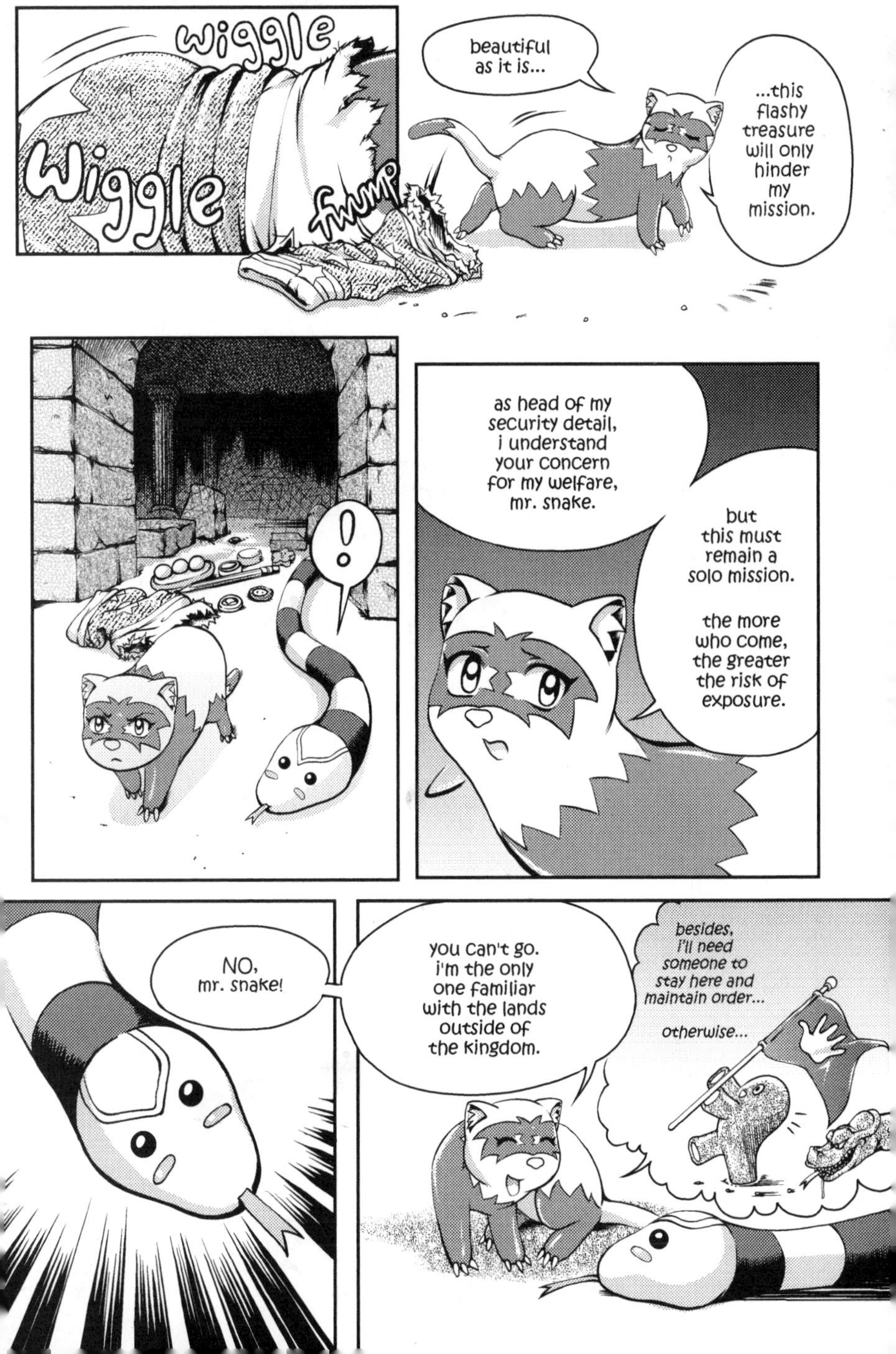
wiggle
wiggle
fwump
beautiful as it is...
...this flashy treasure will only hinder my mission.
!
as head of my security detail, i understand your concern for my welfare, mr. snake.
but this must remain a solo mission.
the more who come, the greater the risk of exposure.
NO, mr. snake!
you can't go. i'm the only one familiar with the lands outside of the kingdom.
besides, i'll need someone to stay here and maintain order...
otherwise...

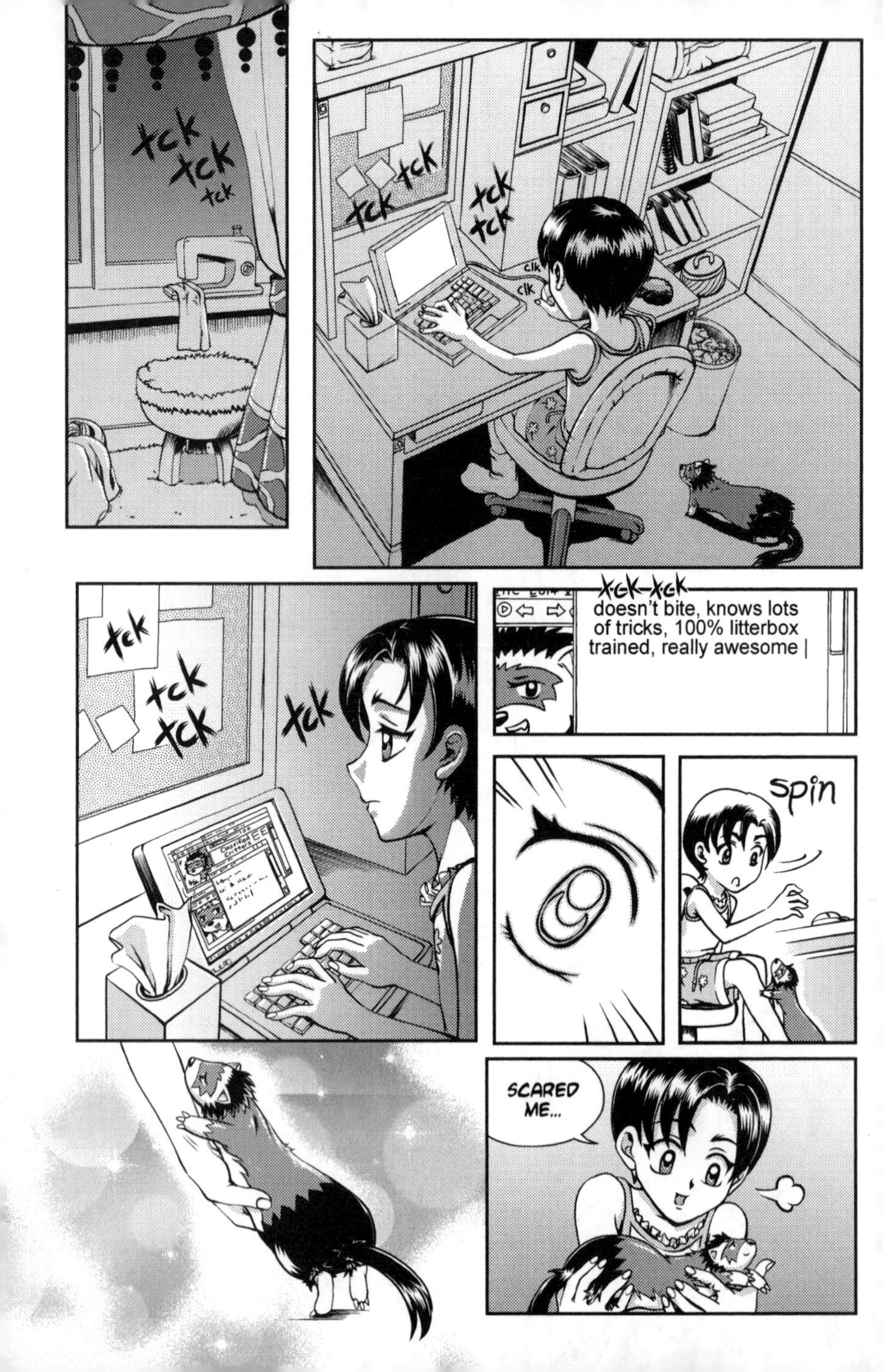
tck tck tck
tck tck tck tck
clk clk
tck tck tck tck
XCK XCK
doesn't bite, knows lots of tricks, 100% litterbox trained, really awesome |
Classified Critters
spin
SCARED ME...

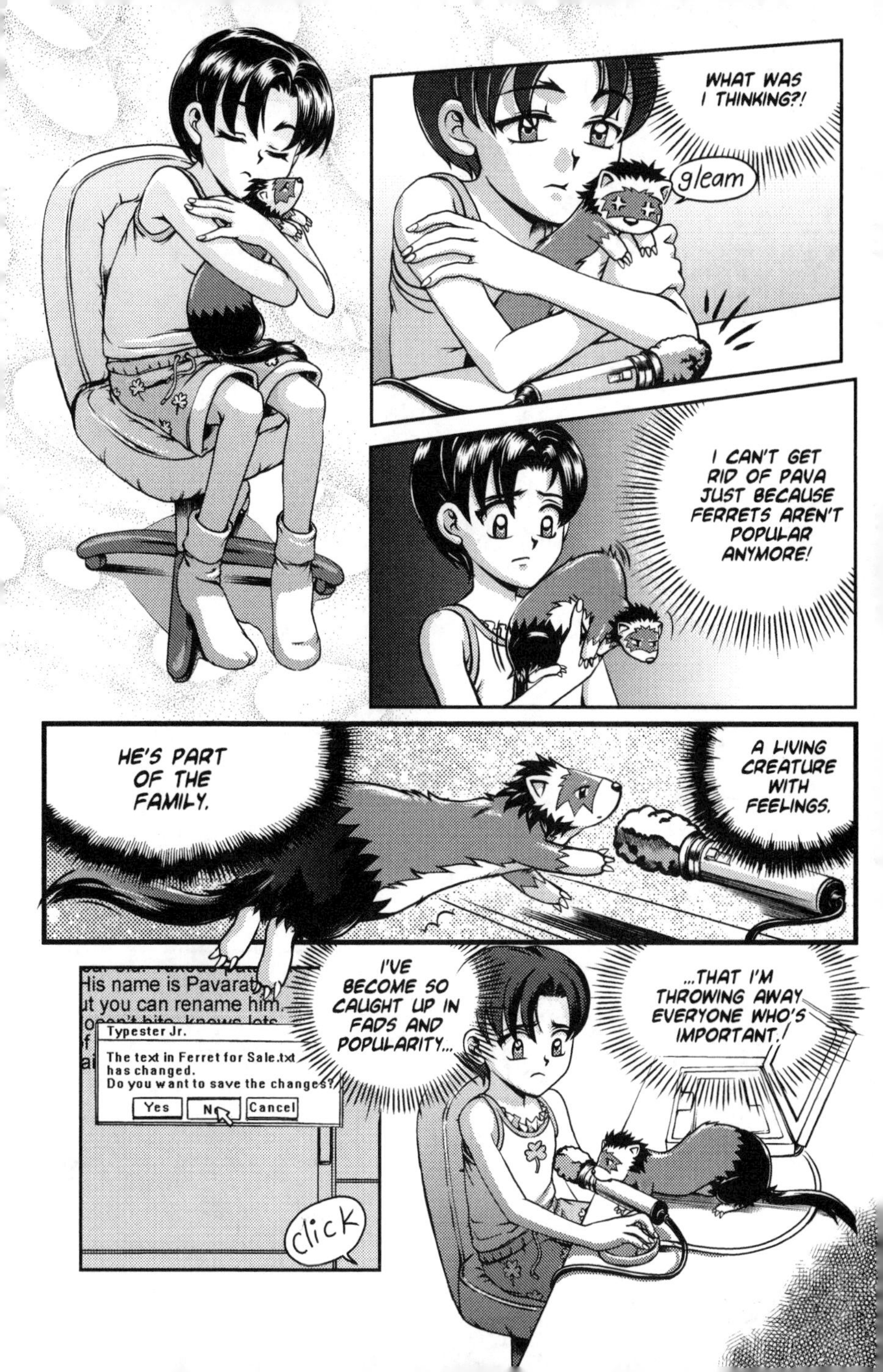
WHAT WAS I THINKING?!
gleam
I CAN'T GET RID OF PAVA JUST BECAUSE FERRETS AREN'T POPULAR ANYMORE!
HE'S PART OF THE FAMILY.
A LIVING CREATURE WITH FEELINGS.
His name is Pavarat
ut you can rename him.
Typester Jr.
The text in Ferret for Sale.txt has changed.
Do you want to save the changes?
Yes
Cancel
click
I'VE BECOME SO CAUGHT UP IN FADS AND POPULARITY...
...THAT I'M THROWING AWAY EVERYONE WHO'S IMPORTANT.

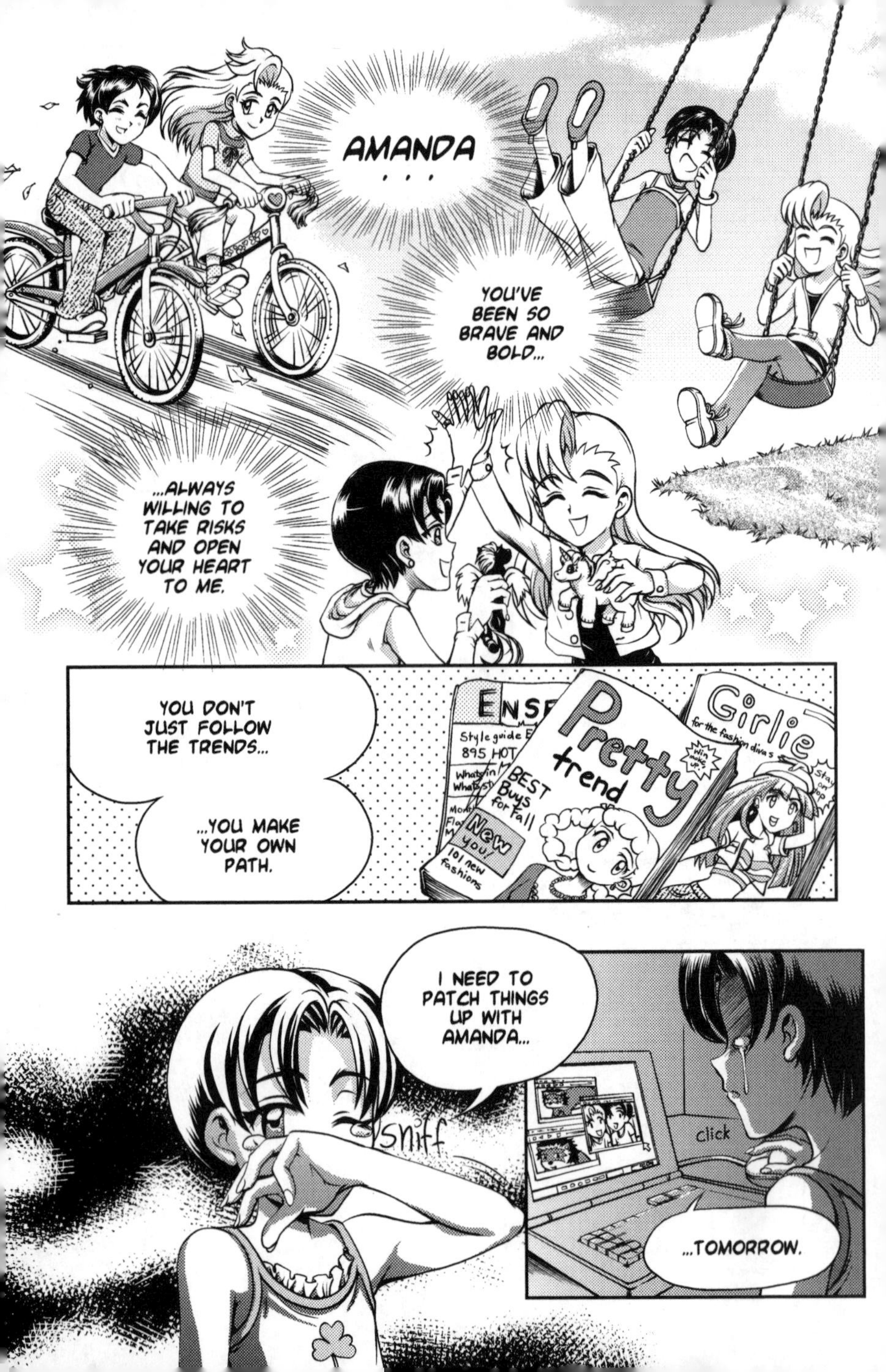
AMANDA . . .
YOU'VE BEEN SO BRAVE AND BOLD...
...ALWAYS WILLING TO TAKE RISKS AND OPEN YOUR HEART TO ME.
YOU DON'T JUST FOLLOW THE TRENDS...
...YOU MAKE YOUR OWN PATH.
Pretty trend
BEST Buys for Fall
New you!
101 new fashions
Girlie
for the fashion divas
Style guide
895 HOT
I NEED TO PATCH THINGS UP WITH AMANDA...
sniff
click
...TOMORROW.

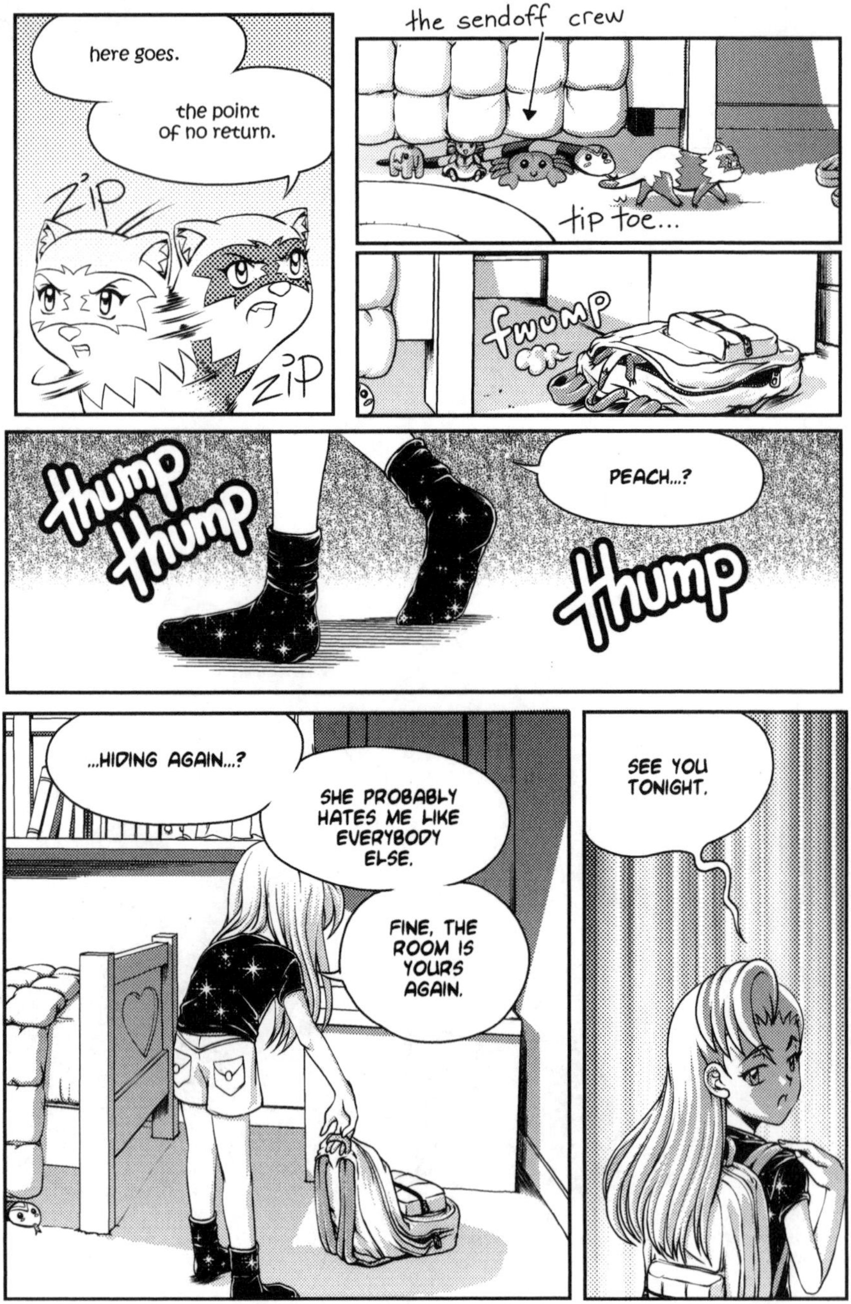
here goes.
the point of no return.
ZIP
ZIP
the sendoff crew
tip toe...
fwump
thump thump
PEACH...?
thump
...HIDING AGAIN...?
SHE PROBABLY HATES ME LIKE EVERYBODY ELSE.
FINE, THE ROOM IS YOURS AGAIN.
SEE YOU TONIGHT.

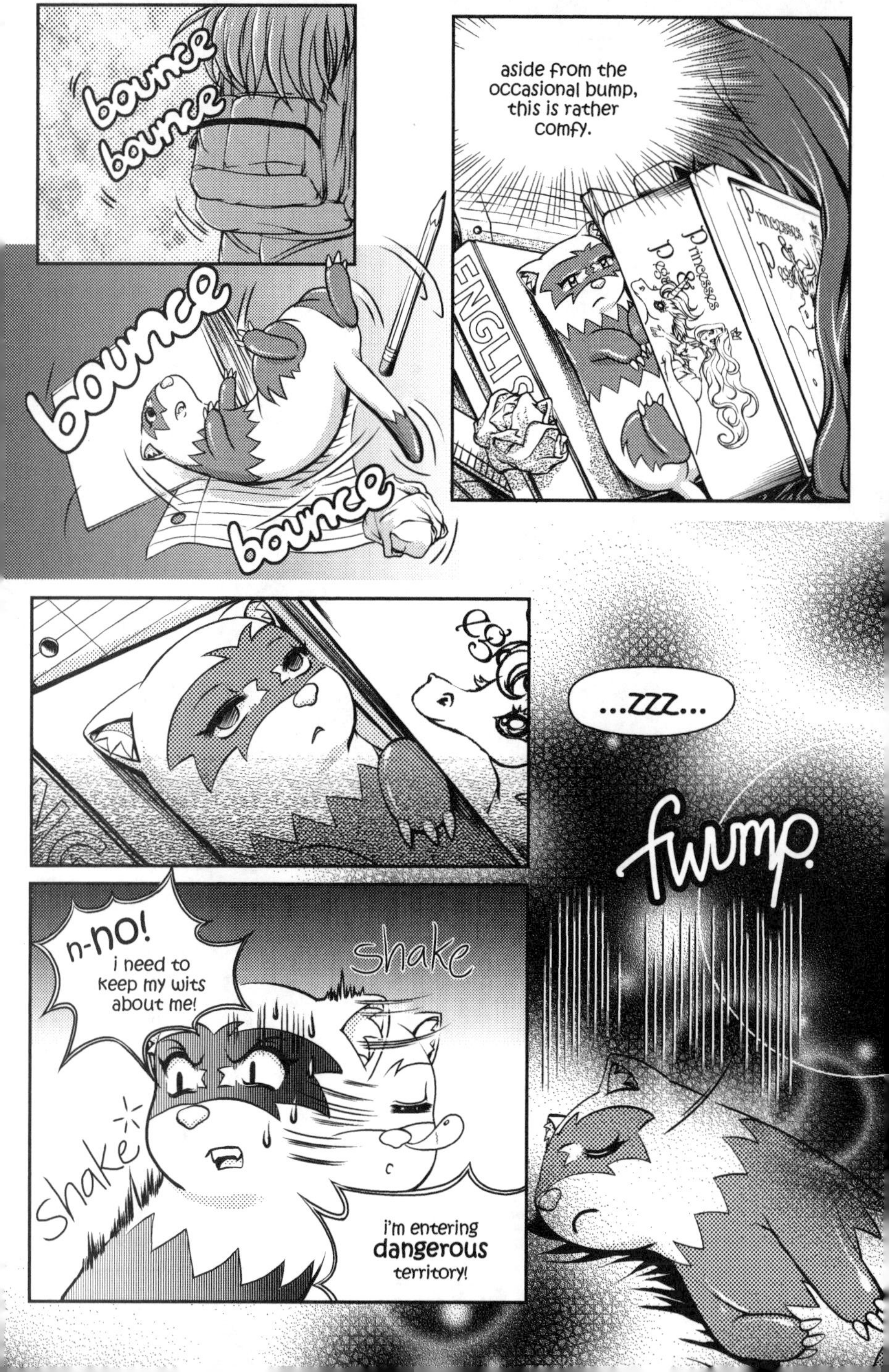
bounce bounce
aside from the occasional bump, this is rather comfy.
bounce
bounce
Princesses & Pegasi
ENGLISH
...zzz...
fwump.
n-NO! i need to keep my wits about me!
shake
shake
i'm entering dangerous territory!

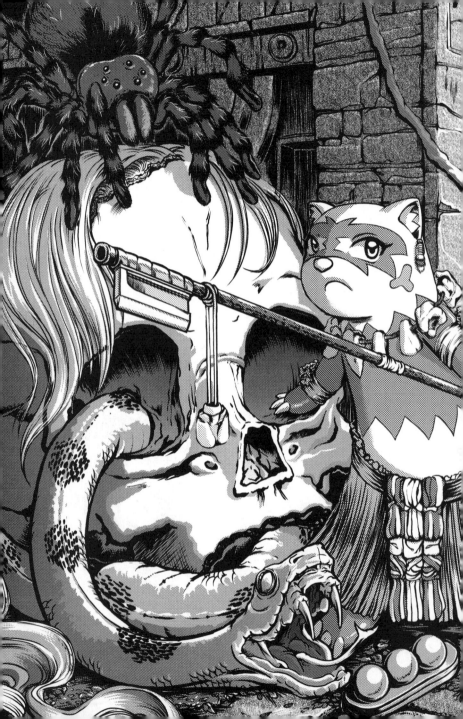

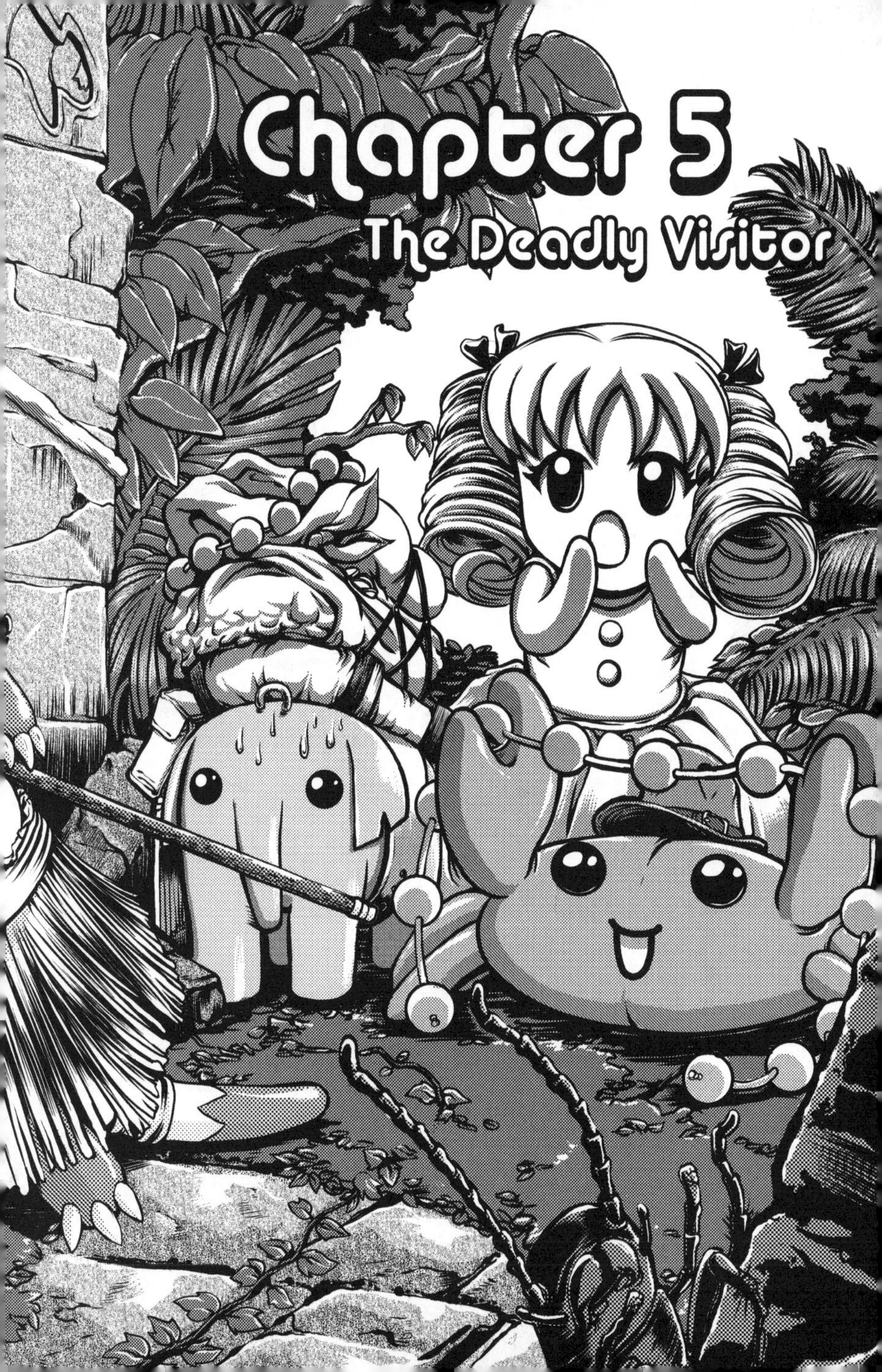
Chapter 5
The Deadly Visitor

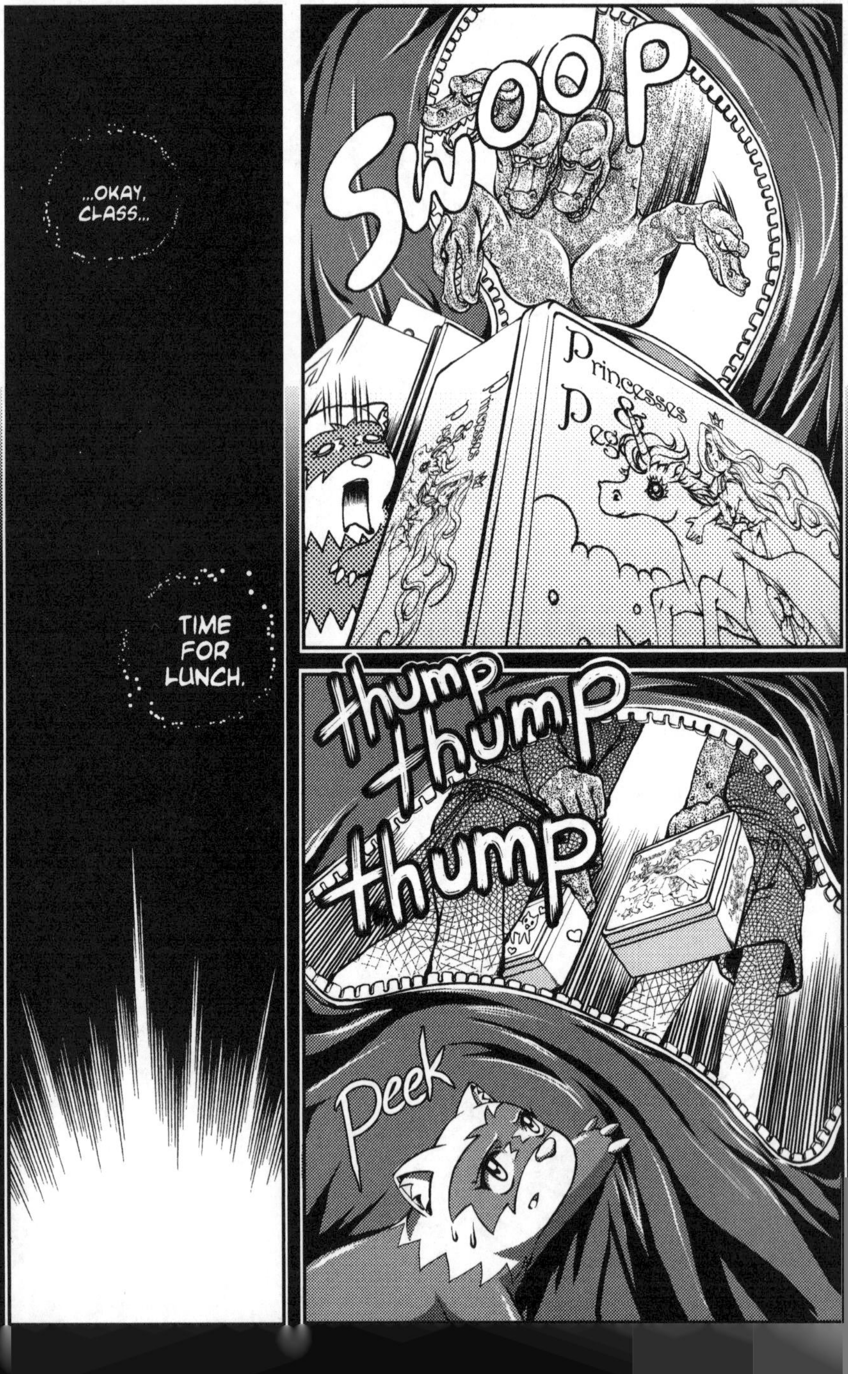
...OKAY, CLASS...
TIME FOR LUNCH.
SWOOP
Princesses &
thump thump thump
Peek

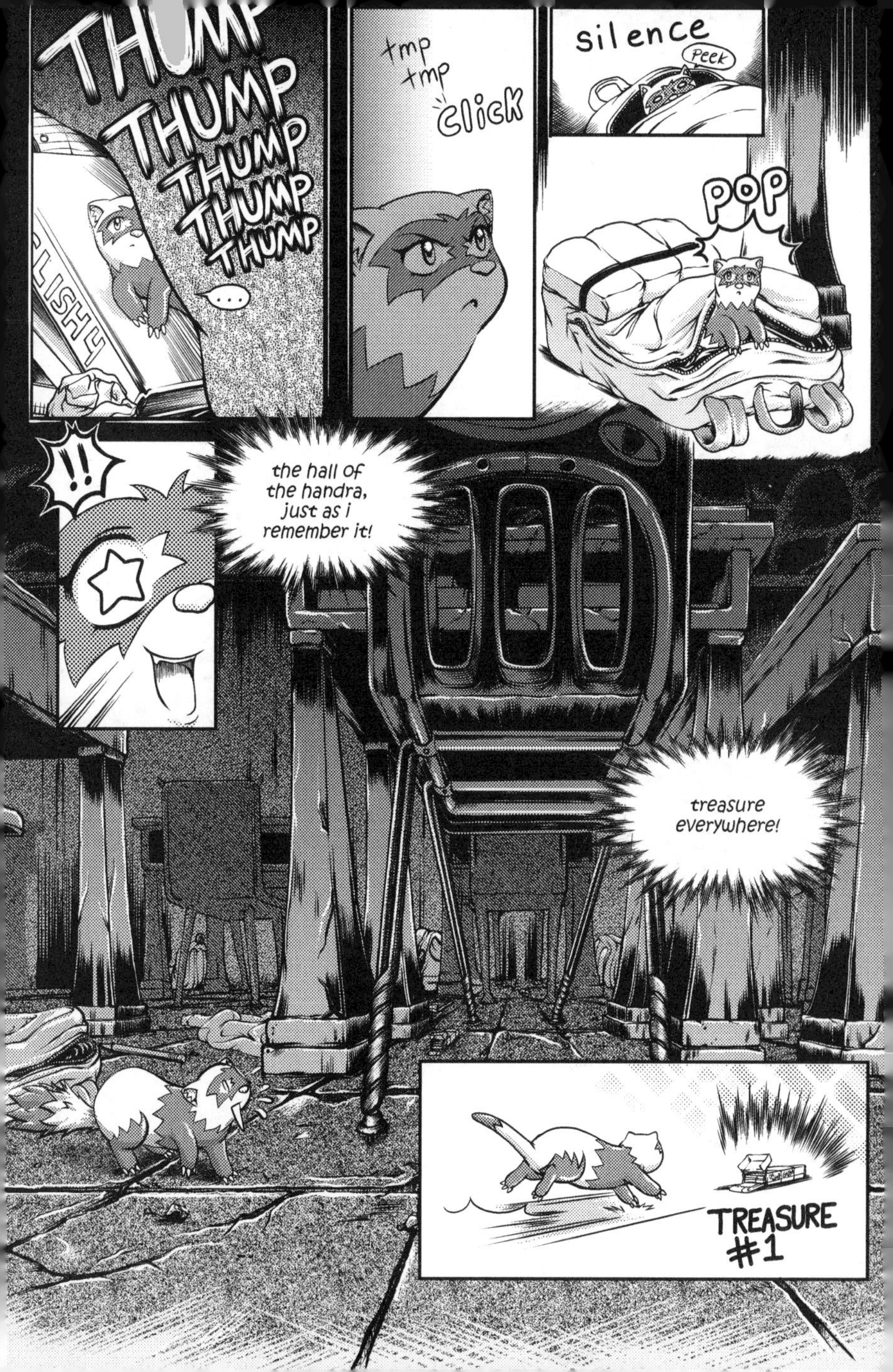
THUMP
THUMP
THUMP
THUMP
THUMP
...
tmp
tmp
click
silence
peek
POP
!!
the hall of the handra, just as i remember it!
treasure everywhere!
TREASURE #1

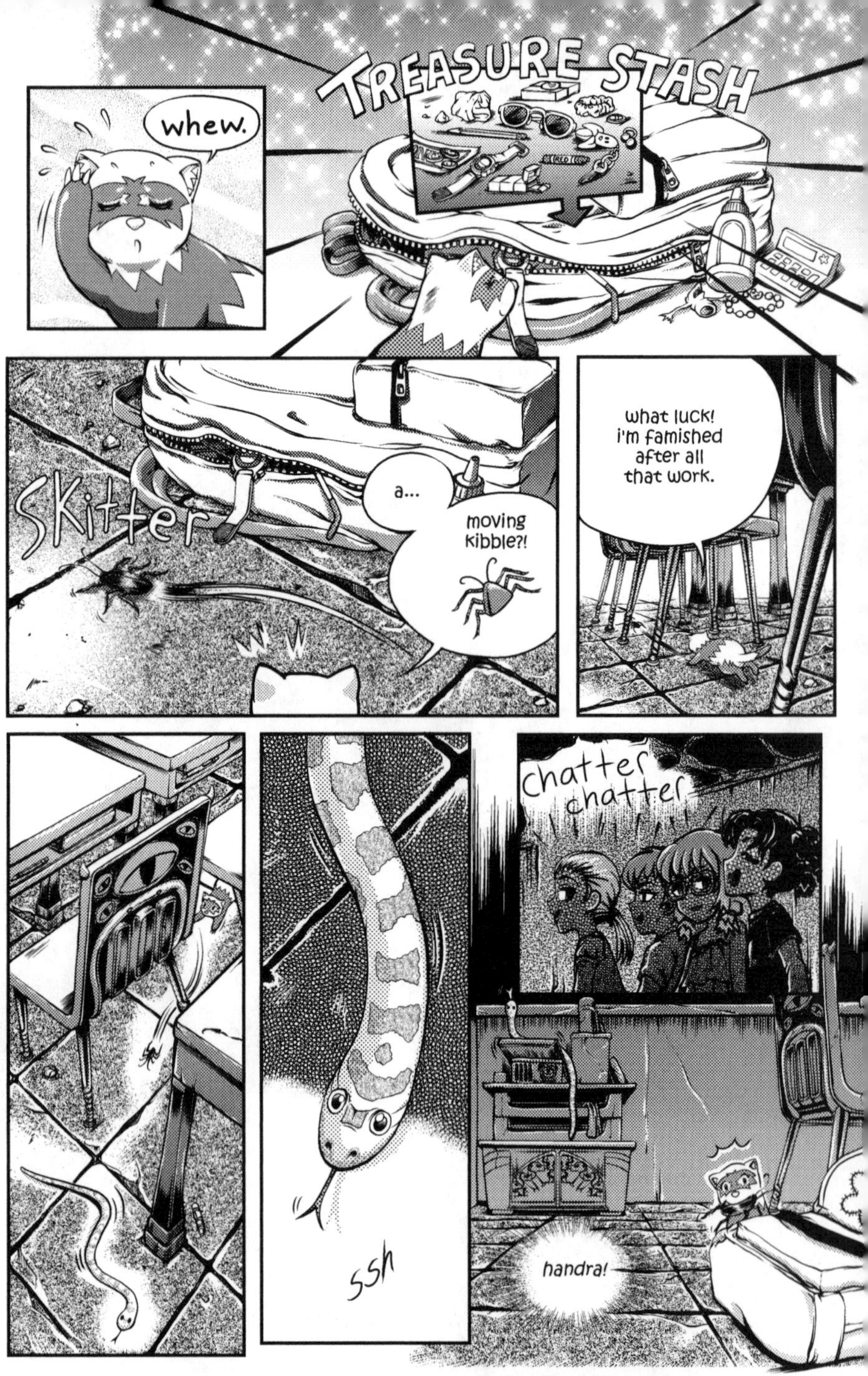

whew.
TREASURE STASH
SKitter
a...
moving kibble?!
what luck! i'm famished after all that work.
ssh
chatter chatter
handra!

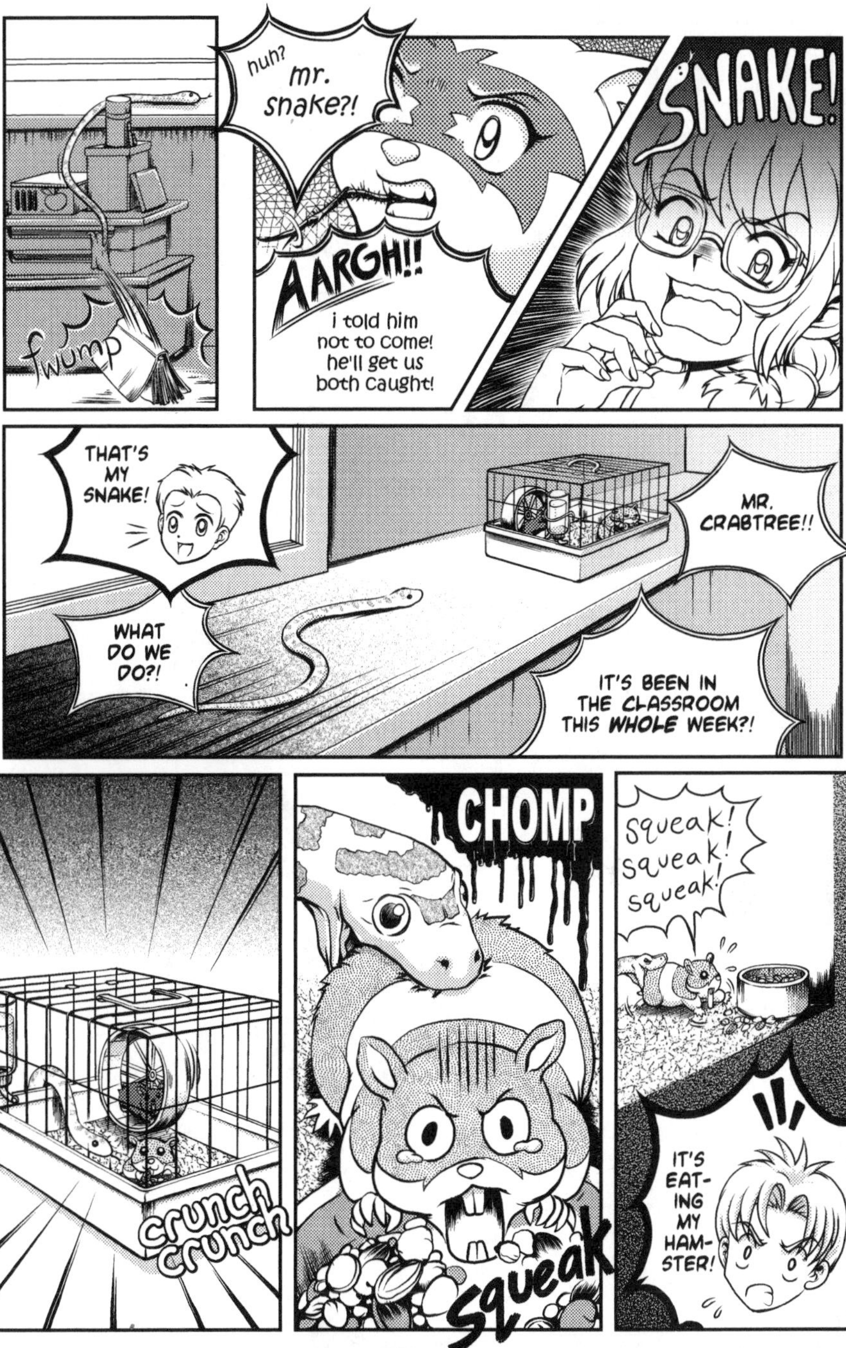
fwump
huh? mr. snake?!
AARGH!!
i told him not to come! he'll get us both caught!
SNAKE!
THAT'S MY SNAKE!
WHAT DO WE DO?!
MR. CRABTREE!!
IT'S BEEN IN THE CLASSROOM THIS WHOLE WEEK?!
crunch crunch
CHOMP
squeak
squeak! squeak! squeak!
IT'S EAT-ING MY HAM-STER!

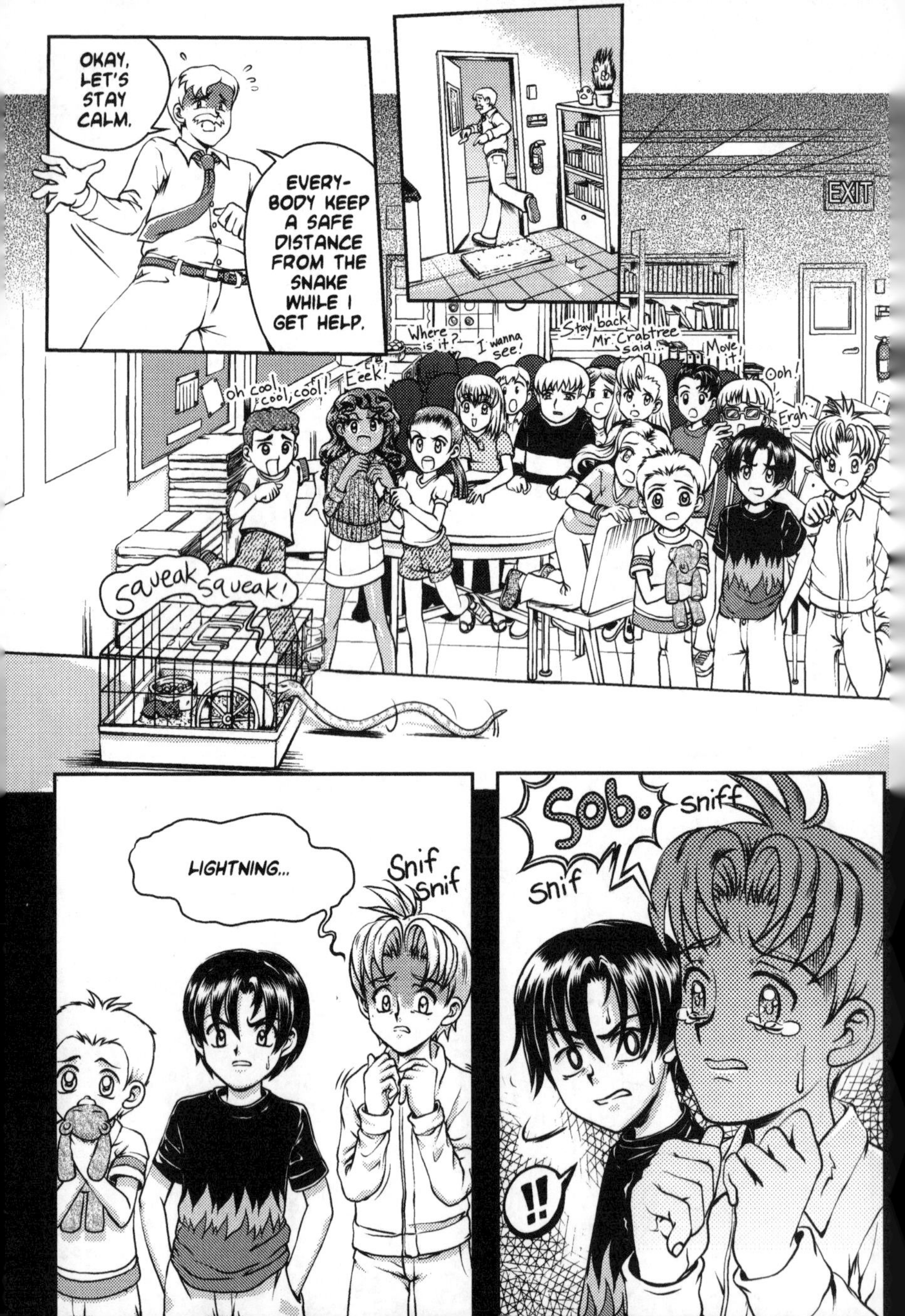

OKAY, LET'S STAY CALM.
EVERY-BODY KEEP A SAFE DISTANCE FROM THE SNAKE WHILE I GET HELP.
EXIT
oh cool cool, cool!
Eeek!
Where is it?
I wanna see!
Stay back Mr. Crabtree said...
Move it!
Ooh!
Ergh
squeak squeak!
LIGHTNING...
Snif snif
Sob.
sniff
snif
!!

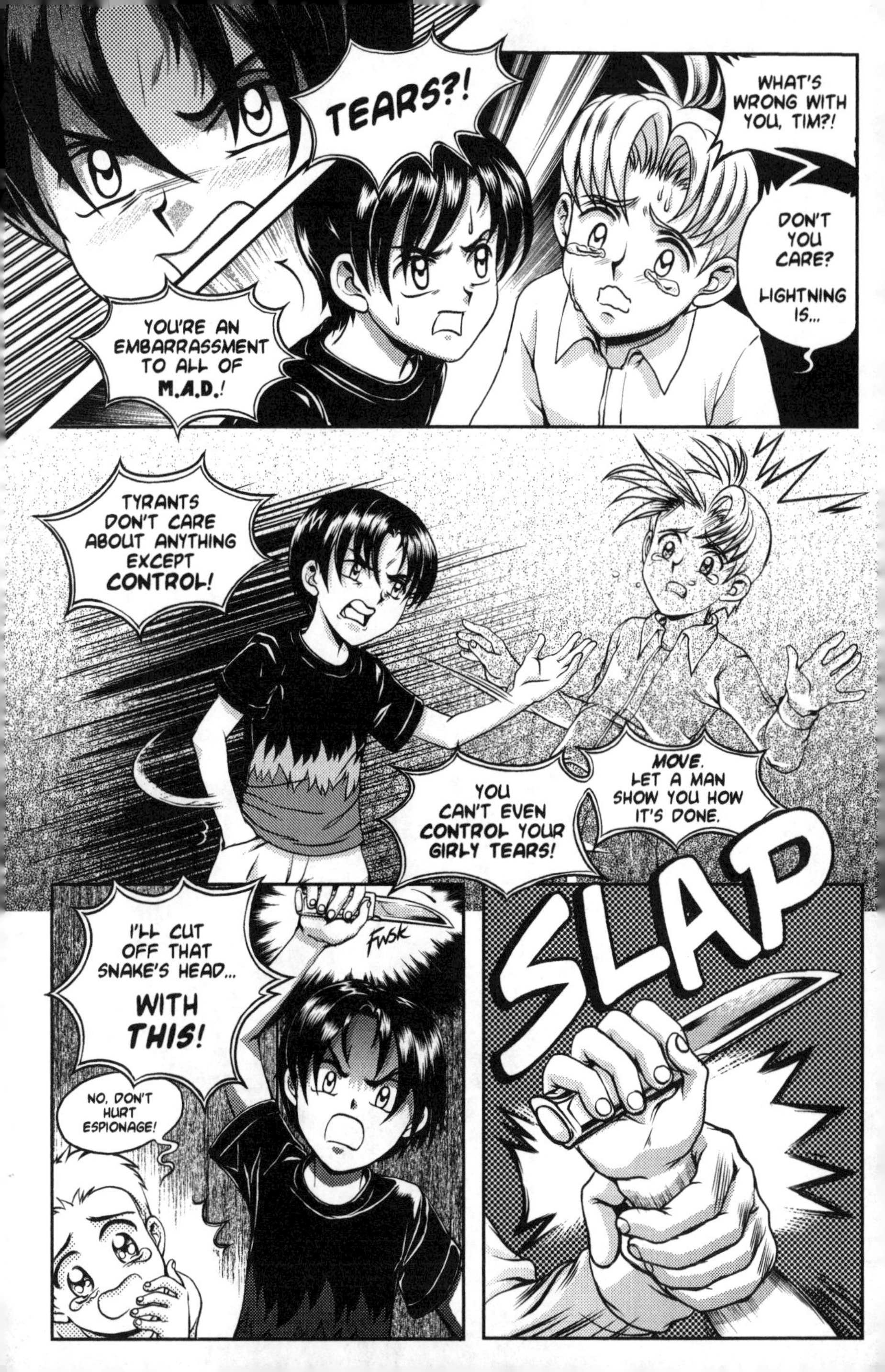
TEARS?!
WHAT'S WRONG WITH YOU, TIM?!
DON'T YOU CARE?
LIGHTNING IS...
YOU'RE AN EMBARRASSMENT TO ALL OF M.A.D.!
TYRANTS DON'T CARE ABOUT ANYTHING EXCEPT CONTROL!
YOU CAN'T EVEN CONTROL YOUR GIRLY TEARS!
MOVE. LET A MAN SHOW YOU HOW IT'S DONE.
I'LL CUT OFF THAT SNAKE'S HEAD... WITH THIS!
FWSK
NO, DON'T HURT ESPIONAGE!
SLAP

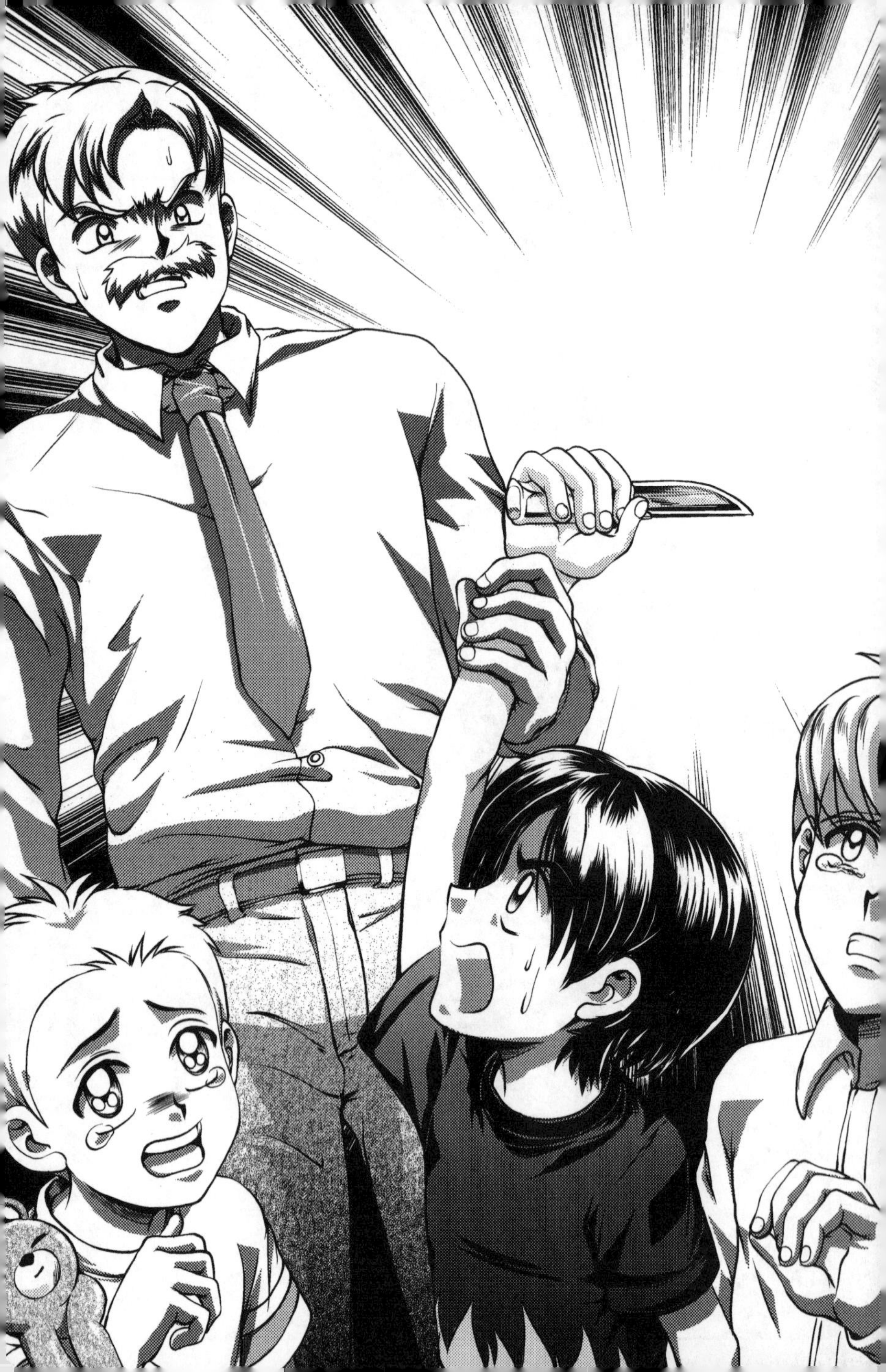

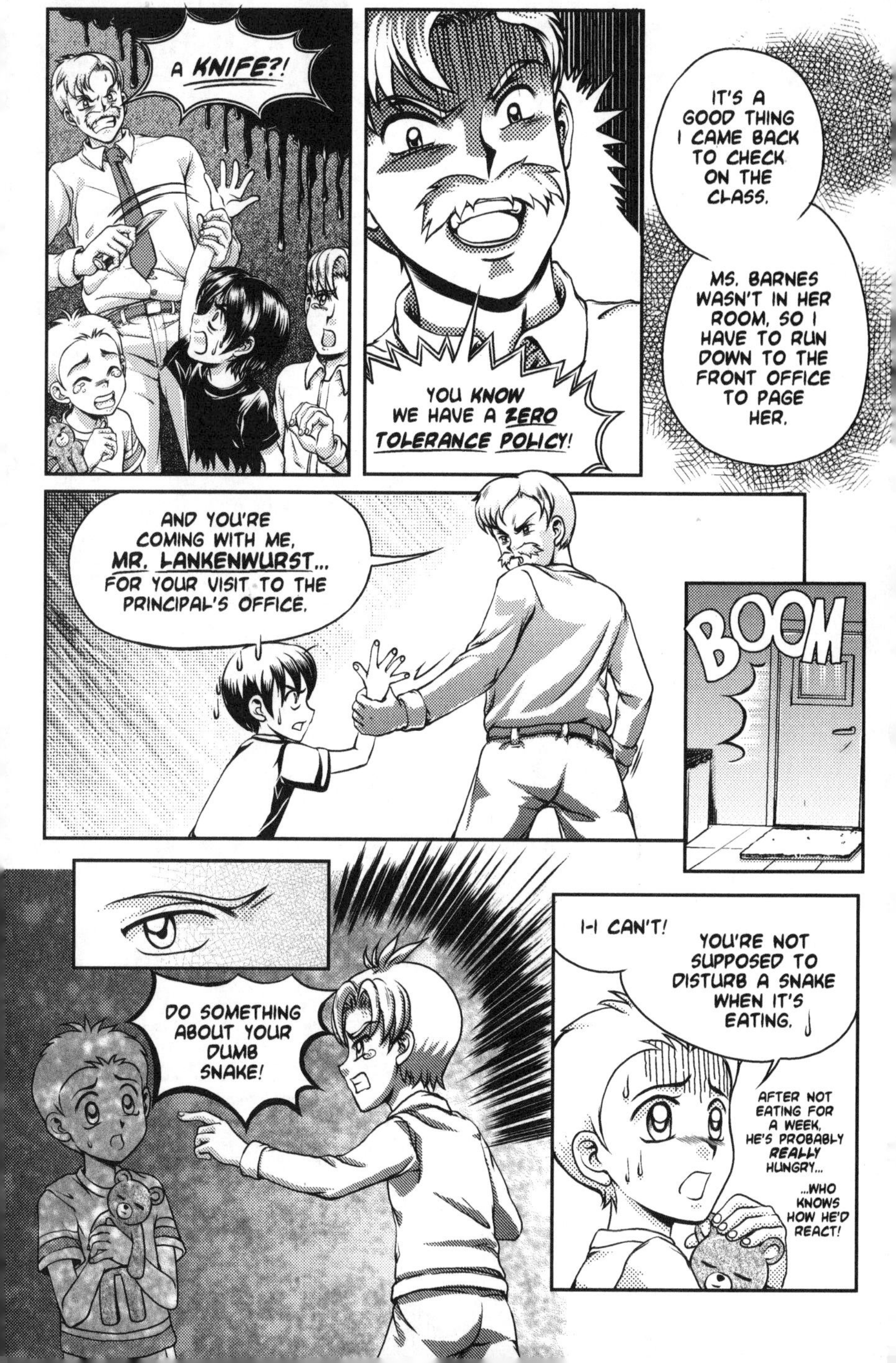
A KNIFE?!
YOU KNOW WE HAVE A ZERO TOLERANCE POLICY!
IT'S A GOOD THING I CAME BACK TO CHECK ON THE CLASS.
MS. BARNES WASN'T IN HER ROOM, SO I HAVE TO RUN DOWN TO THE FRONT OFFICE TO PAGE HER.
AND YOU'RE COMING WITH ME, MR. LANKENWURST... FOR YOUR VISIT TO THE PRINCIPAL'S OFFICE.
BOOM
DO SOMETHING ABOUT YOUR DUMB SNAKE!
I-I CAN'T!
YOU'RE NOT SUPPOSED TO DISTURB A SNAKE WHEN IT'S EATING.
AFTER NOT EATING FOR A WEEK, HE'S PROBABLY REALLY HUNGRY...
...WHO KNOWS HOW HE'D REACT!

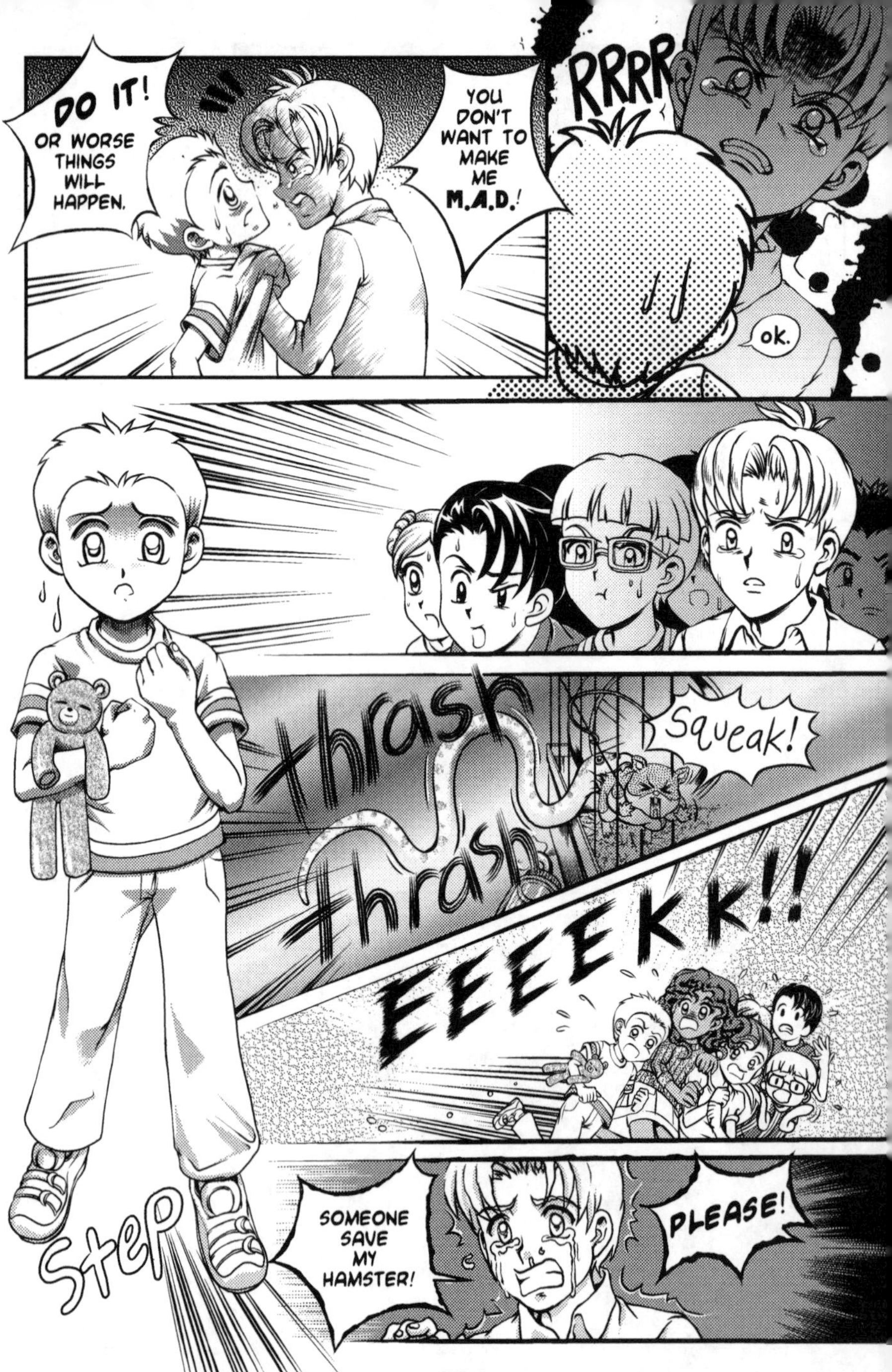
DO IT! OR WORSE THINGS WILL HAPPEN.
YOU DON'T WANT TO MAKE ME M.A.D.!
RRRR
ok.
thrash
thrash
Squeak!
EEEEKK!!
Step
SOMEONE SAVE MY HAMSTER!
PLEASE!

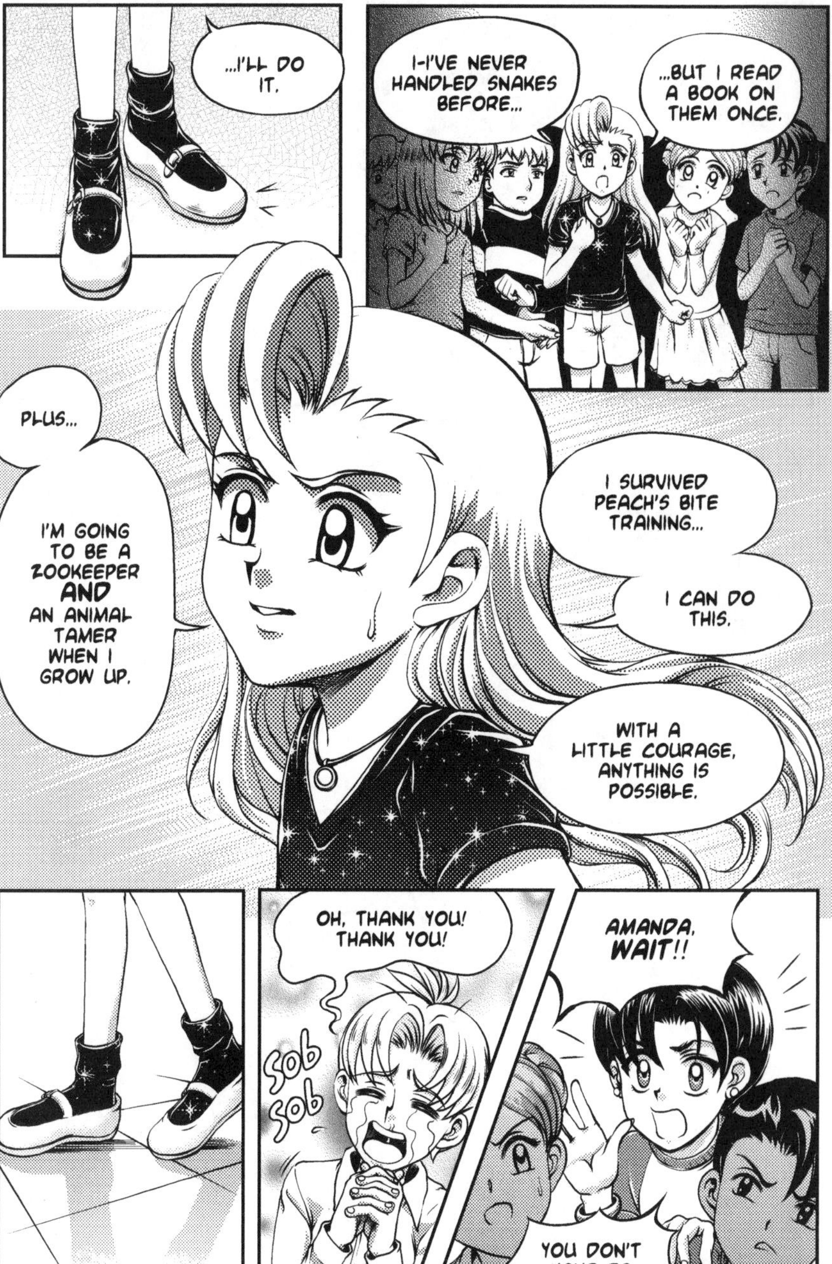
...I'LL DO IT.
I-I'VE NEVER HANDLED SNAKES BEFORE...
...BUT I READ A BOOK ON THEM ONCE.
PLUS...
I'M GOING TO BE A ZOOKEEPER **AND** AN ANIMAL TAMER WHEN I GROW UP.
I SURVIVED PEACH'S BITE TRAINING...
I CAN DO THIS.
WITH A LITTLE COURAGE, ANYTHING IS POSSIBLE.
OH, THANK YOU! THANK YOU!
Sob sob
AMANDA, **WAIT**!!
YOU DON'T HAVE TO DO THIS!

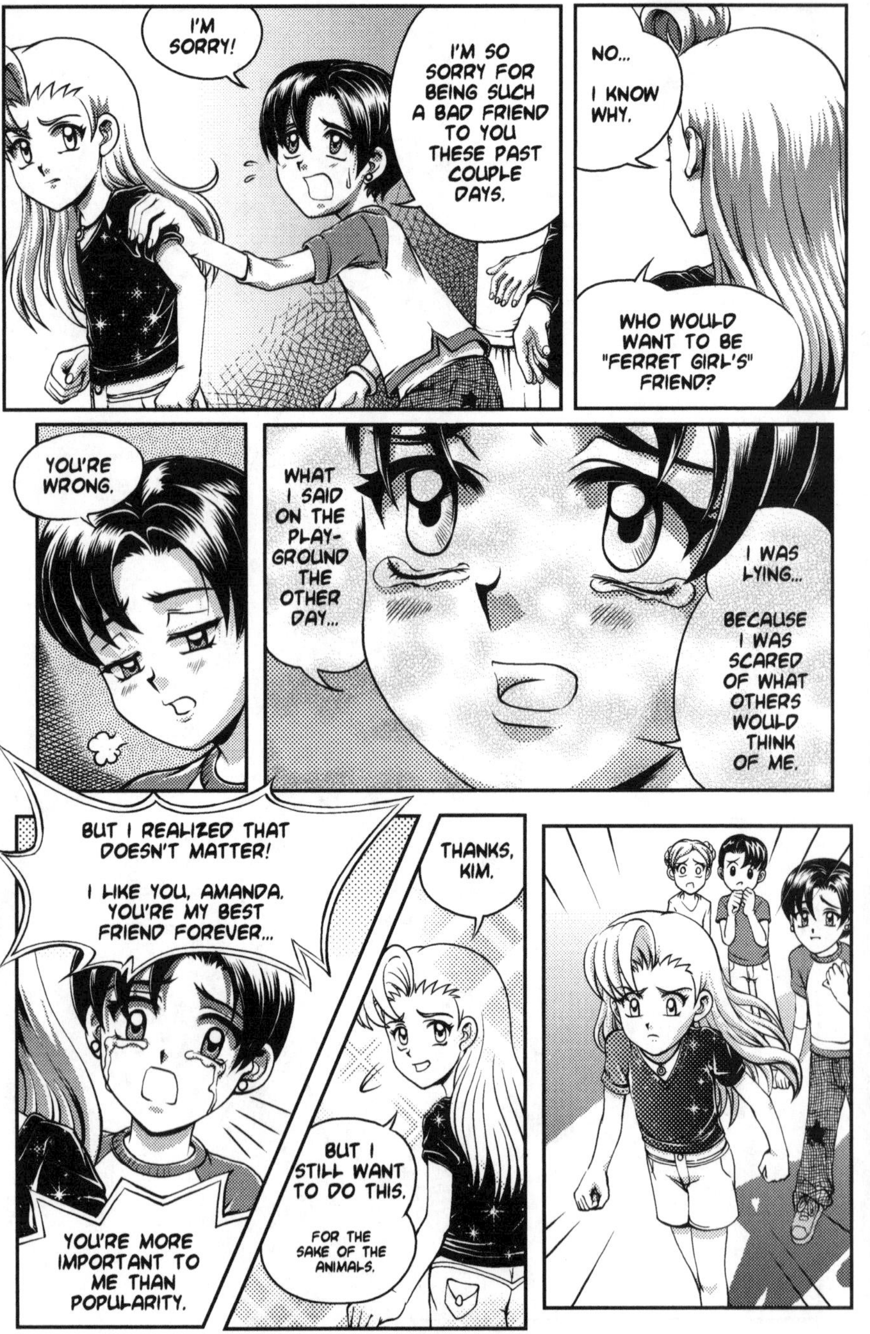
I'M SORRY!
I'M SO SORRY FOR BEING SUCH A BAD FRIEND TO YOU THESE PAST COUPLE DAYS.
NO... I KNOW WHY.
WHO WOULD WANT TO BE "FERRET GIRL'S" FRIEND?
YOU'RE WRONG.
WHAT I SAID ON THE PLAY-GROUND THE OTHER DAY...
I WAS LYING... BECAUSE I WAS SCARED OF WHAT OTHERS WOULD THINK OF ME.
BUT I REALIZED THAT DOESN'T MATTER!
I LIKE YOU, AMANDA. YOU'RE MY BEST FRIEND FOREVER...
YOU'RE MORE IMPORTANT TO ME THAN POPULARITY.
THANKS, KIM.
BUT I STILL WANT TO DO THIS.
FOR THE SAKE OF THE ANIMALS.

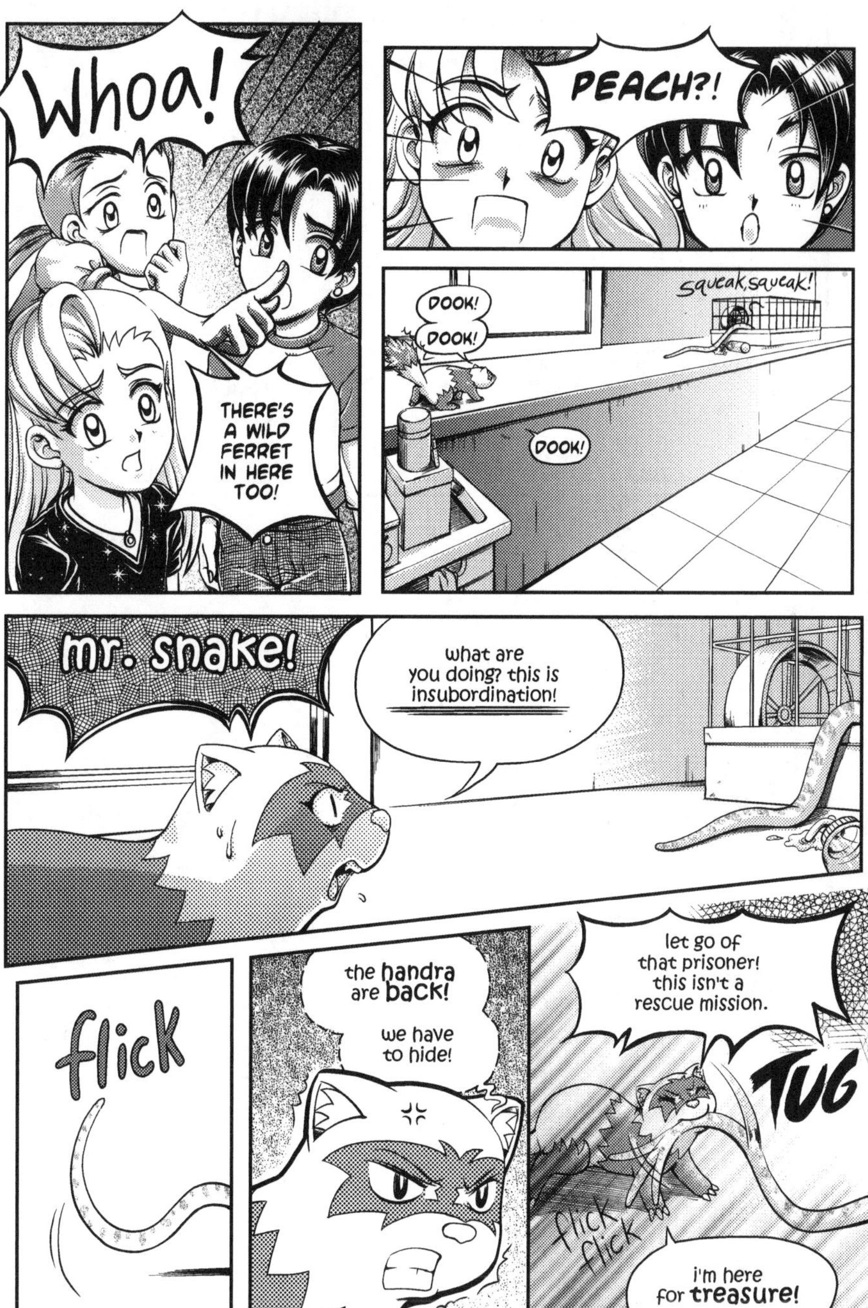
Whoa!
THERE'S A WILD FERRET IN HERE TOO!
PEACH?!
DOOK!
DOOK!
squeak, squeak!
DOOK!
mr. snake!
what are you doing? this is insubordination!
flick
the handra are back!
we have to hide!
let go of that prisoner! this isn't a rescue mission.
TUG
flick flick
i'm here for treasure!

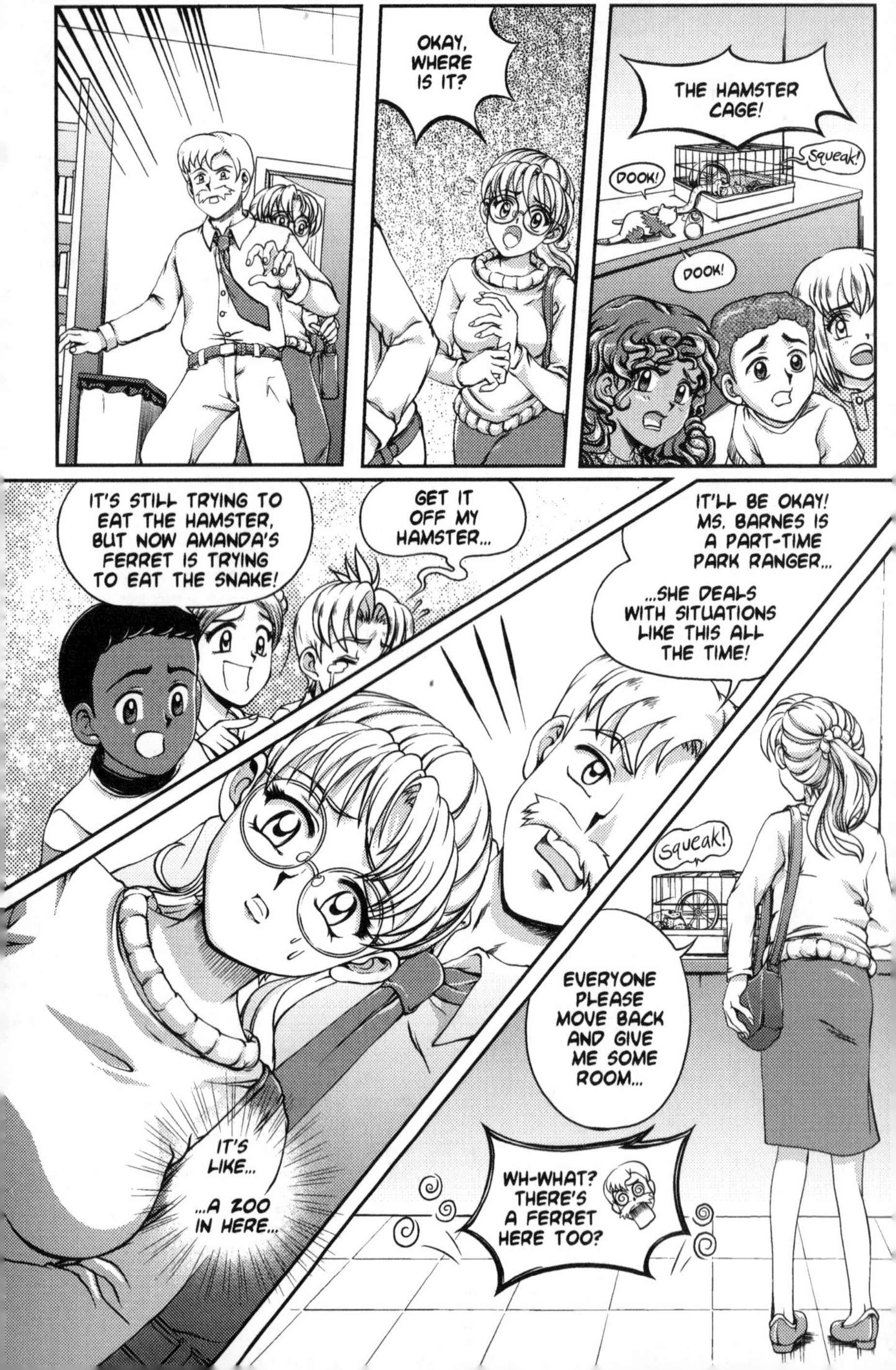
OKAY, WHERE IS IT?
THE HAMSTER CAGE!
DOOK!
Squeak!
DOOK!
IT'S STILL TRYING TO EAT THE HAMSTER, BUT NOW AMANDA'S FERRET IS TRYING TO EAT THE SNAKE!
GET IT OFF MY HAMSTER...
IT'LL BE OKAY! MS. BARNES IS A PART-TIME PARK RANGER...
...SHE DEALS WITH SITUATIONS LIKE THIS ALL THE TIME!
Squeak!
EVERYONE PLEASE MOVE BACK AND GIVE ME SOME ROOM...
IT'S LIKE...
...A ZOO IN HERE...
WH-WHAT? THERE'S A FERRET HERE TOO?

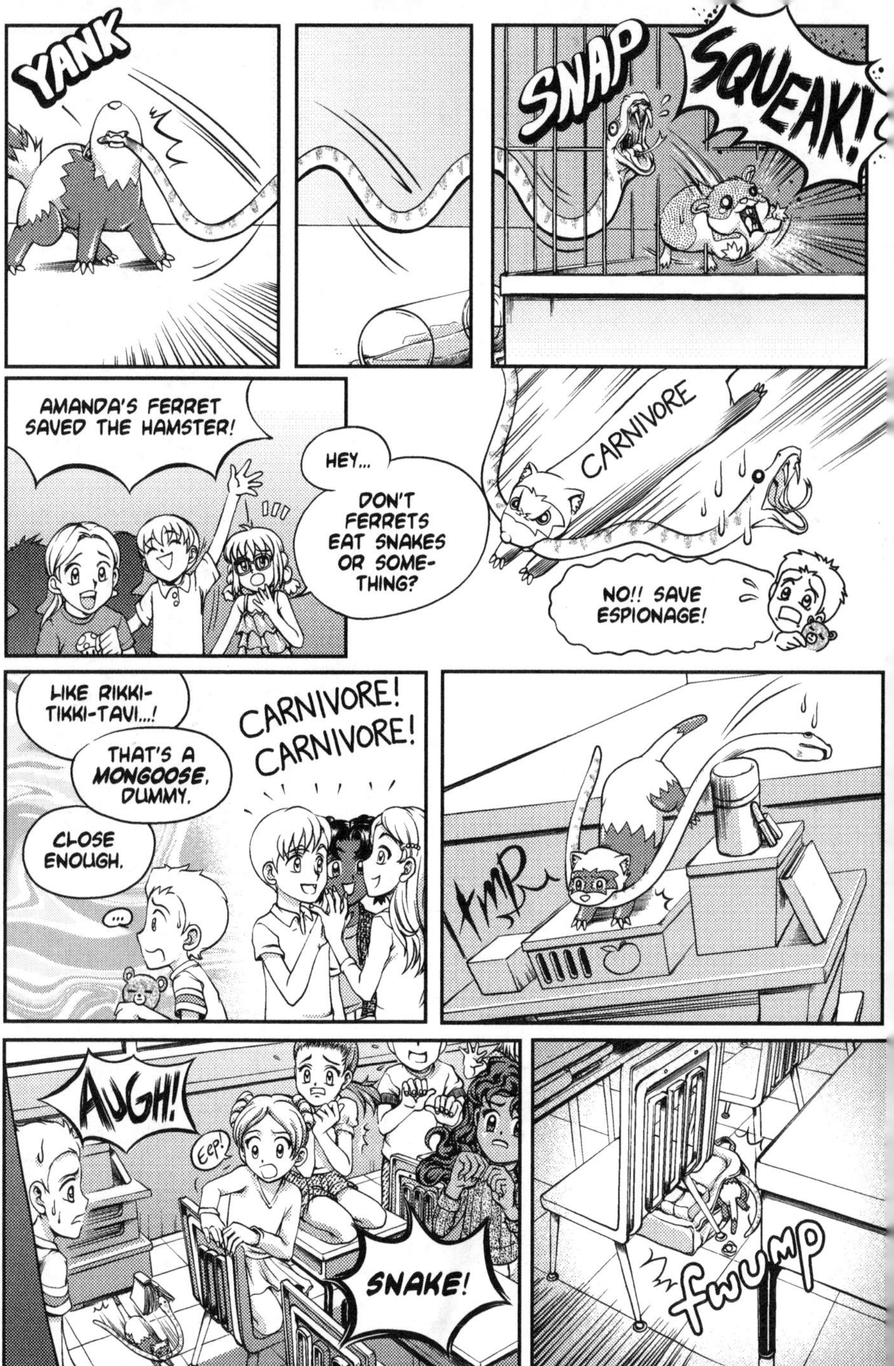
YANK
SNAP
SQUEAK!
AMANDA'S FERRET SAVED THE HAMSTER!
HEY...
DON'T FERRETS EAT SNAKES OR SOME-THING?
CARNIVORE
NO!! SAVE ESPIONAGE!
LIKE RIKKI-TIKKI-TAVI...!
THAT'S A MONGOOSE, DUMMY.
CLOSE ENOUGH.
CARNIVORE! CARNIVORE!
...
AUGH!
Eep!
SNAKE!
fwump

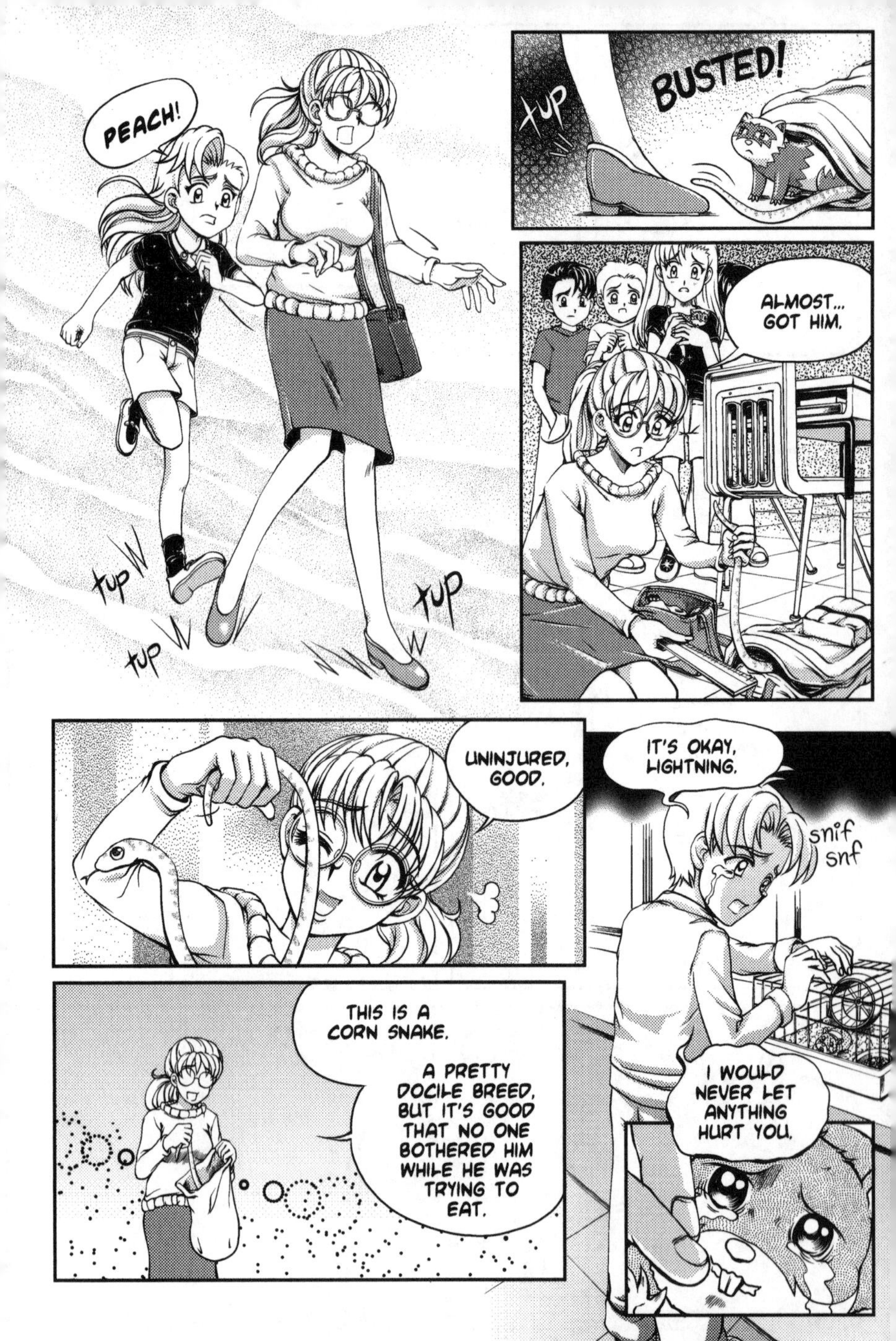
PEACH!
tup
tup
tup
BUSTED!
tup
ALMOST... GOT HIM.
UNINJURED. GOOD.
THIS IS A CORN SNAKE.
A PRETTY DOCILE BREED, BUT IT'S GOOD THAT NO ONE BOTHERED HIM WHILE HE WAS TRYING TO EAT.
IT'S OKAY, LIGHTNING.
snif snf
I WOULD NEVER LET ANYTHING HURT YOU.

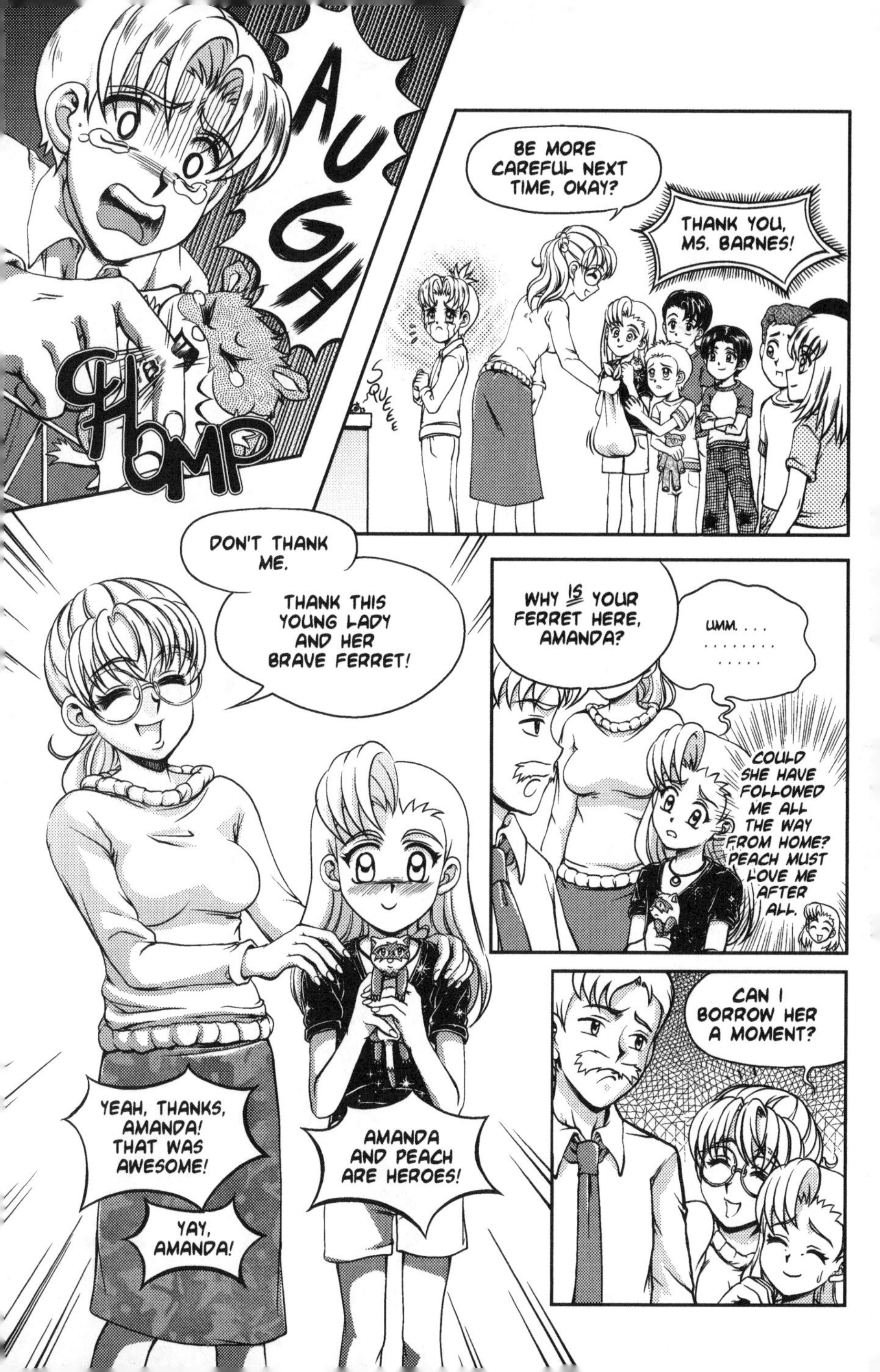
AUGH
CHOMP
SQUEEE
BE MORE CAREFUL NEXT TIME, OKAY?
THANK YOU, MS. BARNES!
DON'T THANK ME.
THANK THIS YOUNG LADY AND HER BRAVE FERRET!
YEAH, THANKS, AMANDA! THAT WAS AWESOME!
YAY, AMANDA!
AMANDA AND PEACH ARE HEROES!
WHY IS YOUR FERRET HERE, AMANDA?
UMM. . . . .
COULD SHE HAVE FOLLOWED ME ALL THE WAY FROM HOME? PEACH MUST LOVE ME AFTER ALL.
CAN I BORROW HER A MOMENT?

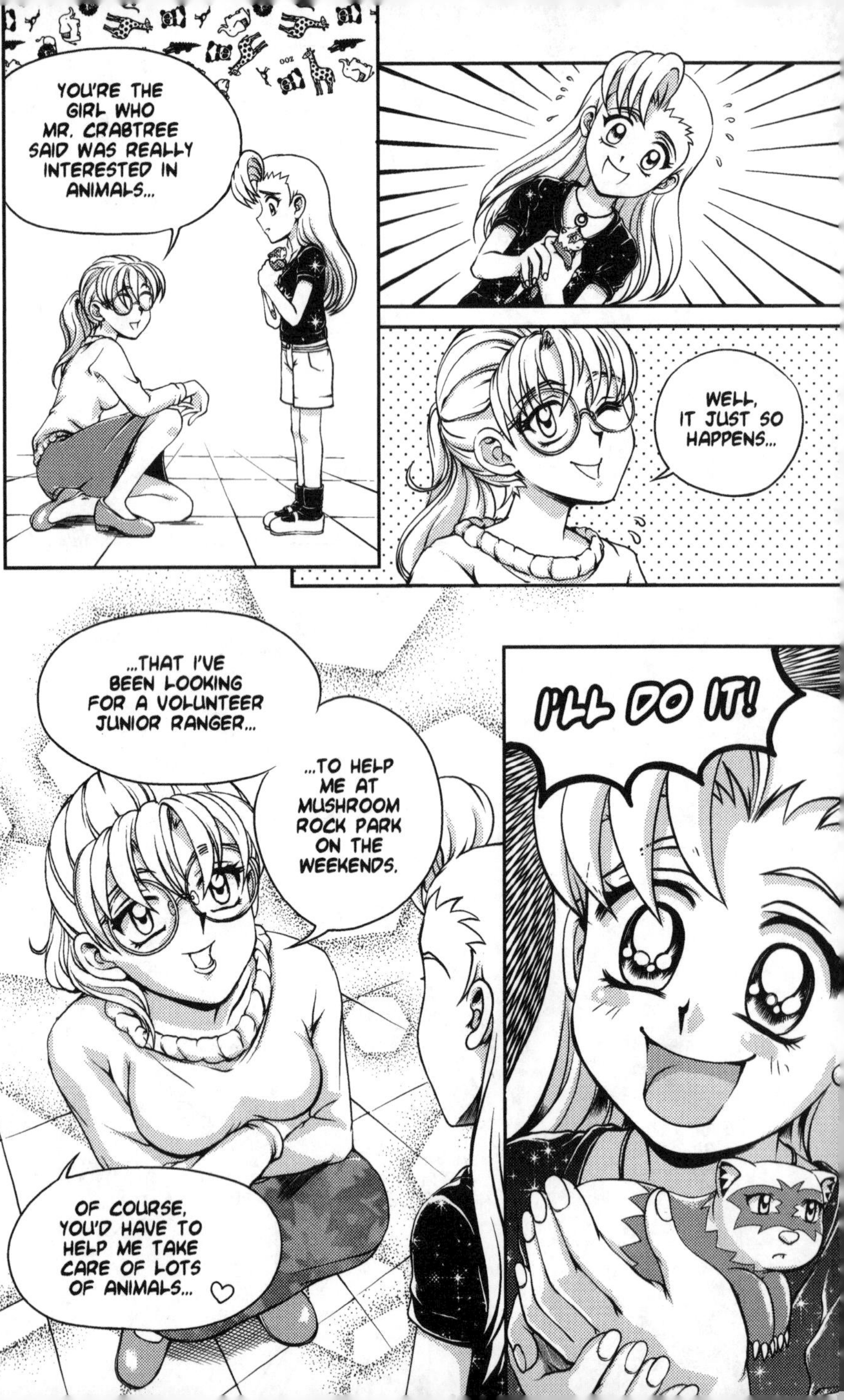
YOU'RE THE GIRL WHO MR. CRABTREE SAID WAS REALLY INTERESTED IN ANIMALS...
WELL, IT JUST SO HAPPENS...
...THAT I'VE BEEN LOOKING FOR A VOLUNTEER JUNIOR RANGER...
...TO HELP ME AT MUSHROOM ROCK PARK ON THE WEEKENDS.
OF COURSE, YOU'D HAVE TO HELP ME TAKE CARE OF LOTS OF ANIMALS... ♡
I'LL DO IT!

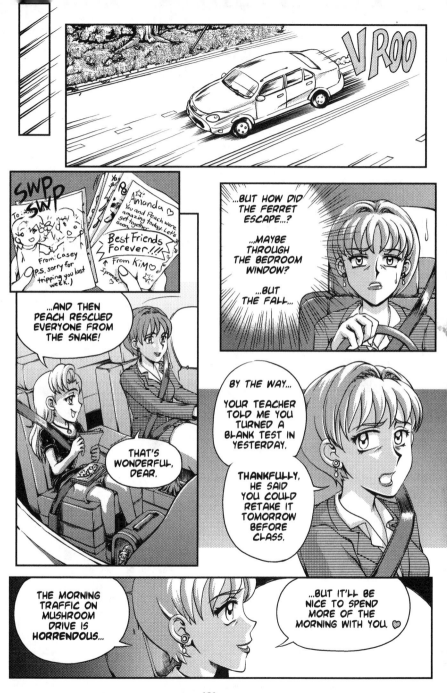

VROO

SWP SWP

To: ...
★Amanda♥
You and Peach were amazing today. Let's get together soon.

From: Casey
(P.S. sorry for tripping you last week.)

Best Friends Forever!!!
→ From KiMO
I promise I...

...BUT HOW DID THE FERRET ESCAPE...?

...MAYBE THROUGH THE BEDROOM WINDOW?

...BUT THE FALL...

...AND THEN PEACH RESCUED EVERYONE FROM THE SNAKE!

THAT'S WONDERFUL, DEAR.

BY THE WAY...

YOUR TEACHER TOLD ME YOU TURNED A BLANK TEST IN YESTERDAY.

THANKFULLY, HE SAID YOU COULD RETAKE IT TOMORROW BEFORE CLASS.

THE MORNING TRAFFIC ON MUSHROOM DRIVE IS HORRENDOUS...

...BUT IT'LL BE NICE TO SPEND MORE OF THE MORNING WITH YOU. ♡

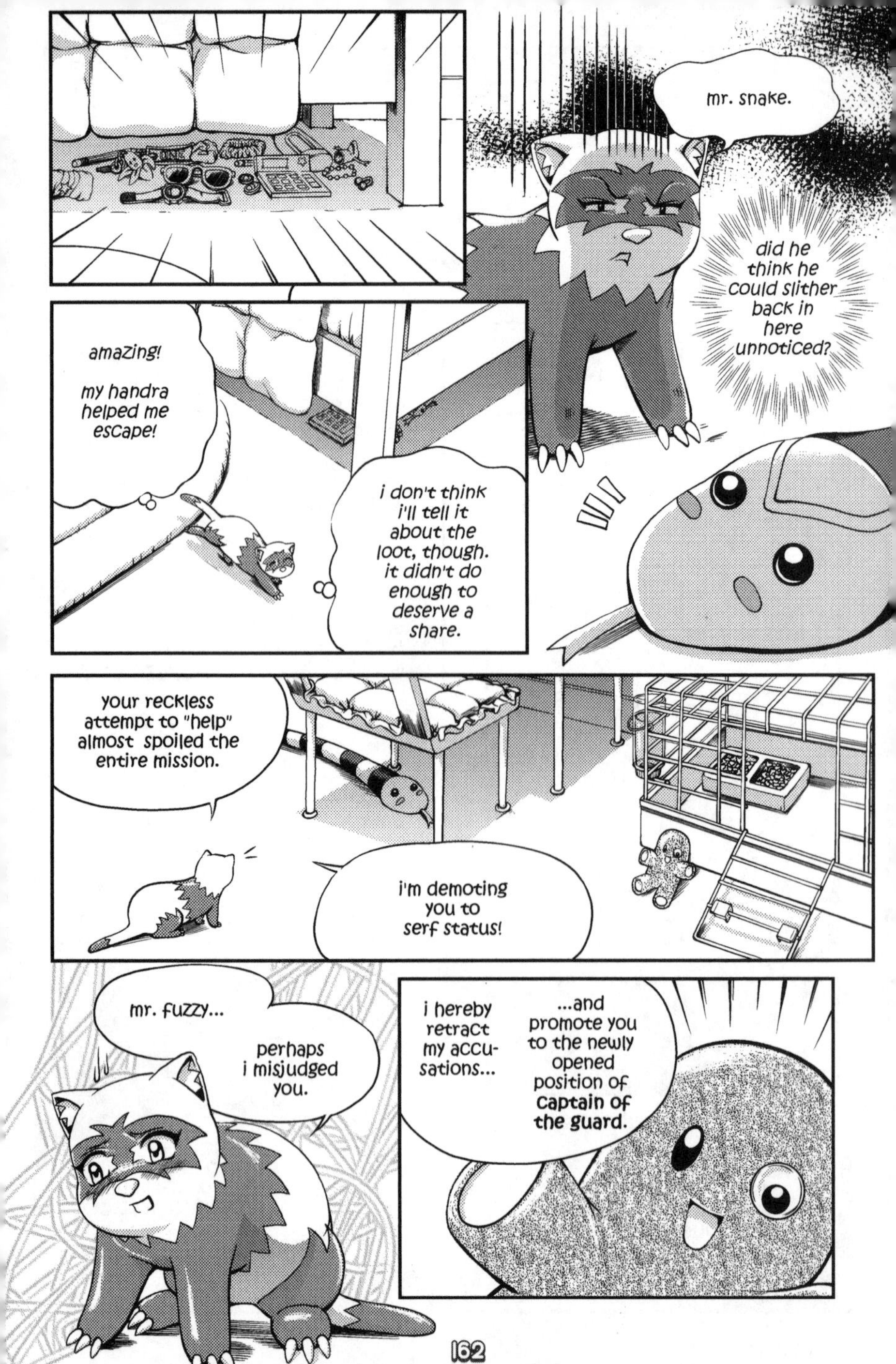
mr. snake.
did he think he could slither back in here unnoticed?
amazing!
my handra helped me escape!
i don't think i'll tell it about the loot, though. it didn't do enough to deserve a share.
your reckless attempt to "help" almost spoiled the entire mission.
i'm demoting you to serf status!
mr. fuzzy...
perhaps i misjudged you.
i hereby retract my accu-sations...
...and promote you to the newly opened position of **captain of the guard.**

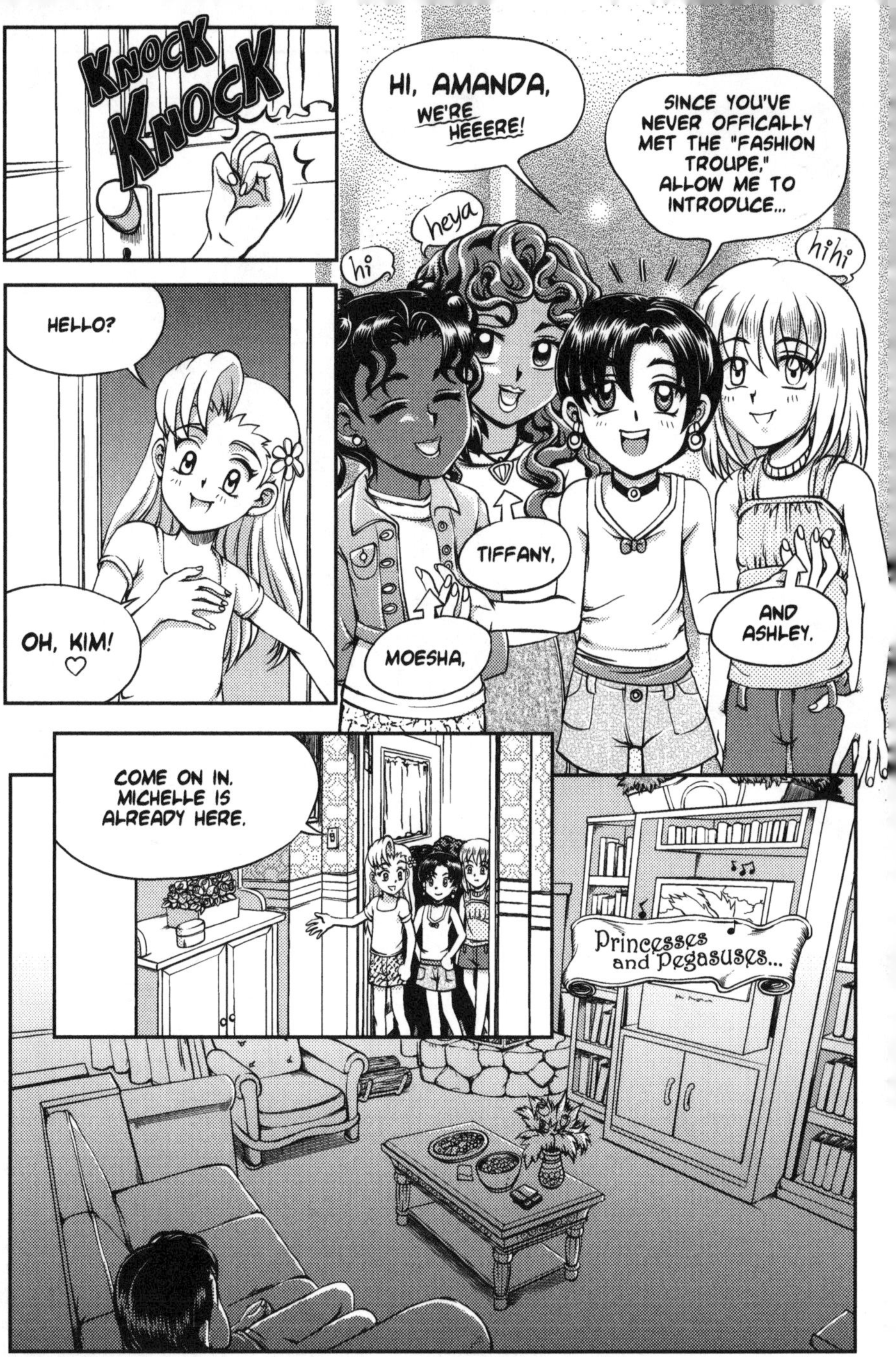
KNOCK KNOCK
HELLO?
OH, KIM! ♡
HI, AMANDA, WE'RE HEEERE!
SINCE YOU'VE NEVER OFFICALLY MET THE "FASHION TROUPE," ALLOW ME TO INTRODUCE...
hi
heya
hihi
MOESHA,
TIFFANY,
AND ASHLEY.
COME ON IN. MICHELLE IS ALREADY HERE.
Princesses and Pegasuses...

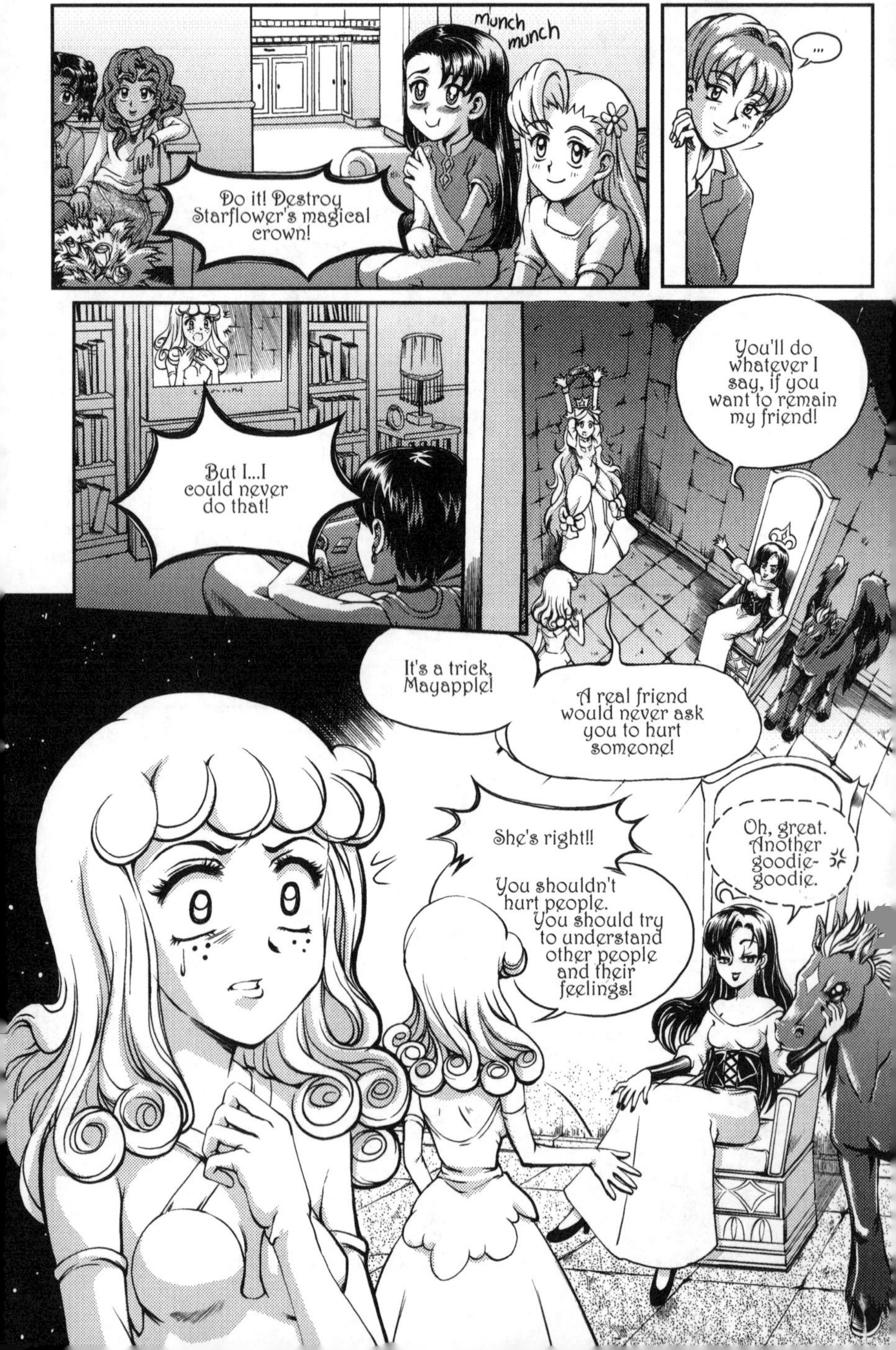
munch munch
Do it! Destroy Starflower's magical crown!
...
But I...I could never do that!
You'll do whatever I say, if you want to remain my friend!
It's a trick, Mayapple!
A real friend would never ask you to hurt someone!
She's right!!
You shouldn't hurt people. You should try to understand other people and their feelings!
Oh, great. Another goodie-goodie.

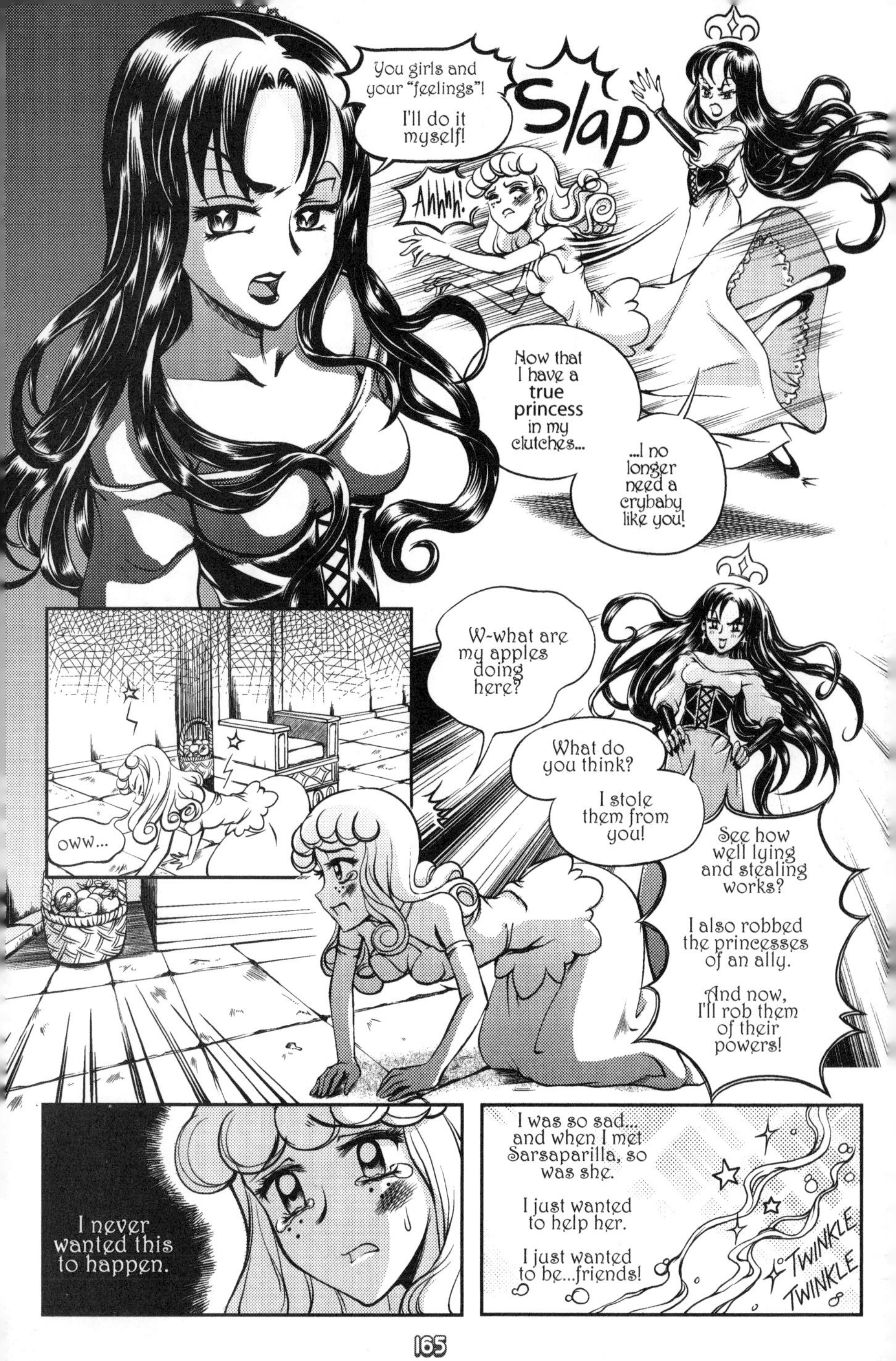

You girls and your "feelings"! I'll do it myself!
Slap
Ahhhh!
Now that I have a true princess in my clutches...
...I no longer need a crybaby like you!
oww...
W-what are my apples doing here?
What do you think?
I stole them from you!
See how well lying and stealing works?
I also robbed the princesses of an ally.
And now, I'll rob them of their powers!
I never wanted this to happen.
I was so sad... and when I met Sarsaparilla, so was she.
I just wanted to help her.
I just wanted to be...friends!
TWINKLE TWINKLE

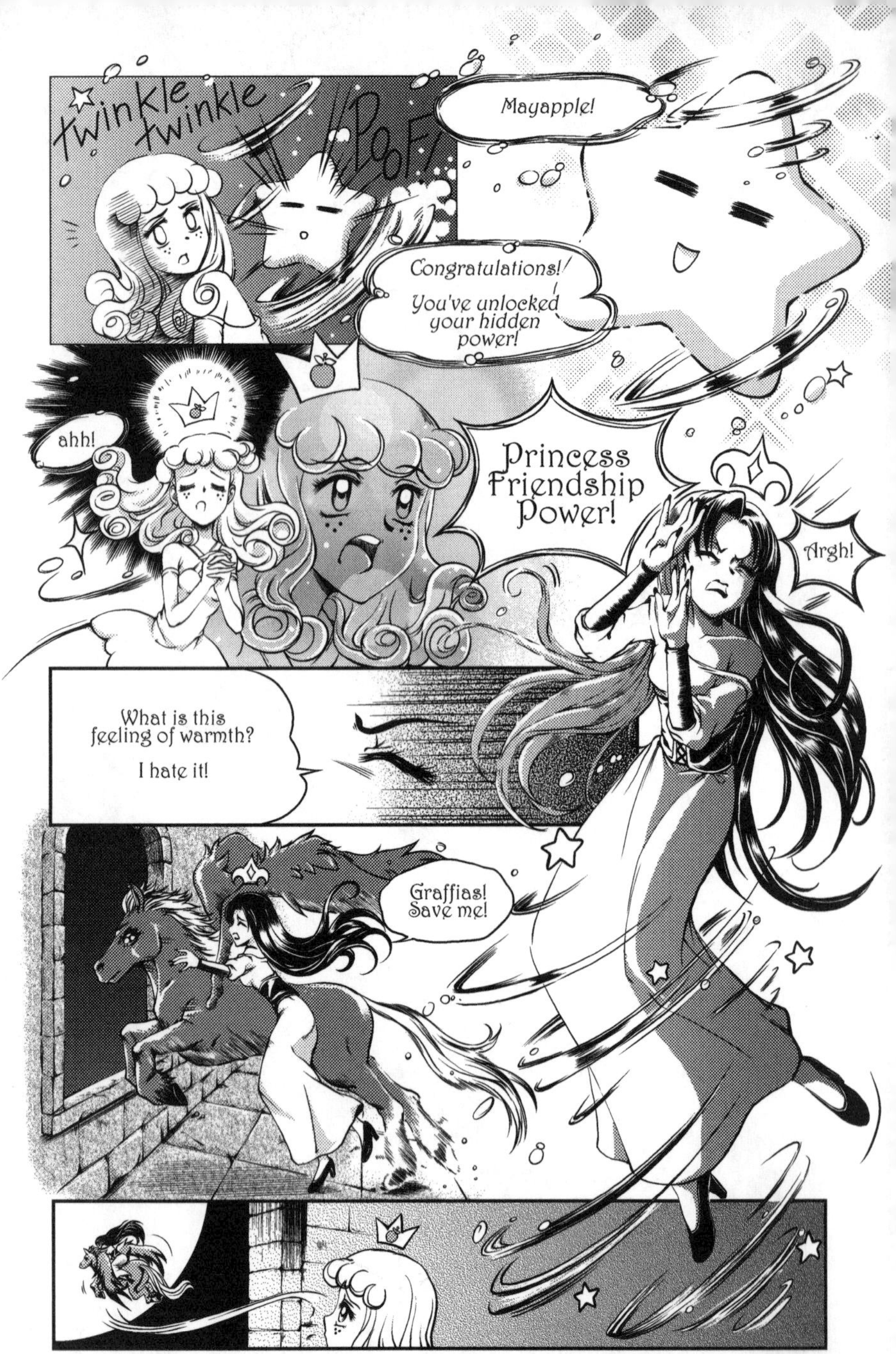
twinkle twinkle
POOF!
Mayapple!
Congratulations!
You've unlocked your hidden power!
ahh!
Princess Friendship Power!
Argh!
What is this feeling of warmth?
I hate it!
Graffias! Save me!

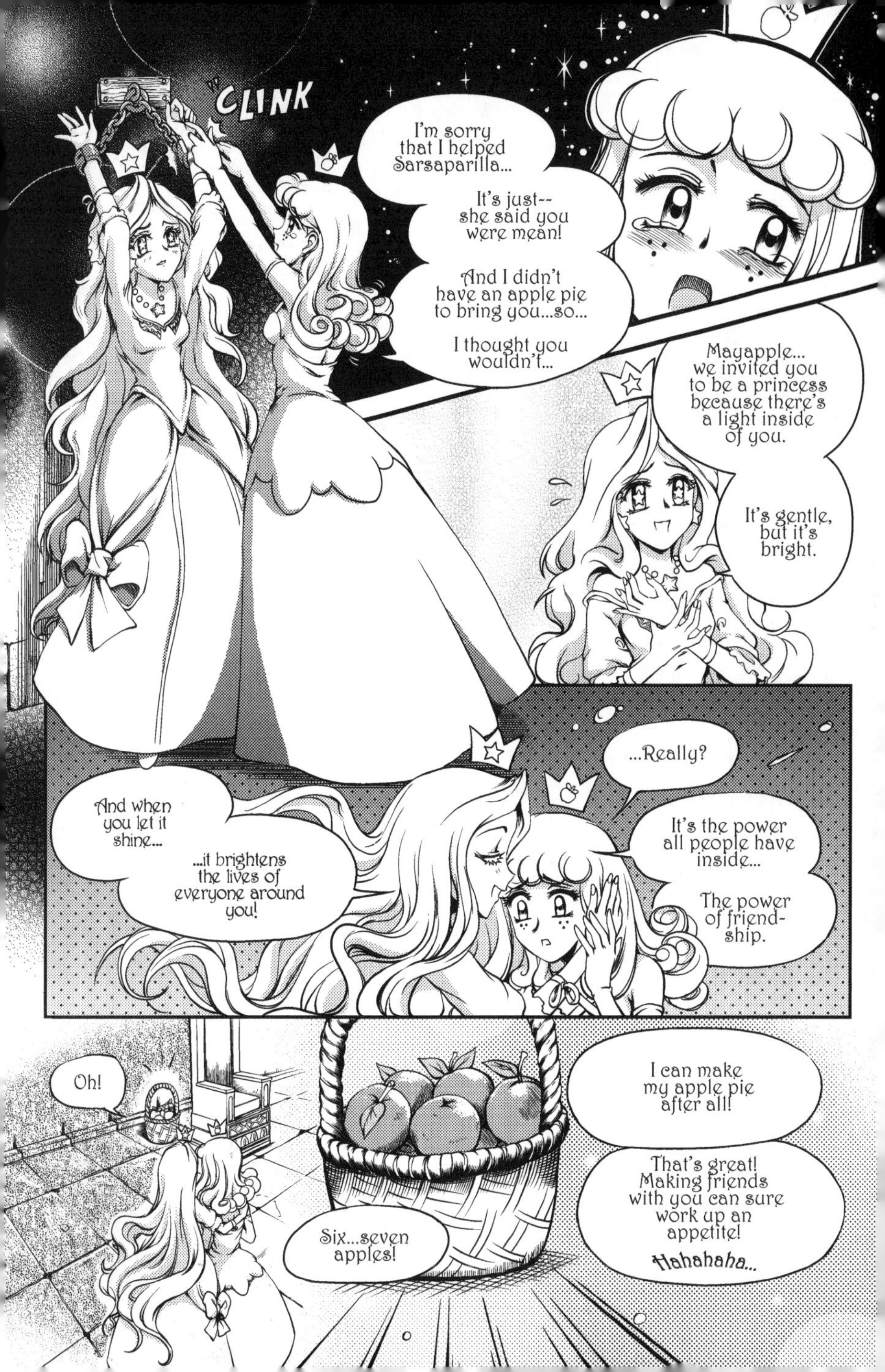
CLINK
I'm sorry that I helped Sarsaparilla...
It's just-- she said you were mean!
And I didn't have an apple pie to bring you...so...
I thought you wouldn't...
Mayapple... we invited you to be a princess because there's a light inside of you.
It's gentle, but it's bright.
...Really?
And when you let it shine...
...it brightens the lives of everyone around you!
It's the power all people have inside...
The power of friend-ship.
Oh!
I can make my apple pie after all!
Six...seven apples!
That's great! Making friends with you can sure work up an appetite!
Hahahaha...

hahaha!
THANKS FOR HAVING US OVER, AMANDA.
TIM SAID YOU WERE STUCK-UP, BUT IT'S CLEAR THAT HE WAS LYING.
I HOPE HE GETS EXPELLED.
I...
I'VE ALWAYS WANTED TO BE YOUR FRIEND, BUT I NEVER KNEW WHAT TO SAY.
WHEN YOU WORE THAT COSTUME TO SCHOOL, IT GAVE ME THE COURAGE TO APPROACH YOU.
AND SO, AMANDA MADE SOME NEW FRIENDS, AND STRENGHTENED HER TIES WITH EXISTING ONES.

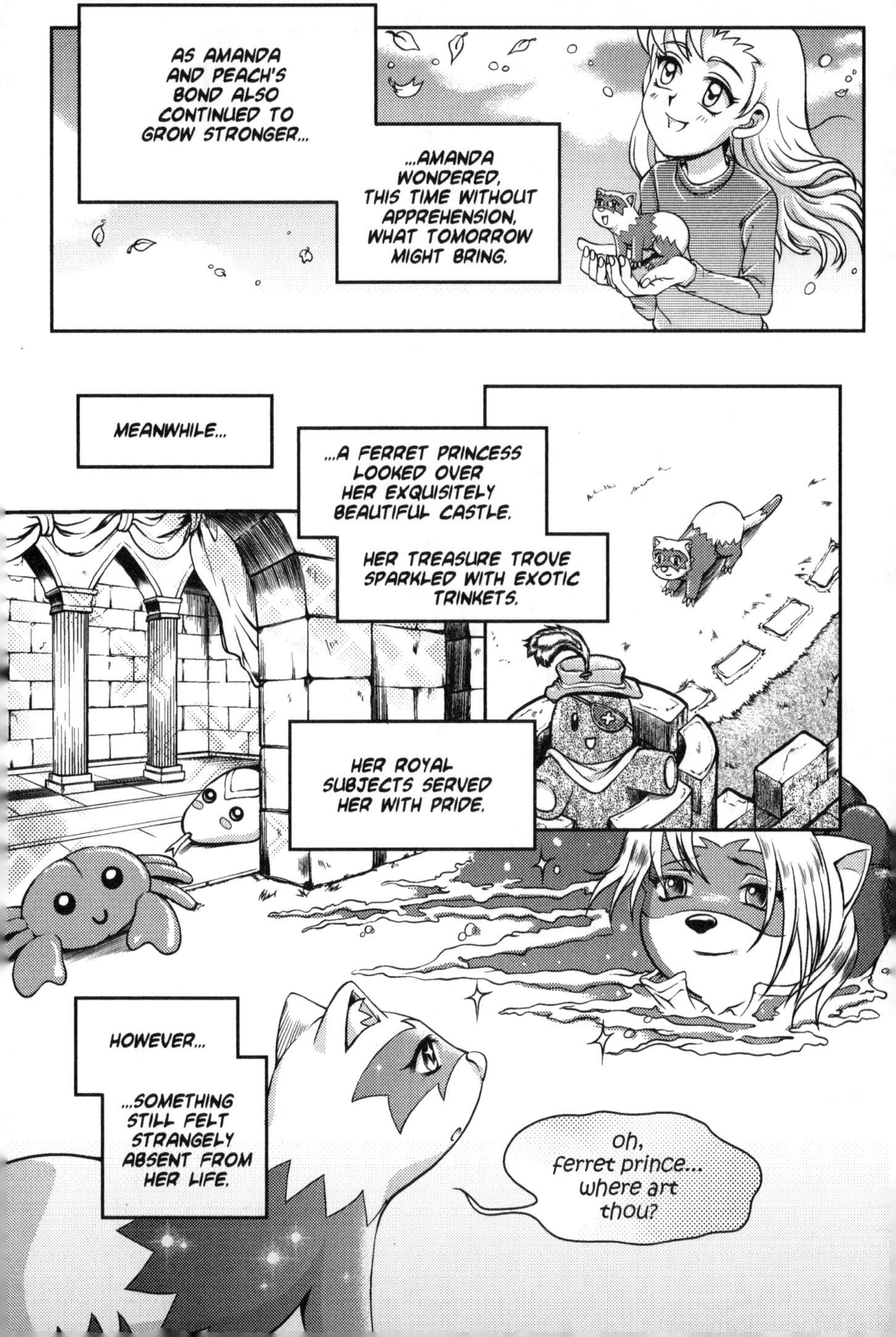
AS AMANDA AND PEACH'S BOND ALSO CONTINUED TO GROW STRONGER...
...AMANDA WONDERED, THIS TIME WITHOUT APPREHENSION, WHAT TOMORROW MIGHT BRING.
MEANWHILE...
...A FERRET PRINCESS LOOKED OVER HER EXQUISITELY BEAUTIFUL CASTLE.
HER TREASURE TROVE SPARKLED WITH EXOTIC TRINKETS.
HER ROYAL SUBJECTS SERVED HER WITH PRIDE.
HOWEVER...
...SOMETHING STILL FELT STRANGELY ABSENT FROM HER LIFE.
oh, ferret prince... where art thou?

Peach Fuzz

presents

Ferret Terminology

starring: PAVARATTY

ferret extraordinaire

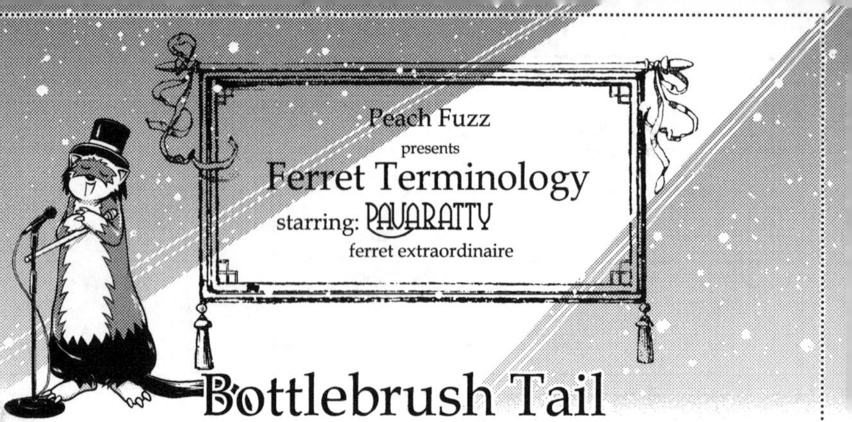

Bottlebrush Tail

(A.K.A. Christmas Tree, Pipe Cleaner, Pinecone)

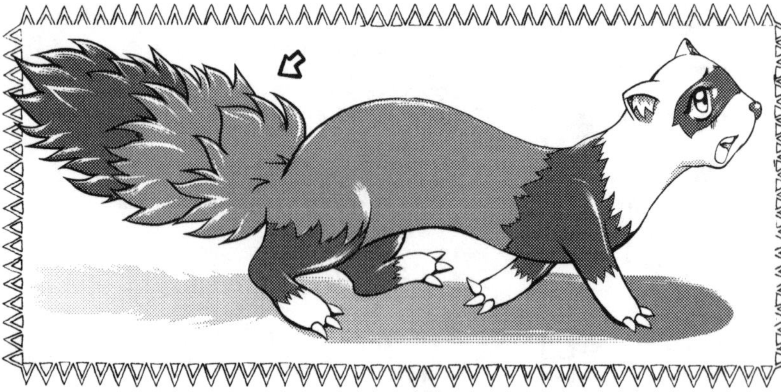

Handlers have so many names for this condition. Bottlebrushing happens when ferrets become excited or scared. All of our emotions go straight to our tails. Our bristly fur puffs up and sticks straight out, demanding attention, and making us appear larger to potential threats.

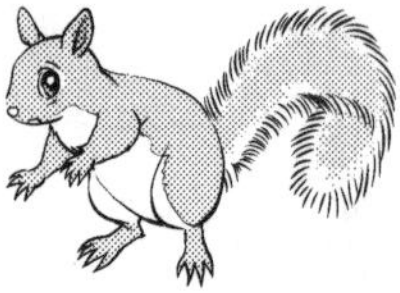

Fig. 1.1
Squirrel.
Bushy tail indicates
a life of constant fear.

This happens often when encountering new sights, smells, objects, and Handlers. It's all too much, and we can't control it! Some ferrets are embarrassed by this condition and would prefer their tail to be left alone until the fur subsides. Fortunately, it does return to normal after a couple of minutes. If it doesn't, something might be wrong. We're not squirrels, after all. (Fig. 1.1)

Handlers should be cautious of ferrets when their tails are puffed, because while it may indicate excitement, it may also mean the ferret is frightened, especially if accompanied by a quick retreat or hissing.

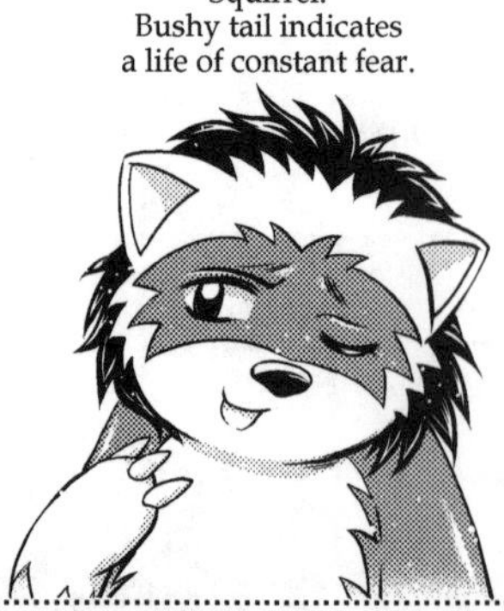

PEACH'S
MONSTER
COMPENDIUM

Note a distinct lack of body hair!

fig. 2.1

No-Fur

Even more mysterious than the Handra, No-Furs are giant ground-traveling creatures. The name No-Fur is a bit misleading. No-Furs actually do produce fur, sometimes in great quantities, but unlike ferrets, they only produce it in a few areas.

No-Furs have large shifty eyes and prehensile mouths, but are typically harmless. Despite their frightening appearance, the No-Furs seem to be mindless and benign, existing only to serve the Handra.

The Handra Connection

Handra seem to be parasites that attach themselves to the No-Fur body and feed off its nutrients. Apparently, the Handra and the No-Fur are two separate entities, with the Handra in control. How else could the Handra perform complicated tasks while the No-Fur has its attention elsewhere?

Despite these distinctions, there is a definite bond between the Handra and its host. One can see this from the way the Handra will defend its No-Fur when under attack. There's also evidence showing that Handra can feel, or are at least aware of pain in the No-Fur.

The Pedra?

Other strange monsters can be found on the bottom of the No-Fur host. They look similar to the Handra, but are strangely stunted in form and range of motion. For instance, their necks are much shorter, and as for movement, I've only observed them flail around. Perhaps these are Handra larvae, or something different altogether.

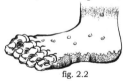

fig. 2.2

In any case, as a daily ritual, most Handra conceal these Pedra projections under a skin, then slide them into small, constricting prisons. They also use them to bear the weight of the huge No-Fur bodies. Perhaps this action isn't as cruel as it sounds. Handra may need to do this in order to incubate the Pedra.

Current Conclusions

The No-Furs are dumb, lumbering animals that provide a habitat for the Handra. It seems to be a mutually beneficial relationship, as without the Handra, No-Furs would never accomplish anything and probably become extinct.

Peach Fuzz

Concept Art Collection

The following pages showcase some of the pre-production work that went into creating the first two volumes of *Peach Fuzz*, including character designs, costume designs, rough sketches, scenery, and story details.

Cover Art Concepts

Rough sketch of Volume 2 cover.

One of the most crucial elements of any book is its cover. For volume 2, I wanted an illustration that was similar to volume 1's top-down view of Amanda and Peach, this time with Kim and Pavaratty.

I came up with four different thumbnail sketches of the idea for Carol, my editor over at TOKYOPOP, to choose from. Happily, my personal favorite, number 1, was selected. This sketch was further refined as a much larger drawing.

Then, Jared inked the completed sketch in Painter. Finally, I colored the line art in Photoshop to produce the finished piece you now see on the cover.
— Lindsay

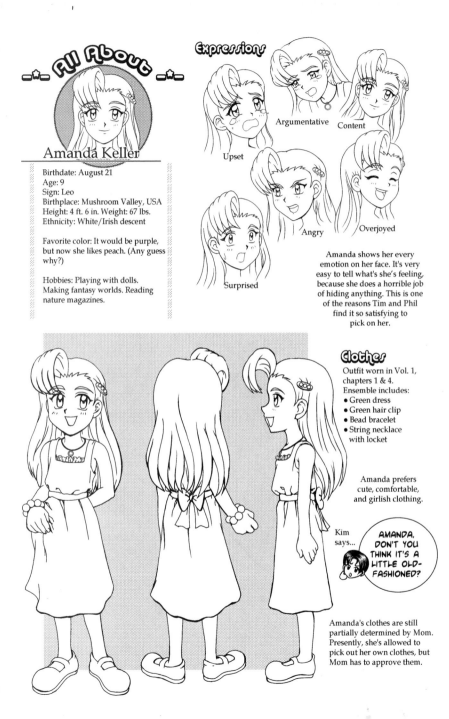

All About

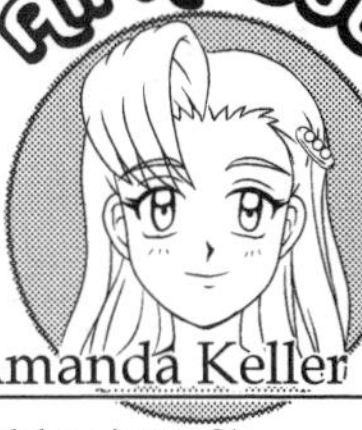

Amanda Keller

Birthdate: August 21
Age: 9
Sign: Leo
Birthplace: Mushroom Valley, USA
Height: 4 ft. 6 in. Weight: 67 lbs.
Ethnicity: White/Irish descent

Favorite color: It would be purple, but now she likes peach. (Any guess why?)

Hobbies: Playing with dolls. Making fantasy worlds. Reading nature magazines.

Expressions

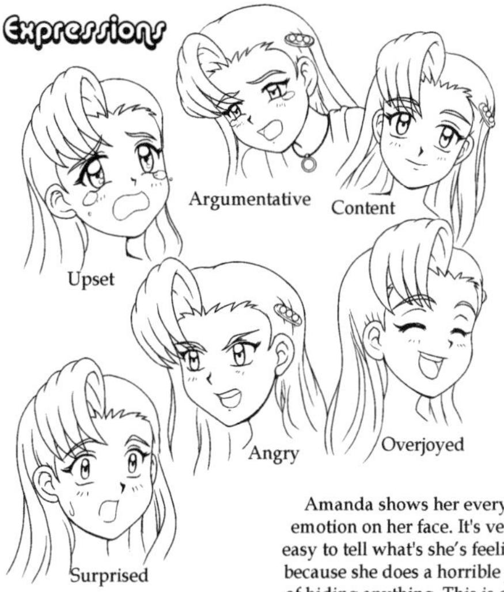
Upset
Argumentative
Content
Surprised
Angry
Overjoyed

Amanda shows her every emotion on her face. It's very easy to tell what's she's feeling, because she does a horrible job of hiding anything. This is one of the reasons Tim and Phil find it so satisfying to pick on her.

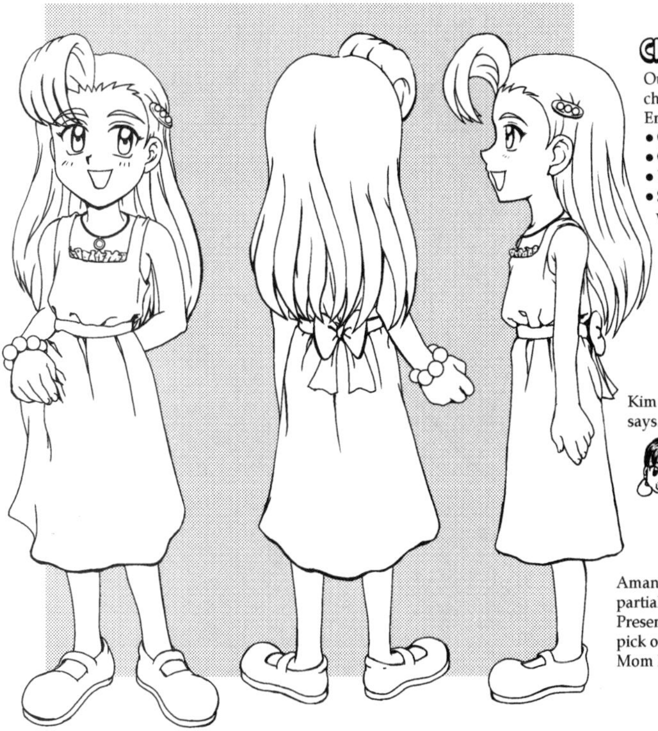

Clothes

Outfit worn in Vol. 1, chapters 1 & 4.
Ensemble includes:

- Green dress
- Green hair clip
- Bead bracelet
- String necklace with locket

Amanda prefers cute, comfortable, and girlish clothing.

Kim says...

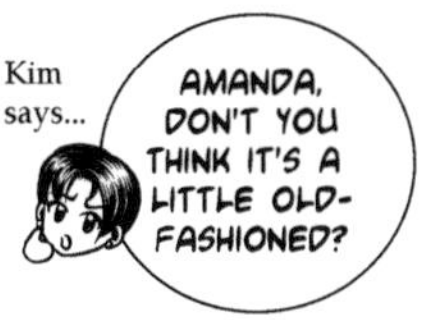
AMANDA, DON'T YOU THINK IT'S A LITTLE OLD-FASHIONED?

Amanda's clothes are still partially determined by Mom. Presently, she's allowed to pick out her own clothes, but Mom has to approve them.

Rough Sketches

For Amanda's clothing, I focused on designing outfits that looked cute and comfortable.
— Lindsay

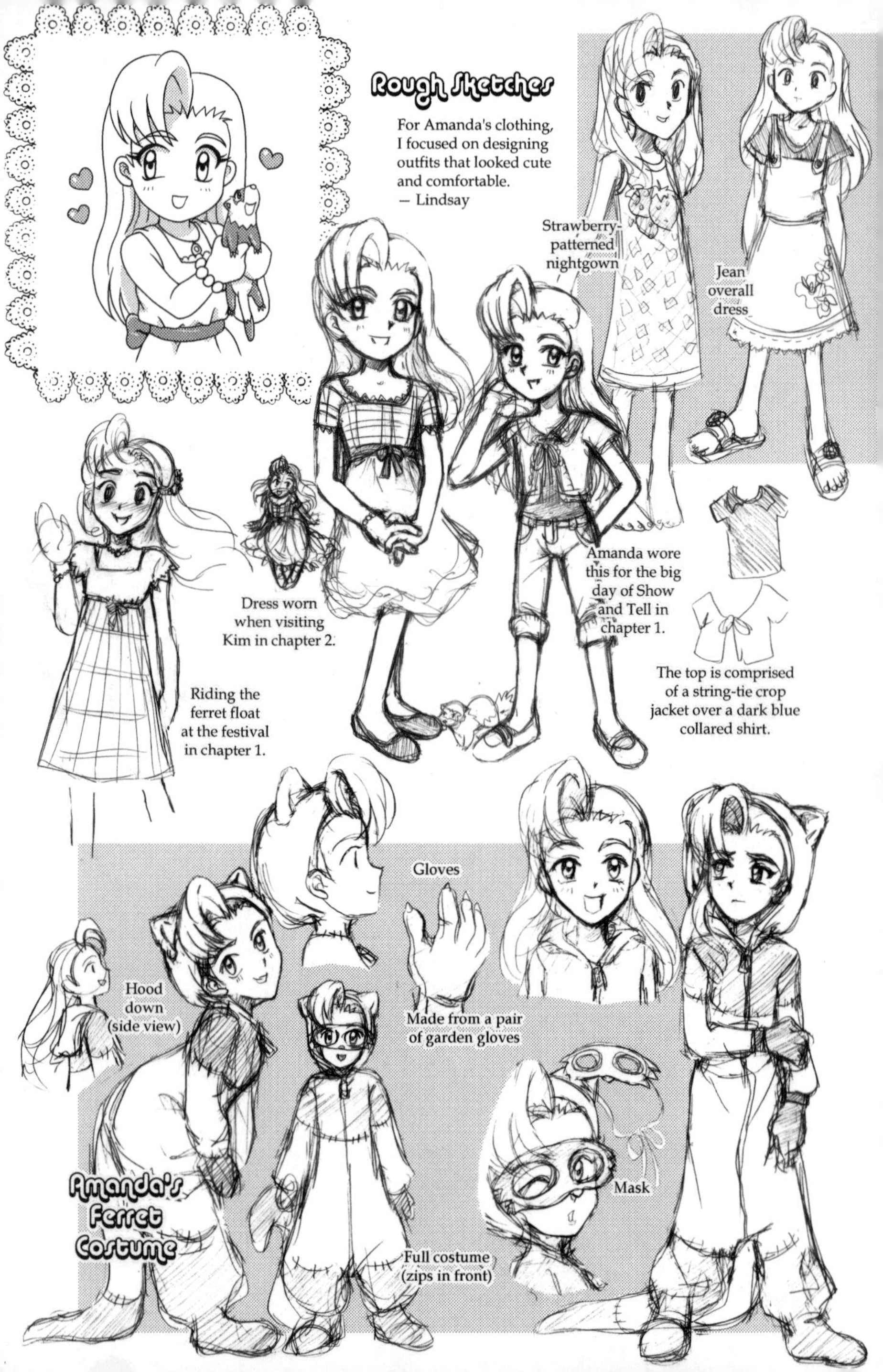
Strawberry-patterned nightgown
Jean overall dress
Dress worn when visiting Kim in chapter 2.
Amanda wore this for the big day of Show and Tell in chapter 1.
The top is comprised of a string-tie crop jacket over a dark blue collared shirt.
Riding the ferret float at the festival in chapter 1.
Gloves
Made from a pair of garden gloves
Hood down (side view)
Amanda's Ferret Costume
Full costume (zips in front)
Mask

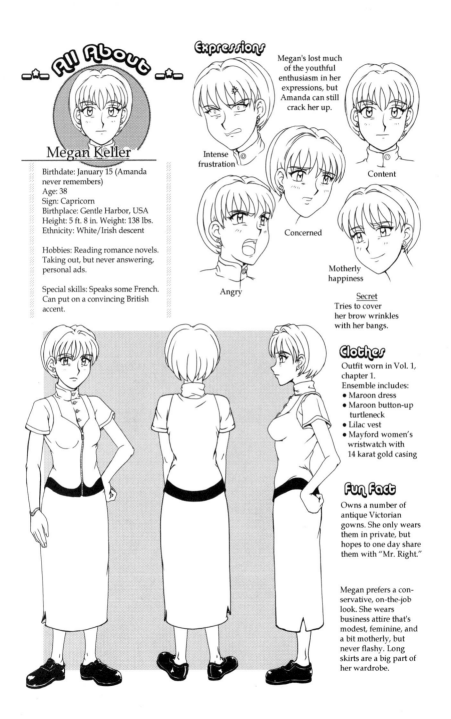

All About

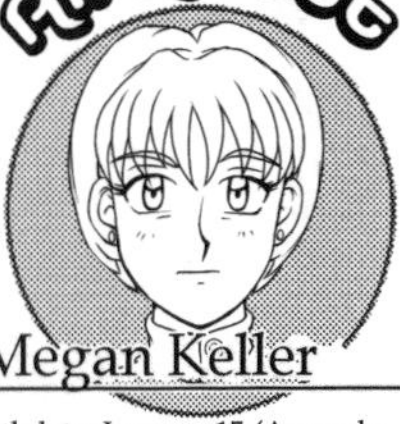

Megan Keller

Birthdate: January 15 (Amanda never remembers)
Age: 38
Sign: Capricorn
Birthplace: Gentle Harbor, USA
Height: 5 ft. 8 in. Weight: 138 lbs.
Ethnicity: White/Irish descent

Hobbies: Reading romance novels. Taking out, but never answering, personal ads.

Special skills: Speaks some French. Can put on a convincing British accent.

Expressions

Megan's lost much of the youthful enthusiasm in her expressions, but Amanda can still crack her up.

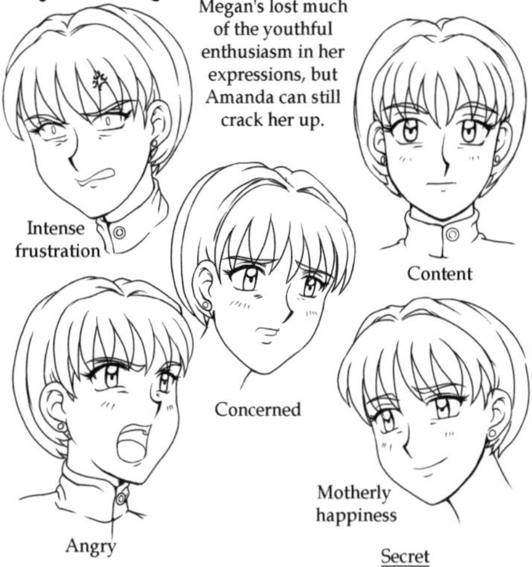
Intense frustration
Content
Concerned
Angry
Motherly happiness

Secret

Tries to cover her brow wrinkles with her bangs.

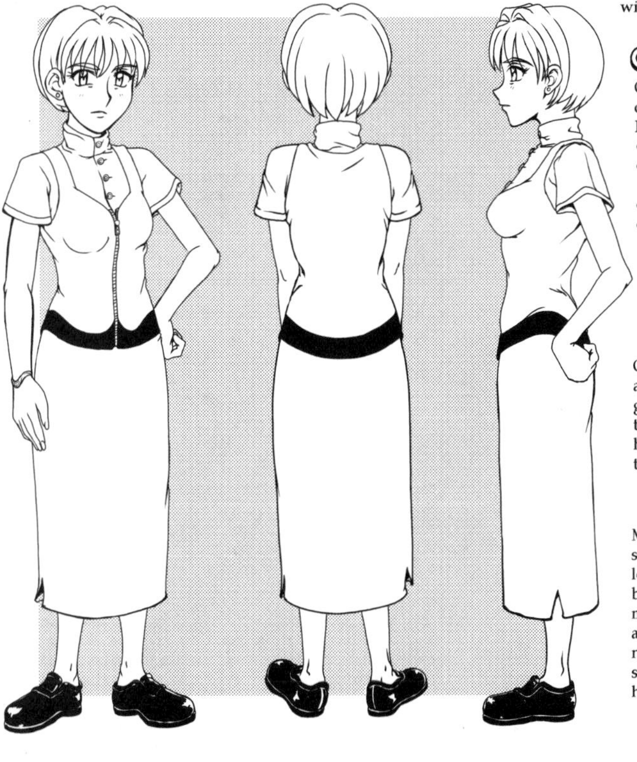

Clothes

Outfit worn in Vol. 1, chapter 1.
Ensemble includes:

- Maroon dress
- Maroon button-up turtleneck
- Lilac vest
- Mayford women's wristwatch with 14 karat gold casing

Fun Fact

Owns a number of antique Victorian gowns. She only wears them in private, but hopes to one day share them with "Mr. Right."

Megan prefers a conservative, on-the-job look. She wears business attire that's modest, feminine, and a bit motherly, but never flashy. Long skirts are a big part of her wardrobe.

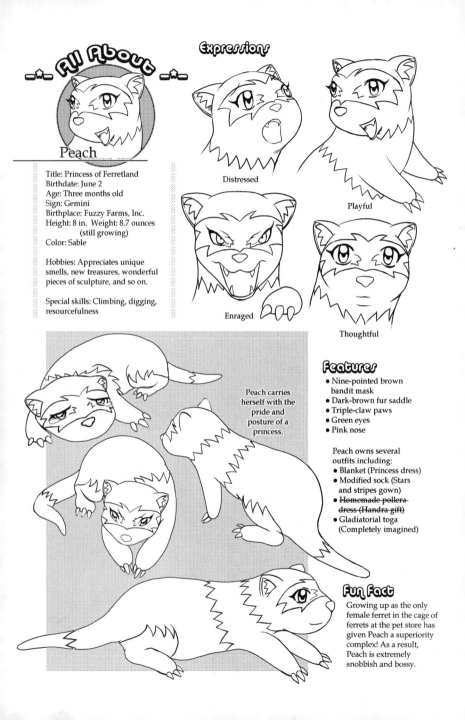

All About

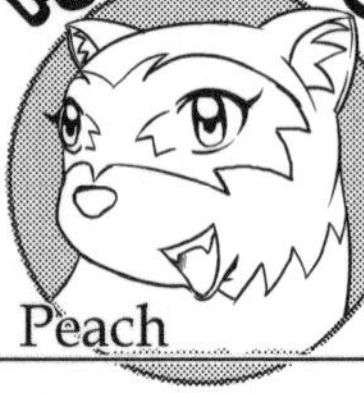

Peach

Title: Princess of Ferretland
Birthdate: June 2
Age: Three months old
Sign: Gemini
Birthplace: Fuzzy Farms, Inc.
Height: 8 in. Weight: 8.7 ounces (still growing)
Color: Sable

Hobbies: Appreciates unique smells, new treasures, wonderful pieces of sculpture, and so on.

Special skills: Climbing, digging, resourcefulness

Expressions

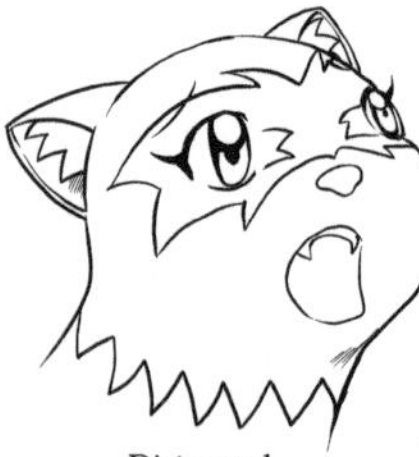

Distressed

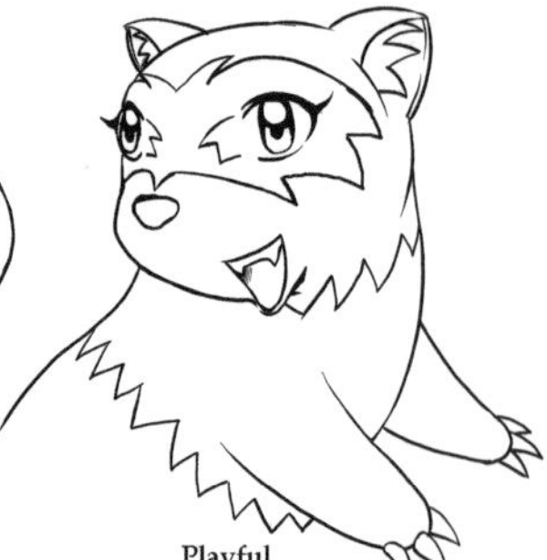

Playful

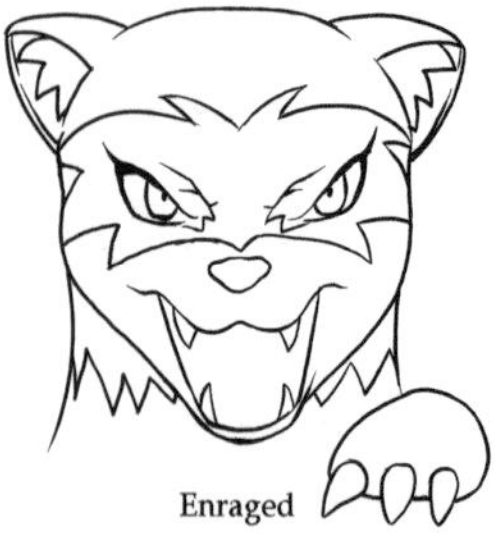

Enraged

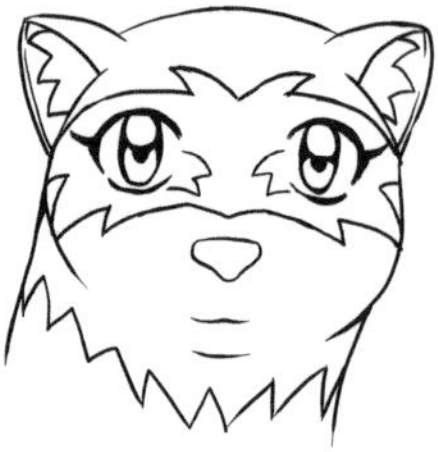

Thoughtful

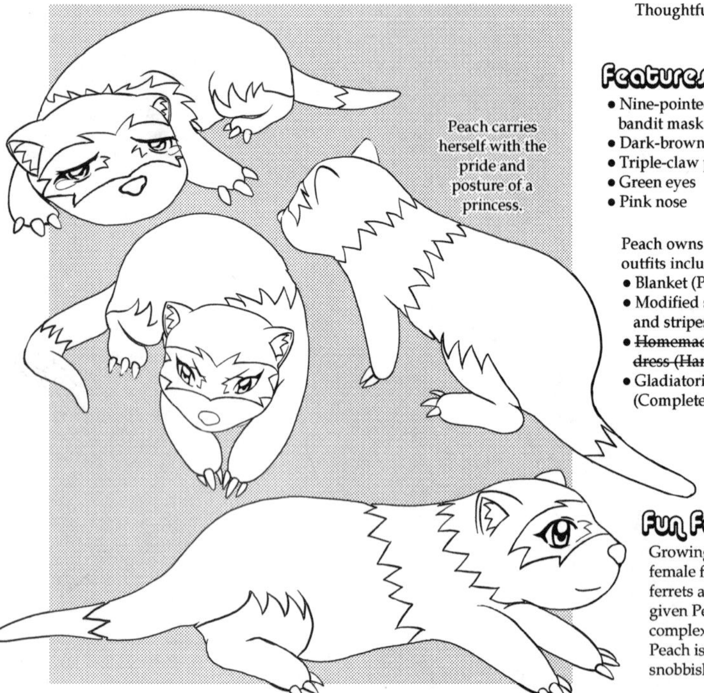
Peach carries herself with the pride and posture of a princess.

Features

- Nine-pointed brown bandit mask
- Dark-brown fur saddle
- Triple-claw paws
- Green eyes
- Pink nose

Peach owns several outfits including:

- Blanket (Princess dress)
- Modified sock (Stars and stripes gown)
- ~~Homemade pollera dress (Handra gift)~~
- Gladiatorial toga (Completely imagined)

Fun Fact

Growing up as the only female ferret in the cage of ferrets at the pet store has given Peach a superiority complex! As a result, Peach is extremely snobbish and bossy.